ACCIDENTAL SAVIORS

JACK A. SAARELA

Can't Put It Down Books

Accidental Saviors
A Novel
Copyright 2018 by Jack Saarela

ISBN: 978-0-9994623-2-4
Printed in the United States of America

This is a work of fiction. All incidents and dialogue, and all characters with the exception of some well-known historical figures, are products of the author's imagination and are not to be construed as real. Where real-life historical figures appear, the situations, incidents, and dialogues concerning those persons are entirely fictional and are not intended to depict actual events or to change the entirely fictional nature of the work. In all other respects, any resemblance to actual persons, living or dead, events, or locales is entirely coincidental.

Published by
Can't Put It Down Books
An imprint of
Open Door Publications
2113 Stackhouse Dr.
Yardley, PA 19067
www.CantPutItDownBooks.com

Cover Design by Eric Labacz
www.labaczdesign.com

This novel is dedicated to my countrymen,
Algot Niska and Felix Kersten,
and all persons of moral vision and courageous acts
of self-sacrifice
on behalf of the oppressed
whose stories, like theirs, are seldom or never told.

*Whoever destroys one life is considered by the Torah
as if he destroyed an entire world;
whoever saves one life is considered by the Torah
as if he saved an entire world.*

—Mishnah Sanhedrin 4:5

*There are certain moments that define a person's whole life, moments
in which everything they are and everything they may possibly become
balance on a single decision. Life and death, hope and despair, victory
and failure teeter precariously on the decision made at that moment.
These are moments governed often by happenstance or accident.*

—Jonathan Maberry

*WAR IS HELL,
but sometimes in the midst of that hell,
people do things that Heaven itself must be proud of.*

—Frederick Buechner

CHAPTER ONE

Berlin: March 12, 1940

Felix Kersten's eyes opened from sleep with a jolt at the ungodly knocking at the front door of his flat. It was six o'clock on a March morning; the sun had not yet risen over Berlin.

"Open the door!" a man's forceful voice shouted through the locked door. "This is the SS."

Why in hell's name is the SS at the door to my home? They must know that I'll be at SS headquarters in just a few hours. Why can't they wait?

Kersten threw off the covers on his bed with an angry force. He hadn't been sleeping well since overhearing the conversation in the SS dining room about Holland. The repulsion of the ugly nightmare of the previous night left a foul taste in his mouth like jungle breath on the morning after a shot too many of the cheap vodka he'd consumed in his student days. He'd been irritable and fretful for a couple of days now.

He fumbled groggily at the edge of the bed with his right foot for his slippers. He grabbed his silk dressing gown off the back of the chair and threw it over his pajamas. He mumbled a curse to himself as he left the bedroom and rushed through his well-appointed living room to the front door.

"Open the door, Dr. Kersten. It's the SS." It was a different, less overtly threatening voice this time. There was further impatient knocking, sounding as though his uninvited visitors were using their clubs against the wooden door.

"Coming, coming. Stop your knocking. You'll wake up everybody else in the building."

When the tall, meaty Kersten opened the door, he found three men there, two privates in the field-gray SS uniform with the ancient ⚡⚡ runes pinned on the front of their collar, and an officer in a shiny black leather overcoat. For a moment, Kersten was overtaken first by surprise, then alarm.

Whatever you say or do, Felix, don't reveal the slightest hint of fear. The SS can smell blood from a mile away.

"Dr. Felix Kersten?" the officer asked.

"Well, now we know you can read the name tag on the door," Kersten countered irritably.

The privates remained impassive. The officer didn't look the least bit amused by Kersten's mockery.

"May we come in, Doctor?" the officer asked with gentlemanly courtesy. Kersten knew that SS officers were trained to begin interrogations with apparent benign politeness, with Aryans at least. Eventually, however, like a cat stalking its prey, sitting absolutely still until the bird is lulled into inattention, the interrogator leaps suddenly just at that moment and administers the fatal attack.

"Do I really have a choice?" Kersten asked as he pulled the door open to let them into the living room.

The officer forced a smile and nodded his gratitude for Kersten's cooperation. The officer was accustomed, however, to an exhibition of more anxiety, even fear, whenever he entered the residence of a host off his guard.

"I am *Leutnant* Rohrbach, Doctor. We have been sent by my superiors to pose a few questions."

"Why don't you have a seat here, *Leutnant.*"

"Thank you. Always stand when I am working, if you don't mind." The officer gave no indication that he would remove his black leather coat.

Good. This isn't going to take long.

Rohrbach remained the epitome of politeness and respect, despite his threatening errand. He nodded to the two privates, who gamboled off immediately in separate directions of the flat.

"I'm at your service, of course, *Leutnant,*" Kersten said in a tone that matched the officer's affected courteousness. He had imagined the SS to be gruffer if not spiteful in their methods of interrogation. Perhaps they were aware of his unique position. "But is it really necessary for your men to inspect the rest of the flat? My servants are asleep and deserve their rest."

"It's just customary and routine procedure, Doctor, on a call such as this. I'm sure that they will return empty-handed, with nothing untoward to report."

Sure enough, barely had Rohrbach finished his sentence than the two privates returned to the living room. One greeted the lieutenant with "*Nichts, Herr Leutnant.*"

"You see, Doctor? They found nothing suspicious hidden in your flat, just as I predicted," Rohrbach said to Kersten with a well-bred grin.

Kersten's head ached. He was growing increasingly vexed by Rohrbach's superficial courtliness and solicitude.

"You said you have been dispatched here to ask questions," Kersten asked impatiently. "What do you need to know?"

"If you're impatient to get right to the point, then, as you wish, Doctor."

"Who is it that wants to know my answers to your questions, if I may ask?"

The lieutenant flashed an indulgent, patronizing smile. "Of course, that you may not ask, Doctor. I'm sure you understand. Instead, let me begin by asking you, do you ever use this residence as a clinic in which to treat any of your patients?"

"*Herr Leutnant,* I am sure that whoever is your superior in the SS who sent you here on this...this...fool's errand has my building under surveillance and has a very accurate record of who enters and who exits the building."

"There's no need for impertinence, Doctor. You must be sufficiently familiar with SS procedure by now to know that we are seeking an answer that corroborates information we have gathered by other means. Or contradicts it."

"Then, since you ask, I'll give you a straight answer. Yes, I do occasionally receive patients in my flat here, particularly if they are from out of town or I do not have access to their residence for some reason."

"Aha, if I may continue, Doctor, why is it that you may not have access to the residences of some of your patients?"

Kersten was beginning to feel more testy. He wasn't consciously afraid of Rohrbach, but he noticed that his mouth was dry.

"As you undoubtedly know, *Leutnant,* some individuals and families no longer have their accustomed residence, but are in temporary arrangements, sometimes with relatives."

"Oh, yes...I vaguely remember hearing something back in 1938 about some families being evacuated to make room for *Herr* Speer's plans to honor the *Führer* by rebuilding sections of Berlin that even Paris could not rival."

"Vaguely remember," my ass! He knows full well the details of the displacement of hundreds of households to make room for Speer's

grandiose architectural delusions. For Hitler's grandiose delusions, in other words. It was the SS that was dispatched to evict the residents.

"As I recall—though, as I say, my memory about the event is only imprecise, I'm afraid—that the households that were appropriated were those of Jews. Am I remembering correctly, Doctor?"

"Yes."

"Then, can we deduce, Doctor, that some of the patients to whose residence you do not have access, whom you therefore need to receive here in your private flat, are Jews?"

It suddenly dawned on Kersten that this was precisely the matter that this circuitous charade was about. Rohrbach had the gratified look of someone about to checkmate an opponent in a game of chess.

These Nazis, and their obsession with the Jews.

"Yes, that is an accurate deduction, *Leutnant*. That's really no surprise, is it? Or a secret?"

"No, indeed, Doctor, we've suspected the same for quite some time."

Rohrbach's face became sterner suddenly, his voice more severe, like that of a drill sergeant. He raised the volume a notch. "You do realize, do you not, Dr. Kersten, that to treat Jewish patients is forbidden, absolutely forbidden?"

"No, actually I do not...Besides, that does not concern me in the least."

Rohrbach had had enough pleasantry, and of this masseur's defiance. His piercing eyes looked directly into Kersten's. "Then you place yourself outside the law of the German people?"

"No, not at all, *Leutnant*," Kersten said with a forced smile. "My driver obeys traffic signals. I pay my taxes. I purchase only my rationed portion of bacon."

Rohrbach's face was turning a shade of crimson now, especially at his neck. "You mock me, Doctor, but you do so, I warn you, at your risk. You are not behaving as a German doctor should behave. It is unlawful for a German doctor to treat Jewish patients. They have their own doctors."

Kersten smiled inwardly as he paused for effect.

"Perhaps so, *Leutnant*. Though among my various medical degrees, one is from Berlin. Nonetheless, I am *not* a German doctor. I believe that this law does not pertain to me," Kersten said as civilly as his glee at evading Rohrbach's checkmate allowed him.

Rohrbach looked at the two privates confusedly, as if expecting one of them to bail him out.

"Dr. Kersten, such insolence and impertinence are unnecessary. They can land you in the kind of trouble with the SS that I would hate to have happen to a man of your standing."

"Surely your superiors know that I am, in fact, a *Finnish* doctor."

An awkward, embarrassed silence overtook the room. Puzzlement was all over Rohrbach's face. The two privates looked back at Rohrbach equally baffled.

"Finnish? So you say, at least," Rohrbach finally said a little self-consciously, though Kersten was humored by Rohrbach's scrambling to reverse the tables and resume his position of strength.

"Then I presume you can afford us the pleasure of inspecting your passport?"

"The pleasure is all mine, *Leutnant.* If you would wait a moment, I will produce it, and anything else you want, for that matter." With that, Kersten nodded at all three SS men to excuse himself, and exited to his bedroom.

After barely a minute, he reappeared holding the oxblood-colored booklet that was his Finnish passport. He handed it to Rohrbach with an air of satisfaction. "Suomi-Finland" was etched in golden letters into the front of it below the new coat of arms of the republic. Though he was trying his best to appear nonplussed, Rohrbach's eyes grew a little larger and revealed surprise mixed with embarrassment.

"It...seems to be in order, Doctor. A Finnish citizen for over twenty years? With temporary stays in the Netherlands and Germany? But not originally a citizen of Finland?"

"Just as it reads right there on the page in black and white." Kersten had to discipline his urge to be mocking.

Rohrbach handed the passport back to Kersten sheepishly, although he tried to maintain a front of official decorum. "Apparently, I have been misinformed. We regret the early hour for this visit, Doctor."

"I will see you and your men out, *Leutnant,*" Kersten said with a feigned smile. "Now if you do not mind, I would be appreciative if you corrected your superior's information."

Rohrbach stood in the open doorway, turned toward Kersten, and said noncommittally, "As you wish, Doctor." Then, he added, with no trace of a smile, "But be aware, Doctor, that this may not be the last time my superiors seek some answers from you."

CHAPTER TWO

Berlin: November 9, 1938

The moment Algot Niska stepped off the train from Brussels at the *HauptBahnhof* in Berlin, he knew that something momentous and sinister was happening. The sky over Berlin was quivering with a malevolent electricity. November was already eight days old, but this evening, for some mysterious reason, a wall of hellish heat cooked the air. As he exited the terminal onto *Friedrichstrasse,* he was almost knocked to the pavement by members of the Hitlerjugend running up and down the street as if let out of school on the last day before summer vacation, boys screaming riotously and pig-tailed girls running beside them. Flames lit the sky a brilliant shade of hot orange. Furniture, beds, dressers, tables, chairs, paintings were strewn and toppled chaotically on the sidewalk; sheets of paper were being carried hither and thither by the wind.

The almost fifty-year-old Niska carried his small valise and walked quickly toward his hotel in the Charlottenburg district, which was in the opposite direction of this insane violence and destruction. He wanted to be as far away as possible from the chaos.

His latest smuggling project had been more hazardous and risky than he had expected. He felt satisfied with a job completed, and gratified that he had succeeded in smuggling the Gottfrieds' jewelry into Brussels and on to the United States, far from the clutches of the Nazis. But he was ready for rest and relaxation. For that, he needed peace and quiet. This evening, Berlin was not cooperating.

He passed a synagogue at an intersection that had descended to all-out, open warfare. Youth were tearing up some of the abandoned objects on the street for projectiles to hurl at people they judged to be Jews. Young men and women were running around with grotesque, wolfish faces, shouting, "There's one! Stone him! Kill her!"

Although Niska was a tall and thin man, he was engulfed in the human congestion on the side of the street opposite the synagogue. The crowd was so densely packed that Niska was prevented from making further progress toward his hotel. Whether he wanted to or not, he was seeing the devastating effects of an unrestrained hatred.

Some of the older people—whether they were members of the synagogue, Niska couldn't tell—were covering their faces with their hands. They could not comprehend the madness. An elderly woman moaned, tears streaming down her cheeks, "Oh, dear God, what are the young *goyim* doing?"

Suddenly an enormous cheer erupted as though a soccer team on a pitch nearby had scored a winning goal. "The synagogue is burning! The synagogue is burning!"

Niska saw an older, bearded man, probably the rabbi, appear on the front steps of the synagogue. His longish locks were gray. He was in his white shirtsleeves, not the way a rabbi was usually dressed in public. There hadn't been time to don his suit jacket. He had his right arm around two large scrolls, and with his left hand he was holding the hand of a terrified woman Niska assumed was his wife. They were trying to escape the burning building. They almost tripped in tandem as they shuffled down the steps to the street.

A renewed burst of rage erupted among the pack of youthful participants. In the next moment, a rainstorm of rocks and projectiles pelted the synagogue. One rock hit the arched frame of the huge, stained-glass window on the front of the building. The remainder of the frame, with what stained glass still remained, came crashing down on the heads of the rabbi and his wife. The mob howled with triumph as the couple became one with the flames on the window frame. In no time at all, the roof of the synagogue collapsed and came crashing down to join the smoldering rubble below.

Niska was literally a very seaworthy man. He had been on boats of one kind or another since at least 1908, not one, in other words, prone to nausea. But now he felt a bitter, abrasive fluid rise into the base of his throat. Niska had to concentrate on not letting the vomit erupt from his mouth onto the others beside him in the crowd on the sidewalk.

Niska ground his teeth tightly together in fury at the youthful violence and wanton celebration. The ferocity of his rage was fueled further when he noticed several middle-aged men in civilian clothes standing before the youth, like directors of an orchestra, urging them on. His stomach turned when he saw a woman of about forty, her face contorted into a thoroughly ugly, almost inhuman, Edvard Münch-like scowl as she yelled out to the destroyers, "Kill them! Kill them all! Bloody Christ murderers!"

As if at her beckoning, a rock flew through the air over the street from the direction of the indignant mob. It struck a young woman holding her small daughter by the hand. As she bent over to shield her daughter, she crumpled in a screaming mass onto the pavement. The orphaned child turned in circles on the one spot desperately seeking her mother. When she saw her body on the pavement, she covered her face with her hands.

Several vans with blue lights flashing and ear-splitting sirens blaring made their way onto the street. One by one firemen and police emerged from the back of the van. Niska began to hope that order would now be restored. Instead, the police laid into the defenseless Jews with their truncheons while, exempt from the attention of the police, the rampaging mob chased and wrestled to the ground any Jews who tried to escape down the street, and beat them. Niska felt the blow of the truncheons, as though on his own skull, his own flesh.

He hadn't been particularly enamored by Jewish contacts with whom he carried on transactions in the past. If anything, they had struck him as rather shrewd and difficult to please, often imperious. But surely no one deserved such unbridled hostility and savagery as he was witnessing. As a Finn living and working in self-imposed exile in Germany for several years now, Niska felt an instinctive racial affinity to Germans, their blue eyes, their fair hair, their tireless work ethic, so familiar in that regard to his own countrymen. But he hadn't learned to understand their visceral hatred of the Jews.

As he stood helplessly on the sidewalk, he felt an unexpected and peculiar compassion for the rabbi and his wife. So, too, for the startled men and women struck by the police, the little orphan girl left screaming on the street, and the would-be escapees wrestled to the pavement and beaten to a pulp.

Some of the Hitlerjugend joined hands and formed a circle and started to dance in the light of the flames emanating from the destroyed synagogue. To what music, Niska wondered. The music of madness and hatred, he supposed, that they, but not he, could hear, but an echo of which he was beginning to discern within the chambers of his own heart toward the perpetrators.

It was a grisly, macabre, godless dance of *death*, Niska thought. The German youth sang a mocking tune, an off-key charade of the Jewish folk song, starting slowly:

Hava nagila, hava nagila,
Hava nagila venishmeja.

Then speeding up and bringing their hands together, they inserted their own obscene German lyrics and cheered lustily at their own cleverness.

Let's burn a Jew boy, let's burn a Jew girl,
Let's burn every last one of them, yay!

Niska had not lived what one could describe as a sheltered life, not even in childhood. But he had never before experienced chaos and violence like this, not even when brother fought brother to the death in the bloodletting of the Finnish civil war after independence in 1917.

Such peach-faced, middle-class youth born with silver spoons in their mouths. Just schoolboys, really. Shouldn't they be out on the soccer pitch, or in their homes playing chess with their grandfathers? Aren't they too young, too childlike, to be chanting such hate-filled verses sated with superstition and ignorance learned from their fathers and uncles?

The mocking voices mixed with the acrid crackling of flames and the unforgettable shattering of glass. It reminded Niska of descriptions of hell he had heard from his pious Finnish Lutheran grandmother. Though he wanted in the worst way to go to his hotel room and not have to see the violence or hear the screams, he stood motionless as though the soles of his shoes were nailed to the sidewalk. His face was lit in the deviant light of the surrounding madness. His eyes were wet and hazy from the heat and smoke...Or were they tears evoked by the lurid spectacle that kept repeating over and over in his mind, of the rabbi and his wife, crushed under the huge window frame and burning to ash to the cheers of the mob, while the youth danced? Was this a portent of a malicious future?

CHAPTER THREE

Berlin: March 20, 1940

Once Rohrbach and the two SS privates were out the door leading out of his flat, Kersten retreated to his bedroom. When he took off the silk dressing gown he was surprised to find enormous, dark splotches of perspiration underneath the two armpits of his pajamas.

It's a damn good thing I put on the dressing gown at the last second before answering the knocking at the door. I am relieved that the SS men could not see the fact that I was perspiring so copiously during the interrogation. If Rohrbach had detected any fear or anxiety in me, he would have turned the screws more tightly.

In the stillness and privacy of his bedroom he was able finally to exhale deeply. He had been in control of his breathing during the interrogation itself, a skill he had learned in his surgical training days in Helsinki. Uneven breathing by a surgeon could cause the hand on the scalpel to move ever so slightly, just enough to cut a nerve or capillary inadvertently. It could be fatal.

He plunked his rear end down on the bed. He was exhausted from the effort to maintain an unanxious affect in front of his SS interrogators.

Kersten picked up the glass of water on the night table beside his bed. He noticed the hand holding the glass was starting to tremble almost uncontrollably. Beads of perspiration formed on his forehead and pooled in his armpits. The close-call nature of the encounter in his living room just moments earlier was beginning to register in his brain.

What was this all about, anyway? Surely, the SS would have done their homework before sending these men? It's not a classified secret that I am a Finnish citizen. What was this, then? A warning of some sort? An exercise in intimidation?

How could they have initiated their mission without my patient himself knowing about it? Very little occurs in the SS without my patient's knowledge or permission.

Or...is that it? Did my patient himself actually order this early-morning social call? For what reason? He's never given me any indication of mistrust in me. Is he going back on his assurance to me that I will enjoy immunity from the usual spying and intimidation tactics of his organization?

When I started out in this profession years ago, I could not have imagined in my wildest fantasies that I'd end up in the private service of a man such as he. My God!

Kersten began to feel the familiar, ancient aching in the pit of his stomach. He began to rub it in an effort to chase away the discomfort.

It's so ironic now, don't you think, Felix, that your expertise in ridding your patient of his fierce stomach spasms is now causing you pains in your own gut?

He thought wistfully of his beloved Irmgaard back in The Hague, and their comfortable flat near the royal palace where he was employed. It wasn't apt to be invaded by the SS like this. He could still remember the sweet aroma of streets in The Hague. It was not just the aroma of the tulips, but of freedom.

I'm nothing but a captive here in Berlin. How did I ever allow myself to get into this damnable situation? Whatever caused me to leave behind that cheery life and exchange it for this surreal, insane existence in the midst of all this folly and madness? What were you possibly thinking, Felix?

Auguste Diehn, as much as I love you, old friend, damn you all the same for your appointment almost two years ago!

11

CHAPTER FOUR

Berlin: November 21, 1938

Even though Auguste Diehn was a captain of German industry, of advanced years, and one of the therapist's oldest patients and dearest friends, he had to wait at least two months for an appointment with Dr. Felix Kersten, just like everybody else. Kersten's physio-neuro therapy practice had experienced explosive growth. It was split between two countries now, Germany and the Netherlands. And there were the occasional trips to Vienna, Brussels, and Rome to see patients.

The fortyish, beefy Kersten greeted Diehn, the president of the German Potassium Syndicate, in his customary warm and expansive manner. The doctor noticed at once, however, that his old friend was nervous and ill at ease.

"Auguste, take a seat, please. Are you working too much again? Ignoring my advice to get some rest? You've come for another treatment?"

"No, I am not here for myself," replied Diehn, avoiding Kersten's eyes for some reason.

"No?"

There was a silence. Kersten was curious why.

"Doctor, I have a favor to ask of you...a personal one."

"We've known each other long enough, haven't we, that you don't need to feel ashamed to ask for one?"

"Well, I'm not sure how to put it...Would you be willing to examine Himmler?"

"What? Who?"

"Himmler . . . *Heinrich* Himmler."

"*The* Heinrich Himmler? The head of the feared SS? The man with no apparent conscience? Do you realize what you are asking, Auguste?"

Kersten shook his head in disbelief. Diehn hoped earnestly that his doctor wasn't refusing.

"Let me ask again just to be sure. Am I hearing you correctly, Auguste? Heinrich Himmler? Me, be his doctor? I should be grateful, I suppose, that you didn't ask me to treat Adolf Hitler. Are you playing some kind of joke? If you are, it's not funny in the least, Auguste."

"Yes, you heard right, Doctor. And no, this is not a joke."

Diehn bowed his head. Kersten said nothing, not knowing what to say. Silently, he studied the man's familiar gray-haired profile.

Diehn continued. "You see, Himmler has orders from Hitler himself to nationalize the potash industry. The *Führer* needs the potash so that German farmers have ample fertilizer to grow the crops to feed the *Wehrmacht* that multiplies every day, it seems."

"I don't see the connection, Auguste. What does that have to do with me? I don't know the first thing about potash."

"Doctor, if your miraculous hands work the same wonders on Himmler as they have on me, in no time he'll be very beholden to you."

"Yes? And...?"

Diehn could see that the famed doctor-therapist either wasn't catching his drift, or was deliberately not understanding something that he was finding unpleasant. Probably the latter.

"I'm asking you to speak a few well-chosen words while treating him. I am confident that you are the only man in Germany right now who can make a dent in Himmler's excruciating pain, which he is keeping a secret, by the way. Your conversing casually with Himmler on behalf of the potash producers of Germany just might convince him to go back to his *Führer* with an alternate plan to nationalizing the entire industry. Surely you see what I am getting at?"

Truth be told, Kersten, indeed, *could* see. But wasn't this an abuse of the doctor-patient relationship?

"You say, he's keeping his condition a secret? Then, Auguste, how it is that it's not a secret to you?"

"Certainly, Felix, you know that industrialists like me have, how shall I put it, information inroads within the Nazi hierarchy."

Kersten rubbed his double-chin and seemed to consider Diehn's request. Diehn knew him well enough not to rush him to a decision.

Finally, Kersten said, "Ah, no! Thank you very much. This doesn't sound like my cup of tea." The black rings that surrounded his eyes seemed to turn even darker.

"I've been able to avoid having anything to do with that insane element up to now, and I have no intention of starting with the very worst of the bunch. I hate politicians and the games they play, hate them with a passion. I just want to be left in peace to be a doctor."

There was another silence, a much longer one. Diehn took up the conversation with a visible effort to suppress his disappointment.

"I understand your hesitation, Doctor. I am sure you will agree, however, when I say that I have never asked you to do anything but treat my condition. In ordinary times, that would suffice. But alas, these are not ordinary times. On the contrary, these are very extraordinary ones. Which is why I come before you with this extraordinary request."

Kersten maintained a reflective silence. He recalled the complete confidence that Diehn had had in him at the start of his career, how Diehn had referred friends and associates to his practice, men and women who could reimburse him generously. He recalled also how Diehn had been instrumental in helping Kersten, an *Ausländer*, get the loan under the table from one of his colleagues to purchase the one blessed place on this earth where he could recharge his batteries, his delightful country estate a little north of Berlin, Hartzwalde.

On the other hand, Kersten reflected, how could he have anything to do with a man like Himmler? Wouldn't that be to take a seat in the devil's lair, a place in the warren of the beast? For his own peace of mind and serenity he had until now forbidden himself even to think about the regime of which the head of the SS was considered the most monstrous personification. The possibility offended to the core Kersten's innate Finnish sense of justice, his love of tolerance, decency, and moderation that had been reinforced by his time in Holland. As he even contemplated the possibility of accepting Diehn's request, he tried to shake off the repulsion he felt in his stomach at the gross arrogance, the primitive racial superstition, the crude police-state tactics, the fanatical blind adoration of the *Führer,* Hitler's promise of easy solutions to Germany's complex problems—everything, in short, about the events and personalities in Germany of the last five years.

"Auguste, partly thanks to you, my practice has expanded almost beyond my ability to handle it all. But you know that for a decade now, I have been retained by the royal family of Holland as Queen Wilhelmina's personal therapist. I'm afraid I would have trouble squeezing Himmler into my normal schedule."

Kersten thought this would surely discourage Diehn from pursuing the ludicrous proposition any further.

Diehn's voice was almost a whisper as he leaned over conspiratorially to Kersten and pleaded, "It would be such a great service…to me, Doctor."

Then, resuming a normal conversation volume and raising his head,

"Besides, is it not your professional duty to treat anyone who is sick?"

The room became silent. Instinctively, Kersten began to massage the area of his stomach. Although he tried to camouflage it, a grimace of discomfort came over his ruddy face. He was gripped by a nascent nausea. He recognized the source of his queasiness, and he knew it wasn't anything physical.

Immediately, Kersten's mind was borne back to a day in the spring of 1922 when he and his classmates were preparing to graduate from the medical school of Helsinki University. How proud he was that he had arrived at the threshold of a medical career. How far he had come from his humble Baltic agrarian roots. He could hear now, as though it were just yesterday, the eminent voice of the dean leading the class in the recital of the ancient Hippocratic Oath. *"Primum non nocere. First do no harm."* He understood that within the prohibition there was an implicit command. *"Secondly, share your medical expertise and knowledge when it requested or needed."*

Kersten had noted then how mechanically and nonchalantly some of his classmates were reciting the oath. *How is it that these future doctors consider this as merely an empty formality, like mindlessly reciting the Lord's Prayer in church, when I recite it so earnestly, solemnly even? The oath isn't a trivial string of words; it's the code by which I am pledging to practice the healing arts, the guiding principle by which I will live my life.*

"Ah, very well, then, I will consider it at least," Kersten sighed. "But with the caveat that it be only *one* session. Is that clear, Auguste? Just *one.*"

CHAPTER FIVE

Berlin: November 22, 1938

It was almost 23:00 when Algot Niska finished a late-night dinner at the *Osteria Bavaria*. Given the late hour, Niska considered hailing a taxi. However, he wanted to refresh himself with a walk to his apartment hotel, even though there was still a residue of the fetid odor of the night of Nazi terror ten or so days prior. Nevertheless, the relatively brisk November air was a welcome relief from the smoke-filled restaurant.

After some forty minutes on the streets of Berlin, Niska walked through the semi-dark lobby of the apartment hotel. He took the stairs to his apartment on the fourth floor. He put the key into the lock. But before he had fully turned it to the right to unlock it, he paused. He thought he heard above him, from the direction of the ceiling, a faint sound like that of the crinkling of paper.

Probably a mouse scampering about in the attic.

But Niska wasn't fully convinced. He heard the sound again. His curiosity made him walk down the corridor to the trap door in the ceiling that led to the attic. He pulled down the wooden ladder connected to it. He climbed up two or three rungs so that he could insert his head through the opening above the level of the attic floor.

In the dim light he could make out a tiny figure, perhaps a child's stuffed animal. The figure was larger than his daughter's teddy bear, but barely bigger than that of a child. He struck a match on the rough surface of the floor of the attic. He was unprepared and shocked to see the outline of a human form. Hesitantly, he climbed the rest of the way into the attic, still holding the match. He saw the stub of a candle someone had left fortuitously on top of an old crate to his right. Before he burned his fingers on the match, he blew it out and struck another one to light the candle.

What he saw in the dim candlelight was not a drunken vagrant, however, such as the one he had discovered trespassing in the building on another occasion. This figure scampered backward on its behind and cowered under Niska's stare. Its eyes were open as large as two silver *Reichsmarks* and emitted a look of panic and fear. The person, whoever he or she was, had found some old newspapers in the attic, apparently, and spread them out on the dusty wooden floor to make a bed. One stocking was torn, but otherwise, the figure was dressed in almost new shoes and fashionable clothes—*female* clothes, even though they were wrinkled. Part of her chest was daringly exposed to the upper part of her snow-white virgin breasts, which heaved as she breathed anxiously.

The girl's shiny black hair covered her shoulders and neck like a silk scarf. Her small hands, in fists, were smudged with dirt, and her carmine-colored lips were slightly apart. From her dark hair and facial structure, Niska judged that she must be a young girl, possibly Jewish. She put her hands over her face to hide it from Niska's view.

Niska tried to calm the fearful girl by speaking to her in as soft and mild a voice as he could make it.

"You will freeze here, girl. The attic is no place for one as slight as you, and with only such dainty clothing."

Slowly, the girl lowered her small, delicate hands from her face.

"Sir, I have nowhere else to go." Her voice quavered like a child's.

"Not your home? With your mother and father?"

The girl just shook her head slowly. As if begging for pardon, she looked into Niska's eyes.

"You can't stay here. Come, my apartment is nearby."

Niska was half-surprised when she pulled herself tentatively off the floor and started to walk slowly toward him at the trap door by the flickering light of the candle.

Niska didn't usually care what others thought of him. But he hoped, now that the girl had complied with his coaxing and descended the ladder behind him, none of his neighbors were up and about in the corridor at this late hour to see their middle-aged neighbor leading a scantily clad young girl into his flat.

A couple of minutes later they were sitting in Niska's cramped living room, the girl in an overstuffed Victorian armchair. She was trying to hide her ruined stocking with her other leg. Her fists were still clenched on her lap. She shifted her position in the chair nervously several times.

Niska went to his tiny pantry of a kitchen and made a couple of sandwiches with the rye bread he had in the ice box, probably stale by now, he feared. There was no milk, so he poured out a couple of glasses of red wine.

She almost attacked her sandwich as though she hadn't seen one in a long time. When she noticed Niska regarding her, she blushed. She released her small hands from their clenched pose. Niska could see a network of minor scratches on them, some of which were still oozing blood. He led her to the closet-sized lavatory and handed her a clean towel.

"On the shelf there to your right you'll find some soap. And a brush if you need one," Niska said as he closed the door behind him, leaving her to her privacy.

When she had re-entered the living room and assumed her seat in the armchair, she didn't pick up the remainder of her sandwich, but sat observing Niska.

"I haven't even asked you your name. I apologize. Mine is Niska, Algot Niska."

She looked a little confused by what to her ears must have sounded like a very foreign name.

After a while, almost as if not sure she should divulge her name to this stranger, she said diffidently, "I am Hannah. Hannah Hirtschel."

"Eat, for God's sake then, Hannah Hirtschel," Niska urged. "It's for you. I can see you haven't eaten for quite some time. Make yourself at home, please. Nobody is going to disturb us here."

Hannah almost threw herself at the sandwich. Niska was caught up in pity for the girl. He stepped back into the kitchen and made a couple of more sandwiches.

"I was out for dinner this evening," Niska explained, for no apparent reason. "The food tastes good even if it's late. I'm really hungry even though I finished a large dinner barely an hour ago."

Niska hoped that casual conversation might allay her fears. It seemed to work.

"I haven't eaten for three days," she confessed.

"Such things are not rare these days," Niska said with a mouth full of food. "These are difficult times. But I am sorry you have not eaten."

She was twirling a lock of her hair absentmindedly with a finger of her left hand. Niska sensed that she was self-conscious about being watched. He got up to brush his teeth and fetch some clean bedsheets for the girl.

When he returned and resumed his seat she looked different somehow. Suddenly, she got up out of the armchair, and with only her slightly torn blouse and her thin underwear on, she approached Niska with a strange look in her eyes, distant, but with a practiced expression of tenderness and gratitude.

She knelt beside Niska's chair and whispered, "You are such a good and kind person, Sir. I cannot in any way compensate you...but if you want..."

Niska lurched back; he had no doubt what the girl intended.

"You little fool!" he said perplexedly. "What are you doing? I am old enough to be your father!"

Niska rose out of the chair and held her hard by her shoulders, pushing her slight body away from his.

"You're just a child, Hannah," he said.

He covered her all the way up to her neck with the coverlet on his spartan couch, as if to protect her from every evil thought... maybe his own.

She stepped back bewildered. Niska gathered his scattered thoughts and feelings strewn about the room. It took him a while to make sense of the sudden, unwelcome change in Hannah.

Why would a fifteen-year-old girl offer herself unbidden to a total stranger, a man well over fifty? There was a time long ago when I might have found the prospect titillating, but not now, not under these circumstances, not with this poor waif. What kind of life has she been leading?

"Now, be a nice girl and sleep well and dream only sweet dreams," he said to her awkwardly. "I'm sorry that I have no other bed to offer you. You'll need to make do with the armchair."

Hannah looked embarrassed and confused at first. Then a smile of relief and happiness spread over her face. To Niska, she looked like what she really was: a young helpless child in an evil and cruel world.

"It's much better than the hard floors of the attics I've been sleeping in."

Niska turned off the light in the living room, and exited to his own bedroom, as though he couldn't retreat there fast enough. He said, "*Gute Nacht,* Hannah."

The following morning, Hannah was awake in her armchair as though waiting for him to emerge from his bedroom. He laid out a small breakfast of slices of rye bread and canned fish on the scarred wooden coffee table.

"Usually, when a woman spends the night in my flat, I ask her to tell me more about herself," Niska said with a friendly, knowing smile.

Hannah caught Niska's drift. She had trusted him thus far so, apparently, she felt she had nothing to lose by reciting a synopsis at least of her story.

She had been raised in a small town in the eastern part of Germany near the border with Poland. Her mother had died when she was eight years old. Suddenly, out of nowhere, her father was charged by the local SS with spying. His barber shop was confiscated and given to a gentile barber in the Aryanization program.

"My *Papa* was grateful that *Mutti* didn't have to endure such humiliation."

Niska shook his head slowly, remaining silent.

"*Papa* and I tried to escape to Poland. But we were apprehended at the border. *Papa* was wounded by a couple of shots by border guards on the German side. He died in the holding cell a few days later."

Her eyes became misty as she related the story.

"And you? How did you survive?"

"I was taken to a camp. An awful camp for Polish prisoners, even though I am not Polish. It was called Ravensbrück. You've heard of it?"

"Yes, unfortunately I have."

A few days after she arrived there, an SS officer approached her and whispered to her, "*Fräulein,* there is a way for you to leave from here. This is no place for you. I can tell you are German. You should be comfortable. I can arrange for you to have accommodations, good food, and warmth. You are a beautiful girl. That is good. How old are you?"

"I'm fifteen, sir," Hannah said in a trembling voice.

"Good. From now on, let us say that you are eighteen years old. It is better. So remember, whenever someone asks you your age, always say that you are eighteen."

Hannah was sent to a beautiful house in the nearby village of Furstenberg. To her, the house resembled a small hotel with individual rooms. One room on the first floor looked like a dim private dining room with a bar.

A dark, elderly lady, rather world-weary and not terribly friendly, led her to a room on the second floor. The door to her room had a number on it as did the other rooms. The corridor was covered by soft red carpet.

"This will be your room now," the woman told Hannah. "You'll find linens and towels in the closet. And use all the toiletries and lotions and perfumes on the counter that you like."

Hannah sensed the woman looking her up and down as if evaluating her.

"You look awfully young. How old are you?"

Hannah remembered to say she was eighteen.

The woman didn't look very convinced.

"Ah, I see. You also? So is everyone else in here. Of course, that is not any of my concern," she said as she closed the door and left.

For a couple of days, Hannah was undisturbed. In the closet she found a couple of dresses, but strangely, no underwear. On the shelves were only a couple of fashionable silk camisoles, stockings with leg straps, and bras.

The next morning, she discovered that her own clothes had disappeared. She complained about the scanty wardrobe to the older woman who brought breakfast in a tray.

"Your own clothes are in the laundry," the woman replied indifferently. "You'll just have to be satisfied for now with what's there in the closet."

An hour or so later the old woman returned with two pairs of shoes for Hannah. One pair had low heels, almost like slippers, the pair she was wearing in the attic when Niska discovered her. The other pair was shiny black and had French stiletto heels. Later in the day she was given a bracelet, earrings, and a couple of rings.

On the second morning, for some reason Hannah couldn't understand, she was photographed by a very uninterested, disheveled man. The dress she wore had a low, revealing neckline, which made her look older than her fifteen years. The photographer had her pose in some of the more daring positions she had seen in some of the magazines the boys had smuggled into the schoolyard at home. One was with her in her pajamas lying face-down on top of the bed, another a close-up of her neck and shoulders with a part of her breast exposed.

These details about her experience practically poured out of Hannah. But then suddenly, she stopped, averting her eyes from Niska, her gaze riveted to the floor of the flat. After a pause, she launched back into her narrative.

"I am embarrassed to talk about this, Sir."

"I understand. But please, go on."

"One night, at around 22:00, there was a knock on my door. I was just getting dressed to go to bed."

"You have company," the old woman announced from behind the closed door, "a *Luftwaffe* officer. For God's sake, remember to behave politely toward him. And don't forget that he is a captain serving our people."

The young, handsome guest arrived in the room a short time later, dressed in a uniform consisting of a blue-gray single-breasted, open-collared jacket, white shirt and black necktie, and blue-gray trousers held up by a black belt. Most impressive to Hannah, and most intimidating, too, were the shiny black leather boots on his feet.

"He looked as proud as a peacock," Hannah continued. "I was afraid of him, but he smiled at me in a way that disarmed my fear. I felt almost naked in my pajamas. He sat down beside me on the sofa. I moved instinctively a few centimeters closer to the armrest at the end of the sofa. Then he poured some wine into two glasses. I was also given a couple of glasses of cognac, which caused me to cough. That made the officer laugh gently."

"'You are a very attractive young lady,' the officer said to me as he moved closer and put his arm on the top of the sofa and then lowered it so that it draped my shoulders. He told me I was not old and ugly and dirty like the Polish women in the other rooms.

"He then leaned over and tried to kiss me and placed his hand roughly on my breast. I tried to resist, but he was too strong. I even threatened to scream for help if he didn't behave himself, but the captain only laughed.

"'Go ahead and try it,' he said. 'You'll notice that there is no help to be had.'

"Finally, the officer cursed in German and violently threw me down onto the bed."

This hell continued for several days before Hannah finally realized what kind of place she had been brought to. When she later became acquainted with several of the other women, she discovered that they had experienced worse, especially the Poles.

"And Jews like me," Hannah added.

"A certain older officer became a 'regular,' a gray-haired retired lieutenant-colonel, he said he was. He called me, '*meine Rosenknöpfchen,*' my Little Rosebud. He did rather strange things with me, but I wasn't afraid of him as I was of the others. He took off his clothes, and I took off mine, just as I had learned was expected of me. But he didn't try to touch or penetrate my private parts like the others. He couldn't, because his small thing remained limp through the whole visit.

"I didn't know what I was supposed to do. I had learned what to do with the other men. But this was strange, I thought.

"He just continued to look at my naked body lying on the bed while he stood up over me and tried to rub his thing. It didn't seem to help. It seemed to take a long time for him to finish. I was afraid that the old woman would come to the door and tell me some officer or soldier was waiting and to hurry up and finish. But thankfully, the old lieutenant-colonel finally gave out a weak groan, kind of like a muffled imitation of the other men when they reach that point. Only, his hands were completely dry. Not a drop fell on the bed or the floor or my body.

"'Thank you, *meine kleine Rosenknöpfchen,*' she said softly as she handed me my bra and panties. None of the others ever did that. 'I know this was probably confusing to you, not to mention very demeaning for me. But you are very dear and beautiful.'"

The old lieutenant-colonel came by her room several more times, and each time, the routine was similar. Hannah was relieved that she didn't need to fear an unknown disease with him, just pose patiently and passively allow him to admire her naked body until he was finished. Afterwards, he was always very kind to her.

"Once, in a moment of weakness, I confided to him my real age," Hannah confessed. "I don't know why. But I started to regret it as soon as the words were out of my mouth.

"'The bastards!' he exclaimed. I was surprised and even a little afraid, because I had never seen him angry before. 'How dare they do this?' he asked. 'That bloody Himmler!'

"I thought that he was confused and that he meant 'Hitler.' I didn't know who Himmler was."

"No, you heard correctly," Niska said. "The brothels are Heinrich Himmler's doing."

"The man just ranted on. 'Himmler's too unmanly even to make love to his own wife. But he opens up these dens of iniquity all over the *Reich* so that his officers can have their lust satisfied. Doesn't he know there are fifteen-year-old girls in these places? The bastard!'

"I was afraid that he was unsatisfied with me and would report his displeasure to the old woman, even though I had always done as he requested. Perhaps now I would be sent to another and altogether worse place."

The old officer, though, had grown helplessly, dementedly in love with Hannah. And what was more, the old man was angered that other men had access to her. He was protective of her. That other men visited her was an affront to his grandfatherly instinct to shield her.

"'*Meine Rosenknöpfchen,*' he confessed one evening to me. 'I have been thinking about your situation. I am a man who can arrange things, you know. I have enjoyed my visits with you. But you do not belong here. My intention is to rescue you from this miserable cave.'

"This set off alarms in my mind, of course."

Hannah did not know what the lieutenant-colonel said, or paid to the old woman to get to her to give permission for Hannah to leave the premises with him. He was a fixture at the house. Perhaps the old woman surmised that such an old man wouldn't pose a danger to the girl. But one morning, after another of their strange but tender sexual encounters, he led her to his home not far away. The old man had never harmed her. But Hannah wasn't sure if this was some kind of carefully veiled abduction of her that would not end well.

"In his comfortable study, he showed me the photographs on top of his large piano. He pointed out his late wife. I could tell from his voice that he missed her. I felt so sorry for him.

"That evening, when the old, kind officer fell asleep on the sofa, I saw my chance to escape. I liked the old man, but he had been, after all, a German soldier in the war. I didn't know if, after he used me, he would turn me over to the SS. So I fled the house and hid in an empty cart at the railroad station—you know, the kind of cart they use to carry mail and other cargo to the freight cars? When I awoke the next morning, I discovered that I was on a freight train. But I had no idea of where it was going. Without knowing it, they must have loaded me onto the train with the other freight."

"You were fortunate that whoever 'they' are didn't turn you over to the police, or the SS."

"When the train halted at a station to pick up the mail in the cover of night, I jumped out of the car on the other side. I had only these flimsy clothes on. People looked at me curiously, but luckily, I didn't run into any police or men from SS or *Wehrmacht*. One kind old lady told me where I was when I asked her. I was in Wandlitz. I walked on country roads through the darkness to Berlin."

"You must have been exhausted from all that walking."

"For several nights I wandered the streets of Berlin. I felt like a tramp, with no food or a place to sleep. I didn't know what to do, where to turn. I was thoroughly drained and in despair—like an orphan, which is what I am, I suppose. I wasn't sure I wanted to go on living. Then one evening, I happened upon the door to your building. Thankfully, someone had carelessly left it unlocked. Maybe it was even you?"

Niska's eyes were getting misty as he listened to her report. He thought of his own daughter, Eeva, back in Finland, just a few years older than Hannah, whom his precarious legal situation prevented him from returning to Finland to see. As a seaman, he knew, of course, about brothels, that they existed, and that some women made a living working in them. But the thought of the girl before him, so much like his own daughter, seized and hoodwinked into becoming a sex slave, both angered him profoundly, and saddened him to the core.

"What will you do with me now?" she asked him, almost as a matter of course, as though she assumed that she was at the mercy of yet another man. "Give me up to the SS?" She was still twirling the lock of her hair girlishly.

Niska felt a sharp pang of disappointment in himself. The girl had no paperwork to identify her. If he tried to smuggle her into Poland, or any country, for that matter, the border guards would detect immediately from her appearance that she is a Jew. It would be pointless to try to convince them that she was his daughter, so little did she exhibit classic Finnish features.

"I can buy you a train ticket back to your town in the east, if you like."

"My family is gone. I don't really have anyone there anymore."

"Do you have others anywhere, grandparents, perhaps, or friends of the family, who might be able to take you in?"

In asking this, Niska felt a sliver of shame because he knew that given the madness of those unforgettable nights of November 9 and 10, it was quite possible, if not likely, that her grandparents or family friends had been rounded up by the SS.

"I do have a great-aunt, in Bautzen, I think, near the Polish border. But I have not spoken with her for many years. I am not sure she still lives there, or even if she is still alive."

"Well, for now, it's the best we have."

Without giving them any explanation, Niska borrowed some clothing from a family on the fifth floor that he knew had a daughter about Hannah's age. Fortunately, Hannah fit into them as if they were her own, and the two walked together to the *HauptBahnhof*. They had to be careful as they walked, needing every now and then to step over shards of glass and charred pieces of furniture that had yet to be cleared off the sidewalks after the nights of Brownshirt fury. Hannah looked apprehensive; Niska was weighed down with a load of sadness and feeling of inadequacy.

On the platform on which the train to Dresden was about to depart, Niska took some bank notes from his wallet and gave them to her so that she could purchase a meal or two. She stepped onto the train without a suitcase. As Niska waved his hand in farewell to her, he could see that she wiped a tear from her eye with a new, clean handkerchief he had given her back at his flat. Niska was overtaken by a feeling of grief. From his pants' pocket, he pulled out his own, less clean handkerchief and blew his nose.

As he walked home, more slowly than usual, oblivious to his surroundings, Niska tried to sort through his muddled emotions and thoughts.

I feel so helpless to help her. I feel like an abject failure. What will become of her? Will she find her great aunt? Will she be received warmly? Will the great aunt even be there to begin with? Can she evade the SS or Gestapo that in time, I'm sure, will catch up to her, maybe eventually almost all Jews in Germany?

What was it that I was feeling as she was telling me her sad story? I've always loved smuggling, because it was a way of helping people get what someone else in authority has used his power to say that they can't have. But alas, I couldn't smuggle her.

Algot Niska, former whiskey runner during the years of Finnish prohibition, was now growing moderately comfortable as a smuggler out of Germany of the property of wealthy Jews. He was a thoroughly pragmatic and opportunistic man, who until that very moment was preoccupied with his own illicit business and livelihood. But that evening, this usually stoical offender of the law on the lam from the Finnish authorities felt an unfamiliar and overpowering tug somewhere within him, or from without, some unseen benevolent power pulling him compellingly outward toward those, like Hannah, who were being victimized and beaten, yanking him irresistibly toward some new version of himself.

CHAPTER SIX

Berlin: December 13, 1938

A superb, shiny, black-as-coal civilian automobile pulled up in front of a house on *Prinz Albrecht Strasse.* Except for its height, this house looked much like the others on that side of the street, old and heavy and gray. Yet, whenever people passed by this house, walking their dog perhaps, or striding to their own place of employment, they hastened their steps, lowered their heads, and strictly averted their eyes from it. They knew this was the general headquarters, the Chancellery of the *Reichsführer SS,* the chief of the *Schutzstaffel,* or SS, the secret police and security force—Heinrich Himmler.

The passenger in the car, Felix Kersten, had been dreading this day. Several nights prior, he had been in his flat in The Hague, fully enjoying in his blossoming romantic relationship with his fiancée Irmgaard. His benefactor Queen Wilhelmina was so pleased with his artful therapy that she requested that he treat her husband, Prince Hendrik, as well. Other requests followed. Kersten's personal and professional life was where he wanted it to be. In The Hague, he had been in his desired home and natural habitat.

The slightly rotund Kersten stepped out of the vehicle and crossed the street. He approached the large, imposing red and black wooden door at the entrance to the repurposed mansion. Whatever anxiety he was feeling was concealed by an exterior of professional poise. Two SS guards, their faces identically impassioned, holding rifles, their heads squeezed into helmets that came down to their eyebrows, stood as a forbidding barrier in front of the entrance. Kersten handed one of the guards a letter of reference addressed to Heinrich Himmler from Auguste Diehn, which indicated the purpose of his visit.

"To the *Reichsführer, bitte,"* Kersten announced as if he expected his words to be received and obeyed as an order.

The guard took the letter and, without saying a word, rotated his erect body 180 degrees on his heels and opened the door for

Kersten, showed him into the foyer, and told him politely to wait there.

Kersten wasn't sure what he was feeling. A little anxiety, certainly, upon entering a realm as foreign to him as if he were getting off an airplane in Papua-New Guinea; a sense of curiosity about this unique, exclusive setting, an inner sanctum of the Nazi apparatus; a hint of defiance, too, a steely determination not to allow the excessive, orgiastic symbols of Nazi power and dominance, staring at him from every surface and corner in the building, intimidate him.

He beheld the enormous black and red Nazi Swastika flag hanging down over the foyer from the ceiling above. Every detail was calculated to inspire praise and glory to the National Socialist party, its leader and his philosophy, just as Notre Dame in Paris, with its supreme interior height, the majestic stained-glass windows and the remote high altar were designed to point to the grandeur of the Christian God.

So this is the den of the beast? This is the home of the notorious outfit that is the most universally feared organization in Germany? I feel as if I am entering a sinister domain of darkness. Such a malevolent, morally rotten presence I sense in the air here. This is the fount from which springs a terrifying new world that has been evolving in the past five years, a world of mistrust, deceit and treachery. It must be impossible for any honest, scrupulous men, if there are any here, to breathe the putrid air.

A few minutes later another guard marched ceremoniously into the foyer, accompanied by a gray-haired officer.

"*Heil* Hitler!" said the officer as a greeting, extending his right arm in the standard Nazi salute.

The tall, stout visitor with the ruddy cheeks stood up, lifted his hat politely, and answered, "Good day, *Leutnant.*"

The officer looked irritated by the calculated civilian greeting in the exceedingly militaristic environment and culture of the building. "Follow me," he said curtly to Kersten.

The officer led Kersten up a flight of stairs and down a very high-ceilinged and long corridor. There was a great deal of activity and movement to and fro through the hallway. Officers of all ranks emerged into the hallway carrying file folders and sheets of paper from offices and disappeared into other ones, exchanging salutes.

Whatever their rank, all men wore gray uniforms, spotless and precise, their black boots polished and shiny, with an insignia depicting two ancient runes on the sleeve cleverly designed to form a stylized spelling of the *ϟϟ*.

Kersten, however, kept his hands in the pockets of his warm woolen overcoat and left his hat on his head almost cheekily. Before they reached the end of the corridor, near the middle, the officer stopped him for a fleeting instant, but long enough for the fluoroscope, hidden in a recess in the wall, to verify that the civilian visitor was unarmed.

Kersten followed the officer up yet another broad staircase, this one an enormous, ornate one made of marble. The ensuing corridor ended before a massive wooden door, again painted in the Nazi red and black. Kersten could sense the officer's demeanor turning graver the closer they got to the door. The officer raised his right hand, prepared to knock on the door. Before he had a chance to do so, however, the door flew open from the inside. A man in the distinctive black uniform of a general of the SS stood in the doorway. He was slight, with narrow shoulders. His black hair was thinning at the crown and above his hairline. Steel-rimmed glasses framed slightly slanted eyes of deep gray. He had prominent Mongoloid cheekbones.

It was Himmler.

His face had deep hollows in the cheeks and temples, and was the color of beeswax. With a clammy and bony hand, he seized Kersten's strong and plump hand, and drew the doctor inside the office. The officer saluted Himmler respectfully and left.

So this is the notorious Heinrich Himmler? This slight, almost puny man? This mouse-like, pitiful creature who has the appearance of an ordinary village schoolteacher, which is logical, I suppose, because, of course, that's what he had been. As a boy, he must have been the last one selected for the pick-up soccer game in the schoolyard.

And yet, how utterly reverential the Leutnant who escorted me here was when he saluted Himmler, how compliantly he stood before this little man, how downright intimidated he appeared before the director of the infamous machinery of terror. Kersten was baffled by the apparent incongruity.

Kersten was barely a meter's distance inside the office when Himmler burst out, all the while continuing to pump Kersten's hand, "Thank you for coming, Doctor. I have heard a great deal about you." The high pitch of Himmler's voice surprised Kersten.

Himmler finally released Kersten's hand. Kersten thought that Himmler's wolfish, unattractive face became even more pale in the yellowish light in the office. Kersten couldn't help but notice the huge, larger-than-life portrait of Adolf Hitler displayed prominently on the wall behind Himmler's desk as though he had his eye on every movement in the office. Even in a still portrait, the *Führer* looked absolutely animated at a podium somewhere giving one of his rousing speeches.

"Perhaps, Doctor, you are the one to be able to relieve me of these unbearable stomach pains that permit me neither to walk nor sit well, not to mention sleep a wink. Sometimes the pain lasts four or five days at a time. I am completely wasted for days afterward. To my disappointment, not a single doctor in Germany, not even our best, has succeeded. But *Herr* Diehn has assured me that where others fail, you obtain results."

Kersten was flattered initially, but silently began to curse his longtime patient and friend for giving Himmler such an excellent review of his work.

"Doctor, do you think you can help me?"

Kersten was struck by how thin Himmler's lips were, like those of a lizard.

Yet, in the doleful features of Himmler's face, in the depth of his dull gray eyes, Kersten recognized the familiar appeal of a suffering human being. Suddenly, Himmler, the thought of whom had repulsed Kersten, was now merely another sick person in need of treatment, just like any other patient.

"Please remove your tunic and shirt, and unbutton the top of your trousers, if you would, *Herr Reichsführer*."

It felt strange and uncomfortable for Kersten to be using the Nazi form of address, making him feel awkwardly that he was collaborating somehow and compromising his own values. But he knew he had to tread carefully inside the headquarters of the feared SS.

"*Jawohl*, at once, Doctor, at once."

Himmler stripped unselfconsciously to his waist. He had rickety round shoulders, narrower than his torso, flimsy skin, slight biceps and chest muscles, and a prominent kettle of a stomach.

One of the "Master Race," this scrawny specimen?
"Please stretch out flat on your back, *Herr Reichsführer*."

Himmler reclined as directed on the divan in front of the Spartan desk that contained only two black and white photos. One, of Himmler looking at Hitler with absolutely rapt admiration, like a little boy meeting his hero for the first time, on a balcony overlooking the mountains, probably at Hitler's retreat in the Austrian Alps. The other was of Himmler and his family, he sporting Bavarian civilian clothes and an Alpine felt hat with a feather, a fishing rod held over his right shoulder, his left arm around the least attractive-looking woman Kersten had seen in a long time, presumably Himmler's wife, with their two young pig-tailed daughters and their stern-looking younger brother in front of them.

Kersten drew up a chair next to the divan and eased himself into it. He placed his hands on the outstretched body.

Kersten's hands were large, thick and fleshy. Each finger had, under its short, close-cut nail, a sort of benign swelling which was much more highly developed, much fleshier, than what one would see on most male hands.

Kersten's hands began to move rhythmically. His fingers glided like a figure skater over Himmler's delicate, white skin. Their tips skimmed in turn over Himmler's throat, chest, heart and stomach. At first their touch was light, barely perceptible. Then the fingers began to stop at certain spots, to seek, to listen. To listen...with those extraordinary small bulges at the tips of his fingers that served as a kind of antennae endowed with unusual sensitivity. They had a kind of second sight into a human body unknown to ordinary men and women, even other chiropractors and neurologists.

Kersten applied all his powers of concentration as he manipulated Himmler's tissue. He switched off his sense of hearing, smell, even sight. The only sense operating was in his hands, in those inexplicable nodules on his fingers.

Kersten's face was transformed by the tide of energy he had released within himself. His eyelids were shut as though in prayer, even though Kersten was agnostic. This was when he felt most fully alive.

Himmler writhed in the pain which tormented him ceaselessly, yet his gaze never left Kersten's absorbed, intensely focused face.

Suddenly, he gave a cry. Kersten's fingers, up to then light and velvety as they glided over the surface of Himmler's abdomen, had just pressed forcefully on a spot on his stomach. The pain burst in Himmler's gut like a wave of fire.

"Good...very good...please hold still," Kersten urged softly. Himmler noted that those were the first words Kersten had spoken since the treatment began.

Kersten continued exploring the flesh near the sensitive spot. Himmler groaned and bit his lip. His brow was wet with perspiration.

"That is very painful, isn't it?" Kersten asked each time.

"Terribly," answered Himmler through clenched teeth.

At last, Kersten withdrew his hands and placed them on his knees and opened his eyes.

"I see," said Kersten. "It's the stomach, obviously; but more interestingly, it's the sympathetic nervous system. It's not anything in your diet, even though I am sure you've been advised many times to change it. No, rather the nerves in your stomach are overstressed."

"I have a nervous system that is *sympathetic*?" Himmler asked with a chuckle. "Don't broadcast that too widely, Doctor. A lot of people would deny that adamantly."

Kersten smiled at Himmler's clever use of the pun. A good sign, perhaps.

"Can you help me, Doctor?" Himmler asked in a pleading tone.

Himmler's wan and lusterless face expressed humble supplication, and the dull eyes were begging for relief.

"We shall find that out right now, *Herr Reichsführer.*"

Kersten reached his hands over Himmler's supine body once again. He saw Himmler's body flinch and his muscles tighten.

"Just try to relax as much as you can."

This time Kersten did not need to grope. He knew exactly where to apply his effort. He thrust his fingers deep into Himmler's stomach at the affected spot, seized firmly and accurately the roll of flesh thus formed, and squeezed it, twisted it, kneaded it like a loaf of dough.

With every movement of Kersten's, Himmler flinched with a stifled cry.

"I'm trying to reach and waken the affected nerves through

your skin, fat and muscle," Kersten explained. "I apologize for the discomfort."

After some more vigorous manipulation, Kersten withdrew his fingers and dropped his arms. His whole body slackened like that of an athlete after a particularly strenuous race.

"How do you feel, *Herr Reichsführer*?"

"*Wunderbar,* Doctor, I feel...yes, it's truly amazing...I haven't felt this good since I was a youngster."

"You can get up now, *Herr Reichsführer*."

Himmler raised his slight body very slowly, carefully, as if in a slow-motion scene in a moving picture. It was as though he might negate the treatment if he rose too rapidly. He fixed Kersten with a look which, behind the lenses of his round spectacles, revealed a kind of bewilderment.

"Am I dreaming, Doctor? Is it possible? The pain is gone... completely gone."

"It is for now, *Herr Reichsführer.* But I warn you that it will most likely return once you are stressed again and the pressures of your life and work return."

"This technique of massage of yours, it's rather unique, isn't it? I see you received excellent training at our esteemed university here in Berlin," Himmler said.

"You're correct, *Herr Reichsführer.*"

"Our German professors are the best in the world."

"They're very learned, to be sure. But this technique you experienced today; it wasn't taught to me by a German professor."

"No, not a German?"

"No, rather by a Tibetan from China, a Doctor Ko." It gave Kersten pleasure to give an answer that undoubtedly would not please Himmler.

"Doctor, you mean to tell me that you treated me according to some inferior, primitive practice developed by those slant-eyed underlings?"

"But you did tell me, didn't you, that you felt absolutely fine after the treatment?" Kersten asked, more in the mild form of a declaration of triumph than an actual question. "Funny, what these 'inferior, primitive practices' can accomplish, isn't it?"

Himmler seemed at a loss for words. Kersten felt he had scored contract points in a game of bridge.

Himmler rose from the divan on which he had been seated and

came over to Kersten.

"You realize that I will now need to keep you near me, Doctor." Now that he had been relieved of his acute pain, the puny, half-naked man, still holding up his trousers with his left hand, had recovered his accustomed sense of glorious omnipotence.

"I'm afraid that's impossible, *Herr Reichsführer,*" Kersten did not hesitate to say. "Did *Herr* Diehn not tell you that I agreed to perform one treatment, and only one?"

"I confess that he did. But I am sure that you are a reasonable man, Doctor, open to negotiation."

"I am fully occupied in the service of Queen Wilhelmina and the Dutch royal family in The Hague."

"*Mein Gott,* Kersten, doesn't a leader of the German people have priority over the queen of a tiny, irrelevant country like Holland? Besides, she won't be queen much longer, let me assure you, Doctor."

Kersten didn't know what Himmler was referring to. He felt a flash of anger at this further display of nationalistic arrogance and supposed clairvoyance.

"I have a home in Holland now. I am contemplating marriage."

"Well, allow me to express my congratulations. To a sweet Finnish blonde? Or a Dutch lady who thinks wooden shoes are the epitome of high fashion?"

Kersten was becoming more and more certain that he would not be able to tolerate being this man's personal masseur.

"Neither, actually. To a young Silesian woman who is working in The Hague, in fact." He said this, aware that he was playing into Himmler's ethnic bias.

"I trust that it is a German woman from Silesia, Kersten, not one of those dirty Polacks or Slavs in the Silesian countryside with pig shit stuck to the soles of their shoes...But I think you will find, Doctor, that marriage is a highly overrated institution. Besides, I happen to think every red-blooded German man should have a mistress, to produce new pure Aryan children. We can find someone suitable for you, if you like."

Kersten had heard the rumors that Himmler had a mistress, not at all a secret even to his wife, who was seven years his senior. Kersten knew he wouldn't have time or energy for another woman, even if he were so inclined.

"That won't be necessary, *Herr Reichsführer.*"

"Well, then, I have other ways to make sure you come back...or better yet, remain in Berlin," Himmler continued with more than a hint of threat. "I would hope, though, not to have to resort to such means with an intelligent, skilled man like yourself."

Kersten felt trapped. He was frustrated, but felt he could not reveal his frustration to a man who, he had to acknowledge, might now hold the power of life or death over him.

"I'd rather not revert to such unsubtle ways to make you stay. Believe me, I do not wish to cause you harm of any kind. You are too valuable to me, and hence the *Reich*. I would much rather appeal to your loyalty to the Hippocratic Oath that you will apply, for the benefit of the sick, all measures that are required."

Kersten felt the familiar, occasional acute spasm of pain in his own stomach again, and the recognizable nausea that always accompanies it. Perspiration began to gather on his forehead and underneath his arms.

Kersten sought to hide his anxiety. He tried another tack. Could a dose of humor have any effect on this singularly dutiful man?

"What would your *Führer* say if he knew you had a personal doctor who is not a member of the National Socialist German Workers' Party, or even a German, for that matter, but a Finnish citizen?"

Himmler looked like a man who had seldom heard anyone refuse him. After a while, fearing perhaps that he had been too insistent, Kersten back-pedaled.

"But should you have acute need of me, I suppose can request Queen Wilhelmina to permit me to return temporarily to Berlin with just a day's notice. I can't guarantee that she would be accommodating to your request, though."

Kersten regretted his words as soon as they hovered in the air between him and Himmler.

"You'll be hearing from me, Doctor," Himmler said curtly. "You can be sure of that...No matter what the trifling tulip-loving queen says."

CHAPTER SEVEN

Berlin: December 15, 1938

In the weeks since seeing Hannah off at the *HauptBahnhof,* Algot Niska had been thrust into an uncharacteristic condition of lassitude. It took him several days to make contact with even one of his contacts in Berlin.

His inactivity surprised him. He had always prided himself on his work ethic, his ability to overlook distractions and to get things accomplished. Part of it, he acknowledged reluctantly to himself, was that now, over fifty, neither his body or spirit could accomplish what he had at the beginning.

He was not particularly a man prone to reflection. But the encounter with Hannah the previous month, and the violence that he had witnessed on the streets of Berlin a few weeks prior to that, the burning of the synagogue, and the overheated hatred of the crowd, had set him on an atypical course of rumination. So, too, had the vehemence of his own visceral reaction to those events. He couldn't remember ever reacting so emotionally to something.

In the past, even at the news of the death of his father in the Finnish civil war, his emotions would skim over the surface of the water like the flat stones he used to skip as a boy over the waves of Lake Ladoga near his Karelian childhood home.

It occurred to him once or twice that perhaps he was a little bit in love with Hannah. Then he quickly chased the thought from his mind and wondered how he could think such a thing.

The image in his mind of Hannah boarding the train alone to an unknown fate continued to haunt him day and night. So did her sordid account of her days as a sex slave. Neither had he been able to expunge from his mind the dreadful memory of the flaming stained-glass window crushing to death the rabbi and his wife.

Niska didn't have first-hand experiential knowledge from the Great War of the acts of cruelty men of warring sides were capable of inflicting on one another. His knowledge of them was strictly from second-hand testimony of drinking companions who had lived through them. However, he was in his late twenties when Finland declared its independence from Czarist Russia in 1917. In the ensuing bloodletting between the conservative Whites and the Reds with their Bolshevik leanings, in which his father was knifed to death, he had witnessed what viciousness and vindictiveness citizens of even the same newly formed nation could perpetrate on one another. So Niska was not especially surprised by the intensity of the mob's hatred and violence that night. What he couldn't quite comprehend was why it was on defenseless Jews that they had chosen to inflict their violence.

But that evening had been the first time that he had had a ringside seat to such irrational pugilism. He was quite surprised by how deeply it had affected his spirit.

Then there was that befuddlingly unfamiliar beckoning toward something more righteous and noble that he felt stirring within him in the midst of the brutality. It was such a novel experience for him that he spent many hours lying on his bed trying to make sense of it.

He was in that very supine position on his bed one late afternoon when the telephone rang. The voice on the other end of the line was that of Mr. Bruno Altmann sounding more fretful and anxious than Niska was accustomed to.

"*Herr* Niska, can we meet at the usual place at 21:00? I've got another item of interest for you." Altmann spoke in his native German. German was one of the four languages in which Niska, despite having had only a brief and scanty foreign education, was fluent.

Altmann and Niska always spoke in code in case either Altmann's or Niska's phone was being tapped by the SS. The "usual" place was the Kakadu Cabaret on *Joachimstaler Strasse.* The "item" was another allotment of personal property and goods that Altmann wanted Niska to smuggle out of Germany to relatives beyond the reach of the Third Reich.

Niska agreed to meet Altmann. As he dressed to leave his flat, he welcomed the familiar, delicious taste of intrigue.

At the door of the Kakadu, Niska was greeted by a familiar, smiling hostess, Paula, clad in a black silk top and a short-hemmed skirt accessorized by black net stockings.

"Your usual table, *Herr* Niska?"

"Ah, you know my needs perfectly, Paula. Yes." He gave her a wink of his right eye.

She led Niska through a forest of round tables covered with white table cloths and surrounded by patrons in formal attire. Niska had an evening suit for just this purpose. Niska sat on the chair she offered. She offered him an *Eckstein* cigarette and held out a lighter so that he could light it. He smiled and passed a crisp bank note into the palm of her hand, told her that his guest for this evening would be a certain business associate, *Herr* Altmann, and thanked her as she left.

His usual table was near the stage. A small, very traditionally German-looking band was on the stage. Niska didn't particularly care for the new menu of German folk music that had become a staple at Kakadu and other cabarets since 1933. He thought the unvarnished celebration of Germanic identity in the music bordered on jingoism. Jazz had had a monopoly on music in the cabarets in the previous frivolous decade and the early part of the current one. Things changed with the accession of Hitler to Chancellor when jazz was discouraged and eventually banned as a subversive non-Aryan influence.

He returned the smile of several female patrons at nearby tables as he sat at the table waiting for Altmann. He scanned the other tables in his vicinity for men whose evening suits looked too new to have been worn very often, or whose eyes, like his, were surveying the other tables. These were sure indications of undercover SS men. He was relieved not to have spied any potential candidates this evening, although he knew that they frequented the Kakadu just about every night. Before the evening was through there would undoubtedly be *Wehrmacht* officers around a few tables with their wives or mistresses. The SS would be watching them, too.

Niska glanced up into the many balconies that overlooked the dinner and dance floor, knowing that the SS were often to be found there, where they could get an unobstructed view below.

Altmann was led to the table by Paula herself. He handed her a new-looking bank note for her service. Whether or not Paula reckoned Altmann was a Jew, she gave no indication. A Jewish tip was as valuable as a gentile tip.

The two men shook hands and took their seats.

"Two cognacs, please, Paula," Niska ordered.

Altmann surveyed the Kakadu anxiously.

"It looks pretty clear tonight, Bruno," Niska reported. "Those *Wehrmacht* jokers at the tables over there are too intent on having a good time and too dullened by *Schnapps* already to take note of who might be in their surroundings. We're okay."

Niska thought Altmann's face looked more distressed than usual, nonetheless. He remembered the note of urgency in his voice on the telephone. When the band stopped playing for a short break, and they knew they could be overheard from nearby tables, the men exchanged the normal mundane pleasantries of small talk about the weather and plans for the coming holiday.

After about a quarter hour, the band struck up a particularly energetic polka. Couples got up to dance, and as they did, the volume of the giddiness in the room increased to the point where Niska and Altmann could get down to the purpose of the meeting without the potential for being overheard.

Altmann began barely above a whisper. "I've put some papers and a few small items—jewelry mostly—in a safe deposit box in the Jacquier and Securius Bank in the Red Castle. I have informed my nephew in New York through a gentile courier to expect them soon."

"And you want me to retrieve them and smuggle them out of Germany?" Niska looked at Altmann through eyes that had been rendered as narrow slits on his face by years of squinting at the reflection of the sun against the water.

"That's right. On your next trip to Amsterdam or Copenhagen perhaps?"

"But I would need to liquidate the jewelry and wire cash to your nephew."

Again, the band paused between numbers. Niska and Altmann altered their conversation seamlessly to a back-and-forth about a recent match of two soccer teams in the *Gauliga*. Once the music started again, the men resumed their transaction.

"Yes, that's right," Altmann said. "I know you have a certain knack for that kind of thing. The jewelry should fetch the equivalent of almost 19,000 *Reichsmarks* by my amateurish reckoning. Just take your own percentage off the top and wire the balance to my nephew."

"You're going to allow me to name my own price?"

"Your own Finnish government considers you a scoundrel, Mr. Niska, but one that I have found I can trust to be fair. Isn't that why you're known as 'The Gentleman Smuggler'?"

Niska smiled faintly. The smile enhanced the deep lines and cracks that a life on the sea had burrowed into his face.

"And, before I forget, here's the key for the box. God, I'm so glad to get my shit out of the Jacquier Bank now that it's been taken over by Gentiles."

Altmann checked around to make sure people at tables nearby were suitably immersed in their boozy conversation, then handed the key to Niska underneath the table. The two men held up their cognac glasses as a gesture of sealing the deal.

Niska looked earnestly at Altmann through the smoke rising from the tip of his cigarette.

"I've accepted your commission, Bruno, but I still detect a look of concern on your face."

"How could there not be concern? It's been a difficult five years. Hitler and his thugs squeeze the vice on us Jews tighter with each passing day. I wonder if the synagogue's burning and destruction of Jewish businesses last month are the climax for which Hitler has been lusting. Or is it just another nail in the Jewish coffin in Germany, with much more to follow?"

"It was a disgusting, stomach-turning series of events I witnessed that night," Niska agreed.

The men were silent for a while. Then Altmann raised his head and looked at Niska with the look of someone who had more to request than just the smuggling out of the country of some cash and jewelry. He leaned forward over the table so that his face was just centimeters away from Niska's.

"You, Niska, are a bold man. You could accomplish so much more in Germany than smuggling Jewish property out of the country."

Altmann held up the palms of his hands.

"Not that I don't appreciate your doing that, of course. Don't get me wrong. But quietly and secretively in our little confabs in our flats and at temple, a lot of us are talking about our desire to escape what Hitler is making into a pig sty. And you know how we Jews feel about pigs."

The recurring scene of the rabbi and his wife being crushed and incinerated underneath the fallen window frame flashed through Niska's mind once again.

"We can't just get up and leave, of course. The Nazis hate us. To them, we Jews are spies, criminal, psychopaths, and enemies of the people. You know the drill. But still, they won't let us leave the country. Of course, they don't want us to take our property and wealth with us, nor our testimonials of all that is really going on within German boundaries."

Niska took another puff of his cigarette. He nodded to indicate he was ready to hear more.

Altmann slammed his fist on the table. Kersten was startled. Patrons at the next table ceased their laughter and conversation momentarily and looked over at the two men. Only the tables of the *Wehrmacht* officers and their companions continued their merrymaking uninterrupted.

"Damn it, something's got to be done!" Altmann insisted. Peering straight into Niska's eyes, he added, "And by God, something *can* be done!"

The neon light from the advertising outside shone through the curtain, giving Altmann's livid face an even redder glow.

"I'm too old to try to leave and start life all over somewhere else. But there are others I know, *Herr* Niska—some of them very wealthy, by the way—who would be eager to compensate a resourceful person generously who could devise a way to help them escape."

Altmann leaned back and looked into Niska's face to get a reading of his response.

"You seem to have a golden touch, Algot. All those years of making whiskey runs into Finland have helped you hone your smuggling skills. Skills, I might add, that you could apply to smuggling *human beings* rather than just bank notes and diamond rings. Ever consider that?"

Niska lowered his head and riveted his eyes to the rim of his now-empty cognac glass while he contemplated Altmann's remarks. Altmann was a savvy enough business man to recognize when he might have a willing fish on the line.

"For instance, a young man I know—he's my wine dealer—has asked me on the sly if I knew of any way he could get the hell out of Germany and back to his native Czechoslovakia. The SS are turning the screws very tightly on him. He was a member of our youth movement. In fact, he was there in front of the *Reichstag* to protest with others in '33 when Hindenburg conferred the

Chancellorship upon Hitler."

"That kind of activity does tend to catch the attention of the SS."

"His wine shop was badly damaged by the Brownshirts on that bloody night last month. A shame—his late father was a good friend of mine. He opened the shop, and it passed down to his son when he died. Now the son has received word that the shop will undergo the process of Aryanization. He will have virtually nothing. He wants to hightail it out of here before things get worse."

Altmann paused and stared into Niska's face.

"I think you can help, Algot. The question is, are you willing to help him?"

Niska's eyes were roaming about the room. To Altmann, he seemed uncomfortable—or tempted, but definitely hesitant. It was time to seal the deal, Altmann intuited.

"I will give you sufficient money to make it worth your effort. You can use what you need to bribe a border official on the way out of Germany, or whatever it is you do. Then keep the rest."

Niska broke his silence. "I like to make a living the same as the next man. Smuggling was what the circumstances called for in the '20s and early '30s, so I took advantage. I don't go out of my way to find adventure and intrigue. They always seem to have a way of finding me. Is that what's happening now, Bruno?"

"The money is pretty good, you have to admit."

"If I choose to do as you have requested, it would be for a different kind of reward than the money. I don't want it on my conscience that I have profited unreasonably from another human being's misery."

"Then, I take it I can give the young Mr. Hudak your number?"

Niska stared out into the night through the windows again and was silent. Finally, getting up from the table, he said, almost under his breath, "I'll *think* about it, Bruno. That's all I am promising."

Before he headed for the exit, he turned and faced Altmann one more time, and added, "But tell him that if he calls me, to use a public telephone, not the one in his residence."

~~~

As he walked to his flat, Niska reflected on the conversation with Altmann, and the apparent upshot. Niska always had to keep his attention and alertness at peak level. Hitler punished smugglers without mercy. The tiniest offense against the *Reich's* strict monetary laws resulted in harsh convictions, and new, more severe laws were being created every day. Niska knew that enormous risks hung over him because he was transporting all kinds of items, like gold, silver, and jewelry across the border. The fact that the ones retaining his services were Jews just magnified the risk. Niska had lived with risk since he was in his early twenties, even earlier, and had served a sentence in Finland for his whiskey running.

Now the stakes were being raised much higher, however. To agree to smuggle an actual *human being,* especially a Jew, was accepting a much graver gamble. Should he be apprehended by the Nazis, rather than merely a prison sentence for smuggling inanimate contraband, it would mean the probable loss of his life. Were Niska to agree to help the young Czech wine merchant that Altmann had told him about evade capture by the Nazis to the relative safety of his native Czechoslovakia, he would be participating in an activity that could blow up and hurtle both him and the young Jew into irreversible destruction.

True, Niska did own a boat, currently moored in Amsterdam, and had three alert helpers on board who were accustomed to risk. And if in previous times he had smuggled large barrels of liquor in quantity successfully past inspectors, why could he not likewise succeed in smuggling a less bulky item, like a human being?

But an overriding doubt tugged at him as he turned the corner and crossed the street to his hotel apartment.

I am not a Jew myself. I belong to another race, almost the same as the Germans. I will do what I know best and help them save their goods and property that the Nazis want to get their greedy paws on. That should be enough. But to do any more than that and sign my own potential death warrant? I don't know.

CHAPTER EIGHT

The Hague: February 8, 1939

After his initial treatment session with Himmler, Kersten returned to The Hague. He was glad to resume his duties with the Dutch royal family and other prominent patients. He and Irmgaard deepened their romantic relationship. He hoped that this was where he would stay, perhaps for the rest of his living days. After his hardscrabble childhood and youth with his ethnic German family in Estonia, Kersten was determined to enjoy the wealth and prestige that his highly specialized practice among the European aristocracy was affording him.

Six enjoyable weeks had passed since that first encounter with the peculiar Himmler. Kersten had wishfully banished the memory of the treatment session. He had practically forgotten his own hasty, unpremeditated offer to Himmler to be available in case he was in a crisis of pain. At the time, Kersten considered his offer as a way of throwing a bone to the dogs to ward off Himmler's persistent barking.

One evening, as Kersten and Irmgaard were seated side-by-side on his couch looking at old photographs, the telephone seemed to explode on the other side of the sitting room with the loud, distinctive squealing of the Dutch phones, almost like an ambulance's siren. He stood up and ran to pick up the receiver to silence the intrusive sound. For several seconds, Kersten heard only the buzzing of the telephone wires, a sure indication to him that the caller was farther away than The Hague or Amsterdam.

"Dr. Kersten, I am sorry to disturb you. This is Major Brandt, *Reichsführer* Himmler's personal adjutant."

Kersten felt himself gripping the receiver more tightly. Just the name of Himmler sent a cold jolt of animus down his spine all the way to his shoes.

"The time has come, Dr. Kersten," Brandt continued, very businesslike. "The *Reichsführer* has need for you... And if I may be permitted to be so bold to add my own untrained opinion, Doctor, in my estimation, he has an acute and serious need for your treatment. The attacks are becoming more frequent and intense."

It wasn't until then that Kersten remembered Himmler's promise—or was it a threat?—to call for Kersten if he had need for him. He now regretted his offer to Himmler to be only a telephone call away.

Promptly but reluctantly the next morning, he boarded a KLM flight to Berlin. Brandt arranged to have a civilian limousine and driver meet him at the airport and drive him directly to *Prinz Albrecht Strasse*. Brandt seemed to appreciate that Kersten didn't want to be mistaken by passers-by on the street for a Nazi official.

When Kersten arrived inside Himmler's office, Himmler was doubled over in pain and could barely greet him. Kersten asked his patient to strip to his waist and lie down on the divan as on the first visit. Kersten took off the coat of his suit and rolled up the sleeves of his shirt. He began to knead the flesh above Himmler's stomach.

From Doctor Ko, Kersten had learned that the therapist's first duty was to find out the exact nature of the pain, and to ascertain its source. To aid him in his diagnosis, the therapist had at his disposal the four pulse and nerve centers and networks of the human body that the Tibetans had identified centuries earlier. His only instrument for arriving at a diagnosis was those idiosyncratic nodules of flesh on the tips of Kersten's fingers. They had become expert in detecting the malady lurking under the patient's skin fat, and musculature, and determining which nerve group was affected.

So now, with Himmler in a supine position on the divan in front of him, Kersten applied just the proper degree of pressure, precisely the appropriate kneading action, and made exactly the correct delicate twists and turns necessary to alleviate Himmler's excruciating pain. Once again, when Kersten had finished the manipulation of Himmler's flesh, Himmler bathed in an infinite ocean of relief and pure bliss. He was downright effusive with his declarations of wonder and gratitude to Kersten. "You're an absolute magician, Doctor, a sorcerer!"

"Oh, it's not magic, *Herr Reichsführer*. It's strictly science developed by the people of the Far East before the time when Jesus walked this earth."

"I suppose they are, after all, the people who invented gunpowder," Himmler said with a smile.

"Actually, that was the Chinese. But you've got the general

region of the world correct."

Himmler requested that Kersten prolong his stay in Berlin and administer daily treatments for the time being. Himmler complained of chronic discomfort of the most acute kind, almost daily attacks. Grudgingly, Kersten agreed to a two-week stay in Berlin.

"Very good, Doctor. I knew you were a man with whom one could negotiate. I'll have Brandt arrange a comfortable flat for you in the Hotel *Kaiserhof.*"

The next day, in their second session of the current series of treatments, Himmler became very talkative during the breaks in the massage session. He chatted freely about himself and his illness.

"I've always been deadly afraid of cancer, Doctor. My father died an ugly death to the disease."

"There's no need to fear that your condition is caused by cancer, *Herr Reichsführer.* You might say that I have a handle on your condition, if you'll excuse the pun." Himmler seemed physically relieved. The sense of reprieve encouraged further confession from Himmler.

"I have to admit that I am ashamed of this illness. I hide my pain fiercely, Doctor. Please don't let anyone, except Brandt, of course, know about the inconvenient nausea, the debilitating stabbing in the stomach. Certainly not the *Führer.*"

"But why, *Herr Reichsführer?* It is no disgrace to be sick.*"

"It is when you are in charge of the SS, Doctor, the elite of the German people, which is to say, the elite of the whole world."

Kersten looked down at Himmler, making no reply.

"I choose the recruits myself, and always on the identical model: tall, athletic, blond and blue-eyed. They must be tireless, disciplined, and as hard on themselves as they are on others. You see, Doctor? How can I let those below me in rank see my bodily misery, and my surrender to it? I cannot afford to be perceived as weak."

Kersten raised his bushy eyebrows, but didn't respond otherwise, though he understood Himmler's secretiveness about his illness. Kersten was beginning to notice the paradox that this man, second in power, only to Hitler himself, perhaps, one whose duty was to keep the highest and most terrible secrets of state, could be so unbelievably indiscreet with him after a treatment. After Kersten's treatments with his expert hands, perhaps this normally morbidly suspicious man was in a kind of drunken forgetfulness in which his caution was suspended.

When a man is consciously on his guard, he will be careful to say what he wants others to hear; when he is off guard, his words reveal his real character.

Kersten had begun to establish a pattern of pausing every five minutes or so to encourage his loquacious patient to converse during these intervals.

Himmler seemed to jump inexplicably to a new subject.

"We will soon be at war, Doctor."

Kersten's hands, which had been lightly interlaced, locked tightly together, but he did not move. In dealing with Himmler, Kersten was learning to manipulate not only his patient's nerves, but also, sometimes, his psychological reactions.

"War?" Kersten exclaimed. "Good heavens! Why on earth?"

Himmler raised himself slightly on his elbows and answered excitedly, like a child breathlessly explaining to his father his latest discovery.

"There will be a war, because the *Führer* wants one. He believes it is for the good of the German people. War makes men stronger and more virile. Surely, you're not so naïve, Doctor that you believe that the world will ever know real peace until it has been purified by war and enlightened by National Socialist philosophy? And until it is totally *Judenfrei?*"

Kersten walked over to the sink which Himmler had had installed in his office to cater to his fetish for clean hands at all times and circumstances. Kersten now felt the need to wash his own hands. Was it because his hands had been massaging a patient? Or was it because of what excrement had been pouring out of his patient's mouth?

Himmler lay back down the full length on the divan and added, a trifle condescendingly, as though he were reassuring a frightened child, "Anyway, it will be a little war: short, easy, and victorious."

Kersten had remained silent and skeptical as Himmler spoke. Now he felt that he ought to respond somehow, however, lest Himmler misinterpret his silence as assent to the Nazi lunacy. It required something of an effort for Kersten to ask in an even, neutral tone, "Don't you think that flirting with war would be like playing with fire?"

"The *Führer* knows exactly just how far to go before we get burned," said Himmler.

Kersten marveled at the intellectual simplicity of this very complicated man, perhaps more feared by the military and the public than even the *Führer* himself. But lying there half-naked on the divan, Himmler seemed to shed the skin of the commander of the special troops and secret police, and take on the identity of a rather ordinary patient, giddy with relief from his pain.

"It sounds as though your *Führer* is not only a military genius, but an expert in human psychology as well," Kersten said, trying his best not to exaggerate the ironic tone.

"Yes, Doctor, you speak the truth," Himmler retorted enthusiastically. "That, he is, indeed."

CHAPTER NINE

Berlin: February 10, 1939

Kersten felt like an animal trapped in a cage. It had been several weeks since he had been able to return to his home in The Hague and be with Irmgaard, and free from Nazi politics. He was concerned that the patience of the Dutch royal family with his long absences would run out, and he would be relieved of his cushy, lucrative position as their personal massage therapist.

He lamented his vulnerable position. He was ensnared in a web of dangerous circumstances from which he wished to extract himself—if only he could. The Dutch royal family could not intercede on his behalf because he was not a Dutch citizen.

Yet, it boiled down to a choice between imprisonment or limited freedom as Himmler's masseur. Freedom, even proscribed and partial, was preferable.

He was a Finnish citizen. It was time to pay a visit to the ambassador at the Finnish legation. He suspected that as head of the SS, Himmler would have been remiss if he hadn't assigned an agent or two—probably plainclothes—to keep track of Kersten's movements. He had to be careful about the places he frequented and the contacts he made. No one should be surprised, however, that a Finnish citizen visited his country's chief diplomat.

Kersten began his private audience with the ambassador, T.M. Mäki, by describing his professional relationship with Himmler.

"We weren't aware of your relationship with Himmler," Mäki confessed, his face looking like that of a shopkeeper who discovers that the innocent-looking little boy who had been coming into his shop every day had been pilfering chocolate bars.

"I can't continue in what I am doing. I just can't," Kersten said. "Sometimes I feel Himmler thinks he *owns* me. I have to be on call at all times. He feels he has the right to loan me out to other prominent Nazis who are experiencing abdominal pain. Like Foreign Minister von Ribbentrop, for instance, who is a damnably dull and distasteful fellow. A few of the others aren't much better."

"And now, you are appealing for our help?"

"Well, yes. With the whole SS under his command, Himmler is in a position to decide the fate of almost everyone in Germany. Now, Austria, too. Surely, he can wield power over the life and death of a defenseless expatriate such as I."

"But from what you tell me, I gather you're too valuable to him for him to do you any harm."

"Well, yes, underneath the intimidating SS uniform, I grant he does possess an unexpected humanity. But when anyone of us is relieved of unyielding chronic pain, we can turn congenial in the presence of the one who alleviated it. The graciousness may be only temporary."

"You're saying that the Himmler's ferocity and brutality leave the room when you are treating him?"

"Yes, it appears so."

"But that at any moment they might return announced and uninvited?"

"Sometimes I fear that, to be quite frank."

"Very interesting, Dr. Kersten...Here's something for you to consider. It strikes me that you are in a very unique position. He seems to consider you his confessor for his soul and doctor for his body. You have a very privileged vantage point from which to see and hear otherwise classified tidbits of the Nazis' strategy. That could be very valuable to your country, if not the family of nations, if we were to be kept abreast of it."

"What I have noticed, though, Mr. Ambassador, is that my proximity to Himmler is being noticed by some of Himmler's associates, Heydrich and Kaltenbrunner, mainly. I see the suspicion in their eyes. I don't think Himmler is even aware of it. To be quite frank, I'm not exaggerating when I say I fear for my life in the Chancellery."

"I can empathize, Dr. Kersten. You are in a precarious position, I agree. But since you have made me aware of it, I'm afraid I must insist that you stay right where you are—by the *Reichsführer's* bedside. It's only a matter of time when war will break out. Germany will be at the center of it. Finland is not directly affected at this juncture. When Germany turns over in bed, however, the rest of Europe shakes. The strategic information you may be able to overhear, or pump from your patient, is too important for us to remove you from your unique tactical position."

Kersten left the embassy feeling doubly trapped. He wanted to scream his utter vexation at the top of his lungs.

~~~

Auguste Diehn came to the clinic once again. Kersten was immediately guarded.

"I am going to ask you again for a favor that only you, Doctor, can do," Diehn began.

Kersten remained his usual gracious self on the outside. But internally he was irritated. The last time Diehn had asked for a favor, it led to a serous interruption to his agreeable life. Now, another request?

"I had working for me in the kitchen at the potash mine a fine old foreman, honest, conscientious, loyal, and peace-loving. But alas, a Jew. And a Social Democrat."

Kersten didn't want to think where this was leading.

"For this, my old friend has been sent to Dachau. I am afraid that he may never come out alive."

Kersten tried to hide his frustration in his voice as he spoke.

"That is a shame. But what can I do about it?"

"Come now, Doctor. I think you know what I am getting at. You have Himmler's trust and confidence as even his closest associates do not have. I am confident that you can persuade Himmler to have this man freed, just as you convinced him once not to nationalize our potash mines."

Kersten felt a tightening in his stomach. All he had ever wanted was to be a doctor, a healer, a husband who enjoys the company of his wife and enjoys watching his children grow up.

But he had learned that the stomach sends signals to his brain to pay attention and listen. Instead of ruling the request totally out of hand as he might have wished, he remained silent for a time and listened internally.

This would be raising the stakes much higher, too high. To persuade the head of the SS to have a Jewish member of the Social Democratic Party released in the current insane climate? Preposterous! The request might just awaken the monster within Himmler that goes to sleep during the treatments. The idea of intervening frightens the shit out of me.

Kersten didn't share his fear and doubt with Diehn, however. Before he spoke again, something inexplicable nagged at him, objected to his rational thinking, and moved him to turn his thoughts about the request upside-down and regard them from a different perspective.

Hmm. This idea has never occurred to me in the times I've been with Himmler. Is perhaps Himmler not the only one here who has power over a man's life and death? Do I really want such power? But if it's given to me to save a human life...Isn't that what a doctor dedicates his life to do?

Diehn was persistent.

"Think about it, Doctor, and if you are a praying sort of man, pray about it. In any case, here is a memorandum with all the facts in the case."

~~~

A few days later, Himmler had an excruciating attack of abdominal cramps. Kersten rushed to the Chancellery, and as usual, quickly relieved the *Reichsführer* of his agony. But this time, instead of getting up briskly, Himmler remained lying down on the divan, half naked, basking in the relief.

"Dr. Kersten," Himmler said, "what in the world would I do without you? I think I would die of pain."

Kersten nodded humbly, accepting the gratitude.

"It's what doctors do."

"The other ones who have come to see me don't seem to be able to," Himmler countered. "I will never be able to repay you commensurately. I have a very guilty conscience about you, Doctor."

"Guilty conscience? But why?" Kersten asked in astonishment.

"You take such good care of me. But I still have not compensated you a single *pfennig* for your invaluable service."

"But you know, *Herr Reichsführer* that I do not charge by the session, but only after the cure is complete. It's not time for that yet."

"Yes, you told me that at the outset. But that doesn't keep me from feeling guilty. You still have to live. You now have a wife to support as well. You must tell me how much I owe you."

This man is a man of surprisingly modest means. He doesn't even pilfer a single Reichsmark of the secret slush fund he established for special SS campaigns. His single-minded fanaticism for Hitler is irritating, to say the least. But he's the only honest man in the Nazi command. Queen Wilhelmina and other European aristocratic patients have made me a much richer man than Himmler. I don't want to take his money. Perhaps while he seems to be in a giving mood, I should ask him for my freedom instead.

Suddenly, Kersten had one of those serendipitous, spontaneous flashes of intuition that turn out to be momentous and determine the course of the rest of one's life.

The image of the stooped, elderly Diehn appeared in Kersten's mind. He recalled Diehn's request. Like a man inspired, he intuited that the time was now or never; this was the moment to take the risk.

If this goes badly, it could pose a threat to Diehn. I must not mention that the Jew in Dachau is in any way connected to him. Diehn is a rare gentile these days who has compassion for a former employee who happens to be a Jew. He has stuck out his own neck by confiding in me and naming his request to me explicitly. If what I may be about to do arouses Himmler's ire, he can have Diehn arrested, or worse. Nonetheless, Diehn took a risk, and now I must also.

Kersten felt the moisture of perspiration in the palms of his hands. Taking his portfolio, he slowly pulled out the memorandum that Diehn had given him.

Kersten looked at the cover of the memorandum as though he were undecided about what to do with it now that it was in his hands.

I can stop myself right now. But if I let him see it, there's no turning back.

A resolved smile grew on his face. He closed his eyes as he paused one more time for moral fortification. Then he handed the memorandum to Himmler.

"Here is my bill, *Herr Reichsführer.*"

Himmler took the memorandum and began perusing it. Himmler's slack skin and muscles under his chin quavered slightly.

"I don't understand," Himmler said, confused. "What's going on, Kersten?"

Kersten felt his heart beating more rapidly in his chest.

He's growing angry, I can see it. If I tell him why I showed him the memorandum, he might erupt. I would be sacrificing opportunities to extort anything else from him in the future. Felix, you've stuck your foot into it. Now it's all or nothing. Think quickly, make up a story, something Himmler would accept. Anything, but fast.

"My bill is…this man's freedom."

"His *what?*" He chuckled. "Are you insane, Kersten? This man is a Jew, a Social Democrat, to boot."

"But isn't he a human being before he's either of those?"

The new courage and conviction was overcoming the anxiety in Kersten's heart. It felt so good to say what he felt.

Himmler considered the Jews to be *Untermesnchen,* sub-human at best, and Social Democrats enemies of the *Reich.* A man like Himmler could hear Kersten's gutsy question about the Jew in Dachau as incendiary and a form of outright apostasy.

"Why the hell should you be asking for the release from Dachau of such a man?" Himmler asked in disbelief. "Who is this man to you? A relative? A friend? He's been sent to Dachau for a reason. What concern is he for you?"

Kersten felt a tingling at the tips of his fingers. He knew from experience as well as physiology textbooks that such tingling is often followed by numbness. That he couldn't afford. Those fingertips were the essential tools of his trade.

This is not going as well as I had hoped. Perhaps I overestimated his sense of euphoria following his treatment. Surely, I need to back-pedal somehow, take back what I've said so far. He's going to accuse me of protecting someone from among the people he detests most profoundly. I should have known better. Never have I been able to have a sane conversation with Himmler about the Jews. What was I thinking? How could I have expected him to receive this request with any semblance of reason? This request could set him off. Any access I have had to him will be eradicated.

Diehn's image came into view again.

Nevertheless, Felix, take heart and do what you consider to be right and just. Don't turn back now.

He answered Himmler's question. "The man is a fellow human being to me. He's in Dachau for no other reason than that he is of another race and a political party of whom you and the *Führer* disapprove. That's a bizarre notion of justice. The man is a hard worker who tends to his own business, according to his former employer. He regrets to lose a worker of such quality and character. Aren't such workers good for Germany, *Herr Reichsführer?*"

"This is most unusual, Kersten. You must understand that this causes me great turmoil of spirit. You know that if I submit to this, and if even just one of my opponents, or God forbid, the *Führer* himself, were to catch wind of it, it would cause me more than a little trouble. My career in the SS would be over. Look at what happened to von Blomberg and von Fritsch."

Kersten was resigned, but not surprised. He was concerned only that Himmler remain as calm as he seemed right now and not get incensed any further.

"I must weigh my choices, carefully," Himmler said, more thoughtfully, it seemed to Kersten, than usual. "Risk the rage of my

Führer and therefore my career. Or risk losing the only doctor who has ever succeeded in alleviating my pain."

Kersten was hopeful again that he had a foot in the door. Himmler had left a tiny sliver of light. He felt a new verve.

"But my dear *Herr Reichsführer*, the odds are small that the *Führer* would ever know. Doesn't he give you sole authority in the realm of your responsibility? Isn't Dachau within that realm? After all, isn't Piorkowski a man appointed by you personally to be *Kommandant* of Dachau? I am certain that when he receives your order for the man's release, like a good SS, he will have no reason or inclination to speculate about the motives of his superior's command."

"You should have been a barrister, Kersten. No, ignore that advice. I am grateful you became a doctor…Because it is you who asks me, for whatever reason," Himmler continued with a resigned smile, "perhaps against my better judgment, I approve."

Himmler shouted out toward his administrative assistant's office. "Brandt! Come take this memorandum, and have the man named there released from Dachau."

Then, looking at Kersten, he said, "Our good doctor wishes it." Himmler obviously didn't want Brandt to think that he was softening his views about the Jews. Brandt gave Kersten a very quick glance, one that Kersten interpreted to communicate approval.

When Kersten walked to his car from the Chancellery, he felt infinitely lightened. He knew he might have dodged a bullet. He wasn't usually a smoker. But he asked his chauffeur Henrik for a cigarette, sat back in his seat and took intentionally long drags in relief and gratitude.

He instructed Henrik to wait in the car while he went for a brief celebratory walk. He was stunned by what he had accomplished. He had actually extracted a *life*, that of a *Jew*, from one of Hitler's chief executioners. He was a healer, but in the case of this one man at least, he was the savior of a human life.

He found it utterly exhilarating. All that the other ears on the street that early evening heard was the sound of automobile wheels on the brick pavement of *Prinz Albrecht Strasse* and the angry honking of car horns. The ears of Kersten's heart, though, heard an orchestra launching into a version of Eugen Malmstén's *Old Mariner's Waltz* that had been a hugely popular hit in Finland the previous year. His feet were advancing on the concrete sidewalk, but it felt as though they were dancing on air to the beat of the orchestra.

CHAPTER TEN

Berlin: February 17, 1939

Bruno Altmann's young wine merchant, Jiri Hudak, did indeed call Niska from a public telephone as requested. Hudak urgently needed to get to his native Czechoslovakia to escape the tightening chokehold of the SS. With his wine shop expropriated for Aryanization shortly after *Kristallnacht*, he felt he had nothing to lose.

"My friend," Niska said over the telephone, "don't make the mistake of assuming that the tentacles of the SS don't reach even into Czechoslovakia. They quite likely have plainclothes agents there, too. You'll need to be observant. But I agree. You'll probably be safer there."

Niska gave instructions for Hudak to meet him the next day in the grand hall of the *Lehrter Bahnhof* where they would purchase two-way tickets on a night train to Prague. Niska told him to dress in the style of a German businessman to deflect suspicion.

In the meantime, Niska stepped into high gear to make arrangements with contacts in Finland for the supplies necessary to conduct an operation of smuggling persons out of Germany. That meant Finnish passports.

An accomplice with whom Niska had worked in his whiskey running days was a genius in creating a counterfeit of any kind of document. She agreed to supply Niska with forged Finnish passports. Only, she said, due to heightened security measures it would take some time—more time than Niska preferred—for her to get surreptitious nighttime access to the printing plant of the Ministry of Foreign Affairs, where she worked. Once the Finnish passports were printed and embossed to look official, the Finnish contact was to mail them to Niska in care of an assumed name and a post office box.

However, the shipment of counterfeit passports from Finland had not yet arrived in Niska's post office box when Hudak called again for further instructions. Niska went by the post office the day after Hudak had made contact the second time. The mailbox was empty. He'd have to wait longer.

Every day until the day he and Hudak had set for their departure, he returned to the post office. Every day, he was disappointed and more concerned. Each time he walked back from the post office more despondent than the day before. He had experienced many unforeseen delays and other snags in his smuggling operations before. They came with the turf. However, the consequences for presenting incomplete documentation at a border crossing for material goods like whiskey or vodka could be handled in creative ways. With the delay of a passport, however, the potential hazards were much more menacing.

In their next telephone conversation, Niska apologized for the tardy Finnish passport, and explained the practical problem that it entailed.

"You have only a German passport, Mr. Hudak?"

"Yes. But you can call me Jiri, *Herr* Niska."

"Well, all right, Jiri. Is it stamped with the prominent red letter "J?""

"Like that of every other Jew in Germany now, yes."

"Then, the passport has been rendered useless. It may pass muster with the Czechs, but the German agents on this side of the border will not permit you to exit the country. I propose we postpone the attempt."

"No, I beg of you, *Herr* Niska," Jiri exclaimed with a sense of urgency.

"The risk of apprehension is too great without a non-German passport."

Hudak continued in a less plaintive voice. "I know you are the expert here, *Herr* Niska. You are better informed and more experienced to make the decision." But the plaintive tone returned.

"Please understand, I feel the SS rope tightening around my neck. The Nazis are demanding reparation payments from us for all the damage their hooligans inflicted on November 9 and 10. The amount is so high there's no way I can pay it. I've applied for insurance to repair my shop, but the insurance money went directly to the Nazis. They're rounding up all us Jews who are unable or refuse to pay."

Niska imagined what the Nazis did with the ones they rounded up.

"Can they possibly catch up with all of you in the next week or so?" asked Niska, hoping to hear agreement.

"*Herr* Niska, surely you know of the efficiency and thoroughness of the SS and *Gestapo*. It's only a matter of time before they throw me onto the back of a lorry."

Niska acknowledged to himself that Hudak was right.

"You can't be absolutely sure of that. But if we attempt an escape and get caught at either border with our pants down, imprisonment, yours and mine, or maybe worse, is a 100% certainty."

"I have nothing to lose by trying to flee, maybe everything to gain, *Herr* Niska. No delay, please."

Yes, Hudak has nothing to lose. But what about me?

But Hudak sounded so desperate. Niska swallowed hard, and then said, against his better judgment, "We'll manage together somehow. Full speed ahead."

~~~

The ornate grand hall of the *Lehrter Bahnhof* seemed to be teeming with uniformed *Wehrmacht* as though war had already been declared. Niska surmised that there were plenty of plainclothes SS agents strategically placed as well. As eager as the Nazis had been to encourage Jews to emigrate before 1938, now they were as obsessed with preventing their departure out of the country.

At least a dozen uniformed *Wehrmacht*, rifles slung visibly over their shoulder, walked back and forth on Platform 5 where Niska and Hudak waited to board the train to Prague. One could cut the tension and suspicion in the air with a knife. Though their nerves were as taut as the E string on a violin, Niska and Hudak tried to look natural and casual as they rose the four steep steps into the train.

Niska pulled out a cigarette and took a long drag to calm his nerves. He offered one to Hudak. "Thanks anyway, but I don't smoke."

Once the train was on its way, however, Hudak looked over to Niska.

"Can I take you up on that offer of a cigarette?" he asked, slightly embarrassed.

The closer the train came to the Czech border, the more frequent were the drags Hudak took on the cigarette, and the closer to his fingers he smoked it. He asked Niska for another, and then another.

"Try to calm down, Jiri. Or at least try to look calmer. You're a dead give-away the way you are fidgeting around."

Hudak noticed that Niska was jangling the change in his pocket nervously. Hudak gave Niska a look that was a wordless reprimand to him to be less noticeable with his anxiety himself.

To be caught at a border without proper documentation for inanimate goods risked only the confiscation of the goods by border guards, Niska thought. What would happen to impounded human contraband, or to someone trying to smuggle such contraband, Niska didn't quite know, but he could imagine. Rumors were circulating about the detention camps, the *Konzentrazionslager*, that had been opened in the past five or six years.

The train lowered its speed, and then came to an abrupt stop that caused the passengers to lurch forward in their seats. Niska and Hudak gave each other a glance that communicated alarm, but encouragement at the same time. They were at the inspection station on the German side of the frontier.

Two German border guards entered the car through the door from the car in front. At the late hour, they appeared tired and not a little irritable. That did nothing to alleviate Niska's and Hudak's nervousness.

"Remember, Jiri, to assume the confident posture and demeanor of a typical German businessman." Niska pulled out his Finnish passport from the breast pocket of his gray suit jacket. He looked over at Hudak expectantly, as if to say, "Now, take out your passport, Jiri."

Hudak started to dig around in his rucksack. His face turned white. He took out each item from the rucksack one at a time. He was becoming frantic. But still no passport.

"Shit, I must have forgotten it."

"Don't panic, Jiri. Your passport had that damnable 'J' stamped on it. It would have been a detriment to our plan."

Hudak didn't appear wholeheartedly convinced or comforted by Niska's attempt to reassure him. Niska, for that matter, wasn't sure the effort at calming Hudak was for Jiri or himself. The closer the border agents came to the rear of the car, the more fatalistic Niska became that his career as the smuggler of human beings to safety would be over before it started; that, in fact, this doomed effort was to be his very last smuggling act, period. Why had he let Hudak talk him into making this trip prematurely? Why had his usually dependable good judgment deserted him? Why had he allowed his heart to overrule his head?

The border agents were clearly growing bored and impatient with their task. The *Deutsche Reichsbahn* system had become terribly over-subscribed by the transport of *Wehrmacht* toward the Austria border for some reason. Consequently, the Prague train's departure from Berlin and its arrival at the border had been delayed by almost an hour. The *Reichsbahn* paid its employees overtime, but the *Zollverein*, the customs and immigration department, had promised to begin doing so to its employees as well when the Nazi party assumed control of it, but hadn't. These men were working past their quitting time, and their faces and demeanor indicated they were none too pleased.

The agents were examining the documentation of the passengers seated in front of Niska and Hudak. Hudak couldn't get his shirt collar loose enough for all his efforts. Niska glanced back furtively at the door at the rear of the car. He had a sudden and overwhelming urge for them to get up quickly and slip through the door unnoticed into the car behind them while the agents were occupied with the passengers in the seat in front of them.

Escape now, while you still can!

But he had immediate second thoughts. What was he thinking? Trouble was, he wasn't thinking, just obeying an innate instinct to flee. They were seated in the very last car of the train. There was no car behind them into which to escape. What did he think they were going to do? Jump off the train? They'd be seen and apprehended—if not shot—before they could count to five by another agent sitting in the guardhouse. That would defeat the whole purpose of the journey, not to mention abort their lives. No, there was no other viable option but to await their turn with the border agents and hope for…what? A miracle?

Niska and Hudak both overheard one of the agents say to the other, "For Christ's sake, Heike, let's get the hell off this bloody train and go home. Our work is done. Just enter 'No irregularities' in the book, and then let's head home."

The other agent let out a tired, conspiring laugh.

As the agents approached their seats, Niska began to furnish his Finnish passport to a hand he expected would be waiting for it. But the agent dismissed it with a wave of his hand and wished Niska and Hudak a good trip. Then he followed his colleague back down the aisle toward the exit.

~~~

On the Czechoslovakian side of the border, however, the border guards were much more meticulous and conscientious. Jewish refugees and other travelers had been causing a lot of concern to Czech officials recently. There was the fear of spies, especially from Germany. A lot of unconfirmed reports were in circulation about an imminent action by Hitler against Czechoslovakia, at least into the primarily German region of Sudetenland.

Niska and Hudak watched the border agents warily from the last row of seats in the coach. The agents were the usual unsmiling, humorless functionaries one had come to expect, conscious of the power they were exerting over and anxiety they were rousing in even the most honest passenger. One by one each passenger put himself or herself into the hands of these nitpicky and diligent officials.

Niska and Hudak gave each other an apprehensive glance when they noticed the border guards shake their heads emphatically as one couple tried vigorously in vain to explain away whatever inaccuracy the guards had detected in their paperwork. Hudak translated the Czech for Niska as the agents ordered the two passengers to gather their belongings and to remove themselves from the train, much to the vocal chagrin of the couple.

The incident caused Niska's and Hudak's hearts to beat faster. They were the next to be inspected by the agents. Niska did his best to push his anxiety aside and appear as relaxed and nonchalant as he could. Hudak couldn't get his shirt collar loose enough for all his efforts to loosen it during the last stages of this leg of the trip.

The border agent seemed to take more than the usual official interest in the document. Niska appeared unperturbed, but he could almost sense the heightened pulse of Hudak's heart, as though it was migrating toward him through the padding of the seat.

Surprisingly, a smile came over the face of the border agent.

"Ever been to *Salpauselkä*, my *suomalaiset ystävät?*" the agent asked the two passengers, pronouncing the Finnish words for "Finnish friends" with a thick Slavic accent that almost made the words incomprehensible.

"Why, yes," said Niska in German, much relieved. "You appear to know my language. Impressive. How do you know about such a prominent physical feature of my home country?

"Yes, in Lahti. At a ski meet there."

"I haven't had the good fortune to be there for the ski competitions," Niska replied, "but I've followed them in the sports pages. But I gather you have skied there?"

"You bet! At three separate meets. Brought home a ribbon from one of them. You Finns produce some terrific skiers."

Niska tried to conjure up all the he knew about cross-country skiing in Finland, and cross-country competitive skiers. Niska and the border agent spent the next quarter-hour in an amiable conversation about skiing, and Finnish athletics in general, the legendary victories on the track of the Flying Finns Paavo Nurmi and Hannes Kolehmainen in prior decades, and the prospects for the ski jumping world championships later that month in Lahti.

The official's partner was growing impatient with this gregarious delay at the end of their work day. The affable skiing border agent didn't seem to notice. Finally, he looked at his pocket watch, got up suddenly, bid a hasty farewell, *"Näkemiin,"* in a passable approximation of the Finnish. He and his partner managed to get off the train just before the locomotive resumed its chugging toward Prague.

Hudak slumped down into his seat and let out the breath he had been holding in his lungs in a long sigh of relief. Niska looked as though a huge weight had been taken off his shoulders. The inspection of Niska's and Hudak's suitcases and documentation was thereby fortuitously overlooked.

Algot Niska couldn't believe their luck…Or was it the invisible machinations of the goddess of fate, or whatever force it was that had enticed him into this daring operation? He didn't know. He resolved at that very moment that he must not rely entirely on similar luck the next time, that he'd make sure he was better prepared for unforeseen eventualities.

In any case, he had smuggled his very first Jew out of Germany.

CHAPTER ELEVEN

Berlin: February 27, 1939

The Finnish passports finally arrived at Niska's post office box in Berlin. Bruno Altmann invited him to his amply and fashionably adorned flat in Charlottenburg to meet with several couples, all distinguished Jewish businesspeople, attorneys, and other professionals.

The Jewish population of Berlin formed a veritable "village within a city." News and rumors traveled with ease within and through such a village. Most of the gathered guests knew of Niska and of his success in smuggling young wine merchant Hudak out of Germany into Czechoslovakia just a week earlier. They were inquiring whether he could smuggle not only their valuables to safety beyond the grasp of the Nazis, but themselves as well.

Niska realized that he was entering a high stakes poker game in which he was gambling with his own personal freedom, perhaps even his own life. He addressed the three couples after dinner from his seat at the end of Altmann's mahogany dining table.

"I'm sure Bruno has told you about the absolute confidentiality of this gathering. Nothing—I repeat, nothing—that is said here this evening is to be repeated beyond these four walls. You understand, I am sure, that were a single word of our deliberations to reach the wrong ears, it could mean imprisonment—or even death—to any or all of us. That includes me."

"We have learned to be wary of the SS and *Gestapo* particularly, *Herr* Niska, we assure you," said a man in a dark suit and prominent bow tie.

"That's a very prudent precaution, *Herr...*"

"Goldberg, the jeweler."

"*Herr* Goldberg, thank you. I trust that before you came here this evening, *Herr* Altmann passed on to you the instructions I related to him. These days, as successful Jewish citizens, you simply have to assume at any given time that agents of the SS and *Gestapo* have their eyes on you, and probably their ears, too. Do any of you have any reason—even the slightest—to suspect that you were being watched or even followed as you traveled to *Herr* and *Frau* Altmann's residence? If so, it is absolutely vital to this operation for you to express your suspicions right now and not hold anything back. Is that understood?"

The group was silent, each seated around the table looking nervously at the others. Niska paused a long time to give time for anyone who might be needing to gather courage to speak up to do so.

"Hearing none, then good," Niska said, but glanced slightly dubiously at Altmann. "We will proceed, then, on the assumption that, for this evening at least, it is safe to do so."

He explained to those gathered that he was able to arrange for forged Finnish passports for about ten of them.

"But there are ten couples who have expressed interest in being smuggled out of Germany—that's twenty people," protested Goldberg. "How will you decide who the fortunate ten will be?"

Niska didn't want to think about that possibility. He had never been any good at playing God.

"I am sorry, but until I and my contacts in Finland have worked out a smooth and watertight system, ten is all I can procure at this time. I leave the decision about who goes this time, and who stays, to you.

"I need to emphasize to you that at any given time, things can go wrong. I urge you to underscore that in your communication with the others. I know that some of your people think smuggling people is always as easy as they might have heard it turned out in the end to be with *Herr* Hudak. I do not want you to have any illusions. Every passport has to be imprinted with valid stamps and notations. These can be acquired usually only by bribing a German immigration official here in Berlin in advance. That's the responsibility of each individual or couple. In wartime, it seems, money is required over and over again. Bribery involves significant risk, as I'm sure you appreciate."

Altmann and the others swallowed hard. The jeweler Goldberg was the first to speak again.

"We've become accustomed to bribery, *Herr* Niska, just to get our fair ration of beef or lamb at the butcher's."

"True enough, I'm sure," Niska replied. "Most often,

immigration officials can be trusted to act out of self-interest and not call attention to an attempted bribe. After all, they need to buy beef and lamb, too. But occasionally there's an absolutely conscientious, strictly-by-the-book alumnus of the Hitlerjugend who has swallowed the Nazi line about the *Volk* above private gain hook, line, and sinker."

"A definite pain in the ass, those Nazi straight arrows are," Goldberg said. His wife looked over at him disapprovingly.

"Yes, they can be. That is why you need to be absolutely sure not to walk straight on up to an immigration kiosk without having taken time to observe each agent carefully. You can usually tell who the straight arrows, as you call them, are by their demeanor."

"But," interrupted Altmann," at the same time, you will have to be careful not to be too obvious about your scrutiny of the agents."

"Absolutely right, Bruno." Niska concurred. "The simple fact that this is a group of ten Finnish tourists leaving Germany is bound to draw some attention, to be sure. It's vital that if one or more of you runs into complications, the others do not in any way seek to interfere. They'd be looking for unnecessary trouble. But we Finns are fortunate. We look Nordic. We have a history of keeping our noses clean. Usually the immigration people are happy just to pass us along and send us on our way."

"*Some* Finns, at least, have kept their noses clean," Goldberg inserted with an attempt at humor to lighten the tense mood.

"If you're referring to me, *Herr* Goldberg, mine is rather unclean, I admit." Niska chuckled self-deprecatingly.

"But it's from *Herr* Niska's brave experience in evading the prohibition laws in Finland that we are benefitting now, Simon. You should be more grateful."

"No, I am, I am. I didn't mean any disrespect, I assure you, *Herr* Niska. My wife, Galia, can tell you that I tend to inject humor in all the wrong ways and at the wrong times."

"*Das est sicher,*" Galia concurred, to the light laughter of all. "That's for sure."

"No offense taken, Simon," Niska assured him. "But I have more precautions you will need to know if you're still willing to volunteer for the journey in spite of all the risks."

"Go on, Algot, please," Altmann said.

"Each person will need to get a valid photograph for their passport."

"How in heaven's name do we do that?" asked the other male guest, a tailor named Aaronssohn. "An Aryan photographer is not allowed to take them. Even to request such could arouse grave suspicion. The Jewish photographers have all been driven out of business by Himmler's henchmen."

"Just be patient, Samuel," Altmann urged. "I'm sure *Herr* Niska has thought of that."

"Indeed, I have, Samuel. I have a contact right here in Berlin who can take reasonable facsimiles. But I warn you, nothing is foolproof. The German authorities have become quite sophisticated in detecting false papers, especially, I'm afraid, if the bearers appear to be or are Jewish."

"Remember how poor Marek and Rebekah Horst were caught at Hamburg trying to board a ship to England with false papers?" Aaronssohn's wife, a nervous Nellie if there ever was one, asked the group.

"And yes, remember that they were carted off to the camps, Marek to Dachau and Rebekah to Ravensbrück," Altmann interjected.

"That's precisely the kind of risk you would be taking," Niska added. "My passport forger in Helsinki is the best there is, and my photographer contact here is an excellent, and most importantly, an absolutely discreet one. But there's no guarantee of success, you must understand."

He told them that all the information in the passports would have to be proper and correct. The only exception was that their names would be modified to the extent that they appeared to be Finnish. They would travel by train as couples to Travemünde on the Baltic, and board a Finnish steamer there for Helsinki with tickets he would secure and provide.

"Begin thinking of yourselves as tourists from Finland who have come for a short visit to Germany. Because that is what you will say to the officials in Travemünde. And, better start trying to imitate my German spoken with the obvious Finnish accent. You're Finnish tourists, right?"

Once safely on Finnish soil, they could choose to remain and rebuild their lives there. Or as he learned, some of them desired to try to continue their journey from Finland to Britain, or even the United States.

"*Hyvää matkaa.* Good travels," Niska told them cheerfully a week later when he handed them their passports. "On the other side of the Baltic, life is worth living again. The freedom in the air there is intoxicating."

On his walk to his flat, Niska appeared totally relaxed and in a light mood. But he had entered his high stakes game. He had laid down more chips on the table than ever before. When does a gambler not fret?

~~~

A week later one of Niska's contacts in Helsinki wired to inform him that nine of the refugees had arrived safely and passed through customs and immigration with no problems. But where was the tenth, Niska wondered. He had given out ten passports.

Through a friendly informant in the customs house in Travemünde, Niska learned that one of the ten for whom he had helped secure passports had been overzealous in observing the immigration agents and had become paranoid that the SS or *Gestapo* were observing him. He sold his precious passport to freedom to another Jew. He had tried to be discreet and secretive when making the deal. But he was plainly just an amateur in undercover activities. Who knew who might have observed and taken note of the transaction? Certainly, the SS or *Gestapo*. But who else?

Niska's heart plummeted when he read the wire. Just as it was beginning, Niska's clandestine work had been betrayed. He feared that now, it might even have been compromised.

CHAPTER TWELVE

Berlin: March 12, 1939

Kersten sat on the bed in his flat in the Hotel *Kaiserhof*. The room was amply decorated in an overly ornate Victorian style. Only after accepting accommodation there from Himmler did Kersten learn that the *Kaiserhof* was where Adolf Hitler had stayed on the eve of his assumption of power as Chancellor in 1933. Kersten wished he had remained ignorant of that fact. The knowledge seemed to blemish his own stay there, making him feel contaminated, somehow.

It didn't matter today, however. His heart and mind transported him to another room, the richly textured wood-paneled den of his forest manor on Hartzwalde, north of the capital city. In his daydream, his mind and entire body were still luxuriating from the long-awaited relaxed love-making with his bride. Now, post-coitus, Irmgaard was in the room with him. The pleasing aroma of the flowers Irmgaard had placed in the vase sweetened the whole room. He was reading the *Deustche Zeitung in den Niederländen* in a leather easy chair; Irmgaard was across the room on the sofa reading a novel by the banned Thomas Mann. His novels had been banned and burned—in Germany, that is—but not in the Netherlands. Felix had been able to locate a copy in Dutch for his wife in a bookstore in The Hague. The feeling of defiance when he bought it was extremely delicious.

Bright sunshine streamed across the carpeted floor of the den through the huge window overlooking the verdant garden in which the two of them liked to dig their hands. The sound of the springtime morning birds drifted in.

Abruptly, Kersten's mind was carried back against his will to his Berlin flat. Yet, he was filled with a warm sense of gratitude that he had been able to escape the mounting bedlam of Berlin, if only for a fleeting moment, and if only in a daydream from which he needed to awaken.

He telephoned the royal palace in The Hague to check up on the condition of Queen Wilhelmina and the royal family. The queen's secretary assured him that she was faring well, as were others in the family. In that case, he told the secretary, he would extend his stay in Germany. He didn't divulge why.

He performed a series of almost daily treatments on Himmler. At each session, Himmler was doubly overcome. First, by the piercing pain in his abdomen when Kersten arrived in his office for the session, and then, by the pain's defeat. After each treatment, the *Reichsführer,* whose whole life was devoted to the obsessive planning and performance of the most top-secret, sordid tasks, had a seemingly unquenchable desire to talk.

"I've been wondering, Doctor, if you don't mind me asking. How is it that a man with a German surname is a citizen of Finland?"

"I'm rather surprised that with all your sophisticated and advanced German tools for surveillance, you do not know the answer to your own question. Surely, you've had both the Chief of the *Reich* Security and the Director of Intelligence check me out."

"Indeed, you are right, Doctor. Kaltenbrunner and Heydrich both did a thorough check when you first started treating me. I know every detail of your story."

"Well, then, why don't you tell me what their intelligence uncovered? I will either confirm each finding or refute it."

"Very clever, Doctor. You catch onto these games very quickly. But no, I want to hear your story directly from the horse's mouth."

"You still want me to repeat it to you? To see if my story corroborates their findings, is that it?"

"No, it's not that. It's like prayer. Do you ever pray, Doctor?"

Kersten was taken aback by what seemed like a non sequitur. Before Kersten could respond, however, Himmler filled the brief silence with his words.

"I do sometimes, Doctor. Haven't you ever wondered why we pray when, being omniscient, the Almighty already knows what we need even before we ask?"

Himmler paused, as though waiting for an answer from him, Kersten thought. But he could see that Himmler was engrossed again in one of his monologues.

"I think the Almighty simply wants to hear our need uttered on our own lips, don't you think, Doctor?"

Kersten had never heard Himmler talk in these terms.

He prays? Now, that's a surprise. Apparently, he hasn't totally abandoned his pious Catholic upbringing by his devout Bavarian parents and sacrificed it all at the altar of pagan National Socialism. A faded remnant remains.

"It's a long story, *Herr Reichsführer*. The long and short of it, however, is that I was in Berlin for post-graduate training with Dr. Ko when the Great War broke out."

"I don't prefer the term, 'Great' War, Doctor," Himmler said rather sternly. "There was very little about it that was 'great' for Germany, especially the ending and aftermath in Versailles."

"Would it shock you, *Herr Reichsführer,* if I confess to you that I am now a Finnish citizen because I didn't want to serve in Kaiser Wilhelm's army in 1917?" Kersten had a glimmer in his eyes.

Himmler raised his head off the divan to look disconcertedly at Kersten.

"If you weren't so adept at alleviating this pain of mine, I rather think I would be very upset about that. That's treason, as I am sure you know. However, I have no choice but to let it go. I may be sorry, but please tell me more."

"To be quite frank, *Herr Reichsführer*, I was put off by the showy Prussian uniforms, the whole ostentatious demeanor of the Kaiser's army." He left unsaid that he wasn't any less put off by all the Nazi militaristic exhibitionism now. "I just wanted to complete my training and begin my practice."

"You are being quite frank and brave, Doctor. Aren't you the least bit afraid of me?"

Kersten sidestepped the question.

"I found a compromise. I learned that some ex-patriate Finns in Germany were forming a legion to assist their native land to throw off Russian domination. Although I was born in the German Baltic province of Estonia, I was pretty confident I didn't have a drop of Finnish blood in me. Nonetheless, I enlisted with the Finnish adventurers."

"It seems I remember hearing something about that Finnish legion."

"I served in the regiment that routed the Russians and their Finnish Bolshevik comrades from Helsinki in 1919. That, for all intents and purposes, cemented independence for Finland."

"I was just a seventeen-year-old student then," Himmler said. "But I well remember how elated I was entering in my diary how the Bolshevik devils were defeated."

"The new Finnish government was very grateful for our legion's part in the victory. I was offered honorary Finnish citizenship. They recommended me for a post as a reserve officer in the newly formed Finnish army. I said, 'Why not?' The Finns were very good to me. I developed a real love for their gutsiness. But really, what did I know about being an officer in the army?"

Kersten paused to take stock of Himmler's reaction to his account. Himmler simply continued listening.

"I was hospitalized in Helsinki for wounds endured in the skirmishes with the Bolsheviks. There, I saw the work of medics. So I decided that I would become a surgeon. I shared my plan with a mentor, the chief of the medical staff at the military hospital. He warned me about how long and grueling the training to become a surgeon was. All the while the doctor was speaking to me, however, I noticed that he kept looking at my hands. Finally, the doctor took hold of one of my wrists, and said, 'This hand is ideally suited for massage.' He recommended Dr. Ko. There you have it."

"I'd say that that military doctor deserves a medal. He gave you very good advice."

"I didn't think so at the time. *Massage*? What the hell? I wanted to be a doctor, not a masseur. I had my sights set on something higher and more dignified."

The familiar sharp pain shot once more in Kersten's stomach. He hadn't wanted to revisit his brief, unpleasant stay in the field of surgery, even in his memory.

"You have discovered a very high calling, Doctor. By the way, I am a great admirer of the Finns. Very few composers are in touch with the tragic and melancholy dimension of human life as intimately as Sibelius. Of course, our German composers are supreme, Beethoven, Brahms, especially Richard Wagner. But I make an exception for Sibelius."

"Not to mention Bach and Mendelssohn," Kersten added enthusiastically.

"Bach, perhaps, but he wasted all that talent on the church. But for God's sake, Kersten, *not* the Jew Mendelssohn. Jesus, we had his statue removed from the square in Leipzig. Don't bring up his name again!"

Kersten wondered if he had simply forgotten that Mendelssohn was a Jew. Or was this an instance of what that famous Jewish psychiatrist in Vienna referred to as a "slip" in which our apparently careless speech reveals a deeper unconscious intent.

"And the heroes in your *Kalevala* remind me a lot of our Aryan heroes."

Kersten had to hold back his irritation at the nerve of this Kraut in daring to co-opt for the Nazi cause the protagonists of one the world's greatest epics.

"While we are talking about your being a citizen of Finland, I have a question to ask you, Doctor," Himmler said. "Several of my lieutenants have mentioned to me the name of a troublemaker here in Berlin, a Finn. His name is Algro Niska. Something like that."

"*Algot* Niska?"

"Yes, I think that's it. Do you recognize the name?"

Kersten did, although he was reluctant to say so to Himmler. Niska had a reputation among Finns for being an intrepid whiskey smuggler during the years of prohibition. Kersten thought he remembered reading something about Niska's having served a short prison sentence in Finland for his crimes. In Sweden, too, as he recalled. But he hadn't heard Niska's name mentioned since prohibition ended in 1932.

"Seems that this Niska character has been smuggling the property of Jews out of the country, a capital offense."

Niska, out of jail? Right here, now, in Berlin? Not surprising that he's back in the smuggling business, though.

Himmler's face had become sterner now, his voice more conspiratorial.

"Now we have reason to believe that he's smuggling actual *Jews* out of Germany, some of them apparently to Finland."

Kersten tried to hide the anxiety that was suddenly churning in his stomach.

"As a matter of fact, Kersten, Heydrich informs me that a Jew tried to sell a forged Finnish passport to one of Heydrich's undercover *Gestapo* agents in Travemünde. Not too smart, was he? The *Gestapo* used their unique methods to interrogate the Jew until he was able to wring the information out of him that he had originally received the passport from this Niska in Berlin."

Kersten felt an attack of alarm, though he didn't even know Niska. But Niska was a fellow countryman whom he imagined being tortured by the Nazis if they ever caught him.

"We've put out a bulletin alerting all our detachments throughout the *Reich* about Niska. He won't get far. We'll catch this damned Jew-lover, you can depend on that...By the way, Doctor, what would you recommend as a particularly Finnish form of punishment for him once we have caught him?"

Kersten couldn't tell if Himmler was serious or not. The SS had its own notorious punitive measures. Why ask about a distinctly Finnish measure? So he tried to put a period after this conversation with some humor. Mind you, he didn't expect a non-Finn like Himmler to appreciate the joke.

"Put him in a room," Kersten said with a straight face, "with a group of extremely extraverted, incurably talkative strangers."

Himmler looked totally flummoxed by the answer. But it occurred to the introverted Kersten that he was enduring a form of the same punishment himself whenever he was in Himmler's office.

~~~

Habitually a deliberate man, Kersten left Himmler's office feeling unusually restless and agitated. He couldn't explain his sense of urgency to get word to Niska somehow about the danger he was in. For some vague reason, he felt responsible for Niska's situation even though he hadn't had anything to do with it. Surely, it would not be news to Niska that he was now a wanted man throughout the entire *Reich*. After all, Niska was a smuggler accustomed to being on the run. What more could Kersten possibly do to help his renegade countryman? What new information did he possess of which Niska was not aware? Was it even any of his business?

Or was the root of the current inexplicit anxiety something else? Was it the possibility that Niska's flouting of the Nazi Jewish emigration laws might now draw attention to any and all Finns and their activities in Berlin, including his own, attention he neither needed nor desired? It could lead the SS right to him. It would seriously jeopardize his new mission, if not end it completely. It would most likely be the end of him, too, for that matter, although he was surprised pleasantly that his own survival didn't seem to be the supreme priority now.

~~~

Kersten's discomfort led him back to the Finnish legation and the office of Ambassador Mäki. Kersten repeated to the ambassador what he had learned about Niska's predicament from Himmler.

"I think you know, Doctor, that we can neither confirm nor deny that we know of this Algot Niska. Yes, we know about his past in Finland, of course. That is public knowledge. But as to whether we know of his exploits after his departure from Finland for his self-imposed exile, we cannot, as I say, confirm or deny. I am sure you understand, Doctor. We would answer in precisely the same manner if someone came to us seeking information about you."

Kersten did understand, but still, was irritated and impatient with the diplomatic cageyness.

"Surely, Mr. Ambassador, since Niska is a Finnish citizen in this country, you must know of his whereabouts...an address, or something?"

"If you insist, Doctor. His last known address in our records is a boat registered in his name in Amsterdam harbor."

Maki kept his eyes on Kersten absentmindedly while he contemplated the matter some more.

"You seem unusually interested in making contact with him. Since that is so, you might pursue the matter with the Finnish legation in The Hague. I warn you, however, Dr. Kersten, that your position is already quite delicate. It probably wouldn't improve any by enmeshing yourself with the fate of Algot Niska."

Kersten sat silently and waited for the ambassador to offer more. Mäki, however, returned his focus to the stack of papers on his desk. Kersten uttered a formal, if half-hearted, thanks, rose from his chair grudgingly, and headed in the direction of the door.

"Oh, by the way, Dr. Kersten," Mäki said from behind his desk without looking up from his papers. "We appreciate your service to us with regards to Heinrich Himmler. I am sure it is not always pleasant...As for the whereabouts of Algot Niska, you might try your luck with his physician, a Doctor Josef Singer in Charlottenburg. But you didn't hear it from me."

~~~

Kersten found Dr. Singer at his small clinic on *Otto-Suhr Allee,* not far down a steep hill from the imposing castle named after Queen Charlotte of Prussia. Charlottenburg exhibited telltale signs that not long ago at all, it had been a comfortable, affluent and bustling sector of Berlin. Many of the formerly elegant shop windows were boarded up. The shops themselves stood empty and abandoned. Evidence of destruction by fire and vandalism was all around.

The massage practice Kersten had inherited from Dr. Ko when the Tibetan master retired and returned to China was located in the Schöneberg sector, adjacent, ironically, to Charlottenburg. But non-Jews seldom had business in that primarily Jewish enclave, so Kersten had never sauntered to the neighborhoods to the west and north of

Kurfürstendamm Strasse. This was his first crossing into the mysterious neighborhood of Jewish professionals.

Josef Singer appeared wary, suspicious even, when Kersten caught him at his clinic between patients.

"Whether I know of *Herr* Niska, I am not allowed by medical ethics to divulge," Singer replied when Kersten asked if he knew Niska or had an address for him. "I am sure as a doctor yourself, you are familiar with that, and follow the same practice with your own patients...That is, if you really are a doctor, as you say you are."

"Yes, of course, Dr. Singer, under normal, routine circumstances. But as you know, the days we are living presently are not the least bit normal or routine. Neither is my business with *Herr* Niska."

"He has never mentioned to me that he is under the care of a masseur."

"He's not, as far as I know. At least, not with me."

Kersten could see he was not making much headway with the quiet, unassuming but shrewd, guarded doctor. He couldn't blame him if he suspected that Kersten was an officer of law enforcement.

"If it's not medical, then may I ask what your business is with *Herr* Niska?" Singer asked warily.

"I acknowledge the fact that I am not a friend of his, nor even an acquaintance. Just a countryman of his concerned about his safety at this time. We're engaged in the same kind of enterprise."

Singer's dark eyes softened and eyebrows rose slightly at this news. He looked directly at Kersten's eyes. He seemed to comprehend Kersten's code language.

"If, then, you are engaged in the same enterprise as *Herr* Niska, I welcome you to my clinic. And warn you, as well. I apologize if my reception of you has been so cautious. Perhaps you have interpreted it as cold and unfriendly. I am sorry. But as you say, the days we are living are not the comfortable, secure ones we knew just a few years ago, especially here in Charlottenburg."

"No apology necessary, Dr. Singer. I fully understand the circumstances. You were prudent to be judicious with a total stranger, especially at this time a non-Jew."

"*Herr* Niska has never divulged his actual address to me, for perfectly good reasons of security, I'm sure. His own, and mine as well. If I don't know his address, should the authorities come looking for him here, I can honestly and credibly say that I do not know where he resides."

Kersten was disappointed initially. But Niska's strategy seemed like a wise one. He wouldn't push the doctor any further.

"I thank you for your time, Dr. Singer."

"I am sorry I could not be more helpful, Dr. Kersten."

Kersten shook the frail doctor's hand, turned toward the door, and headed toward it.

"I can tell you this, however, Dr. Kersten," Singer called out before Kersten had opened the door to leave. "I do know that he is out of the country at present. I don't know exactly where. But I am confident that he is engaging, as you put it, in the life-preserving enterprise you say you share with him."

CHAPTER THIRTEEN

Litomerice, Czechoslovakia: February 17, 1939

In September of the previous year, British Prime Minister Neville Chamberlain and French President Edouard Daladier traveled to Munich in an effort to convince Hitler to rein in his alarming expansionist tendencies. The leaders of the two Western nations still had fresh, painful memories of the bloodshed of the Great War, and so were eager to maintain peace in Europe, or at least some semblance of the status quo.

They, it turned out, were prepared to sacrifice the western corner of Czechoslovakia bordering Germany in their wager for peace. With what Hitler saw clearly as their consent, he marched virtually unopposed into the Sudetenland in Czechoslovakia. The pretext given was that he was moving in to offer protection for the German-speaking population. It was unveiled as a ruse six months later when the Nazis marched beyond the Sudetenland and occupied the entirety of Czechoslovakia.

Niska was infuriated by those developments. His mind was on fire with his native skepticism.

Can Hitler be anything but contemptuously cynical when he announced to the German people and the world that the country's name now was "The Protectorate of Bohemia and Moravia"? Does he really expect the people to swallow as truth that von Neurath is now to be addressed as Reichsprotektor?

I must say I am rather surprised at the credulity of the German people. They seem to be convinced that something is a verifiable, historical fact, just because their Führer tells them it is, and that is that. If they don't hear directly over the radio from their Führer, his twisted version of the truth is promulgated through his mouthpiece Göbbels. What a brilliant manipulator of facts, half-truths, and outright lies until the gullible Volk digests them as absolute truth. What insanity and plague of make-believe has taken over this nation?

The day after the Nazis rolled into Czechoslovakia, German

newspapers boasted of measures the Nazis would be taking there to "keep the Jews in line." When Niska read about them, he hated to imagine what some of those measures might be.

The news troubled Niska because by no means had he forgotten Jiri Hudak. The young man believed he was returning to a country where he could live as a free human being again. The Nazi occupation of Czechoslovakia negated Niska's smuggling of his first Jew to safety. He couldn't sleep at night knowing that his job had been rendered null and void. Was it time now for an unscheduled trip to Czechoslovakia to try to rescue Hudak once more?

Since one of the ten Finnish passports he had secured for Bruno Altmann's Jewish associates in the previous month had fallen into the hands of the SS, his Finnish passport would be suspect now. He communicated with a friendly contact in Sweden from his smuggling days. Several weeks later, a new forged Swedish passport arrived. His new travel identity was Sven Ovesen. He got on another Prague-bound train, telling the wary border agents he was going to Czechoslovakia to reestablish his interrupted business dealings now that this nation was under German rule.

Niska went to the address he had for Hudak, not at all certain he would still be residing there. Fortunately, when Niska knocked on his door, Hudak himself answered warily, opening it only part-way. Hudak looked as though he had lost ten kilos. His face was thin and gaunt despite his youth. Not a split second had elapsed, however, before Hudak's face erupted into a smile. He swung both of his arms around Niska and almost smothered him in a bear hug of an embrace at the threshold to his less than modest flat.

"*Herr* Niska, how relieved I am to see you! I was afraid of contacting you in Berlin, lest the Germans are opening my outgoing mail or tapping my telephone, or yours, for that matter."

"That's prudent of you, Jiri," Niska said, stepping into the flat. "But unfortunately, the Nazis have been made aware of Algot Niska's activities already. I'm Sven Ovesen now." He opened his passport to the identity page and held it up for Hudak to see.

Jiri looked a little confused initially. "Pardon me? Sven who?"

Almost immediately, however, Jiri's face registered comprehension.

"We have to get you out of here," Niska said, to which Jiri was nodding his head in fervent agreement. "The SS are pissed off when a Jew escapes their clutches from Germany. They must be doubly pissed off when he tries to evade them a second time from an occupied country. I warn you: If we're caught, the consequences would be twice as unpleasant, to say the least."

"Once again, *Herr* Niska…"

"Ovesen."

"Yes, of course. *Herr* Ovesen. I have nothing, no shop, no job, no freedom, no future here now. So what have I got to lose?"

Niska cautioned Jiri that he would have to exit Czechoslovakia somehow with no papers. He couldn't risk using one of the Niska's false Finnish passports. An alert had been disseminated to all the Nazi border patrols in Germany, Austria, and now Czechoslovakia.

"Well, aren't you and I old hands now at slinking through border patrol with no passport at all?"

"I don't know for how long, but Poland is still independent," Niska said. "We'll try to slip through the border there. But I wouldn't advise staying in Poland. The Poles don't exactly have a sparkling record in their treatment of Jews. And besides, we can't know how much longer Hitler can resist the temptation to march into Poland in search of *Lebensraum*."

Jiri let out a sarcastic snort. "Is that what he's calling his voracious hunger for conquest?"

"Once we get you to Poland, you can continue on your way to Danzig and catch a ship to Finland. I can arrange for one of my contacts in Helsinki to meet you there. It's just that right now I don't have any idea of how to get us into Poland in the first place."

"Maybe we'll run into a Polish border guard this time who also happens to have been to a cross-country ski meet in Finland," Hudak joked.

"I'm glad that under the circumstances you can still laugh."

"We Jews have learned the hard way over the centuries to laugh whatever our plight. Otherwise, we'd die of despair. But *Herr* Ovesen, whatever we have to do, I'd rather be laughing in Finland, or even Poland, than here or Germany."

Indeed, Niska thought. This Jiri had seemed as cool as a cucumber back in Berlin when they first discussed possible escape. He had seemed earnest but patient, almost serene, when Niska had described the process and explained the obvious risks. But today, here in Czechoslovakia, he seemed more agitated and desperate, almost bursting with a frantic doggedness to get as far from the Nazis as he could. Yesterday wasn't soon enough to leave.

They boarded a train bound for Krakow at the central station in Prague. This one would take them only as far as the border, where they would have to transfer to a Polish train. Once again, the two men were fellow travelers on a train bound for what they hoped was freedom.

After several hours of uneventful travel, the train came to a stop at the border to allow Nazi border agents to board and begin the process of inspecting passengers' paperwork.

"*Reisepasskontrolle!*"

The Nazis had in such a short time trained the Czech guards to bark their orders in German. Jiri looked anxiously at Niska.

Niska handed him a package of cigarettes adding, "I see you're still a non-smoker, Jiri." He was hoping some humor might reduce Hudak's obvious anxiety that could give them away.

Hudak didn't bother to answer other than by taking the package into his hand almost greedily. Niska maintained his familiar Finnish stoical face, not letting on that beneath his stony exterior, his veins and arteries were coursing with a rush of adrenaline.

Niska and Hudak sat deliberately in the last row of seats once again, just in case there were instances such as this one. As the border guards made their way down the center aisle, they were preoccupied with their official duties. Niska grabbed Jiri lightly by the elbow of his right arm and made a subtle nodding gesture with his head in the direction of the door at the rear of the coach. These two border agents must have been new to the job, because they hadn't posted one of them at the rear door to prevent a passenger from making a hasty exit.

Niska and Jiri rose from their seats slowly and quietly in an effort not to attract the attention of the agents. When they were sure that the agents were sufficiently focused on the paperwork of another passenger, first Jiri, and then Niska stepped into the aisle as casually as someone rising to go to the restroom. Only they scampered past the restroom door, quietly opened the exit door, and jumped the meter and a half or so down to the ground. Niska's wasn't a smooth landing and tore the left knee of his trousers.

"*Saatana!*"

"I don't know what that means," Jiri said slightly above a

whisper, "but it sounds obscene enough."

"You'll learn a bunch of such helpful expressions once you get to Finland, believe me, Jiri." They both chuckled.

While jumping, Jiri had managed to hold on to his suitcase. Niska pointed to the scrub woods lining the tracks. The two men crouched so as to avoid being seen and crawled into the shelter of the trees.

Fortunately for them, spring had come early to Czechoslovakia and Poland that year. Their passage through the woods was not hindered by remnants of the winter's snowfall. There were fallen branches and limbs everywhere, but they proceeded as silently as possible. The early morning sun was still low above the horizon. There was little reason to fear any unwanted encounters, at least until the agents on the train noticed that two passengers were missing, and alerted their colleagues in the tiny border station.

Niska had made it a point to study a detailed topographic map of this particular border region in the central library in Prague before they left. He recalled that if they made their way down the steep embankment, they would soon come to a small river, just a creek really, that formed the natural boundary between Czechoslovakia and Poland.

But now, Niska began to think that his memory was misleading him. The closer they came to the creek, the stronger the sound of rushing water. Standing at the brink, they realized that the creek had accumulated a lot of water from the winter snowmelt. Its current had become rapid and deep; it was impassible, and there was no footbridge in sight. Only the call of a cuckoo accompanied the sound of the angrily gushing rapids.

The men discussed their situation.

"I think we have to wait out the day until evening," Niska offered. "We can move under the cover of darkness."

"But we can't just wait *here* in broad daylight like sitting ducks." It was the first time in their relationship that Hudak had dared to contradict Niska. "At any moment, a border patrol alerted to our disappearance can greet us with an unpleasant surprise."

So they hatched a new plan.

Jiri looked upstream. "I'll go along the edge upstream. You go in the opposite direction, downstream. If I come upon a bridge or a ford, I'll find a large piece of birch bark and throw in the stream as a sign."

"You're assuming my aging eyes can see it in a rushing river," Niska said. "But yes, that might work. Now, if I should discover a place to cross over into Poland, I'll imitate the call of the cuckoo four times. You know, that bird we keep hearing. Hear it?"

"Yes."

Niska chanted an approximate facsimile.

"Your imitation is not that perfect that I won't confuse it with the call of an actual cuckoo and get confused," Jiri said, almost laughing despite their situation.

"We have lots of cuckoos in Finland. They never let out four calls in a row. Once you hear four calls, you'll know it's me, signaling you to come back toward me. Answer my call with an imitation of your own so I know you got the message. Let me hear one now."

Jiri tried a couple of times.

"No, it's got to be the imitation of a healthy cuckoo, not a sick one. Like this."

Niska made the sound again "Now, try that."

Jiri's next imitation was closer.

"Now, if we lose track of each other," Niska continued, "we each have to do the best we can independently. Figure out a way to enter Poland undetected. Then make your way to the train station in Katowice. It's just a few miles inside Poland, within a moderate walking distance. I'll meet you there. We'll board the next train together for Krakow."

"Then what?"

"Don't get too far ahead of yourself," Niska said. "In the meantime, I assume that a fresh shipment of Finnish passports will have arrived in my post office box in Berlin, I've left a key to the box with a trusted contact in Berlin. I'll call him from Krakow and instruct him to put your name in it and then to mail it to us in care of Sven Ovesen at the Finnish consulate in Krakow. We'll get it right, Niska."

"And make up the rest as we go along."

Hudak seemed satisfied with the plan and started slinking upstream along the bank.

"Leave your suitcase here," Niska said, grabbing Hudak's arm. "It'll just weigh you down as you negotiate the creekbank."

Niska watched as Jiri disappeared empty-handed among the

trees along the creek. Niska was just about to head in his appointed direction when, instead, he encountered another obstacle. His heart stopped.

"*Aufstieg!* Stand up!" came a crisp, insistent voice in German. "What are you doing here by the border?"

Niska turned around slowly and saw two border guards staring at him.

Should I say that I am fishing? No, that won't wash. I'm wearing a business suit and shiny black shoes, for Christ's sake. Besides, I'm not carrying the requisite equipment. Just Jiri's suitcase.

"There can't be more obvious evidence that our friend here was on his way to cross the border into Poland illegally, can there?" the cynical border guard said to his partner, pointing to the suitcase.

Niska had nothing to say.

"Come with us."

That evening, Niska was escorted by two SS men on a train to Ostrava, a nearby market town where the SS had set up district headquarters. The following morning, he was interrogated.

"I was lost," Niska answered in German to the interrogator's questions. "I belong to a small group of Swedish tourists from Prague on our way to Krakow. It's a beautiful city, I'm told."

The beefy interrogator looked doubtful.

"The others had gone with the car to get petrol while I waited," Niska continued hopefully, although he could feel the water leaking out of his alibi. "They were delayed for some reason. I was thirsty and hungry. I heard the sound of the stream down below. So I made my way down the slope to the creek. I thought maybe I could drink the water. I was overcome by the beauty of the place and lingered. Just about then, the guards arrived."

The interrogator looked no more convinced than before.

He motioned to a subordinate to inspect the suitcase. Niska held his breath. His eyes followed the suitcase while trying to appear casual.

"It appears from the contents of your luggage that you are a Jew," the interrogator confronted Niska. "And yet, I don't get it. Maybe you can help me understand. It seems strange that these photos are obviously of a much younger man, a Jew, to be sure, but a slimmer one than the man who stands before me. I must deduce that you have some kind of connection to Jews. Perhaps you have an explanation, *Herr* Ovesen."

Niska's mind fumbled for an answer. He found none. He was growing resigned that the grains of sand were almost finished sifting through the neck of his hourglass.

The interrogation over, Niska was taken by two SS to a camp of some sort out in the woods not far from Ostrava. It was clear that most of the inhabitants of the camp were Jews.

The camp *Kommandant* came to Niska's small barrack at the camp around midday and introduced himself gruffly.

"I understand you are claiming that you are not a Jew. Certainly, *Herr* Ovesen, your passport confirms this. It says here that your occupation is international business. In Czechoslovakia on business, were you, *Herr* Ovesen?"

"You'll notice that I possess a Swedish passport, Sir. You cannot hold the citizen of a neutral country against his will like this. I protest."

"For the time being, you may protest all you want, for all I care. But we will hold anyone we choose. You haven't answered my question. Citizen of Sweden?"

"Yes, as a matter of fact, I was in Czechoslovakia on business. The recent occupation of Prague had caused an interruption in my operations—a very inconvenient one, I need to add. I was in Prague to get things up and rolling again."

"That may be so. However, is it not rather strange that on a business trip to Prague, you, by coincidence, were found in the woods near the border between Czechoslovakia and Poland?

The *Kommandant* didn't wait for Niska to reply. "And that a couple of our border guards caught you sitting on a suitcase? Is that the kind of place where you are accustomed to conducting your business? Furthermore, the suitcase does not belong to you, but to a Jew who seems to have disappeared. How do you explain that strange fact, *Herr* Ovesen?"

"The suitcase was by the creek where I found it. Someone else must have come down to get a drink and left it there by mistake." Niska felt he was losing track of his concocted alibi.

The commandant gave a faint, skeptical smile. "I'm afraid your story is not very imaginative, *Herr* Ovesen. Why do I sense that you are making it up as you go along?"

Shit! That's because I am making it up as I go along. Face it. I am going down. It is only a matter of time before they discover that Herr Ovesen is, in fact, Herr Niska, a wanted criminal, an enemy of the Führer.

"That's enough for today," the commandant said brusquely and abruptly. He nodded at the subordinate to take Niska back to his barrack.

Niska shivered in the fog the next morning when he was led outside to the train siding and ordered to board the train along with a large crowd of camp guests, as the *Kommandant* called them, Jews, all of them. A very crowded, uncomfortable two hours later, the train disgorged its passengers at another camp, a larger, more forbidding one.

All the passengers had to wait seemingly interminably before being processed by the personnel from the registration of new arrivals. Niska stood at the end of the long line, still holding Hudak's incriminating suitcase. His legs were asleep from having sat awkwardly on them in the aisle of the crowded coach. The tear in the trousers of his business suit had grown. He leaned against the wall of one of the wooden barracks.

Directly in front of him was a group of children, a juvenile with four small siblings. Their clothing was in tatters. All of them were dark-haired and pale-looking, typical Eastern European Jewish children. When it was their turn to be processed, they were pushed together violently into the barrack—needlessly violently, Niska thought. A guard slammed the door behind them.

That left Niska standing alone in a small inner yard, unable to go either in or out. The camp personnel seemed to have retreated to some other part of the compound. The door to the barrack was locked tight, as was the wire gate through which the passengers had been funneled into the camp.

It was late in the afternoon. Niska had been alone in the yard for several hours. He tried to push out of his mind his fear of what being singled out in this way might mean, what special punishment awaited him.

Suddenly, he heard the sound of a key opening the door through which his unfortunate young companions had been pushed. Niska expected to see a uniformed guard coming to fetch him, or perhaps the *Kommandant* who had interrogated him earlier. But instead, it was a man in civilian tradesman's clothes, appearing startled that someone should still be standing in the yard so late in the day.

"*Was...? Was wollen Sie?*" What do you want?

In a flash, the situation became clear to Niska. He could hardly believe it. The man had absolutely no idea that Niska was part of the large group that had been transported to the camp. Perhaps the business suit, as torn as it was at the knee, confused the man.

"What are you doing here?"

"*Ach,*" Niska responded. "I came here to try to visit one of the apprehended ones, a familiar tailor from my town. But I am told that is not permitted. Now I'm only waiting for someone to open the gate for me so that I can return home in Ostrava."

The man apologized for what he surmised was some other person's neglect.

"My shift helping maintain the electrical system is over. I'm ready to go home, too." They walked together toward the gate.

The man waved a thumbs-up to the guard in the tower near the entrance. The guard returned a thumbs-up signal. The man opened the gate by manipulating a metal bar. He bowed deeply and asked Niska to pass before him through the gate.

Niska was still worried that despite the exchange of thumbs-up signals, the guard in the tower would open fire on them.

"My car is right over there, *Mein Freund.* The trains to Ostrava have stopped running for the day. I am happy to drive you."

The man did not need to ask Niska twice. He directed the man to drop him off near a residential area close to the train station, thanking him profusely as they reached the destination.

The next morning, Niska took the short train trip across the Polish border—using Sven Ovesen's passport—and to Katowice. It had been several days since he and Hudak went separate ways by the stream. He managed to track down Jiri Hudak through a synagogue that was housing a group of the Czech refugees who had, each in his or her own way, managed to flee from Czechoslovakia into Poland.

"I had given up on you, *Herr* Niska. When you didn't show up in Katowice the first few days, I was sure that you had been apprehended by the Nazis, maybe even executed."

"You got part of it right. I was apprehended. I've added a couple of other anxious episodes to my collection of adventures. But as you can see, here I am, alive and well. By the way, here is your suitcase. Good riddance. It was almost the death of me."

~~~

The two boarded a train to Krakow to fetch a Finnish passport for Hudak at the Finnish consulate there. A polite secretary reached into a mailbox labeled "Sven Ovesen." "Here, this must be it, an envelope postmarked in Berlin."

It was difficult to tell who was more relieved, Hudak or Niska. "Thank you very much," Niska said on behalf of both of them and flashed a charming smile.

"It's a good thing, Mr. Niska, that you came to retrieve the passport today," the secretary said.

"Oh?"

"We might not have been here tomorrow."

"Some kind of Polish holiday?"

"No. More serious than that. Helsinki has ordered us to evacuate the premises and return immediately to Finland."

"Sounds rather drastic. Are the Poles taking back their welcome?"

"Word is that Hitler is on the cusp of invading Poland from the west," she informed him. "We've got to get out of the country before he mistakes us for the hated Poles."

"What?" Niska was genuinely surprised that Hitler was actually going ahead with what he and many others had suspected he might do. "He's gambling that neither France nor Britain will dare to come to the aid of the Poles?"

"There's more, I'm afraid," the attractive secretary added. "We're told by our people that Stalin is sending armored and infantry battalions toward the Polish border, too, from the east. It appears that Poland is going to be squeezed in a deadly vise, I'm afraid. We don't want to be squeezed along with it."

Jiri was not able to follow the conversation in Finnish. He didn't need for Niska to translate, however. The grave look on Niska's face sufficed as the conversation with the secretary ended. The blanched look told Jiri that it was high time for him to catch the train to Danzig

Niska handed Hudak the Finnish passport hurriedly. He wished him a good trip. "May good fortune follow you as you sail to out-of-the-way, off-the-beaten-track Finland. I don't think Hitler will have much interest in following you there."

They shook hands. Hudak released Niska's hand, and

proceeded to embrace him, not a form of farewell to which the solitary, seafaring Finn was accustomed.

Weeks later in his Berlin hotel apartment, Niska tried to picture in his mind Hudak boarding the steamer, waiting for arrival in Helsinki, finally stepping on Finnish soil. At least, he hoped so. The daydream filled him with a depth of satisfaction that he had seldom felt before. In his whiskey smuggling days, there was always the sense of completion when the booty had been delivered successfully to its destination, a relishing of winning the cat and mouse game with the authorities. More than once, Swedish maritime police had pursued him to the end of Swedish territorial waters, all the while firing bullets at him and his boat. Once in Danish waters he would laugh derisively at his frustrated Swedish trackers. But next time, he might not be so fortunate.

But the escapade of helping Hudak escape the Nazis, not just once, but twice, all the moments of uncertainty and foreboding, and even despair, in the process, yet sweet escape nonetheless—nothing he had ever experienced in his fifty years could compare to this feeling of elation and gratification.

Niska knew from his own experience what confinement and surrender of freedom were like. He had known freedom, too, especially out on the open seas, the whole world before him, his choice where to land limited only by weather and the wind.

But it was a novel kind of freedom he was experiencing now—the freedom from concern for his own safety, the freedom to assist others like Jiri attain their freedom using his distinctive skills and unique history.

He was convinced in the deepest part of him that he was now doing what he was put on earth to do.

CHAPTER FOURTEEN

Berlin: February 28, 1940

Auguste Diehn couldn't have been more effusive in his utterances of gratitude to Kersten for having rescued his faithful foreman from Dachau. He came to see Kersten at his clinic in his flat with increasing frequency, just incidentally for treatments. Each time, before Diehn left, he handed Kersten a handwritten note containing the names of other Jews in need of rescue that had been made known to him.

Kersten received these names with a different attitude than he had Diehn's earlier requests for "personal favors." It seemed that all the rational arguments against taking these risks had evaporated with time. The euphoria of his first success in extracting from Himmler the freedom of a human being still warmed his blood a month and a half later.

Himmler had granted to Kersten a short leave so that he could return to his wife in The Hague. Once he got off the train at the elegant central terminal there, Kersten breathed deeply of the free, fresh air. His emotion on returning to the city he loved so much was even stronger than he had anticipated. The reunion with Irmgaard was a pleasant interlude in which they alternated between making love, fine dining in the best restaurants in The Hague, and quiet evenings together in their luxurious flat.

He made use of the time to reintroduce himself and his services to the royal family.

The extraordinary gift of time and freedom from the watchful eyes of the SS and *Gestapo* enabled Kersten to organize a veritable secret network of informants and associates throughout the Netherlands. Before he was summoned back to Berlin he had accomplices in most strategic sectors of Holland's political and business life.

One morning after his return to Berlin, Kersten stopped at Rudolf Brandt's desk in the anteroom to Himmler's office. He noticed that someone else had had the same idea, so he stood back to await his turn to talk to Himmler's personal assistant. A tall, fit, almost aristocratic-looking SS officer was finishing a conversation with Brandt. He was meticulously dressed in his uniform. There was something about the man's aspect, however, some subtle form of uneasiness in his otherwise correct posture, that suggested that the man was not entirely comfortable for some reason wearing the uniform. When the officer finished his conversation with Brandt, he turned to leave. As he did so, he looked directly into Kersten's face and gave a slight hint of a smile. The man's face didn't register even a hint of suspicion. Kersten was accustomed to a kind of hostile glower from other Himmler's lieutenants. They made no attempt to hide their unfriendly glares that amounted to querulous warnings. "Watch yourself, foreigner. You may be Himmler's personal doctor, but we've got you in our sights."

Kersten wasn't sure exactly what this officer was communicating, but he responded to him with a friendly nod of his head and an uncertain smile. Once the officer left—without the ritualistic "*Heil Hitler*" salute—Kersten approached Brandt.

"I'd advise you to not overlook that officer," Brandt said to Kersten, nodding his head in the direction of the door. "He might be of some help to you."

"Who is he? I don't believe I've encountered him before."

"That's SS Lieutenant-General Walter Schellenberg. He is the head of the SD—the *Sicherheitsdienst*—the secret intelligence service that the *Reichsführer* arranged to be folded into the SS itself late last year. He's one of the *Reichsführer's* most trusted lieutenants. Has he not mentioned Schellenberg to you?"

"No, the only men he mentions are the ones he's not so sure he can trust, like Heydrich and Kaltenbrunner. I guess he's more focused on potential enemies than allies."

Brandt nodded his head and smiled knowingly. Kersten filed Brandt's advice for possible future reference.

"I've got a little personal request to make of you, Rudolf," Kersten began in a voice barely louder than a whisper, as though he were about to confess something. "It's rather sensitive, if you catch my drift."

Brandt moved his chair closer to his desk, a move that indicated his willingness to hear the confession.

"I met some interesting women while back in Holland," Kersten confided. "Very beautiful ones, at that." He smiled devilishly at Brandt.

"I'm sure you have a good eye for the most desirable ladies, *Herr* Doctor."

In point of fact, Kersten had not had encounters, at least not romantic or sexual ones, with any women in The Hague other than Queen Wilhelmina and Irmgaard. But he was enjoying this little exercise in fantasy.

"I am sure these women will want to write to me here in Berlin. I'm sure you understand, Rudolf, how it pains me to think that these delectable personal letters will be read by the censors if I correspond back and forth with them through the *Reichspost.*"

Kersten didn't have to wait long for Brandt to take the bait. Since Kersten was in such good graces with his boss, Brandt no longer bothered to conceal his liking for the doctor.

"Then, Doctor, use the *Reichsführer's* postal box."

"What? Himmler's mailbox? That would be very risky, would it not?"

"No, not at all. I'm the one who sorts the *Reichsführer's* mail every day. I'm not sure, in fact, that he even knows where his official postal box is located. I will be sure to pass on to you privately any mail that is addressed to you."

"Is this really safe, Rudolf?" asked Kersten.

"Trust me: It's the only safe postal box in all of Germany."

~~~

When Kersten came into Himmler's office to perform another treatment, Himmler's mood was unusually jovial for a man in pain.

"Kersten, how good to see you. I hear that you have been very busy in The Hague. I was glad to hear what Brandt passed on to me this morning."

Himmler made a very awkward attempt to wink at Kersten. A spasm caught in Kersten's throat.

Himmler smiled broadly. "Every man deserves an occasional discretion. I'm proud of you, Kersten. I'm delighted that you don't consider yourself above the rest of us who dabble in love affairs from time to time."

"Brandt told you this?" Kersten asked, totally flummoxed, his anger at Brandt beginning to simmer.

"Well, yes, of course. Brandt had to secure my permission for your use of my official postal box. I had to sign off on it, or else the Chancellery postmaster would begin asking questions of people who shouldn't be asked. Suspicions grow like a cancer in the Chancellery. I was overjoyed to affix my signature to the request."

"Then, no one else but you and Brandt know about my amorous liaisons? Or that I have such generous access to your private mailbox?"

Kersten asked.

"There are few things of which you can be more certain, Doctor…Now, are you ready for my treatment? I've been in terrible pain."

Kersten had scanned the titles of books once on the small bookshelf in Himmler's office. Hitler's *Mein Kampf* was there, not surprisingly. There were also titles like Willibald Hentschel's *Varuna: The Origins of the Aryan Race; The Crusade Against the Holy Grail* written by one of Himmler's SS recruits; Otto Rahn, and a series of other volumes of stories of the medieval Teutonic Knights. That helped explain, thought Kersten, why Himmler had chosen the Renaissance-era Wewelsburg Castle in Westphalia as the locale for his SS Officers Training School. Against the resistance of several others in Hitler's inner circle, Himmler had insisted on a grand redesign of the interior as a replica of a castle of the old Teutonic Order. The former schoolteacher would appear before a classroom of officer recruits dressed in the full attire of a Teutonic warrior and, much to their chagrin and embarrassment, would insist that his senior deputies Heydrich and Kaltenbrunner do the same. Himmler wished to identify himself with Frederick Barbarossa, Henry I, the Fowler, and other emperors and princes of that epoch. Himmler believed himself to be their reincarnation in the twentieth century.

Himmler confided these fantasies more than once to Kersten, who saw an opportunity in turning Himmler's almost childlike hero worship to his own use.

"*Herr Reichsführer*," Kersten began near the end of a therapy session. "In the centuries to come, I am sure you will be called the greatest leader of the German people, the equal of Barbarossa and Henry the Fowler."

"Doctor, you are much too kind to have such a high opinion of me," Himmler said in response. But Kersten could tell that Himmler was enjoying the comparison immensely.

"I mean it sincerely, I assure you, *Herr Reichsführer*. You know yourself that you are so much more gifted for leadership than your colleagues."

"Like Heydrich and Kaltenbrunner?" Himmler asked. "More rivals than colleagues, I'd say. The *Führer* is right to put more trust in me than in the others."

"That he is, *Herr Reichsführer*."

Kersten paused strategically, then continued and finished the massage session. He waded into these waters of obsequiousness with caution—and a nausea akin to seasickness. But he had to be careful to remain credible to Himmler. When the session was over and he knew Himmler would be almost inebriated with relief and pleasure, his head swollen by the flattery, Kersten resumed his stratagem.

"You must remember, *Herr Reichsführer,* that those admirable heroes like Barbarossa and Henry the Fowler did not owe their greatness to force and courage alone."

"What do you mean, Doctor? They were knights."

"Well, I am sure you are aware that knights were known for their sense of justice and generosity. To truly resemble these valiant cavaliers, a man must be as magnanimous in victory as they were, would he not?"

"They slaughtered their enemies," Himmler objected.

"Yes, but from what I know—and admittedly, that is not as much as you—they slaughtered only the ones who were necessary to liquidate, and spared the rest." Kersten cringed internally as he used the term "liquidate." It had become the Nazi euphemism of choice for their widespread murderous activities. "That may be so," admitted Himmler. "I didn't know you had an interest in our Teutonic heroes."

I might have as a thirteen- or fourteen-year-old.

"I tell you this, *Herr Reichsführer,* because I am thinking of your reputation in the centuries to come after this war is over and the history books are written."

Kersten took a careful look at Himmler's face. It was beaming with pride. Kersten could tell that Himmler was swallowing the bait wholeheartedly.

"My dear Dr. Kersten," Himmler said. "You are my only friend, the only one who both understands me and helps me."

Strike now!

"You're a valued friend, too, *Herr Reichsführer.*"

"Good Doctor, do you realize how long it has been since anybody said that to me?"

"Considering all the favors you have extended to so many people, all the farmers like Höss and filing clerks like Eichmann that you have chosen and elevated to their current heights, I find it strange that you would feel as though you have few friends."

"They would all prefer that I disappear so they could have my position," Himmler said sadly. "My only friend is you...and perhaps

Brandt."

"I have a favor to ask, *Mein gut Freund.*"

He reached into the bottom of his portfolio and produced two small folded pieces of paper, and presented them to Himmler.

Himmler looked down the two lists of the names given to Kersten by Diehn. "I don't think I need to ask you to explain this time, Kersten," Himmler said resignedly. "These are obviously the names of Jews. Aryans don't name their children Moshe or Danka or Isaak, as a rule. And what is it you would like me to do with these names?"

"You've been saying for quite some time, *Herr Reichsführer*, that the life of the one Jew you had released from Dachau at my request was hardly remuneration enough for all I've done for you with my treatments. So I compiled a modest list of several others to serve as the balance of the compensation."

Kersten immediately regretted having said "the balance of the compensation," just as Himmler was simultaneously lamenting his remark about one Jew's life not being sufficient payment.

"Modest list of several others?" Himmler repeated. "I count at least a dozen names here. You are beginning to be beyond the price range I can afford."

The stratagem is backfiring. I chose the wrong time. Perhaps I should have presented only one of the lists.

Himmler summoned Brandt once again.

"My good Brandt, please draw up an order list for the immediate release of the names designated by Dr. Kersten on these slips of paper and bring it in for me to sign." Brandt took a quick glance at Kersten with as much of a hint of a smile that he could risk.

Kersten didn't hazard a smile back to Brandt in response. But he slowly let out his breath in relief.

"You realize, I'm sure, Kersten, that it might be easier for one of my so-called 'friends' within the SS to take notice of a dozen Jews being released than just the one and trace it back to me. But such are the things we do for true friends, I suppose."

This procedure, or ones much like it, was repeated several times through the summer of 1939 and early spring of 1940. The rescue of Jews he had never met was extremely gratifying for Kersten. However, at the same time, it was also a source of acute anxiety. Himmler had supreme command, of course, in the matter of the fate of the Jews. Kersten wondered how long before Himmler's immediate subordinates, like Heydrich and Kaltenbrunner, or perhaps even Hitler himself, began to wonder what was causing Himmler to sign pardons for all these Jews. They were not accustomed to leniency from such a quarter. Surely, they would investigate on the sly. Himmler had always demanded of his subordinates an implacable, unrelenting fury in persecution and terror. Surely, one or more of them is asking himself: Why, now, this sudden change in the Chief himself? What role does the Finnish doctor play in the *Reichsführer's* unpredictable behavior?

CHAPTER FIFTEEN

Berlin: March 27, 1939

Algot Niska felt relieved to be back from Poland and resettled in his Berlin flat. Smuggling Jiri Hudak out of Czechoslovakia had taxed his energy and given him a fright to boot.

Niska wasn't given much time for leisure and rest, however. Bruno Altmann had discovered a new vocation, too: as a broker connecting Jews in Berlin desperate to escape with Niska, who had proven several times that he as inventive enough to discover ways to save them. Altmann and Niska met several times a week at the Kakadu. Each time, Altmann would present Niska with the names of Jews who had approached him secretly and requested his help in escaping the hell that Germany was becoming.

There was the young merchant, Hans Friedländer, wanted by the SS for purported espionage, whom he helped cross the border into Holland, and his beautiful nineteen-year-old fiancée Hella, who when she discovered Hans had fled without a word in advance to her, pleaded desperately with Niska to help her join him in Amsterdam. She told him that she had absolutely no means by which to compensate him, but that she would be eternally grateful if he helped her. Niska remembered being offended by her assumption that he wouldn't help her escape unless she had hard currency as remuneration, as though his compassion had a fixed price.

There was Simon Gluschner and his wife who wanted help to get to Finland. Only Simon's eyebrows were so dark and bushy, and his wife's face so prototypically eastern European Jewish, that they would have a hard time convincing the emigration officials on German soil that they were Finnish. So Niska found a way to neutral Portugal instead.

Altmann had also connected the widow Ester Neumann with Niska. She wanted to be reunited with her son Josef, daughter-in-law Sarah, and toddler grandson Eli whom Niska had helped escape to Belgium. Ester had developed a serious skin disease that disfigured her feet and made it well-nigh impossible for her to walk. Niska experimented with the strategy of bribing an ambulance driver to transport her from Berlin to Brussels. He had a contact forge the proper paperwork for Ester, including a medical directive that the patient needed to undergo serious surgery that could only be performed by a Dr. Piet Vanbiesbrück in Brussels because every orthopedic surgeon in Germany had been requisitioned to treat *Wehrmacht* soldiers wounded in the invasion of Poland. The driver was to give the directive to the SS exit guards as well as the Belgian immigration officials on the other side of the border. Niska had held his breath anxiously back in Berlin. The following morning, however, he received a very brief, coded telephone call from the driver indicating that the bold experiment had been successful. Suddenly, Niska had a new tool in his smuggling toolbox.

These and other adventures in the rescue of Jews were a source of tension for Niska at the time. However, whenever he had occasion to recall the faces of his "clients" and the relief and high spirits he felt on their behalf when he'd heard that they had made it safely to their destination, he concluded that the felicitous result compensated many times over for whatever risk he had taken and anxiety he had endured.

~~~

The German newspapers made little mention of Hitler's and foreign minister Ribbentropp's diplomatic antics. True, much ink was devoted to the previous autumn's appeasement by Chamberlain and Daladier, and the subsequent annexation of the Sudetenland. The further advance into the rest of Czechoslovakia was hardly mentioned, and when it was, Niska read the German explanation with skepticism.

The Finnish papers, however, made no effort to shield the Finnish people from the growing threat of German expansionism and the resulting potential war that threatened to engulf most of Europe. The *Helsingin Sanomat* was available at a newspaper kiosk within a comfortable walk from Niska's flat, but it was usually last Saturday's edition, so the news he read was a week out of date. Nevertheless, the dispatches of the *Sanomat* correspondents in Berlin were surprisingly bold in relaying information leaked from within the Nazi government. Their anonymous sources reported that there was a growing fervor to continue expanding the German borders farther eastward. Given the relatively anemic protests from Western governments of Hitler's appropriation of Czechoslovakia, the loyal Nazi acolytes nodded their heads whenever Hitler suggested that there would probably be an equally feeble response by the Western democracies should Germany infiltrate their eastern neighbor Poland in the same way.

What made the editorial staff of the *Sanomat* particularly anxious was the rumor of a potential non-aggression pact between Germany and the Soviet Union. That the two dictators should even consider such an agreement was more than curious to Niska.

Does such a piece of paper have a snowball's chance in hell of lasting as long as either of them needs to take a leak? These two characters hardly have a sterling record in keeping their promises.

If, indeed, Hitler had his sights set on Poland, the pact made sense, the editorialists maintained, because it might pave the way for Hitler to march into Poland without Russian military interference.

Sanomat correspondents reported that apparently the Hitler-Stalin treaty effectively divided Europe into so-called "zones of influence," with Finland squarely in the Soviet sphere of "influence." Niska was both confused and dubious.

Now, what in the hell do they mean by "a zone of influence?" Stalin has wanted to get his dirty paws on Finland again since we kicked them in the ass in 1917. This so-called pact might just guarantee that the Krauts will look the other way while Stalin sneaks back into Finland from the east. Not good news.

But Niska was stupefied by the obliviousness of the residents of Berlin regarding the potential for war. The non-Jewish residents, that is. To be sure, the German population was still resentful, to say the least, about the punishment inflicted on Germany by the victors through the terms of the 1919 Treaty of Versailles. But more recently, life went on for most non-Jewish Berliners much as before, except that the employment rate had improved almost exponentially in the six years since Hitler had become Chancellor. The insanely rampant inflation of the previous decade had been tamed. Niska found the general population to be quite content. The cabarets were still filled to overflowing, even on weeknights. The liquor flowed freely. Decisions made at Hitler's headquarters on *Wilhelmstrasse* were totally unknown. Sure, certain violent acts against Jews occurred regularly, but that was the Jews' concern, not that of "real" Germans.

Shortly after his return from Poland, his physician, Dr. Singer, discovered that the source of increasing pain in Niska's abdomen was a stomach ulcer. Using a fake identity, Niska was hospitalized as Sven Ovesen in a small clinic in Charlottenburg near Dr. Singer's office.

Once word circulated throughout Charlottenburg that the *goy* patient in the clinic named Sven Ovesen was, in fact, Algot Niska, several relatives of Jews he had helped escape came to visit and express their concern for him. Niska received his visitors graciously, even though their visits put him in greater risk. For one thing, there might be a Nazi collaborator among the Jews who had learned of his new identity, and would pass the information on to the SS. Or just the fact that there were Jews visiting this Swede named Ovesen might not be overlooked by the SS. If, as he feared, he was being monitored by the SS, these prominent Jews would be putting themselves in great danger, incriminating themselves, in effect. Hell, they were in danger in any case.

The flowers and sweets that his visitors brought to Niska he routinely passed on to Singer's nine- or ten-year-old daughter, Angelika. Angelika sometimes tagged along on her widower father's rounds in the hospital. She would wander back to Niska's bedside where she knew she would be given either flowers or candies. In return, she would pass on bits of news to Niska about others she knew in the Jewish community, especially ones she had heard about that were escorted from their residences by the SS or *Gestapo*.

One afternoon, when Angelika came by his bedside, Niska asked her why she wasn't in school at that time of the day.

"Don't you *know*, *Herr* Niska? I haven't been at school since the awful burning of synagogues and smashing of store widows this past November. The laws were changed so that we Jewish pupils could no longer go to the public schools."

"Oh, my, you're right. I should have known that. I'm not surprised, though. What about attending one of the Jewish schools?"

"*Herr* Niska, you're so silly. How can I go to a Jewish school when the three of them in my neighborhood were burned down that noisy night when I couldn't sleep? Our rabbi holds class in his flat, but that is only for boys. So my father tries to teach me at home, but lately he's been so busy with new patients who have lost their regular doctor."

It was from Angelika that Niska learned about the accumulation of indignities and humiliation visited upon Angelika's friends and other Jewish children. They were no longer allowed to visit movie theaters; they were prohibited from riding on the streetcars, and the swings in the playgrounds were reserved for the exclusive use by gentile German children.

Niska wondered why she seemed to have few objections about having to wear a yellow Star of David on her coat. In fact, she wore it as a badge of honor.

"Daddy says that no matter what the Germans say about us, we are as good as they are. In some things, even better. I had better grades in school than any of the pure children."

Nonetheless, sometimes when she came to visit, Niska could detect that she had been crying not long before entering his room. One time, she came into his room, her blouse torn to shreds.

Quite concerned, Niska asked, "My dear girl, what in the world happened to you?"

"Oh, it's nothing. I ripped it accidentally when I tried to climb a fence."

Angelika tried to smile. But she couldn't hold back the tears. She turned away from Niska to hide her embarrassment.

These children, thousands of them, are all behind a fence, as it were, kept out from a wonderful world, only because they are Jewish. God damn these Nazis, many of whom are rewarded with titles and medals for dreaming up new infernal laws every day, it seems.

When Niska was close to being discharged, Angelika returned his favors and brought him a handful of wildflowers. Niska was deeply touched by the humble gift and the love it expressed. They were just about to begin their usual friendly conversation about whatever was on the child's mind. They were interrupted by a very loud conversation in the corridor beyond the closed door.

Angelika quickly put her index finger on her lips as a signal for Niska to keep absolutely quiet. She tiptoed to the door. A centimeter at a time, she opened the door very slowly and quietly and took a furtive peek up and down the hallway.

This child is not unfamiliar with unpleasant surprises. How often has the poor girl experienced or heard about brutal house searches by the SS? She knows that something evil could befall us at any second.

She returned to Niska's bedside and leaned her little body toward him.

"I think they are some kind of soldiers or policemen," she whispered. "They are wearing uniforms." She noted the unfamiliar look of alarm on Niska's face, and added, "My father has told me that you have done good things for Jewish people and that you may be in trouble."

Niska's brain shifted into high gear. He understood immediately that it was for him that the soldiers—most likely the SS—had come to the clinic. He asked Angelika to stay posted at the door while he, with some effort to hold back pain, slipped on socks and shoes, and then his coat over the hospital gown he was wearing.

"They've gone into the nurses' office," she informed him.

They sneaked stealthily out the door into the corridor. They could see that the door to the nurses' office had been left wide open. Niska deduced that the agents were checking the nurses' log. At any moment, they would come out of the office into the corridor.

What could Niska and Angelika do? The way to the exit meant passing by the nurses' office. *Where can we go? Think quickly, Algot! For your own sake, but mainly for hers.*

Niska grabbed Angelika's hand and they sneaked toward the door leading to the back stairs used by the cleaning and maintenance staff. Before they could reach the door, they heard the sound of heavy footsteps coming out of the nurses' office. Niska quickly pushed open the door to the bathroom and dragged Angelika in with him before they were spotted.

For the moment, it was silent in the corridor. Quite possibly, Niska conjectured, the soldiers were still nearby, listening for the sound of footsteps—Niska's and Angelika's footsteps, or other movements. He and Angelika were like mice in a trap without an escape route. They heard the sound of male voices apparently talking to one of the nurses.

"He could be anyone among the male patients," a deep voice said. "We must question all of them one by one." Then, raising his voice to the level of a shout, "Nurse, lock all the doors to the patients' rooms."

It's only a matter of time before we're discovered here.

Just then, Niska was surprised by the initiative of the little girl. Hurriedly, she reached for the faucet on the bathtub and began to run the water that came out in a rush. She took off her blouse, and then the rest of her clothing.

Niska felt immensely self-conscious, even though this was a pre-pubescent girl he was observing. He looked into Angelika's eyes with a look of comprehension mixed with admiration.

Without losing a split second, Angelika jumped into the bathtub and submerged her body up to her neck in the hot water.

In just several seconds, Angelika rose from the water and stepped out of the tub. Niska handed her a large towel with which she began drying herself urgently.

Steps out in the corridor were closing in toward the bathroom. Niska stepped into one of the stalls, and climbed up onto the toilet seat so that his feet would not be seen underneath the stall door.

"*Was gibt es da?*" What is there? The voice was coming from just beyond the bathroom door.

"Sir, that is the female bathroom," the head nurse announced to them from down the corridor. "A patient must be taking a bath."

Water was still gushing from the faucet into the tub. Angelika left it on deliberately. The door to the bathroom opened. Angelika turned toward the male intruder, pretending to be caught totally by surprise. She dropped the towel to the floor, revealing her naked body.

"*Ach! Bitte um Verzeihung.* I beg your pardon, *Fraulein*!" the male intruder uttered. "I didn't mean to violate your privacy."

He stepped back out into the corridor in a panic of embarrassment, his face as white as a ghost's, and slammed the door behind him. His partner laughed.

Niska, still crouching on his haunches on the toilet seat, was curious about what was transpiring. When the man had exited the bathroom, Angelika told him it was safe to come out of the toilet stall. She was still wrapping the towel around her wet body. Niska was able to put two and two together. In his relief, he marveled at the cleverness and quick thinking of such a young girl.

"We have to inspect the rooms of the female patients," the man with the deep voice said to the nurse. "He may be hiding in there."

The steps were fading away. Soon they sounded far down at the end of the corridor.

Angelika dressed herself in a hurry. She and Niska opened the door cautiously and peeked out. They glimpsed the backs of the nurse and two men walking through the door leading to the female ward.

He turned to Angelika. "Wait. We had to leave my hospital room in such a hurry that I forgot to grab my passport. I don't believe I could be so thoughtless. I have to go back. Wait here in the bathroom until I get back."

Angelika shook her head. "No, don't go back. You mustn't try. What if the men come out from the ladies' ward and see you?"

"No, I have to fetch the passport. In today's Berlin, if you don't have the proper papers or ID, you are as good as gone."

Angelika didn't argue any further. She watched through a door cracked slightly open as Niska tiptoed quickly along the wall of the corridor, and then disappeared into his hospital room.

Suddenly, one of the men came out through the door from the

female ward. He headed directly in her direction. She was relieved as he passed by Niska's hospital room without looking in. He continued toward her hiding place. Quietly, carefully, she pulled the bathroom door shut all the way, kicked off her shoes, and wrapped the towel over her fully clothed body. If the man entered the bathroom, he might think she was still drying off after the shower.

She breathed more easily when she heard the man's footsteps walk past the women's room. Suddenly, they stopped. Or else she could no longer hear them. Was he standing outside the bathroom door? She held her breath and stood absolutely frozen.

In a minute or so she heard what she imagined was the flushing of a toilet and the running of water in a sink from behind the bathroom wall. The man walked out into the corridor again, finished tightening the belt of his uniform trousers, and marched past the women's bathroom. The footsteps gradually grew fainter and more distant.

"Please, God, please let *Herr* Niska stay in his room until the man has passed and gone back into the ladies' ward," Angelika fervently prayed. She feared for him, and for herself, lest he be caught and she be left alone to cope.

Finally, after what seemed to Angelika like an eternity, Niska stepped into the bathroom. From deep inside her, Angelika let out a long breath of relief.

"Did you get the passport?" she asked.

"Got it. And a few *Reichsmarks*, too, so that if we manage to escape the building, we can catch a taxi and take you home. Is the coast clear?"

"I don't see anybody in the hallway."

Niska took Angelika into his arms to carry her into the corridor. He took long strides toward the door to the stairs to the emergency exit. By some miracle—or the carelessness and forgetfulness of a clinic employee—the door was unlocked.

They exited the building into the backyard. Niska looked back to make sure that no one was following them. Suddenly, Niska remembered that from his room, he had looked out over the backyard. Then, the windows in the female ward must look out over the street at the front of the building.

"I can't go out to the front to hail a taxi. I must not be seen from the window. They are looking for a man, not a little girl."

Niska had barely completed the sentence when Angelika was headed out the backyard toward the front of the building.

"I'll get us a taxi," she said breathlessly with her back to Niska.

"Angelika, no! Come here! It's too dangerous out there for you. The SS may have an agent waiting in a parked car for the other two."

But Angelika was already beyond earshot.

Niska waited in the darkness of the backyard. Every few seconds, he looked over at the emergency exit, expecting one or both of the SS agents to emerge. Minutes passed that felt like hours, but no sign of Angelika. It was an unusually warm evening, given that it wasn't even the end of March. But the tension of waiting for Angelika to return safely was making him tremble from the cold. Would Angelika be able to get a taxi without being apprehended as an accomplice of a smuggler of Jews? Or as a Jew herself?

A moment later, Niska felt his heart relax. Angelika returned to the backyard.

"*Herr* Niska, I have a taxi waiting out front." She took Niska by the hand and led him the front of the building.

"Run for the car, hurry!" she instructed Niska.

Niska did as he was commanded. Angelika followed him into the taxi.

Angelika had been taught some English by her father. "Someday, you may get to England or America where it is safe for Jews. They speak English there," he had said by way of explanation. So she and Niska spoke only English so that the taxi driver would not understand their conversation.

"No, we must not go to your father's home. I am sure that the nurses' log lists me as a patient of your father's. The SS might go there when they cannot find me in the clinic."

"Oh, then I'll give the driver my aunt's address on *Friedrichstrasse*," Angelika said. "We can be safe there."

The aunt graciously invited both of them to spend the night. She figured out that it was not safe for Niska to return to his flat at his hotel either, since the nurses' log would list his address.

"Here, *Herr* Niska," the aunt said as she handed him a bundle of clothes. "These are my late husband's. I haven't had the heart to throw them out or give them away until now. You can't go back out into the streets in that hospital gown."

"Thank you...Frau..."

"Schwartz. Hilde Schwartz. But it's you we should be thanking...for what you have been doing for our people."

He borrowed *Frau* Schwartz's telephone to report on the evening's events to Dr. Singer. He could not praise highly enough the ability and initiative of the doctor's daughter. Niska didn't spell out all the details for the time being. But he emphasized that Angelika most probably saved his life.

"You and your late wife gave her a truly appropriate name."

It occurred to Niska as he spoke to Dr. Singer that the doctor may not be as thrilled by his daughter's actions that evening as Niska was.

~~~

Niska's contacts located another flat for him the very next morning in a different section of Berlin. Comprehending his situation, they even moved his meager belongings from one flat to the other. Niska's close call at the clinic with Angelika reinforced that he needed to make sure that the new flat had a front *and* a rear entrance, and instructed his contacts to that effect. You never knew when a rear exit would be the difference between life and death.

For the next several weeks Niska hibernated in the flat, leaving only for the briefest moments to buy cigarettes at the nearby kiosk. But the pain in his stomach raised its ugly head again. He called Dr. Singer's number, but there was no answer.

Needing medical care, he called for a taxi and gave the driver an address a couple of blocks from Dr. Singer's. This was another precaution he had learned from prior events. The driver was Aryan, and made no effort to hide his reluctance to wander into Jewish Charlottenburg.

"I'll have to charge you extra for entering a *Yid* neighborhood, Sir."

When they were near Dr. Singer's office, Niska jumped out of the taxi and paid the driver, adding a generous tip. He began walking toward the doctor's residence which also housed his surgery. As he got closer to his destination, he noticed immediately that something was amiss. Dr. Singer had a tastefully enameled sign beside the entrance door to the house naming the practice and listing the hours of his practice.

Niska stopped and stared at the sign. All over it was glued a sheet of paper on which was scrawled just one word in capital letters: "*J-U-D-E.*" Jew.

Niska was totally disheartened. While Dr. Singer, like a significant percentage of Berlin's physicians, was a Jew, and thus vulnerable, Niska couldn't help but feel responsible somehow for this.

Did the Gestapo do this to punish Dr. Singer because a patient of his, a wanted criminal in the eyes of the state, had eluded them? And what about little Angelika? What has happened to her?

Upset and angry, Niska went up the three steps and rang Dr. Singer's door bell. After an unusually long time, a middle-aged woman opened the door part way.

"Yes, can I help you?"

"I'm here to see Dr. Singer."

"I don't know," the woman said. "The doctor is having some difficulty seeing visitors today."

"I am an old patient of Dr. Singer's, really, an old friend. Please tell the doctor that Mr. Algot Niska is here to see him. He'll know who I am. Please, it's quite urgent."

"Just a moment," the anxious woman relented.

She came back five or so minutes later. She looked guardedly out onto the street before opening the door to allow Niska to enter. She led Niska to a room at the back of the house.

Upon entering, Niska could tell that Dr. Singer was shaken. He looked pale and haggard, not his usual self.

"Dr. Singer, what has happened? Are you all right?"

"Oh, *Herr* Niska. I don't want you to see your doctor like this. Nothing has happened to me that hasn't happened to most Jewish doctors in Berlin. Perhaps all of Germany."

"But I am relieved that you appear safe. And physically unharmed."

"I am relieved, too. German patients are forbidden to come to me, now. I will see Jewish patients for as long as I can. But for now, I am grateful that I have not been beaten...or worse."

"Where is Angelika, Doctor?" Niska held his breath in anticipation of Singer's answer.

"I sent her to her late mother's sister Hilde on *Friedrichstrasse*. You know all about her, Mr. Niska. Angelika can be safe there...for the time being."

"You have an amazing daughter. So intelligent, so courageous."

"I'm afraid she will need all of that and more to survive this insanity."

"The noose is tightening for many of us, now. I cannot move about freely either."

"I know of the good you have done for Jewish people, *Herr* Niska. But you must be careful."

"So far, the mouse is winning the cat-and-mouse game. Thanks largely to Angelika."

"I don't want to boast, *Herr* Niska, but until now my reputation as a prominent specialist who has successfully treated even wives of Nazis, has been to my advantage. How long it can go on like this, I don't know. The sticker on my sign downstairs is the first warning. But it will not be the only one, I am sure. They gave me this yellow Star of David to sew on the front of my coat. My name now must be 'Israel Singer.' Josef, the name given to me by my parents, is no longer acceptable to the powers that be."

Remaining there any longer constituted a potential danger for both Niska himself and Dr. Singer.

"*Herr* Niska," Singer said with a sad resolve. "You had better find a German doctor to consult from now on, for your safety, and mine, too."

Niska nodded in reluctant agreement. He thanked the doctor for all he had done for him as his physician and took his leave.

As he walked back to the location where he had exited the taxi, Niska looked back at the vulgar placard covering Dr. Singer's classy, attractive sign. He wondered if he would ever see Dr. Singer and his cherubic young daughter again. He came to the sad conclusion that probably not.

The madness was well on its way to infecting all of Germany.

CHAPTER SIXTEEN

Berlin, August 16, 1939

Niska was confined to his flat like a restless prisoner on house arrest. One afternoon he listened with a great deal of both fascination and visceral repugnance on his radio as Adolf Hitler gave a rousing speech to the filled *Sportplatz* where he had hosted the Olympic Games in 1936. Hitler sounded no less enraged than usual. He railed against recent incidents of violent resistance against German officials and soldiers. He claimed that the perpetrators of the murders were Jews.

"I have decreed, that commencing at 5:20 am this morning and onward, one hundred shots will be returned for every shot fired against a soldier of the *Reich.*"

Niska's physical condition was rapidly declining day by day. He visited a physician—a gentile this time, at Dr. Singer's urging. The new diagnosis was two serious ulcers instead of just one.

"You are in need of care," the elderly physician told him. "I'm afraid I cannot treat you, however. Not because I do not want to. No, it's rather that every available doctor in Germany is being called up, either to report in person near the Polish border, where our troops are mobilizing, or be transferred to a military hospital in Germany, Austria, or Czechoslovakia."

Niska wondered how the land of Beethoven, Göthe, and Kant could be so intent now on mobilizing for yet another war so soon after their ignominious defeat in the previous one, so recent, earlier in the century.

"The best thing is for you to leave Germany and get care elsewhere," the doctor continued. "In a matter of weeks, days even, almost every hospital in Germany will have been converted into a military hospital where you do not qualify for care. Try to get to your own country. I am sure that in Sweden everything is still in full functioning order."

Initially, Niska was taken aback by the doctor's reference to Sweden as his "own country." Then he realized that this doctor knew him as Sven Ovesen, the name on his own forged Swedish passport.

Niska's situation was becoming more desperate each day. It was clear that his only remaining hope was to return to his actual home country, Finland. He faced legal problems there, probably imprisonment, that lingered from his smuggling years. But even in a Finnish prison he could receive much better care than as a foreigner in a German one.

Ambassador Mäki at the Finnish legation in Berlin was aware of Niska's outlaw past, of course. He was also cognizant of the rumors circulating among some of Berlin's Finns that Niska had a new calling now: smuggling Jews out of the clutches of the SS. Mäki might have to face consequences eventually for overlooking Niska's past crimes against the government of Finland. But consequences be damned. He had had it up to his neck with the presumptuousness and self-importance of his German hosts. He was not going to allow this Finnish savior of Jews to end up in Dachau, or worse. He secretly arranged for Niska to board a German merchant ship in Danzig bound for Helsinki.

On the first part of the voyage, Niska writhed in pain in a supine position on a hard bench down below. It became almost unbearable as the steamer was near the mouth of the Gulf of Riga in the Baltic. The steamer's doctor discovered that Niska had begun hemorrhaging.

The captain ordered the ship to be diverted to the port of Riga in Latvia. Even if it was a detour and would delay the arrival of his cargo in Helsinki, he was not going to allow his fellow seafarer, a captain in his own right, bleed to death on his vessel.

It would not be a day in Niska's life, it seems, if, in addition to such serendipitous moments of grace, there weren't further obstacles as well. At the behest of the occupying Soviets, the Latvians had just imposed a new ordinance that no Latvian was allowed to leave the country, and no foreigner was permitted to enter, whether they had a valid visa or not. Niska had jumped from the German frying pan into the Russian fire.

The German captain himself carried Niska into the customs building and laid him on a counter where Niska lay almost unconscious from the severe pain.

"You're familiar by now of the prohibition of foreigners entering our country," a young Latvian customs clerk informed the captain.

"I don't give a damn about your prohibition. I don't appreciate your mouthing the bloody Bosheviks' prohibitions. This man will bleed to death right here on your counter, if he does not receive some medical attention," the German captain barked at the clerk. He angrily handed him Niska's passport.

The clerk looked intimidated by the angry German. He regarded the passport.

"This man, Mr. Ovesen, is a Swede."

"I don't really give a rat's ass if he's a Hottentot. He needs immediate attention!"

The clerk responded, "We don't have a Hottentot hospital in Latvia, but we do have a Swedish one. They might take him."

"Well do you want to take responsibility for the bleeding death of a citizen of a neutral country like Sweden?"

Immediately, the clerk called over to a colleague, even younger than himself, "Get this man over to the Swedish Hospital. Not in the morning! Now!"

The Swedish hospital had been spared the worst of the damage of the Soviet reoccupation of the city. Niska lay on his bed seriously underweight, his usual angular facial features rendered even more bony. He had been given intravenous fluids and been fortified for surgery. Surgeons were shocked at the condition of his stomach and how close to death he had been.

It wasn't until September morphed into October that he was strong enough to be discharged. Since Sven Ovesen had a Swedish passport, he was informed that the government of Sweden had paid the substantial tab for his medical care and stay in the hospital.

The Latvians were gracious to Niska. When Niska was exiled from both Sweden and Finland because of his vodka runs in the previous decades, he had taken refuge briefly in Riga. There he taught himself a few practical phrases in Latvian, which he used to his advantage now with the nurses and doctors. The government granted him an exit visa to travel to Estonia, not his desired destination, but one nation closer to Finland.

As the train chugged toward Tallinn, the capital of Estonia, Niska thought about the people he had smuggled out of Germany. Eleven had begun new lives somewhere other than Germany, Austria, or Czechoslovakia. A few, like Jiri Hudak, had remained in Finland, while others had taken advantage of the relative freedom and peacetime conditions in Finland to travel to more far-off destinations, probably figuring that the farther away from Germany, the safer and happier they would be.

Niska brought to mind the face of Jiri Hudak.

How is the young wine merchant faring? Does he feel safe now? Are the Finns receiving him warmly and helpfully? Are the Finnish people free enough of their innate suspicion of outsiders to recognize what an asset a young, ambitious entrepreneur like Hudak is to their country?

He recalled Hannah Hirtschel as well, of course, the forlorn Jewish street urchin he had discovered in the attic of his hotel. He relived the profound regret he felt about his inability to help her. It was a feeling of utter helplessness that he had had many times since. He had a hard time accepting that it was impossible to save them all, especially Hannah. This dark cloud of failure hovered over him and haunted him, not just whenever his memory resurrected the sweet face of Hannah, but whenever he had walked the streets of Charlottenburg and saw what seemed to him like a million Jews, each looking more fearful and desperate with each passing day.

~~~

Once on Estonian soil, Niska was depressed by how the beautiful, medieval town of Tallinn in which he had taken refuge from time to time was deteriorating into chaos. The country had enjoyed twenty years of independence from Russia. But now a dark, foreboding cloud moved over the skies of Estonia. The threat of invasion by the numerically superior Soviet forces loomed over the tiny nation like a heavy lead-colored thunderbolt that was poised to strike any day. In June, it did.

When Niska made his way to the Tallinn harbor, he was not totally surprised, therefore, to find fourteen Soviet naval vessels just off shore. They had been busy all night rounding up Estonians who were abandoning their homes and fleeing the dismal prospect of a brutal occupation by their former masters in any vessel that could float.

He had made it thus far against the odds; so close was he now, a mere eighty maritime kilometers to Finland from which he was exiled. But the imposing, seemingly impenetrable wall of Soviet naval vessels formed the barrier that potentially caused his connection to his homeland to be severed.

Seeing a tall wooden figurehead in the shape of the head and shoulders of a bear affixed to the bowsprit on the prow of one of the moored Estonian fishing boat made him think of the beautiful, almost erotic, figure of *Vellamo*, the goddess of the lakes and seas of traditional Finnish and apparently, Estonian folklore. Her carved image adorned many a Finnish fisherman's skiff as its figurehead. They prayed to her to calm the waves and tame the winds. The typical *Vellamo* figurehead depicted her with long blond hair that flowed suggestively down to her chest to barely cover her enticing breasts. *Vellamo* was the balm of men out at sea for weeks or months without the comfort and warmth of their wives or girlfriends.

Instead of merely inspiring in him erotic thoughts and instincts, Niska had always thought of her as an angel. Most days he wasn't sure if he believed that there really were such sublime messengers from the Divine. But whenever the cold winds of the autumn started to blow across the water and the waves swelled, in his solitude he had looked to *Vellamo* to shed her favor on his rickety boat and his worried soul. Each time, though tossed about and buffeted, the boat had weathered the storm, and his soul had rejoiced.

Though he and she hadn't been out in open waters, it occurred him that Angelika Singer had been a juvenile Vellamo for him at the hospital in Charlottenburg.

Now, looking anxiously at the Soviet armada, he wondered, was this how it was going to end. There were some close brushes with death before, such as the hell-raising twenty-meter waves on the Baltic in '28 that he was certain were going to engulf and capsize his boat. Or the time the Swedish coastal police surrounded his boat in '31 and took shots at his boat as he was about to leave Swedish territorial waters with a cargo of vodka. A bullet had grazed his left arm. Had the projectile struck him just a few centimeters to the right, it would have gone through his heart. *Vellamo* had preserved him to sail yet another voyage.

Isn't that precisely what makes the life of adventure so thrilling, the ecstasy of the chase so exhilarating, the satisfaction of the success so rewarding? The inescapable reality that we die, that sometimes we can outsmart death or outrun it, but that in the end, no one, not even the most artful adventurer and ingenious escape artist, can evade it? Even Vellamo must concede defeat to its inevitable power eventually.

For that matter, isn't life itself so precious because we know it doesn't last forever? Isn't that why the immortal Greek gods envied humans, namely, that humans weren't imperishable? Is this now my time to encounter death, my moment of truth?

Even now, Niska's lifelong habit of suppressing anxiety or depression with action, however, was too deeply ingrained for it to disappear. He scoured the harbor region for anyone who might accept the few

Estonian *kroona* he had in his pocket for a boat at least moderately seaworthy. He got his hands on one, though to call it seaworthy would be an exaggeration; it was in its middle stages of decay, leaky, with a poor excuse for a sail, only a pair of oars and one steering oar. The man, a retired fisherman who sold it to him, agreed to keep it in his shed by the water until Niska had need of it.

Every morning, he went down to the harbor to check conditions, but he had been disheartened by the sight of a mid-size Soviet ship unloading its cargo of dozens of Estonians who had tried to escape. Niska knew that despite the discouraging scene of refugees being forced to return to the mainland, he'd wait until his gut told him it's the opportune time and then make a break for it somehow.

One morning, Niska woke up in his room in a dilapidated old rooming house and was pleased by the thick fog over the lower part of the city. When he found his way—more by memory than actually navigating the fog-draped streets—he deemed the impenetrable conditions over the Gulf of Finland to be ideal for his purposes.

He retrieved his wobbly boat from the fisherman's shed. He decided the safest route was the ten-meter gap between the vessel farthest to the right and the sea wall. That way, he figured, he would be seen from only one of the ships. He rowed the skiff slowly and as quietly as he could toward the gap.

When the small rowboat emerged out of the fog, Niska was beyond the last vessel and on the open sea before him. His entire body was trembling. He hadn't had much realistic hope of succeeding, but hope in what is seen isn't really hope at all. *Vellamo* had pulled him through yet another crisis.

The fog remained behind in Tallinn. When night came, Niska was able to utilize his skills as an old seaman in navigating by the stars. The wind blew from the southwest, ideal, Niska thought, to convey him to Helsinki. Niska had no choice but to go where the wind was taking him and hope that it was to somewhere near Helsinki directly across the Gulf of Finland from Tallinn, rather than, God forbid, the eastern end of the gulf at Leningrad.

Now Niska was on an open sea somewhere between where he'd departed and where he hoped to arrive. These in-between times were the ones on his alcohol smuggling runs that were the most challenging. He recalled some of them now when all he could do for himself was put himself at the mercy of the wind and the waves. Strangely enough, he had often experienced fear more acutely at junctures like this than on any other point in his run. When he had been pursued by Swedish border police in their motorboats at the onset of an escape, he had to drive his boat faster and keep his body low to the floor to avoid bullets from the police pistols or rifles. Cortisol and norepinephrine rushed through his body and made his heart beat faster and his brain think more clearly and quickly and sharply.

Once he was in international waters, the flood of stress hormones subsided and his heart relaxed. His brain was no longer focused solely on survival as he bobbed in the waves between Sweden and Finland. That is not at all to say that his mind had switched to an "off" setting. Rather, it was as though other intangible and less easy to evade fears rushed into the vacuum. Gratitude that he'd made it out of danger this time, yes, but fear, too, that sooner or later his luck would run out. Fear of Finnish border police up ahead and their scrupulous protection of Finnish waters and their firm determination to protect them with violence if necessary. More unnamed, indistinct existential fears, too, the fiercest kind: fear at age fifty that this way of making a living is not sustainable over the long haul; fear and a measure of shame that what he was doing was merely providing for the indulgent gratification of those who could afford to purchase his illegal booty; most of all, fear that if this was all there is, then when all was said and done, his life would not have made much of a difference in the world—a foretaste of death.

Now, bobbing up and down in a rowboat on a different gulf, his mind was downcast, his heart and soul strangely empty. The adrenaline high of the adventure, the thrill of the successful passage through the Russian naval blockade in Tallinn harbor, were over and done. He felt flat; his mouth tasted stale. He longed for his mind to be vacant. He didn't want to squander mental energy trying to predict the unknown and unknowable future and think about what fate might be awaiting him if and when he arrived in Helsinki. He could only think about what he'd lost and left behind: the new vocation he'd arrived at accidentally, and the new purpose he'd been given in smuggling living human beings for their survival in this dark, dangerous time, instead of vodka or whiskey to help just a few forget and deny the darkness momentarily. He thought wistfully of people who had sparked his soul to new life: Altmann, Hudak, Hannah, and most longingly of all, Angelika to whom he owed his life.

He saw now that this voyage was not just from one country to another, from an adopted home to his homeland. It was a farewell voyage, really, from a life he was just learning to appreciate and cherish when it had to come to this abrupt end with two life-threatening inflammations in his gut. It was the unceremonious journey from the Algot Niska who had been to the Algot Niska who just beginning to be born.

After more than a day and two nights, Niska was exhausted in all corners of his body and mind. He could not hold off sleep any longer. If he was apprehended now, at least it was by his countrymen rather than the SS or the Soviets.

Niska could not tell if he had been asleep half the night and half the next day when he was awakened by the boat's banging now and then against a cliff that rose up out of the water. Not until he had rubbed the sleep from his eyes did he realize how dangerous it would have been if the wind had increased while he slept and flung the boat against the cliff.

He had so frequently sailed the coastal waters of Finland that he could orient himself immediately: He was at the foot of the cliff adjacent to the lighthouse on the tiny island of Harmaja—a stone's throw from Helsinki harbor.

Bless you, Vellamo.

CHAPTER SEVENTEEN

Helsinki: September 23, 1939

Niska stood still as a lamppost in the square facing the central train terminal in Helsinki. He thought of catching a train to Turku where his daughter Eeva lived. But her husband was such a tight-ass who bore his wife's resentment on her behalf that Algot had abandoned the family in order to flee to Germany. He'd likely report his father-in-law to ValPo, the state police, before Algot was prepared to face them.

He wondered if his sister, Aino, still lived in Helsinki's *Eteläinen* district. He rummaged through his memory for a mental map of the district. It had been such a long time since he'd been there. Had she been relocated like some others to make room for the construction of the stadium for the 1940 Olympics, which were cancelled, as it turned out, due to the outbreak of war? He couldn't remember his sister's address, but figured that he'd remember the street by its appearance and her ancient stone apartment block once he saw it, if it was still there.

Indeed, he did. Once he decided which block was hers he stood on the sidewalk within range of the locked front door. A resident exited the building. Niska nodded his head slightly, pretending that he was another resident of the building and knew the man, grabbed the front door before it shut, and let himself into the lobby.

He recalled that she and her husband lived in an apartment on the second or third floor. He patrolled each floor and examined the metal nameplates on the door of each flat until he found his sister's.

His brother-in-law Heikki answered the door and was opened-mouthed and mute when he recognized their visitor. Heikki called Aino to come to the door. Aino stopped in her tracks when she saw Algot standing at the threshold. Her eyes were larger than chestnuts. She raised a hand to her mouth and began to weep.

"Algot, is that you? My God, you're alive! Since we hadn't heard from you, we were sure that you'd breathed your last long ago."

"It is indeed your long-lost brother, Algot, alive and in the flesh. Shame on you for thinking that I'd died. I couldn't write or call on the telephone because I was sure that if ValPo wasn't opening my mail and tapping my telephone, then the SS was. True, I've more than a few close calls. But more than one person says that I'm like a cat. I have nine lives."

"Yes," said Heikki, "but how many of the nine have you used up? For God's sake, come on in."

"Now that you mention that, I've got to get to a doctor soon. I've got two nasty ulcers in my stomach that burn like hell."

The next day, Heikki called their family doctor and made an appointment for Algot. The doctor prescribed an antacid and emphasized the need for rest, counsel that after his eventful sea journey to Finland Niska was quite ready to accept. As the older sister and a professed teetotaler at that, through their younger years, Aino had often expressed her displeasure at Algot's outlaw activities in the past. Nevertheless, she was gracious now when he had nowhere else to go and nursed him for many days in her flat.

When she left him alone, Niska was busy preparing a lengthy "sea declaration" of all that he had been doing in Germany since 1932, particularly his activities on behalf of German Jews in the past year. He didn't withhold any of his own hardships or obstacles he had faced. He worded his declaration truthfully but strategically with the intent of provoking leniency from whatever judge he would have to face in a trial for his smuggling of liquor and other contraband a decade and more earlier.

He and Heikki lingered after breakfast in their underwear over several cups of Aino's coffee. Finland wasn't rationing coffee yet, unlike Germany, which had begun doing so the moment the *Wehrmacht* had rolled its tanks into Austria. Niska hadn't enjoyed the taste of real coffee since.

"How are your ulcers today?" Heikki asked.

"Thanks to the rest, better each day. I'll get out of your way soon, though, and give you your flat back to yourselves."

"The shenanigans in Moscow are giving me more than ulcers," Heikki said cheerlessly. "You've heard, haven't you?"

"Well, it depends on which shenanigans you mean. My little Estonian rowboat didn't come equipped with a short-wave radio, remember."

"Paasikivi has been recalled from the embassy in Stockholm to head a Finnish delegation to Moscow."

"Not to see the Bolshoi or tour St. Basil's Cathedral, I presume?"

"That's for sure," Heikki said, adding a sarcastic snort. "The President is sending him there on a futile mission of trying to convince Molotov and Stalin that Finland isn't going to allow them to adopt us forcefully as a Russian satellite as the Lithuanians, Latvians, and Estonians were obliged to do."

"No, no, we don't want that. I've just had a little unplanned holiday in both Latvia and Estonia. Riga and Tallinn aren't the grand cities they were the last time I was there. The Russian occupiers have made sure of that."

"Molotov and Stalin were ridiculous with their demands," Heikki complained, shaking his head indignantly. "They want us to redraw the map of our borders with Russia so that Viipuri becomes a Russian city and most of Karelia becomes a Russian timber plantation."

The antacids were easing the pains in his stomach. Consequently, each successive day added to his restlessness. One Friday morning in mid-November, he told his hosts that he was going down to ValPo headquarters and turn himself in.

"Are you sure you ought to do that, little brother?" Aino asked.

"I don't think ValPo would take to you kindly for harboring a wanted whiskey smuggler in your flat," Niska explained. "It's time I said 'Thank you' and left your flat and faced the consequences of my past actions."

"I can't let you go to see the police in those old clothes you're wearing." Looking at her husband, she said, "Heikki, look through your closet for one of your suits that would fit Algot."

Algot came out of his bedroom looking almost comical in an ill-fitting suit. But he virtually luxuriated in its cleanliness and freshness after having ditching his sea swept and tattered sweater and pants that he had been wearing since he left Latvia. When he was ready to leave, he and Heikki gave each other a self-conscious handshake at the door. Aino was tearful as she put her arms around her brother.

"You just got here after years away, and now you'll be holed up in jail somewhere."

CHAPTER EIGHTEEN

Berlin: March 1, 1940

Kersten was taking lunch alone at the ornate general staff dining room in the Chancellery.

He observed at a nearby table the formidable Richard Heydrich, Himmler's deputy in charge of the *Gestapo*. Kersten did not recognize the other plump officer sitting with Heydrich.

It's a common phenomenon that in a public space such as the dining hall, where various indistinct conversations are taking place at the same time, one never makes out a single word from any of the conversations...until either the overhearing individual's name or some other such piece of identifying information is mentioned. Kersten heard nothing specific except the general buzz of lunchtime chitchat and light clanking of china. But then Heydrich spoke the word "*Niederlände,*" and Kersten's ears stood at attention immediately.

Kersten had developed a liking and admiration for the hard-working, peace-loving Dutch. He was a citizen of Finland, to be sure; but he had not resided there for more than a month at a time since 1924 when he left to study Dr. Ko's method of neurological therapy in Berlin. But Holland had been home for Kersten almost since he entered practice, and it had assumed a primary place in his allegiance.

"The *Führer* has his mind set on the Netherlands," Heydrich said to his colleague.

"Does he have matters so well in hand in Poland and Czechoslovakia now that he can set his sights to the west?" the other officer inquired.

"Apparently so. I've heard through the grapevine that he's looking northward as well, particularly at Denmark and Norway."

"I wouldn't be surprised if he'll also have Russia in his crosshairs before too long. He worships Napoleon."

"Yes, anyone who has read *Mein Kampf* would know Russia is his ultimate goal. A lot of *Lebensraum* there," Heydrich said. They both chuckled knowingly.

"The *Führer* envisions hundreds of German settlements in Russia, and thousands upon thousands of Germans there," his conversation partner added.

"But to get back to the Netherlands..." Heydrich said, virtually ignoring the other's addenda.

"Yes. You were saying?" The man was hungrier for more information from Heydrich than for the food on his plate, which was virtually untouched.

"I have been informed that the end of April—maybe on the *Führer's* birthday, or early May at the latest—is the target date to move troops into the Low Countries."

"Seeing how easily we moved into Poland and Czechoslovakia, Hitler ought to make light work of them."

Heydrich seemed to have remembered suddenly that they were not in a private office but in a cafeteria. His eyes quickly scanned the room for curious listeners. Kersten looked down at his newspaper to act as though he were minding his own business. Heydrich leaned his head over the table toward his dining partner, who reciprocated. Heydrich lowered his voice, but Kersten caught the gist.

"Hitler wants my boss to begin implementation of a plan to transplant undesirable Dutch citizens to new camps in Poland, forcibly if necessary."

"Your delicate boss would have the stomach for such a messy operation?" the other officer sniggered.

"Not by temperament, certainly," Heydrich said. "I would think the *Führer* would have the wisdom to assign it to someone with balls, men like you or me. But one thing I can say for the *Reichsführer SS* is that he is more eager to obey and impress the *Führer* than the *Führer's* mistress is." They joined in a salacious laughter.

~~~

Kersten put down his knife and fork on his plate with the partially eaten schnitzel, rose as nonchalantly as his seething anger permitted, and went promptly to Himmler's office. The way was so familiar to him by now that he could find it blindfolded. It's a good thing, because Kersten's mind was in such turmoil that he didn't focus the least on where he was going.

As usual, Himmler had stretched out on the divan in anticipation. He was more than ready to surrender his slender body into Kersten's strong and skillful hands. As for Kersten, however, he envisioned the gruesome parade to the hell in the east of what Hitler considered to be

Dutch slaves, some of them friends Kersten knew. No smile of greeting from Kersten. None of the usual good-natured preparatory banter before the treatment.

Somehow, by sheer muscle memory, the distracted Kersten was able to manipulate Himmler's body sufficiently to bring about the usual relief.

"You seem unusually glum today, Kersten," Himmler said as he raised himself on one elbow from the divan.

Kersten shot straight to the point. He asked sternly, "*Herr Reichsführer*, what is the exact date that you plan to begin the deportation of the Dutch Jews?"

Himmler seemed taken aback, and then smiled. "I see that information travels fast in the Chancellery in spite of all our efforts at utmost secrecy."

"I overheard Heydrich and some tub o' lard of an officer discussing a potential attack on the Netherlands."

"If the officer you so disrespectfully refer to was Hans Rauter, you overheard correctly. I'm considering making him head of the SS in Holland when the time comes."

"That time comes...when?"

"The invasion and occupation will commence as a birthday gift to the *Führer*. I advise you to stick around Berlin and not return to The Hague in the immediate future."

"On the 20th of April then? You've got a very roundabout way of answering my simple question today."

"A little patience, Kersten...The *Führer* is incensed at the stubborn insistence on neutrality by the Dutch and their refusal to come to Germany's aid in the Great War. He wants to make them pay a special price."

"Occupation of the country by Germany and Holland's humiliation is not enough for your *Führer*, is that it? Didn't your *Führer* give a stirring speech on the radio assuring the world that Germany would not only honor, but also safeguard, the neutrality of the Netherlands, Belgium, and Luxembourg? What's happened to that promise?"

"Well, yes your memory serves you right, Kersten. But that was in 1937. Conditions change with the passage of time. A study of history will show that treaties are made to be broken. That is the case now."

"This doesn't speak well for German dependability and integrity, does it?"

"Victory in war will erase any memories of broken treaties and promises. I have been commanded to begin making preparations immediately for the SS to identify, round up, and transport what the *Führer* calls 'irreconcilable' Dutch to the eastern front for resettlement there."

"An order for you to direct the *whole* operation? Good Lord! How large is this group of 'irreconcilables'?"

"The plan is to resettle eight and half million in various stages. The first stage will be to relocate some three million Jews."

"Three million!? I don't understand it. What have the Dutch Jews ever done to Germany to deserve this? What have the Jews done except grow businesses that bring wealth to Holland?"

"He says that the Jews are always the first ones to form cells in resistance movements. They'll do so in Holland, too. The Jews are like a rock in the stomach of Europe. It's impossible to digest them…"

"So you have to spit them out? Is that it? Your *Führer* has credible evidence to that effect? Most Jews I have known in Holland are happy to mind their own business."

"He has classified evidence of a Jewish conspiracy in Holland."

"Which he has shared with you?"

"No, that's why it's called 'classified'."

"The Dutch Jews, relocated thousands of kilometers?? To do what, in heaven's name?"

"To work in the labor camps we've begun building in Poland. The Jews are good tailors. The women are good at the sewing machine. They'll make uniforms for our troops."

"I see you wasted no time building camps in Poland. You must have something you don't want the German people to know about them that you'd build them outside the country."

Kersten was surprised with the anger in his voice. He knew he'd better tone it down. He continued the therapy session with the characteristically Finnish sulk and silent treatment instead.

"And, Kersten, I almost forgot to mention this. I've also been informed by the *Führer* that I will be held personally responsible to make certain that many of the Dutch Jews being transferred to the east never reach their designated destination…or any destination. I'm to recruit local men with unbridled hatred for the Jews to form Einsatzgruppen to kidnap some of them. What they do with them after that is out of our hands."

Kersten wasn't sure he could believe what he'd just been told. He almost despaired completely.

"That sounds like an absolutely chickenshit mode of operating."

Himmler smiled slyly, almost devilishly. "No, it's a rather efficient mode of operating, isn't it? Why should the SS reserve all the unpleasant dirty work for ourselves when there are ordinary civilians in both Germany and Poland who are happy to do it for us?"

Kersten could hardly contain his contempt and disgust. "Then I must conclude that your *Führer* is not envisioning an increase in the number of German troops in the future since he orders you to deliver fewer tailors and seamstresses to the camps?"

Himmler said nothing. He turned onto his side on the divan and gave Kersten a look of frustration bordering on total befuddlement. Was it befuddlement at what his therapist had just said? Or as Kersten hoped, at the essential illogic of the order handed down to him from on high?

~~~

After the session, Kersten made immediate contact with friends in the Dutch resistance. He felt a keen obligation to do something to help his adopted country. He instructed them to make contact with him by addressing letters to Himmler's private mailbox. Kersten realized some would be puzzled by such a directive, but he had learned to trust Brandt to pass on mail addressed to him unopened. Kersten was careful not to inform the queen and prince yet, lest they do something impulsively, thereby alerting Hitler that the Dutch had been forewarned of an invasion.

In the following days, Himmler's abdominal torture grew progressively more acute. In despair, he pleaded with Kersten to do everything he could to alleviate his suffering.

Then a strange thing occurred. For the first time in two years, Kersten's treatments on Himmler stopped working. The fingers that had been able to banish Himmler's pain were suddenly impotent to assuage it more than slightly.

Kersten knew that there were times when the state of the therapist's own heart and mind could nullify his skill and render his care ineffectual. For the slightest instant, the thought occurred to him that the torture Himmler was suffering as a result of his inability to perform the usual miracle was some sort of inherent justice, that the man who had been directed to perpetrate so much anguish and terror on others now deserved to suffer mightily himself. Kersten asked himself if he was deliberately underperforming as Himmler's therapist that day as a way of inflicting punishment. Yet, Kersten's professional conscience, so deeply ingrained, made it his absolute, almost sacred, duty to give a suffering patient, whoever he was, the best and quickest relief he could unconditionally. "First do no harm."

Besides, Kersten was almost certain that Himmler was not suffering from any organic source in his body.

"Has your magic deserted you, Kersten?" Himmler grimaced in pain. "For God's sake, do something about this God damned pain of mine!"

"To advance, or even just survive, in your *Führer's Reich,* you find it necessary to be thoroughly and devotedly obedient to his commands, do you not, *Herr Reichsführer?*"

"Kersten, you know very well I do," Himmler answered grouchily. "Why are you asking me such questions at this particular time when you know the answer?"

"Well, the same goes for our therapist-patient relationship. If you want to advance in well-being, as I know you do, you'll have to obey your therapist's orders strictly...or find a new therapist."

"Nonsense, Kersten. I'll do what you ask if you promise doing so will bring back your power."

"Well, then, I remind you that I warned you," said Kersten. "Your duties are too great an ordeal for your nervous system to handle. Have you ever tried to put ten amps on a circuit made for six?"

"You are full of riddles today, Kersten," Himmler said impatiently. "No, I haven't because it would blow the fuse and sink us all into darkness."

"Good. You're following my logic."

"Where are you headed with this electricity lesson?"

"Listen, this is important, *Herr Reichsführer*: You've told me of your ambitious plan to increase the number of the SS—what did you say, tenfold? I would think that that's more than enough work and responsibility for one man. But now you have this insane order to organize the deportation of an entire Jewish population of a country."

Kersten controlled himself and lowered his voice. "I know your *Führer* has a high estimation of your abilities. But does he think you're some kind of superman? Look, renounce the order and focus on your original project of strengthening the SS and I guarantee that then I can cure your pain."

Kersten couldn't believe he was advising a fortifying of the hated

SS. But under the circumstances, the alterative was worse.

Through his agony, Himmler rustled enough strength to say, almost in a sob, "Impossible! It's an order from my *Führer.* I cannot possibly refuse it."

"Then, it's absolutely impossible for me to do anything about your pain," Kersten said angrily. "It's either follow my order, or the *Führer's.*" At that, Kersten walked over to the sink to wash his hands. He put on his overcoat, picked up his familiar felt hat, and exited the office without a word, slamming the door behind him emphatically. The consequences be damned.

~~~

Before he was awake the next morning, Kersten's telephone rang irately. It was Himmler's voice, no more than a gasp, interspersed with sobs.

"Come, come quickly, Kersten. I can no longer get my breath."

Accustomed as he was to seeing Himmler in agony, Kersten was amazed when he entered the office at the violence of his suffering that morning. "Try again, Kersten. Please…try again. Perhaps today your magic has returned."

"I will try," Kersten said. "But I am sure it will be useless."

And it was at first. Kersten tried mightily to shove aside his resentment at the horror of the impending deportation.

Felix, let the resentment and anger go. This is a patient on the divan in front of you, just a patient, not a monster. For this treatment, he is not even your enemy. Do for him what you know well.

Kersten took a chair, brought it close to the divan, sat down, and bent over the tormented patient until their faces were almost touching. This time, he did not argue. He did not try to chastise. In a tone that was humble, affectionate, almost imploring, he said, *"Herr Reichsführer,* you know that I am your friend. I only want to help you. But listen to me. I beg of you: Put off this Dutch thing until later. You will soon be better, I promise. Your suffering is of nervous origin. Usually I can keep your nerves under control, except when too great and constant an anxiety eats into them like acid. For you, the acid is your unexamined discomfort about this matter of the Dutch. You were doing relatively fine, weren't you, until the order to see to it that a significant number of Jews die on the journey? I'm not really convinced that you really want to do that. Find a way to disregard that order. If you do, you won't feel this pain, I swear. Remember how effective the treatments were before this order was given to you? It can be like that again…if only you would go to your *Führer* and ask him to postpone the deportation until the war is won."

Kersten was expecting pushback from Himmler. Instead, Himmler grabbed one of his hands convulsively. "Yes, yes, Kersten. I really believe you are right…But what am I going to say to the *Führer*? What in heaven's name can I say?" He was almost sobbing.

It was all Kersten could do to downplay his hope. "It's very simple, *Herr Reichsführer*. Just tell him that you cannot fulfill both responsibilities at the same time. Remind him that neither can the *Wehrmacht*. If the rumors are true that he is preparing a plan to attack Moscow and Leningrad, this is no time to overtax Germany's logistical capability by mass-moving people eastward across an entire continent at the same time. Mention the fact that this superhuman work threatens your health, and that if it continues, you cannot guarantee the completion of your first priority, to reorganize the SS."

"Yes, Kersten, you are right. Napoleon discovered the same truth. The *Führer* intimidates me sometimes. But I fear this pain, and Germany's possible defeat, even more."

"Then, you have made up your mind? You won't change your mind when you feel better? Because I warn you: If you get cold feet, I will not be able to help you."

"You have the word of a German officer," groaned Himmler. "Just give me the strength."

Never had Kersten been so confident of success. The blood flowed freely from his wrists to his fingertips. Himmler found solace immediately in Kersten's hand. "I think…yes, the pain is going away," he uttered exultantly.

"Only because you have decided to talk to Hitler," said Kersten. "You must do so at once; one never knows when the cramps will return."

"I am going immediately," Himmler promised. "But to you, it must always be *Herr* Hitler, or the *Führer*, not just Hitler."

Feeling elated and particularly generous at the moment, Kersten replied, "Of course, *Herr Reichsführer*, it won't happen again."

Later that evening, Himmler telephoned Kersten again at the *Kaiserhof*. "The *Führer* is as generous as he is brilliant, Kersten. He is sympathetic to my poor health. I have it in writing. The deportation will be postponed indefinitely."

"Indefinitely? That is wonderful news to a Dutchman," Kersten said. "But your *Führer* did not agree with our warning about fighting on two fronts simultaneously?"

"He said not a word about it. He is supremely confident of victory on both fronts."

Kersten wanted to ask Himmler whether he was as supremely confident of that as Hitler. But he had accomplished at least as much as he had hoped.

"Alas, Kersten, though there will be no mass deportation for the time being, the invasion and subsequent occupation of your adopted homeland will proceed as planned."

CHAPTER NINETEEN

Berlin: March 1, 1940

When he got to his flat at the *Kaiserhof*, Kersten was feeling simultaneously ashamed, fearful, and deeply cleansed and purified by his frank, cathartic display of anger at Himmler earlier that day. Despite his sense of accomplishment and victory, Kersten was totally exhausted from his session with Himmler. He didn't even bother to brush his teeth before collapsing onto his bed, a very unusual violation of his usual strict discipline.

He didn't fall asleep immediately. Perhaps it was the abnormally early hour in the evening when he was retiring for the day. The longer he lay on his bed, the more he tossed and turned, and the more often he had to rearrange the tangle of fine sheets the hotel provided for him.

He got up one time to urinate. Then, as if to compensate for the fluid he eliminated from his body, he went to the liquor cabinet in the living room and poured himself a full glass of Finnish vodka, gulped it down greedily, and returned to bed, hopeful that the vodka would induce sleepiness. He opened the Finnish novel he had been reading in the past week and tried unsuccessfully to focus his attention on the words on the page.

Sure enough, in a few minutes, his eyelids were beginning to droop. When he woke up several hours later to empty his bladder again, he found the book open on his chest at a page he didn't remember having read.

Between his falling asleep and his revisit to the toilet, he was suspended in that delicious, but simultaneously confusing and even frightful, liminal state where his mind was pleasantly idle and at rest, but strangely still aware of the world from which his mind was seeking temporary retreat. His ears could detect the consistent ticking of the alarm clock on the night stand to his left. Tick, tick, tick, tick. The relentless drip-drop of water from the tank into the bowl of the toilet. Drip, drip, drip, drip. A door being shut loudly in the distance. An angry woman's muffled voice from a flat down the corridor. The insistent buzz of an incandescent lightbulb on the ceiling of the corridor giving notice of its intention to malfunction. The impatient honking of two car horns from *Mohrenstrasse* below.

The air in the *Kaiserhof* was charged with unease. The sounds were distressing. The automobile lights from the street below were projecting unfamiliar ominous shadows that moved across the wall and reflected partially onto his face. Kersten turned onto his side on the bed.

Heydrich's shrill nasal voice intruded. "The *Führer* intends to invade and occupy the Netherlands and eliminate the 'irreconcilables.'"

Kaltenbrunner's savage laughter echoed through the corridor and became louder the farther away it traveled. Kersten heard Himmler saying, "Treaties and promises are made to be broken."

At that, Kaltenbrunner's laughter grew more sinister and echoed in Kersten's mind.

Kersten tossed in his bed but remained in his liminal state.

He was transported to a city street with pavement wet from the rain. Was it the denuded Hague? Fog hung like a curtain in the air above the street. It was night. A faint nimbus formed in the anemic light from a couple of lonely streetlamps. Kersten saw a shallow puddle at the junction of the concrete sidewalk and an old edifice. The liquid was not the clear color of rain, however, but bright red.

A woman dressed in some coarse material like burlap was coming directly toward him on the sidewalk on a bicycle. Her bare head was bald in spots, yet covered in others with lonely short tufts of hair. The tunic hanging loosely over her inhumanly thin body had faded gray stripes. The cloth material was torn in places. Even in the misty darkness, Kersten could see with horror the irregularly shaped red stains and stripes on the tunic. He saw similar bloody scratches on her emaciated face. She seemed to be aiming the bicycle right at him. Kersten didn't have time to curse. He jumped off the sidewalk onto the street to avoid being struck. The woman looked back defiantly and swore in Dutch, and then cried out, "I am an irreconcilable," as she faded from view.

A black car honked its horn irritably. Kersten's heart skipped, and he hopped back up onto the curb. The automobile missed hitting him by a matter of centimeters. A rowdy voice from inside the car shouted in German, "Get out of our way, you fat bag of shit."

Kersten caught his breath, and resumed his walk. On the sidewalk up ahead, he spied a short dark figure. The figure's back was turned toward him. It was covered in a dark overcoat. Its head was obscured by a hood. Kersten swallowed his fear and passed the figure warily.

From behind him he heard his name being called in a grotesque voice. "Hey, Kersten, Finnish doctor, Dutchman, whatever you are. You are an enemy of the *Reich.*"

Kersten turned to face the figure. In the fog and dim light, he couldn't make out its face. Uninvited, the figure pushed the hood off its head. It had short, straight hair as dark as the night, with a surprisingly neat part down the right side of its scaly scalp. A sinister caricature of a red swastika stared out at Kersten from the figure's chest. It held out a limb toward Kersten. Kersten held out his own hand to return the gesture. He was repulsed and backed away instinctively. The appendage was furry and bony, a ghastly paw dripping with blood.

The figure was a black wolf.

From its sheath by his right side, Kersten pulled out his curved golden ceremonial sabre awarded to him by the government of Finland in 1919. He grabbed the hilt firmly in his right hand. He swung the sabre at the figure, which stepped back quickly to evade the blade. The figure laughed at the failed attempt. It ran out of room to back up on the sidewalk. It was caught against the wall of a grand, ornate official building. The figure now had fear and panic etched on its face. It held up two huge paws, first in a gesture of threat and attack, then in an effort to defend itself from Kersten's sabre. To no effect, as Kersten swashed the sword in the air and thrust it through the overcoat deep into the flesh of the wolf. A blemish of yellowish-orange blood formed on the overcoat. A hideous pool of the figure's discolored blood was forming at its feet. Kersten cut off the buttons of the figure's overcoat with the sabre. Underneath was jet black fur, stained with the abhorrent fluid.

The figure fell into the rank, revolting puddle on the sidewalk. Kersten thrust the sabre into the torso again once, twice, three times, until the figure was a heap of repugnant bloody meat.

After an untold number of stabs of the sabre, Kersten's eyelids burst open with a start. His heart wanted to beat out of his chest. He was breathing heavily. The sheet underneath him felt damp. His mouth felt as though he had swallowed sour milk.

The horrifying dream scene flashed through his awakening memory, leaving his conscious mind to ask, *Are you capable of such brutish butchery, Felix? Is there a seething well of violent hatred deep within your heart that you have tried to condition with reason, science, and civilization? Where is this thing with you and Himmler headed?*

CHAPTER TWENTY

Karelia: March 9-10, 1940

The whole world seemed to be thundering and shaking under their feet as the shells whirred overhead. The fighting had been bloody, cold, and fierce at the Kollaa River in western Karelia where Jiri Hudak's 12th Division of the Fourth Army had been badly outnumbered by Soviet troops. For every infantryman the Finns were able to kill, there would appear three or four fresh Soviet replacements. The Soviets were firing nearly 40,000 artillery rounds from the ridge on the eastern side of the river at the Finnish defensive line. All the Finnish artillery could manage was a paltry 1,000 rounds a day.

Jiri's company had been at the Kollaa for a week. Most of the 12th Division had been trying to hold back the Soviet war machine since the second week of the war in early December. Several times, the Red Army had been able to penetrate the Finnish defensive line, pushing the Finns out of their positions. But each time the Finnish boys systematically counterattacked to restore the integrity of their line. It had been a brutal, bloody, and costly tennis match that was lasting over two months.

The most effective weapon for the Finns was Corporal Timo Haula, known among the Russians at Kollaa as "The White Death." A world champion marksman in his pre-military days, he proved to have a deadly aim as a sniper from the tops of the pine and spruce trees. The others in his company marveled at the idiosyncratic procedure followed by their thoroughly unassuming mate. He insisted on using an iron sight on his rifle, by now old-fashioned, instead of a telescopic sight, which one would expect would enhance the accuracy of the shot. No, Haula pointed out, it would not. In these glacial conditions, the telescopic sight glass would fog up easily, rendering it practically useless. Should sunlight reflect off the glass, his location would be exposed to the enemy. When sniping from the ground, Haula resourcefully packed dense mounds of snow to conceal himself while also providing padding for his rifle and reducing the telltale billow of snow stirred up by the rifle blast. What his mates thought rather counterintuitive initially was his practice of stuffing his mouth full of snow as he aimed his rifle; but they quickly realized that the snow prevented steamy clouds of breath that would give away his position in the frozen air.

The Finnish forces ran a pool—a half-pack of cigarettes got you in the game—to see who could predict the number of fatalities Haula would inflict each day with his M/28-30. The men learned quickly not to pick a number less than five.

Russian casualties were heavy. Without cross-country skis and dressed in olive-colored coats, which stood out against the snow, the Russians slogged on foot through two-meter-deep drifts and were as easy targets as ducks in a carnival shooting gallery. With fewer troops to begin with, the smaller number of casualties on the Finnish side made more of a lethal difference. Jiri's company and others had been deployed to Kollaa as reinforcements.

Most days, however, it appeared to the Finnish commanders that the number of reinforcements had not been enough to staunch the bleeding. The division commander sent a daily request to his Fourth Army superior for more reinforcements to shore up the defenses. Each day, the message came back: "None available. We have three separate fronts to defend."

If the Soviets were to succeed in penetrating the Finnish line with finality, the result for Finland would be severe, probably disastrous. The Russians would have a clear, unhindered passage through the remaining fifty or so undefended kilometers to the town of Kitee within Finnish territory, and the road and rail networks and endless chain of navigable lakes and rivers of eastern Finland. Above all else, it was imperative to limit the Russian advances to Karelia and not allow them to penetrate further west into the rest of Finland.

One day, the runner from the Fourth Army headquarters came with the news that the division commander's entreaties for reinforcements had been heard and heeded finally. Companies of the 13th Division were being sent to Kollaa. For the men of the 12th Division, yesterday was not soon enough for them to arrive.

There was a lull in the artillery barrage from the Soviet ridge the afternoon the 13th Division appeared from the west. The troops of the 12th let out a spontaneous cheer and shout of welcome at the arrival of the first reinforcements. The commander made no attempt to order the men to stifle their cheers. Surely the Soviet troops could hear the loud cries of jubilation and relief from across the river. On the other hand, just as surely the Finnish revelries would thrust an unwanted shot of despair and fear into the freezing Russian hearts.

In the makeshift mess tent men shook the hands of strangers and patted the backs of familiar men whom they had not seen since before the conflict had started back at the end of November. They related tales of their tussles with the enemy elsewhere on the Karelian front, some obviously stretching the truth a little to outdo others with accounts of their heroic exploits.

Jiri couldn't remember when he had last laughed. From amidst the laughter and general racket in the mess tent, he could make out a particular laugh that somehow was familiar. Some men chortle when they laugh, others cackle, still others shriek with delight. This man's laughter was like a full-bodied guffaw. Jiri had known a man with such an idiosyncratic guffaw once.

Jiri looked around the mess tent to see where the hearty whooping was coming from. Once Jiri thought he had isolated the one with the familiar laugh, the man had his back to him. Jiri couldn't see the face. But the back of the man's head had a small, round, bald spot surrounded by a ring of thinning, dirty blond hair. This would not be uncommon in the officers' tent. But in the conscripted men's mess, full as it was with men in their early twenties, and some even as young as nineteen, it was a very unusual sight.

Jiri had a happy hunch. He arose from his seat and carried his dented metal mug of coffee over to the table where the man was conveying his husky laughter.

Jiri's hopeful intuition had been an accurate one. Sure enough, the man slapping his thighs in almost obscene enjoyment and raising his deep and loud gusts of laughter to the canvas ceiling was none other than Algot Niska.

Before Jiri could get close enough to greet him, Niska himself caught sight of Jiri's eager face in the distance.

"Is that you, Jiri?" he shouted gleefully in German in Jiri's direction. "What the hell are you doing here?"

Jiri took a few steps toward Niska and reached out his hand to shake Niska's enthusiastically.

"I was about to ask you the same question," Jiri said in German. His Finnish had improved only slightly since Niska had last seen him in Poland over a year earlier. "Why are *you* here?"

Niska threw his long arms around Jiri, conveying how very

relieved and glad he was to see Jiri alive and well. He embraced Jiri not only because of their history together, but because Jiri represented the best of Algot Niska, the honorable smuggler of Jews that he had had to leave behind in Germany. Seeing Jiri again, his first rescue, helped him feel validated once more as a worthy person.

The two pulled away from the others and a found a table where the previous occupants had finished dinner and moved on.

"I know, I know; you think I'm too old for this, too, right? Why not? Everybody else does. It's a long story."

"This is one story I want to hear, for sure."

Such was Jiri's surprise at seeing his old friend in such an unexpected place, such was the fullness of his gratitude for what Niska had done for him, that Jiri had a lump in his throat that rendered him speechless. Tears of joy welled up in his eyes.

Finally, his tears turned into a broad smile, "Good God, it's great to see you, Algot."

"I'm sorry, Jiri, that I didn't follow up and try to ascertain your whereabouts in Finland. I simply couldn't under the circumstances, you understand?"

Jiri nodded. The chatter and laughter in the tent had run its course. Men were finishing their cup of coffee and getting up to leave.

"But that doesn't mean I hadn't wondered about you, about how you are doing in Finland, or indeed, whether or not you were still in Finland at all."

"I wondered about you, too, after we went our separate ways in Poland. Did you go back to Berlin?"

"For a short time, yes. Not long afterward, I developed the damnedest ulcers in my gut. A doctor recommended that I get out of Germany and seek treatment in my home country."

"You picked a hell of a time to come back."

"The Russians dropped their first bombs on Helsinki not long after I arrived. I made it back to Finland by way of Latvia and Estonia—just barely—in a rowboat. Can you believe that?"

"If it was anyone else telling the story, I wouldn't believe it. But I have learned, Algot, that you are like a cat. You have nine lives. Obviously, the bombs over Helsinki did not kill you; you're here now."

"That's not all, Jiri. It's precisely because of the bombs that I'm here in the flesh before your eyes."

"I don't follow." Jiri chuckled and playfully slapped Niska on his left shoulder.

"The bombing was what kept me out of prison. After my ulcers started to heal, I went dutifully to ValPo headquarters to turn myself in and face the music for my liquor smuggling. The whole place was abandoned like an empty matchbox. The cops had all taken refuge in the bomb shelter down the street."

"What? No one minding the store?"

"Not even the janitor or night watchman. I did run into a couple of the officers when I took cover in the bomb shelter myself. They told me that given the turn of events in the country, they had bigger fish to fry than a small-time booze smuggler from a time before the Depression."

"They let you go scott-free, just like that?"

"They gave me a choice: Either go to prison or join the Finnish defense forces at the front, even though I'm past the age of enlisting."

"So you chose this frozen hell?"

"The anti-aircraft guns shot down a few of the Russki planes in Helsinki. I figured that if I chose prison, I might end up sharing a cell in *Sörnäinen* with a damn captured Bolshevik."

"You are one lucky man, Algot."

"Yes, but not everyone was so lucky in the bombing. About fifty civilians were killed on the first day. Tragic. But you know, Jiri, there have been times in my life when some good fortune emerges out of misfortune, even if it's just a single match flickering in the darkness."

Jiri listened eagerly for more. He needed to hear about light and good fortune, so much darkness and misfortune had he endured in the war.

"Someone up there is looking out for me, that's for sure," Niska continued. "Some angel, maybe."

Jiri was silent for a moment. He didn't know quite what to make of his rescuer's newlyfound cosmological and religious leanings.

"You're probably thinking that Niska has been buffeted by too many gales, or that he's endured one too many bouts of sunstroke. I don't blame you if you are...Let me ask: Have you lost a buddy in this war, Jiri?"

"Of course."

"Then have you asked yourself why your buddy got a bullet in his brain while you survived to see another battle? I don't pretend to understand this stuff. I didn't pay much attention in my confirmation school. But isn't some higher power mixed up in all of that somehow?"

During occasional lulls in the fighting, Jiri had, in fact,

contemplated that very question more than once. But the memory of his God-fearing, Torah-abiding Bohemian grandfather's slaughter at the hands of unruly young gentile Czech ultra-nationalists led him to conclude that if some higher power did, in fact, intervene to save some, he, or she, or it, or whatever, was not very consistent since so many are not saved.

"I suppose you could say I chose to freeze my ass in the Karelian forest over rotting in prison," Niska said. "But I also consider my enlisting as an act of gratitude for all my good fortune in still being alive."

"I admire that, Algot. But when the Russian shells start coming over the ridge soon, I think I would trade a year in jail for one day here."

"Jiri, how is it that you're wearing the white snowsuit of a Finnish private?"

"When the Nazis attacked Czechoslovakia I was ready to volunteer for the defenses. But the Czech army didn't want me. Remember, I lived in Berlin for many years. The Czechs thought I was spying for Germany. Shit. Can you imagine that? After what the Germans did to me?"

"That's laughable." Niska guffawed once again before he took another sip of his coffee.

"But I suspect the real reason they wouldn't take me is that I am a Jew. When the Nazis stole the Sudetenland, the Czech government tried to appease Hitler and keep him out of the rest of the country. They started to turn the screws on us Jews."

"That's better than what the Czech government did *after* Hitler annexed all of the country."

"I know. It's why you came to get me back out, remember?"

"The Finnish army doesn't care if you're a Jew?"

"No, they don't have enough manpower for this fight with the Russians. They don't care if a volunteer is circumcised or not. I signed up in the foreign volunteer corps. Stalin just looked the other way when Hitler snatched Czechoslovakia. This gives me a chance to help the country that welcomed me as a refugee. I want to get my revenge on Stalin, for the sake of Finland, but also of my home country."

~~~

The morning of March 10 was one of the coldest in decades. The air was so silent and still that any sound from the tents could carry through the frigid space across the river and over the ridge.

Niska, as usual, was the first man out from his tent. He hummed a folk song out of tune to himself as he stood with his feet apart behind a birch tree some twenty meters from the colony of tents and urinated, wondering if his stream would freeze in motion before it hit the snow.

Suddenly, Niska was startled by a terribly loud *crack* of a single gunshot that echoed through the frozen air. Niska dropped to his stomach on the snow to be a less vulnerable target to whomever had shot the rifle. His heart was pumping furiously with the rush of adrenaline released into his blood. He remained on his stomach and scanned the horizon. Not hearing a follow-up shot, he rose slowly, first to his knees, then to his feet.

Aalto, his platoon commander, hurried out of his tent. "What the fuck was that?"

Before Niska could answer, the two men heard the plaintive groaning of a man trying to shout from the riverbank.

"That must be one of our snipers," Aalto said. "I sent Haula and Hämäläinen out to keep their eyes open lest the enemy climb over the ridge before the sun came up."

"Good God, let's hope it's not Haula. He's our ticket out of here," Niska said.

Aalto closed his eyes, in disbelief and perhaps regret, and shook his head slowly. In any case, this was not good. "He or Hämäläinen must have been hit by an enemy sniper."

Aalto ran back to the entrance of his tent. He pulled away the threefold flap and poked his head into the tent.

"Salminen: Haula or Hämäläinen has been hit by a sniper by the river. It may be both. But I hear someone's voice so at least one's still alive. Make your way over to retrieve them. Take another man with you. Now! On the double."

Niska wondered at the wisdom of sending anyone to get them and possibly exposing two healthy men to the Russian sniper's view.

Nonetheless, Niska shouted to Aalto, "I'll go as the second man."

He started to run back to his own tent to retrieve his rifle.

"No, private. I need a younger man for this assignment, a faster one. Salminen is one of our most able. You won't be able to keep up."

"Damnit, I'm the oldest man in this outfit," Niska replied defiantly. "I have the least to lose."

Before he could be refused by Aalto, Niska had crept over beside Salminen, and the two set off on their stomachs toward the river bank.

"I think he was hit over there, near the small birch," Niska said to Salminen.

They headed in the direction of the birch. The tree stood on top of a small ridge that led down to the river. They could see a trail of blood in the snow, and the marks of someone's having dragged himself through the snow to take cover underneath another tree on the riverbank. Haula apparently had enough strength to have maneuvered his wounded body from his mound of snow in the unprotected part of the riverbank.

Salminen and Niska followed the trail of blood, still on their stomachs. Salminen was the first to see him. The white-clad sniper was lying with his face down in the snow, no longer moving. Salminen crawled over to the body and started to rise to his knees.

"Stay down!" Niska urged Salminen.

Niska finished crawling to the body. He forced his right arm below the man's chest and tried to turn him over. The body was too heavy to turn while Niska was prone on his stomach. Contrary to his instruction to Salminen, Niska pushed up to his knees. He managed to pivot enough to turn the body onto its back. It was Haula. Though barely recognizable, Niska knew it was Haula by the thirty-four-year-old's receding hairline he'd seen in newspaper photos.

Another *crack.* A figure in white fell from the top of a tree on the near side of the river, breaking several branches as it plummeted and landed with a muffled thud on the snow.

"Must have been Hämäläinen," Niska whispered.

When Salminen saw Haula's face, he immediately turned his own face in the opposite direction. Haula was moaning weakly. At least he was still alive. But where Haula's face would normally be, there was only a grotesque red mess of shredded flesh. The sniper's bullet had gone into Haula's left cheek and blown off the left side of his face until it was barely identifiable as human.

Niska averted his eyes for a few seconds, but then sprang into action.

"Come, we have to try to carry him or just drag him to the tents. But for God's sake, keep your body as low to the ground as you can."

Together, they took hold of Haula under each armpit and, while still on their knees, began to drag him toward the cluster of tents. Progress was painfully slow through the deep snow. Both men's strength was flagging the closer they got to their destination. In the frigid air, Niska had trouble getting his breath. They were only a few meters away from one of the tents, so very close. Niska was sure they had succeeded in their arduous task and that they were safe. He rose up from his knees on to his feet to drag Haula the rest of the way.

Crack! The sound of another single shot reverberated across the surface of the frozen river and over the ridge. Niska fell face first into the snow. He raised his head slowly and cautiously and looked back to see if Salminen had been hit.

Salminen, though exhausted, shouted at the top of his lungs, "Medic! We've got bad casualties here! Medi-i-i-c!" As though he himself had been shot, Salminen buried his face into the snow and wept aloud like a wearied, whimpering child.

A contingent of the 12th Division had crept from the tents in the direction from which they had heard the cry for a medic. Platoon commander Aalto ordered the men to remain behind a snow embankment. "Keep your eyes peeled toward the trees on the opposite side of the river. If you spy a sniper, take aim at the son of a bitch. But make sure you don't miss and give away our position."

Crack! A second bullet from across the river ricocheted off a tree trunk just a meter from where Niska was prone on the ground. He knew he was still an exposed target. Lest he invite another shot, he remained absolutely still, face-down in the snow like a dead man.

The men of the 12th launched a blistering volley of shots toward the tops of the trees. Niska wondered if anyone of them had actually spotted the sniper, or if they were merely shooting blindly in the hope that at least one bullet would find its way to the hidden target.

Aalto ordered the men to cease fire. There followed a long pregnant silence. Niska dared to raise his head slightly. He was still less than a few meters from the entrance to one of the tents. This pause in the shooting was Niska's opportunity to make his way on his stomach to the tent.

"Salminen, you've still got Haula? Need my help dragging him to the tent?"

"No, I think I can do it alone."

Salminen's voice sounded exhausted and anemic. Niska turned and began crawling in the snow in Salminen's direction. *Crack!* The silence was shattered. Niska stopped in mid-crawl. "Damn! I'm hit."

A cannonade of gunfire erupted from behind the snow embankment to Niska's left. Niska's head was back down in the snow. Salminen continued to drag the limp body of Haula with much breathless effort. He paused where Niska lay to check on his condition. The white snow beneath Niska's left side was turning a brilliant red.

~~~

Two days later, on March 12, Finnish President Ryti spoke to the nation on the radio and announced that hostilities between Finland and the Soviet Union were over. The two nations were preparing to sign the Treaty of Moscow. The terms of the Finnish surrender were still being negotiated, but they would be severe. The depleted surviving troops had broken down and packed up the encampment of tents and began the long walk on the snow-covered floor of the pine and birch forest back to Finland, depleted and defeated.

Jiri Hudak and Eemil Salminen were among them. Hämäläinen's corpse was placed in a sledge. Niska and Haula, however, both still clinging to life, were being prepared by intrepid medics to be borne by the same sledge to a field hospital.

CHAPTER TWENTY-ONE

Berlin: March 12, 1940

Kersten was livid over the surprise early-morning visit by *Leutnant* Rohrbach and the two other SS personnel at his flat. He needed to vent to Himmler. That could backfire, of course, but he felt strongly enough about having been scrutinized and his privacy invaded that he would take his chances.

At noon the same day, Kersten walked into Himmler's office at the time Himmler was expecting him for a treatment. Even before taking off his overcoat and hanging up his hat, Kersten said to Himmler, only half-jokingly, "When you want to find out something about me, you don't have to bother sending the SS. You have only to ask me directly yourself."

Himmler had been approaching Kersten with a hand outstretched to shake his, stopped cold, as if he had been hit in the *solar plexus.*

"What did you say? You had a call from someone in the SS? Without my knowing about it? That is impossible."

"A *Leutnant* Rohrbach and two subordinates went through my flat. They were courteous enough, but I was annoyed, to say the least." Kersten spoke unusually rapidly as he related the whole incident. He hadn't finished before Himmler angrily picked up his telephone receiver. Not trying in the least to control the vexation in his voice, he grilled the recipient of his call about the confrontation. Once he stopped to listen, Himmler's face turned the color of laundered linens. He put his left hand over the mouthpiece of the receiver and spoke to Kersten, "It seems they were going to arrest you for treating Jews."

Abruptly, Himmler took his hand from over the mouthpiece and, his face now the color of scarlet, shouted, "I forbid anyone to interfere with Dr. Kersten. I don't care about the reason. This is an order. The doctor is answerable to me directly, and only to me. Is that understood?"

He waited for the affirmative response of the person on the other end of the line.

"Now, please make sure that this order is communicated to General

Heydrich and *Obergruppenführer* Kaltenbrunner. Remind them, in case they have forgotten, that they are subordinate to me. Neither is to send officers of the SS or *Gestapo* to Dr. Kersten's address, in Berlin or at his country estate, on any pretext whatsoever, without my express knowledge and permission. Understood?"

Himmler slammed down the receiver on its cradle. He struggled to catch his breath. His glasses slipped down the length of his nose. He began pushing his spectacles up to their proper position without being aware of it, but they just continued to slide down the sweaty surface. Kersten could tell that Himmler had not exhausted his anger. Himmler raised his head to look into Kersten's face.

"You cannot be my doctor and still treat Jews," he said flatly.

"How the hell am I supposed to know my patients' religion?" Kersten asked. "You know I never ask them that. Jews or non-Jews, they are all my patients."

"Jewishness is not just a religion, Kersten. Don't you understand? They're a filthy race, different from all the rest. Jews are the enemy. You can no longer be treating Jews! The German people are engaged in a war to death against the Jew-infested democracies."

Kersten said quietly, "But you forget, *Herr Reichsführer*, as apparently *Leutnant* Rohrbach and whoever sent him to my flat did as well, that I am not one of the German people. I am a Finn. My country is not at war against the Jewish people."

"As someone in the employ of the head of the SS, you are not permitted to treat Jews."

"Then perhaps I will have to resign my post in the employ of the head of the SS. I will have to wait for my government to prescribe the next line of conduct for me."

Himmler seemed to be flummoxed by Kersten's resistance. He did not want to lose his healer. He paused to choose his words carefully.

"This is a silly way to argue," Himmler said in calmer voice. "You know very well what I mean. I have been given the assignment of tracking down, punishing, and weeding out the Jews. So do me a personal favor, Doctor, and leave the Jews to their ailments and pains."

If Kersten yielded now, if only outwardly, he would be denying everything he had come to stand for.

In a half voice, he said, "I cannot do so, *Herr Reichsführer*. The Jews are humans subject to illness and pains like everyone else. If one needs my help, I cannot refuse. They don't have their own doctors any longer. You may, in fact, have had something to do with that."

"I must insist, no!" Himmler shouted. "The *Führer* has said no. He says there are three categories of creatures: men, animals, and Jews. And the last will have to be exterminated so that the other two can continue to exist."

"I must ask, is that your *Führer's* absurd anthropology alone or is it yours, too?"

Before he could shout an answer to Kersten's provocation, Himmler's wan face suddenly took on a greenish tinge as though he were about to vomit. His brow broke out in beads of perspiration. His hands clutched his stomach.

"Here it comes again," he groaned.

"The cramps have returned?"

"No, the stabbing of the knife."

"I have warned you many times not to let yourself get worked up this way," Kersten chided as if he were talking to a naughty child. "It is very bad for your cramps." Rolling up his shirtsleeves, pointing at the divan, he commanded, "Come now, you know the routine. Take off your shirt."

Obviously in acute pain, Himmler obeyed and made himself prone on the divan. Kersten launched immediately into the massage therapy. Himmler would be impossible to bear until his pain was alleviated.

When the therapy session was nearing its conclusion, but while still massaging Himmler lightly, Kersten thanked him for convincing Hitler to postpone indefinitely the hair-brained scheme to force Dutch "irreconcilables" to march to Poland.

"I think I caught the *Führer* on a good day. He had just come in from the courtyard and playing with his precious Blondi."

"Who is Blondi?" Kersten asked, assuming that she was a mistress, even though Hitler was notoriously austere and traditional about matters of personal morality, especially sex. Besides, Hitler already had his mistress, Eva.

"Oh, yes. Silly of me. How can I expect you to know about Blondi? I apologize for the assumption. Blondi is the German shepherd puppy that Bormann gave the *Führer* as a gift on his birthday last year. The *Führer* is totally charmed by the animal. That's why I say I caught him on a good day. Anytime the *Führer* spends time the Blondi, he is totally relaxed. He was remarkably amenable to the suggestion that we wait until a more propitious time to punish the Dutch."

"I don't imagine that Göbbels or Göring were too pleased,

however."

"No, that's putting it mildly. They were beyond irritated that the *Führer* heeded my counsel instead of theirs. Still, you need to remember, Doctor, the Dutch Jews will still be deported from Holland eventually."

"Allow me to say, *Herr Reichsführer,* that I do not understand this, shall I say, inhumane campaign against the Jews."

Himmler was annoyed by Kersten's comment.

"Come, my dear Kersten. You said you're an *Evangelisch*, did you not?"

"Where I was confirmed, we were known as Lutherans."

"Then I am sure you are familiar with the views on the Jews by the man whose surname gave the name to your denomination?"

"I haven't had much time to read theology, *Herr Reichsführer."*

"I suggest you go to the library and read Luther's treatise, *On the Jews, and Their Lies.* Göbbels directed every library in the *Reich* to order ample copies. I think every *Evangelisch* should be required to read it. Every German, for that matter."

"Why do you think that?"

"Luther learned an important lesson. Initially, he tried following your naïve and sentimental approach, Kersten. He believed that the path of kindness toward the Jews was the right one. Of course, he only wanted to impress them with Christianity and then convert them."

"That's to be expected of a former monk, isn't it?"

"But alas, Kersten. His attitude of tolerance didn't last. He was totally frustrated by the Jews' stubbornness. I could have told him that. They refused to see the superiority of Christianity. That's when he sat down and wrote the famous treatise. He damned them to hell and called them 'the devil incarnate.' The *Führer* got a lot of mileage out of Luther's words."

Kersten felt he couldn't pursue this line of conversation much further since he hadn't read the treatise, nor had he ever even heard it mentioned in his Lutheran circles.

"What most people don't know, Doctor, especially the Jews," Himmler continued, "is that in the *Führer's* inner circle, I am the best friend the Jews have."

Kersten thought this highly unlikely. One rumor had it that it was by Himmler's command that the violent revenge was exacted on the Jews on *Kristallnacht.*

"How so, *Herr Reichsführer?*"

"*Ach* Kersten. I never wanted to destroy the Jews. I hate them, to be sure. Just name any problem in Germany: inflation and the banks; unemployment before the *Führer's* rise to power, the outlandish reparations Germany had to pay after the Great War, the loosening of sexual mores in our cities, the mixing of the races, the monopoly and corruption of the banks. I could go on and on. Each and every one I attribute to the sinister, cancerous influence of the Jews. Nevertheless, I had quite different ideas than others as to how to handle the matter. It's Heydrich and Göbbels who will have to have it all on their conscience."

Kersten stopped his massaging and looked at Himmler with genuine astonishment.

"You'll have to tell me what you mean."

"The history books will probably say that I ordered the chaos of November 9 and 10, 1938. But it was Heydrich and Göbbels who gave the order for retribution, Heydrich behind my back and without clearing it with me, his superior. I would have demoted the disobedient bastard if the *Führer* had not intervened on Heydrich's behalf, a decision that I fear the *Führer* will live to regret."

Kersten maintained a strategic silence, sensing that Himmler was in the mood to divulge more about the inner workings of the Nazi cult.

"Some years ago, the *Führer* gave me orders to get rid of the Jews. I don't remember if it was in '33 or '34. My plan for the Jewish question was to eliminate them from Germany by emigration. They would be encouraged to leave the country and even take their fortunes and property with them...Did you know, Doctor, that in 1938, even President Roosevelt became aware of our intentions for the Jews?"

Kersten said nothing, but raised his eyebrows.

"Yes. And we requested American support for executing our plan. If things had progressed differently, I think Roosevelt might have agreed."

"But..."

"But then vom Rath was murdered by that impetuous young French Jew Grünspan. The *Führer* was incensed. Then, in an effort to kiss the *Führer's* ass, Heydrich and Göbbels took advantage of the *Führer's* absence in München and gave the fatal order. Göbbels never misses an opportunity to curry favor with the *Führer* and stick it to me. Neither does Heydrich. Soon after that, Jews were no longer permitted to leave Germany."

Kersten was trying to assimilate Himmler's information with what he had suspected and garnered by way of rumor before.

"I am sure Göbbels and Heydrich persuaded the *Führer* that the Jewish question could be solved only by means of their extermination. Heydrich and Göbbels couldn't stop talking about an *Endlösung*, a final solution to the problem. I knew exactly what they meant."

"But you were hoping for a different solution?"

"Yes. If we lose the war—unlikely, judging by how things have been going so far—history will judge Germany harshly for killing off the Jews. After all, all the papers and publishing houses in Britain and America are in the hands of Jews. I proposed to the *Führer* that he reconsider the ban on Jewish emigration, and instead give them a large piece of territory and let them set up their own independent state. There they could cheat one another instead of the rest of us. We made inquiries in a number of different quarters, but no one—including Roosevelt—wanted the Jews."

"Where did you envision this independent Jewish state to be? In Palestine?"

"No, in Madagascar, in fact. We'd dispatch an expeditionary force of the SS to Africa to take over the country. Those black *Untermenschen* wouldn't know what hit them."

Kersten was stunned. He didn't know if Himmler was kidding and he should laugh at such an outlandish idea. But no, Himmler looked perfectly serious.

CHAPTER TWENTY-TWO

Jyvaskyla: March 10-14, 1940

The Russians began lustily anticipating a final victory when word reached them that "the White Death" had been stricken down, possibly fatally. Haula had been much more than a minor uncomfortable thorn in the Russians' flesh. Singlehandedly, he had felled almost seven hundred of them. Now the surviving troops at Kollaa were eager to strike a final and decisive blow to the Finns and go home. Almost 89,000 of their comrades had been killed or were still missing in action in the four months since November. The Finns, for their part, estimated that their losses were only one-quarter of those of the enemy. The sheer overwhelming numerical superiority of the Russian forces, however, and their unrelenting pace of adding replacements, finally inundated the Finns. The Finns were in retreat on skis and boots toward the Finland-Karelia border.

Niska and Haula were oblivious to events after they'd been hit by a Russia sniper. As severe as it was, Haula's facial wound was not life-threatening once the bleeding was staunched and the wound stuffed with cotton by the medics. He was transported to the closest field hospital at the recently converted sanitorium at Tiuru.

Niska's situation was more dire. The effusive bleeding from the wound in his chest raised his medical status to critical. The hospital at Tiuru was not equipped with the specialized facilities required for surgery and treatment of his life-threatening condition. He would have to be transported to a full-fledged military hospital farther inland.

Two medics stabilized him in the closest tent at Kollaa all the while troops preparing to evacuate were taking down the other tents. The medics staunched the bleeding and sprinkled sulfa powder as an antiseptic over the chest wound. They applied dressings the best they could in the hellish cold. They resurrected the dying embers in the campfire outside the tent, commanded the orderlies to dig beneath the snow for stones and small rocks and heat them over the revived flames. They inserted the heated rocks into several water canteens and placed them under the blankets on the sledge to protect Niska as much as possible from the threat of hypothermia. To fortify his body further for the sledge transport, they injected morphine to alleviate pain.

On the morning of March 13, Niska sat visibly dazed on a bed in a post-operative ward in a military hospital. His chest was wrapped tightly with strips of gauze bandage. He glanced down at his chest but saw no evidence of bleeding. His eyes grew wide with disgust as he noticed that a plastic tube connected his penis to a bag beneath his bed. He was sufficiently conscious and aware to feel embarrassment when a volunteer *Lotta* nurse poked her head around the privacy screen encircling his bed.

"Dr. Berg will be down to see you soon, Corporal Niska."

A few minutes later, a short, roundish man in the white coat of a doctor came around the screen and saluted. "Corporal, I am Captain Berg, surgeon, Fifth Medical Corps."

Niska answered with a feeble salute. "Where am I, Captain?"

"Why, you're at Kinkomaa Military Hospital. Just beyond the pine and birch outside your window is the city of Jyväskylä."

"Jesus. Jyväskylä? The last place I remember being was a frozen river bank in Karelia someplace."

"Yes, you were at Kollaa. Several of you who served there have been patients here. You were transported by some exceptionally competent medics on a Lapp sledge to a train full of soldiers evacuating Karelia and then brought here from the Jyväskylä station by military ambulance."

"I don't remember a blessed thing about that."

"That's perfectly normal at this juncture. I performed emergency repair of your heart just two days ago. We dug a Russian Mosin-Nagant bullet out of the right ventricle of your heart. You're lucky to still be alive. Your body has been through a lot of trauma, and you are still feeling the after-effects of the anesthetic. I assure you, Corporal, your memory will improve in time."

"I guess I'll just need to take your word for it."

"I'll leave you now so that you can try to get some sleep. Are you feeling any pain in your chest?"

"No, not really, Doctor."

"That's another thing for which to take my word, Corporal. There will be pain, maybe as soon as tomorrow. The *Lottas* are trained to administer morphine in that case."

The next morning, Dr. Berg stopped by Niska's bed once more.

"The *Lottas* tell me that you have been obeying their orders to get out of bed, Corporal, and walk a little. That's good."

"That stout farmer's wife…Kettunen's the name, isn't it?..she's quite persuasive, if you know what I mean. I don't dare disobey her. She's as crusty as a couple of the worst sergeants at boot camp." Niska laughed at his own remark, but immediately placed his hand on his bandaged chest and grimaced.

Berg joined in the laughter, which indicated to Niska that the surgeon wasn't overly concerned about the pain in Niska's chest just now, and therefore he didn't need to be either.

"Corporal, you were hit by a sniper's bullet," Berg reported. "But it appears you dodged the sniper's intent."

"I have a vague memory of trying to stay low on the snow to evade a sniper up in the trees."

"I'm told you rescued the famous Corporal Haula. He will live the rest of his days with half a face, but the important thing is that he will live. A whole nation owes you a huge debt of gratitude, Corporal Niska."

"A soldier does what he has to do," Niska managed to say. "Any one of us would have done the same for a wounded brother-in-arms."

"In any case, you seem to be recovering swiftly. Continue following *Lotta* Kettunen's orders," Berg said, and winked at Niska as he left.

The affable Niska was beginning to feel isolated and cut off by the privacy screen. He asked one of the *Lotta* nurses to remove it for the daytime.

A voice came from the man sitting up two beds down from Niska's.

"So soldier, I hear you're Algot Niska. *The* Algot Niska?"

"As far as I know, there is only one of us in the world with that name, and it's me."

"Just wait till I get back home to Vimpeli and tell the guys I was in a hospital ward with the notorious whiskey smuggler, Algot Niska. I'll be the big man in town. Most of us were just boys in '12 when you almost led Finland to a football bronze medal in Stockholm."

"But the thing is, we didn't win the medal, unfortunately. Maybe your buddies would be more impressed if we had."

"No, it was pretty impressive. Imagine. Tiny Finland knocking the mighty Czar's team out in the first round. Then almost doing the same to the Brits in the bronze medal game. We were prouder than hell."

Niska couldn't think of a self-effacing comeback. They were silent for the time being. Finally, seeing that the young soldier looked eager to have more conversation, Niska asked, "Vimpeli, eh? You a farmer? I presume once this bloody war is over, that you'll be going back to your farm in Vimpeli?"

"Well, it's actually my father's farm. He's had a hard time of it working it alone with just the help of my mother and sister, even in the winter, while I've been here on the Karelian front. As soon as the surgeon gives me the okay, I'll be on that train headed toward home."

"They won't send you back to the front? That's where I figure they'll send me."

The young soldier fell into an awkward silence of consternation. He looked disbelievingly at Niska.

"You haven't heard, then?"

"Heard? About what?"

"The peace treaty, of course. The one signed by Ryti and Molotov on the 12th. None of us is going back to the front anymore."

Niska sat on his bed stunned. If what his young mate was saying was true, how swiftly the tide of the war had turned.

"We lost Karelia, then? All that bloody fighting…for what?"

"Viipuri is suddenly a Russian city."

"Damn them! That's my birthplace. No going back there now."

Niska sat mum on his bed. He couldn't believe what he'd just heard. He always knew in his mind, of course, that at some time the conflict would end. But things had started so propitiously the first two months that he naïvely believed just like others that things would continue that way.

Niska slept fitfully that night. *Now what? Where to next?* The medics and Dr. Berg had given him another chance at life, but what was he going to do with it? His estranged wife and children didn't want him back in Finland. He had no desire to go back to Germany. In fact, since Hitler had by now annexed or occupied to much of it, he couldn't go anywhere in Europe either. He woke up from his sleep while it was still dark and felt a yawning void within, a vague emptiness.

The next day, Dr. Berg made another bedside visit. "Good morning, Corporal."

"I guess I should see the morning as a good one. I'm still breathing. So many of my army colleagues are not."

Berg took the stethoscope from around his neck and placed it on Niska's chest. The *Lottas* had unrolled and removed the tight bandages and replaced them with lighter ones. Before they had applied the new dressings, Niska saw that his chest was crisscrossed by red lines sown together with bloodied stitches as though he were several pieces of fabric.

"Your ticker sounds good considering the shape it was in when they brought you here. I frankly wasn't altogether sure that we could patch the punctures."

"You undoubtedly got your first training for this job when repairing your bicycle tires as a boy," Niska joked.

Berg smiled politely but not with much conviction. "Despite your humor this morning, Corporal, you seem less animated than usual. Did you get some sleep?"

"A little yes, until the farmer's wife *Lotta* came in the middle of the night to pull that damn tube out of my baby-maker. Afterward, it hurt like hell to pee."

"That's quite normal after the catheter is removed. You'll just have to grin and bear it for a few more days...You can also expect to experience a touch of depression, strangely enough, as you get closer to a full recovery."

"I admit I feel a little lost. It's going to be hard to find a direction, given what I hear has happened. Strange. This is the moment we had all been waiting for. Yet now I feel life is a little futile."

"From what I've heard about you and your venturesome life, you always seem to find your way out of the fog to a safe harbor," Berg assured him.

Niska pondered the doctor's remark. *The angelic Vellamo with me again*?

Niska had been watching the dancing motion of Berg's unusually dark, bushy eyebrows, so characteristically non-Nordic, whenever he spoke.

His next question seemed even to him a non sequitur. "I've been meaning to ask you about your name, Doctor. One of the Swedish Bergs?"

"No, not Swedish. Jewish, from Russia originally. The former family name was Rosenberg."

"I figured as much." Then, suddenly fearing that this casual remark would be offensive to Berg, he added, "Not that it changes anything as far as I'm concerned, you understand?"

"My grandfather did his twenty-five years of service in the Czar's army mandated for Jews. He married a Finnish woman when he had been stationed at Turku. After his tour of service, he chose to stay and resume civilian life in Finland. I shortened the name to just 'Berg' to make it easier for me to gain entrance into medical school."

"That sounds a lot like the story of the few other Jews I knew growing up or have met since."

"There aren't many of us in Finland, that's for sure. I've learned from my rabbi at the Helsinki synagogue that thanks to your heroic assistance, there are a few more of my people in the country now."

Niska felt his customary bashfulness whenever this topic was raised in conversation.

"I've heard of what you'd done for so many Jews trapped in Germany. You may like to know that a few of them joined the synagogue after they arrived with your help in Finland. You might say that my preserving your life through surgery was the least I could do on behalf of my fellow Jews you saved from the ghettoes and camps."

"I merely did what the situation called for, Doctor. The opportunity found me, not the other way around. That's where I find my joy: doing what needs to be done. Believe me, I'm no hero."

"But you've led a life well-lived, Corporal. The venerable old rabbis used to say, 'If you happen to come along and see what in the world needs repairing, and you know how to repair it, then you have found a piece of the world that God has left for you to complete.' Being a hero doesn't always mean doing extraordinary things, does it, though I hear you've done your share of those? I think it means sometimes doing the ordinary thing that needs to be done, but doing it courageously and faithfully. Yes, by God, Corporal Niska, that's a life well-lived."

CHAPTER TWENTY-THREE

Berlin: December 1, 1941

Kersten was going about the treatment with Himmler in an unusually perfunctory, mechanical manner. This was no longer the exception to the rule; it was the rule. It had been a year and a half since Himmler had laid down the condition that Kersten not treat Jewish patients any longer. Kersten felt his professional independence had been violated. He was still resentful. He wasn't conscious of his resentment every day by any means. Many days, however, he was going about his treatments of Himmler in a less committed and conscientious way.

Kersten knew the map of Himmler's abdomen like the proverbial back of his hand. He knew what areas of Himmler's abdomen to manipulate more gingerly than others because of the proximity of the nerves to the surface of the skin. But on this day, it seemed that Kersten had handled those sensitive areas with a particularly rough touch. Several times, Himmler shrieked in pain.

"Doctor, you're hurting me more than usual today. Can I request that you soften your touch a little?"

Kersten hadn't been aware of his manner.

"I apologize, *Herr Reichsführer*. I must focus more on what I am doing."

Kersten's overly firm manipulating of Himmler's flesh wasn't entirely congruent with his apology, however.

"Indeed, you should...Your mind is somewhere else, Doctor?"

Kersten did not answer at first. He was in turmoil, he acknowledged to himself. But he wondered if it was safe or prudent to voice to Himmler what was roiling in his mind. He was angry enough, however, to risk it. He couldn't remain silent any longer.

"These camps the *Führer* chose you to have built: Gusen, Neuengamme, Gross-Rosen, Auschwitz."

"What about them?"

"Is it true? I mean, that in your labor camps men and women are systematically tortured or worked to death?"

Himmler laughed nervously. By now, Kersten was able to distinguish Himmler's unfeigned laughter at something genuinely funny, and a forced laugh he used on some occasions to try to mask another feeling. This was one of those occasions.

"Come now, my dear Kersten. You are falling for the falsehoods of the enemy's propaganda. The Allies are spreading nasty rumors. These camps are for the reeducation of those not yet convinced of the National Socialist philosophy, and for building the armaments we need for the war effort. You know that, Kersten."

Himmler's remark only served to irritate Kersten further. Lest he express his irritation with his massaging hands, he pulled them back from Himmler's torso.

"No, I am thinking of facts that I have heard from a reliable source."

"Facts? What source? If your source is the BBC, those facts are undeniably false ones. Besides, you know you're not allowed to listen to the BBC."

"You forget again, *Herr Reichsführer,* that your prohibition against listening to *Feindsender* doesn't apply to me, a Finnish citizen."

"As an adjunct to my staff, I explicitly forbid you to do so."

Kersten bristled at the idea that he was considered an adjunct to Himmler's staff. He thought of himself as an independent medical contractor.

"In any case, my source is not the BBC, or Radio *Suomi* from Finland. When I was at the Finnish legation recently I met two Swedish photojournalists on their way back to Sweden from an assignment."

"So?"

"These journalists were carrying a file of photographs. The photographs show terrible torture. Emaciated bodies. Men and women hardly recognizable as human. These were photos of inmates at your camps."

"Someone failed to inform them that the taking of photographs in the camps is strictly forbidden."

"Oh, they didn't take the photographs. They purchased them from several SS guards at these camps," Kersten said with a tone of irony.

Himmler started up from the divan in a poorly disguised panic. At that moment, Kersten realized that the incredible rumors were true.

"Are these journalists still in Germany?" Himmler asked urgently.

"No, they are back home in Sweden now."

"Do you know how I could buy back those photographs? At any price?"

"I don't." Kersten shook his head reproachfully and continued. "You seem very desirous of buying them back, suspiciously so. Wouldn't it be better if you spoke to me openly? Don't you think I deserve the truth?"

"You saw the photographs yourself, Kersten?"

"Yes, I did. I was repulsed."

Himmler remained silent. After a while, he covered his face with both of his hands. Kersten was surprised, never having seen his patient in this pose.

Himmler lowered his hands from his face, but looked away from Kersten. Kersten could see nonetheless that there was guilt and anguish in Himmler's eyes.

"My dear Kersten. I must concede that some unplanned and unfortunate things happen in the camps sometimes. War is messy, after all. A few of the *Kommandants,* one or two, are overly zealous in enforcing the rules. They are merely trying to impress me, thinking that I will reward them by moving them up the ladder of command or transferring them to a camp closer to their home. Or every now and then, one of the guards—usually a Pole or a Ukrainian—gets carried away in punishing an inmate who isn't working hard enough. But once I hear of such exceptions to our usual good order and discipline, I make sure that the perpetrators are duly punished."

Himmler saw the look of disappointment in Kersten's eyes. "I am terribly distressed, my dear Kersten. I cannot say more."

"All that bothers you bothers me, *Herr Reichsführer.*"

"It's not a question of me, Doctor."

"What is the matter, then? Perhaps if you unburden yourself of what is making you anxious, I may be able to help you."

"No one can help me with this, Kersten."

He looked up at the round, florid, reassuring face of his doctor, the good and wise eyes, and said, "I will tell you what I can. You are the only person I can talk to about this. I can't even tell my wife."

Whatever anger Kersten had brought with him when he had entered Himmler's office was replaced now by professional forbearance and consideration for his suffering patient. "I'm all ears, *Herr Reichsführer.*"

He wondered if Himmler actually knew how to push this button in.

"After France collapsed," Himmler began, "the *Führer* made

several offers of peace to England. But the Jews who control Churchill and run that country rejected his kind offers. 'Nothing short of unconditional surrender,' they said. The idiots don't understand that nothing worse could happen to the world than a protracted war between Germany and England. The *Führer* knows that there will be no peace on earth as long as the Jews are in power...as long as the Jews continue to *exist*."

Kersten noted that this time, Himmler's railings against the Jews were not uttered with the same dogmatic certainty and vitriol as usual. Himmler's voice seemed to quaver slightly.

Hitler is beginning to see that he may lose this war. But his madness cannot accept it. He needs a reason for his losses in the east, something that will explain and excuse everything. As usual, pin them on the Jews.

"And so?" Kersten asked.

"So...the *Führer* has ordered me to ensure that the Jews are destroyed. Eliminated from Europe. Entirely. No exceptions."

"But you cannot," Kersten cried, almost involuntarily. "Think of the horror, the suffering. What will the world think of Germany?"

Usually, Himmler was lively, even intense, in his treatment conversations with Kersten. But on this day, his face remained impassive and his voice was dull, flat, resigned.

Kersten wondered if this was the moment to broach a medical theory he'd been mulling over in his mind for quite a while.

"You don't think that horrendous orders such as this from your *Führer* have something to do with your abdominal miseries, *Herr Reichsführer?*"

"What in the world are you talking about, Kersten?"

"What I mean is that your body may be expressing your deep, profound ambivalence of your mind about your *Führer*, at least about his strategies, particularly this unspeakable one."

"My *ambivalence*? I think if you ask any of my colleagues or my subordinates, they would disagree wholeheartedly and unanimously. They would testify to my decisiveness...Kersten, I could have you shot for suggesting that I am in any way disloyal to the *Führer*."

Kersten ignored the implied threat. "Do you remember that you told me once that you felt Gobbles' and Göring's solution to the existence of Jews in the *Reich* was more drastic and unnecessarily severe than the one you favored? Your idea of Madagascar?"

"Of course, I remember. What is all this about?"

"Well, *Herr Reichsführer*, I have observed that whenever your *Führer* seems to side with them, or even take the solution of the matter of the Jews to a more violent extreme, you experience the most violent bouts of pain. I can't help but suspect that there's a connection."

Himmler began to squirm in his chair.

"Doctor, I have the greatest respect for your abilities, as you know. But perhaps you have been working too hard. I've noticed that lately you see distracted, more distant. You're wandering into areas of sheer speculation and conjecture. You said yourself that you have very little interest in politics."

Then, abruptly and decisively, he added, "This part of our conversation is over, Kersten."

Kersten decided that to pursue the matter further would not yield results. Instead, he ventured back into the territory of the liquidation.

"*Herr Reichsführer*, though I have had my suspicions and heard rumors, this is really the first confirmation I have heard of the possibility of mass extermination. I...I have no words..."

"There's more, my dear Kersten."

Kersten's heart plummeted. Himmler seemed ready to pick up where he had left off when Kersten had inserted his theoretical suspicions.

"The *Führer* has demanded... *demanded,* that crematoria be built in many of the camps for which I have ultimate oversight...Dachau, Sachsenhausen, Auschwitz, others. Any new camp will not be built without crematoria."

Kersten's heart was too sickened to hear more. He was beginning to feel nauseous.

"I didn't *want* this horrible assignment, Kersten," Himmler continued, almost pleading for Kersten to believe in his innocence. "'*Mein Führer*,' I begged him. 'I and the SS are ready to die for you...but please do not give me this mission.'

"Then, the *Führer* erupted into one of his awful, awful tantrums. He literally jumped on me, seized me by the neck, and shouted, 'You spineless mouse! I've made you into everything you are. And now you dare refuse to obey me? You are behaving like a traitor.'

"After that, I had no choice but to ask for his forgiveness and to reiterate my utmost loyalty and full agreement to follow his orders."

"Follow his orders...even when they are crazy?"

"The *Führer's* orders are not crazy. His is the greatest mind in all of Europe...if not the world."

"And if the greatest mind on earth ordered you to kill your own wife and son and daughter?"

"I would do it without thinking," Himmler answered. "Because the *Führer* would have a good reason unknown by us to give such an order."

Kersten wanted to hear no more. The acrid taste of nausea began to burn his esophagus. Never had the sickening feeling that he was living among madmen been so strong. He had to take several deep breaths.

"Then, you will *burn* Jews in these crematoria?" Kersten could hardly get the words out.

"Not alive, of course. Only after they have died in the camps."

Kersten's mind was feverish—hijacked by repetitive flashes of the nauseating photographs he had been shown of dog-tired Jews in the camps being struck and kicked mercilessly, of bodies shrunken and shriveled by starvation, of faces horrifically gaunt and withered until barely recognizable as faces of human beings. Now the implausible image of Jewish bodies incinerated. It was difficult to breathe.

"Or killed somehow by your men." Kersten had reached his limit. Turning away and heading for the door, he bellowed to Himmler, "This treatment session is over." He slammed the door shut and stepped into the corridor, feeling faint and nauseous, his heart beating rapidly.

~~~

Kersten leaned all his weight on his right hand against the wall of the corridor outside Himmler's office. With his left, he rubbed his forehead furiously. His mind replayed an old but vivid film of another face...in Finland...twenty years ago...the skin charred and foully pungent...two black vacant spheres where the eyes should have been...the rest of the body scorched like a log on the floor of a forest after a fire...the skin putrefying...the young man's mouth agape but emitting no sound...beyond the strength to give voice to his intolerable pain...the charred face and body brought into emergency ward at Meilahti Hospital in Helsinki on that damned, damning night in 1921...gang-beaten and set aflame by brutish White militiamen for being a socialist...for being born a Jew...the physician on call listed as Felix Kersten, M.D...the undisguised fright on Kersten's own face as he entered the ward and beheld the patient...the putrescent odor in the room...the rancid smell of burned flesh...Kersten's feet immobile as though nailed firmly to the floor...the sacred charge to approach and treat the seared body and try to alleviate the patient's suffering...but his inability, sheer inability, to move...the volcanic, acidic discharge beginning to erupt from his stomach to his throat...Kersten's hand pushed tightly against his mouth...his turning and running from the room...his retching in a patient's commode in a neighboring ward...splashes of greenish vomit on his white doctor tunic to remind him of his cowardice...the anxious glances back over his shoulder to verify he wasn't seen...the furtive, hasty exit along the corridor and down the stairs...the shameful slithering through an empty lobby...the palpable sense, nonetheless, that his spineless retreat from duty was being observed from an invisible gallery by his laughing supervisors and instructors...the pangs of shame in the pit of his stomach...the utter piercing shame of his failure...the disgraceful bankruptcy of his fidelity to Hippocratic pledge...that he did not "apply for the benefit of this suffering Jew all measures that are required"...that he abandoned the man on his sickbed...his deathbed...that he lacked the courage to see and touch the wounds...his misgivings since that at heart he might have an ancient inherent vestige of anti-Semitism...his disgracing of his liberal, tolerant upbringing and education...the shame he has borne over the years and across the distances...even to this day.

~~~

Kersten didn't appear at Himmler's office for the two days after fleeing in a panic in the middle of a treatment session. Himmler's adjutant, Brandt, and eventually Himmler himself, telephoned Kersten, demanding that he come immediately to minister to Himmler's excruciating abdominal pain. When Kersten told a white lie that he himself was under the weather, Himmler softened and revealed a more compassionate side, which never failed to disarm Kersten, even though he knew Himmler could change faster than the fickle sky at sea.

"Oh, better than anyone, I understand how debilitating illness can be, Kersten. I will get through my pain somehow. Take the rest of the day to pay attention to your own health. I'll see you tomorrow?"

Kersten wasn't sure he would be over the hangover and shame from his panic by tomorrow. "I will see how I feel, *Herr Reichsführer*. I assure you I will be there as soon as I feel better."

The panic attack in Himmler's office had seemed to arise out of nowhere. He hadn't consciously thought about the incident with the Jewish patient in the Meilahti Hospital for many years. He was convinced the trauma he experienced had been hermetically sealed in the past. The supervising doctor had been shocked and disappointed in

Kersten's abject difficulty in facing the burned patient, much less treating him. Their next scheduled mentor-mentee consultation was when he recommended that Kersten no longer pursue the track of becoming a surgeon and consider massage instead. At the time, the bubble of Kersten's manly pride had been punctured. But he recalled also how relieved he was to be given an alternative track to pursue, and thus save face.

Had he not been advised to investigate massage, he would not have met Dr. Ko. Consequently, he would not have discovered the priceless gift for healing in his hands.

If I had become a surgeon and not a masseur, I would not have been put into this unforeseen and unforeseeable position where I am the private doctor and therapist for the commander of the SS. I would not have been able to prevent Auguste Diehn's foreman from dying in Dachau. I would not have been able to manipulate Himmler so that he ordered the release of other Jews. Would I have been in a position to save Jiri Hudak?

But now, after the revelation by Himmler of Hitler's unspeakable intention to liquidate all of the Jews in the Third Reich—all of Europe, for that matter—the rescue of a few individual Jews seemed to Kersten utterly inconsequential. Were Himmler to succeed in carrying out Hitler's bizarre, downright satanic command, Kersten's securing the life of one Jew here, another one there, was so negligible. In the face of the annihilation of thousands upon thousands, perhaps millions, his efforts amounted to a spit in the ocean, a mere candle held up in a dark universe.

No, I feel the same as Hitler. One Jew at a time is too slow, too inefficient, such a poor stewardship of opportunity. I must find some means to speed up the process of rescue, to match Hitler's pace of annihilation with the pace of liberation, to save as many as my advantageous and strategic position enables me to do and for as long as I have the opportunity.

He remembered his bold intervention with Himmler to delay Hitler's forced march of the "irreconcilables" of Holland to Poland, probably to be murdered there if they hadn't died on the journey. Himmler had told him that up to three million could be relocated in the first wave, with five to six million awaiting a similar forced removal after them. That was a number his mind could not comprehend. Suddenly, Kersten didn't feel so insignificant. His mind began to focus resolutely and energetically on possibilities rather than on limitations.

By some accident of history or twist of fate, some writing in the stars, or the machinations of some such other force beyond his own power to control or comprehend, he had been placed in this fortuitous, if originally unwanted, position where he could push back against the forces of death that were blitzing across all of Europe. He vowed in that moment of sudden clarity to push the envelope because many lives depended on it, to test the limits of possibility because the stakes had been raised much higher now, to tempt fate, and to the limit of what is possible, to defy the devil incarnate himself.

CHAPTER TWENTY-FOUR

Berlin: June 12, 1942

"Dr. Kersten, the *Reichsführer* is very anxious to see you today," Brandt said over the telephone.

"That makes today a rather ordinary day, doesn't it?" Kersten countered sardonically.

Brandt smiled, but chose to ignore Kersten's irony. "It's not to treat him this time, Doctor. Instead, he has something to show you. He says it's important for you to see it."

Kersten took his time preparing to leave for *Prinz Albrecht Strasse*. Whatever Himmler had to show him, he would see when he was good and ready. He did have to admit to a certain level of curiosity. What might it possibly be?

When Kersten arrived at the SS Chancellery, he was surprised to see that Himmler was not alone in his office. Standing before his desk was the tall SS officer whom Kersten had met briefly in Brandt's office some months before. "He may be able to help you" is what Brandt had intimated to him about the officer: Lieutenant-General Walter Schellenberg, Director of Intelligence.

Schellenberg bowed formally in Kersten's direction by way of greeting. Kersten returned the greeting by extending his right hand to shake Schellenberg's. They looked into each other's eyes almost in a conspiratorial fashion.

Kersten looked over at Himmler behind his desk to see if he had noticed the other two men's mutual cordial greeting. Himmler might not have been summoning him for a treatment session, as Brandt had said, but Kersten saw immediately the look of affliction on Himmler's face.

"You called for me, *Herr Reichsführer*? Brandt tells me you have something to show me."

Without a word, Himmler pushed back his chair and stood, not as erect, Kersten noticed, as he usually did when dressed in his full SS commander's uniform. Then he knelt on one knee above the black safe which had been installed into the floor, so that only its face and combination dial were accessible. He opened the safe, grabbed two identical red and black file folders and handed one to a dumbfounded Kersten, the other to Schellenberg.

"This is to be handled with utmost secrecy, gentlemen."

Kersten looked down at the closed file folder, and back up with consternation.

"Only I and Brandt have seen its contents. Other than Dr. Morell, of course. At least officially. I can't help but suspect that before the file left the *Führer's* Chancellery, Göbbels and Göring snuck a peek at it."

"Undoubtedly, yes," chuckled Schellenberg.

Schellenberg's chuckling indicated to Kersten that Schellenberg was no greater a fan of Hitler's two bootlickers than were Himmler and he himself.

Kersten slowly opened the file folder. The title page read "The State of the *Führer's* Health 1942." Twenty-five densely typewritten pages followed.

"You're a medically trained man, Kersten. Go ahead and read it. I can wait. I've already had the displeasure."

Kersten began perusing the report, not taking the time to read every word. He hadn't gotten through many paragraphs before he had a good idea of what was in the later pages. The first part summarized Hitler's past medical history. It mentioned how Hitler had continued until the present to suffer the negative effects of poison gas in the Great War, and had been for a while in danger of total blindness. Morell also reported that in 1937, and again at the beginning of the current year, certain symptoms had reappeared of the syphilis he had contracted in his youth. Those included insomnia, dizziness, severe headaches. Of utmost concern, Morell reported, was the progressive paralysis, which had the likely potential, sooner or later, to affect Hitler's mind as well.

At this startling statement, Kersten stopped skimming the report. He made no comment, but looked at Schellenberg, who returned the glance.

There just might be a once in a lifetime opportunity here to alter the course of this damned war without firing a shot. Seize it, Felix. For heaven's sake, carpe diem.

"You realize now what anxieties dog me, gentlemen. The world regards Adolf Hitler as a strong man made of iron—and that's how he must go down in history. The greater German *Reich* will stretch from the Urals to the North Sea after the war. That will be the *Führer's* greatest achievement. He's the greatest military man who ever lived.

We're almost at the goal, gentlemen, but there's still a mopping up operation to complete. The *Führer* needs a clean bill of health to finish what he started."

Kersten appreciated how severely anxious Himmler must be that he would share such confidential and possibly damaging information. Kersten took pride in how much the closed, guarded Himmler had grown to trust him. He obviously trusted Schellenberg likewise.

"*Herr Reichsführer,* I am sure you realize what this report means," Kersten commented, trying not to sound too eager. "The *Führer* must resign his position immediately, of course. He needs serious medical care."

He glanced again at Schellenberg to read his silent response. If Schellenberg disagreed, he gave no indication on his face.

"He's already receiving medical care from Dr. Morell," Himmler responded defensively. Then he modified his response by adding, "Granted, I suspect that Morell is a quack. The man was nothing more than a ship's doctor before the *Führer* rescued him from such trivial work. Though no one says it aloud, but some like Göring and Bormann spread whispers that Morell is conducting experiments on the *Führer* with drugs and all sorts of injections."

Schellenberg remained resolutely silent. Kersten thought perhaps he was deferring for the time being to the medical doctor. Kersten was eager to know where Schellenberg stood. He took Schellenberg's silence as his invitation for him to continue.

"Your *Führer* must be convinced by someone close to him, someone he trusts, that he needs to find and name a successor to take over from him—just temporarily, of course—while he seeks long-term medical treatment immediately. You understand, I'm sure, *Herr Reichsführer,* that it is quite possible, with his condition, that at any moment, under any crisis, his judgment could fail. Or at worst, his mind could be clouded by delusions and megalomania." Kersten hoped that he didn't sound too much as if he were exaggerating, which, of course, he wasn't.

"Whoever dares to suggest that to the *Führer* is looking to be out of a job. Or worse," Himmler countered anxiously.

"Actually, I was thinking of *you, Herr Reichsführer*, as the most logical person to give him such advice."

Schellenberg looked at Kersten, who seemed with his eyes to encourage him to continue with this line of argument.

"*Me*? Are you insane, Kersten? The *Führer* has made no provision for a successor. He believes deep in his heart that he has been uniquely called by fate to continue to restore Germany to its deserved greatness, even after the war."

"I am under the impression that *Herr* Hitler trusts you more than just about any of his associates."

"Kersten, even if the *Führer* didn't have me shot on the spot, Göbbels and Göring would be quick to point out to him that I am giving such questionable advice in order to further my own career, that I want to be *Führer* myself. They'll have me just where they want me. Don't you agree, Schellenberg?"

"I'm afraid you are right about them, *Herr Reichsführer*. But Dr. Kersten is making good sense. This report helps explain those inconsistencies and discrepancies in the *Führer's* long speeches in his meetings with us. You've noticed them, too, have you not, *Herr Reichsführer?*"

Himmler looked as though he didn't know how to answer.

"The future of the *Reich* may be at stake here," Schellenberg said very earnestly while looking at Himmler directly into the eyes.

That was Schellenberg's first explicit indication to Kersten of some unspoken, surreptitious alliance between them, even though one wore the SS uniform and the other did not.

"What will you do then?" Kersten asked Himmler in a voice that was beginning to betray a growing exasperation. "Will you simply let the matter alone, for heaven's sake, and wait for Hitler's condition to get worse and worse? Can—"

Himmler interrupted. "I remind you, Kersten, that he is *Herr* Hitler to you."

"Yes, of course," Kersten said dismissively. "But what I want to ask is, can you endure the idea that your beloved German people are being led by a man who is very probably suffering from a progressive paralysis? Good heavens!"

Schellenberg stepped into the conversation calmly, perhaps lest Kersten proceed to mention the term "mental illness." "*Herr Reichsführer*, I remind you that though the campaign in Russia started well last year, and we have surrounded Leningrad, almost a whole year later we haven't succeeded in penetrating the capital itself. Isn't it an ominous repeat of our attempt to take Moscow last winter? We were stalled forty kilometers outside the city, you remember, and then shamefully repulsed. Does the *Führer* really believe that we will be any more successful in Stalingrad, which he has ordered the

Wehrmacht to take next at all costs? The tide may be beginning to turn for the worse in Russia, and therefore the whole eastern front."

Schellenberg grew increasingly animated and impassioned as he spoke. Pointing his head in the direction of the Finnish masseur, Schellenberg continued. "Those who were paying attention in '39 and '40 to the Russians' eventual defeat of the Finns know how capable they are of raising thousands, if not millions, of reinforcements to defend Leningrad, and then mount a counteroffensive."

Kersten gave a nod that was tinged with regret. "We Finns learned that the hard way, to be sure."

Schellenberg paused strategically and looked earnestly into Himmler's eyes.

Go for it, Schellenberg. You're making progress.

"You have said yourself that Göring's *Luftwaffe* is ineffective in defending against Russian airstrikes on our troops. The *Führer* isn't aware of that, of course, and I think you know why, *Herr Reichsführer.* The others in the *Führer's* inner circle are sycophants who share only information with him that they know he wants to hear."

Kersten noticed that Himmler looked unusually pensive. Was at least a part of him agreeing with Schellenberg?

It was Schellenberg's turn now to look over at Kersten for some sign of solidarity as a tag team. In spite of being not quite sure of Schellenberg's own ambitions, Kersten carefully nodded his head slightly in Kersten's direction for encouragement, hoping that Himmler would not notice.

"*Herr Reichsführer*, you are a brilliant leader. Surely, you can discern the signs that we are having difficulty fighting this war on two fronts. But now with this additional information about the *Führer's* health, especially his mental health, the likelihood of victory has diminished greatly, has it not?"

"Do you really have a crystal ball that makes you so sure you can predict the future accurately?" Himmler shot back.

"No, of course not. But we military men are trained to observe what direction the winds are blowing...I am wondering if this may not be the opportune moment to pursue your idea of an independent peace with the Western allies so that we can focus all our attention and deploy all our resources trying to triumph in the east. *Herr Reichsführer*, did you not yourself raise that possibility with me in a conversation? That was when you took protective custody of Professor Haushofer after the

Führer discovered that he had assisted Hess make his daring but ill-conceived flight to Scotland to try to make a secret separate peace with Britain. Do you remember?"

Himmler stared hard at the surface of his desk and adjusted his spectacles. He looked as though convicted by a prosecutor in court. Kersten was surprised at this new information. He admired the forthrightness and candor, the sheer doggedness, of Schellenberg's strategy. Again, Kersten filed it away for future reference. Still, Schellenberg remained an enigma.

Himmler remained silent for a long time. Then he rose from his desk resolutely, adjusted his posture so that he was once again as straight as a board, and announced his decision. "The *Führer's* illness has still not yet gone far enough. I will watch carefully and there will be time enough to act once it's established that Morrell's report is correct. These symptoms—and remember, gentlemen, that they are only symptoms— are likely the effects of the *Führer's* exhaustion from his single-minded carrying out of his heroic duties on behalf of the German people, that's all."

Kersten and Schellenberg exchanged glances that silently communicated their mutual regret that they had been unable to move Himmler off the spot and get him to pull his head out of the sand.

Himmler extended his hand to both Kersten and Schellenberg. "Thank you for coming, gentlemen. That is all. Good day. *Heil, Hitler!*"

HISTORICAL INTERLUDE

Algot Niska and Jiri Hudak participated in the so-called Winter War between Finland and the Soviet Union in 1939-1940 (Chapter Twenty). The Soviet Union had sought to claim parts of the Finnish territory adjacent to the border in exchange for land elsewhere. The Soviets wanted the Karelia region of Finland as a buffer to protect Leningrad. The Finns refused the exchange. Consequently, on November 30, 1939, Soviet forces invaded Finland.

The Finns fought the vastly more numerous and better equipped Russian forces alone. Germany did, however, provide Finland with critical material support and military cooperation during the Winter War as part of its overall plan to keep its options open on a possible eastern front.

On June 22, 1941, Germany launched Operation Barbarossa, an all-out invasion of the Soviet Union. Germany wished to invade the Soviet Union from at least three directions, including the north. Hitler petitioned Finland to grant permission for his troops to transect Finnish Lapland from Nazi-occupied Norway and infiltrate the Russian border from the north. Meanwhile, other German units pinched into the Soviet Union from Poland and the Balkans. In retaliation for the Finns' giving consent to Hitler, the Soviet Union launched a major air offensive on Finland on June 25. The so-called Continuation War, essentially Part II of the Finno-Russian conflict, had commenced.

In response, Finnish leaders sought a mutual assistance arrangement with Germany. The two nations were to become "cobelligerents" working together to defeat their common enemy, the Soviet Union. This was a unique and unprecedented military accord. The Finns were careful to specify in the pact that it was not a conventional military or political alliance, merely a covenant of mutual convenience between two sovereign nations. Finland would participate in the first phase of Operation Barbarossa as "brothers-in-arms" with German forces, but under Finnish command. In exchange, Germany guaranteed promises of military materiel and food supplies.

It was stipulated that once the joint Finnish-German forces had succeeded in recapturing Finnish Karelia and conquering East Karelia, Finnish forces were to halt their offensive. Much to the frustration and disappointment of Hitler and the German generals, the Finns ceased their advance 30 kilometers outside Leningrad at the pre-war Finland-Soviet Union border.

In 1944, Soviet air forces conducted further devastating air attacks over Helsinki, other major Finnish cities, and Finnish airfields used by the Germans. Eventually, in mid-1944, an overwhelming Soviet offensive drove the Finns from most of the territories they had regained. A ceasefire ended hostilities on September 5 and was followed by the Moscow Armistice. Finland agreed to cede its repatriated territories, pay sizeable reparations to the Soviet Union, and forcibly expel all German forces from its soil (The Lapland War 1944-1945).

In its precarious position sandwiched between two major combatants, the Finnish government managed miraculously to maintain its independence from both Germany and the Soviet Union.

CHAPTER TWENTY-FIVE

Vinnitsa, Ukraine: July 16, 1942

Kersten almost tripped on an upraised root as he walked through the copse of pine trees between the cottage he had been assigned and the cottage that served as Himmler's office at the German field headquarters in the Ukraine. Hitler had summoned his top leaders there to receive first-hand updates from *Wehrmacht* officers on the progress of Operation Barbarossa, the massive incursion into Russia initiated in 1941.

Himmler didn't look up from the papers he was skimming at his desk when Kersten entered the makeshift office.

"Good morning, Doctor. In the mood to get some real Finnish home cooking?"

Kersten tried to feign a look of confusion by the question. He had heard from Ambassador Mäki about Himmler's possible imminent mission to Finland. The fact that Himmler even asked the question seemed to indicate that he still wasn't aware that Kersten was serving as an informant to the Finnish delegation in Berlin.

"You look a little baffled this morning, Kersten."

"A little, yes. Where could you possibly get genuine fish pie, Karelian pies, salmon soup and whipped lingonberry porridge here in the middle of the Ukraine?"

"You misunderstand, my dear Kersten. I'm offering you a week or so of Finnish cuisine, which I know you have been missing, instead of all the heavy cabbage rolls and sauerkraut in Berlin."

"Well, of course, I'd love the taste of Finland. But I don't quite understand how."

"The *Führer* has ordered me to Finland to have a little friendly chat with your President Ryti and Field Marshall Mannerheim about the little agreement to cooperate you Finns made with us last year. We leave in a little over a week. I want you to be with me in case my condition flares up."

"Wasn't your *Führer* there just last month?"

"Yes, he was there to charm Mannerheim and thus pave the way for my visit. He warmed up the audience, and now I am to regale them with the punchline."

Kersten couldn't picture Himmler telling a joke, much less delivering a funny punchline. But his own spirits rose as he thought about planting his feet on Finnish soil again. They sagged almost as quickly, however, when he realized that there was no secure way, from the Ukrainian forest, to contact Ambassador Mäki in Berlin to confirm the rumor. He wanted to give him a heads-up.

"You don't look especially pleased or excited, Doctor. Is there something wrong?"

"No, *Herr Reichsführer.*" He fumbled a bit to invent something to say. "It's just that you caught me quite by surprise. Of course, I'm pleased to be going."

"I have other news for you, Kersten, which I think you will consider good. We finally caught up with your elusive countryman, the smuggler, the guy with the name Niska."

"Algot Niska?"

"Yes, that's the one, the one I asked you about a few years ago. He had been smuggling Jews out of Germany and Austria and slipped away right under our noses."

"And you say, you caught up with him? That's good news for you and The *Reich*, but I fail to see how that's good news for me as a Finn."

"Or as a fellow Jew-lover, I'd say. Anyway, we caught up with him, but he managed to give us the slip again. Not on his own, mind you, but rather with the help of that shifty government I am going to talk with."

"Oh?"

"The SS tracked him down to a seaside cabin on one of the small islands off the Finnish west coast. General Buschenhagen ordered them to apprehend him and ship him back to Germany. A military tribunal would try him and sentence him to one of our camps."

Himmler paused to let this sink in Kersten's consciousness. Kersten tried not to let his grave sense of disappointment be obvious. He maintained a stoic face.

"But the Finnish High Command intervened on the bastard's behalf. 'This stalwart man fought bravely in the Winter War against our common enemy, the Russians,' they boasted. 'Now that together we have signed a memorandum of understanding to continue to fight this mutual enemy hand-in-hand and side-by-side, we cannot and will not release him into your custody. Besides, isn't *Herr* Niska on *your* side now after our agreement?'

"Such naïve drivel! So as not to get our agreement off to a bad start, however, Buschenhagen had no choice but salute, turn around and come back to headquarters in Helsinki empty-handed."

The thought that the SS now had headquarters in the capital, Helsinki, was beyond repugnant to Kersten. "No doubt, uttering a few choice German words under his breath as he did so," he said while was sporting a secret expansive smile on his heart.

"The *Führer* has given me a lengthy agenda. I am tempted to register a protest about this with Field Marshall Mannerheim of the Finnish High Command, however. But since he and I have to put our heads together about coordinating our joint advance into Russia, I've got to swallow my pride and let go of that idea. The *Führer* is mad as hell at you Finns. We could penetrate Leningrad and wipe it off the face of the earth if you obstinate Finns would just do as he asks and deliver artillery and ammunition from Karelia across Lake Ladoga to our forces outside the city when we have it in the palm of our hands."

"*Herr Reichsführer,* let me remind you that the Finnish government agreed to accompany German forces only as far as the Karelian-Russian border, no farther. We are your cobelligerent, not your ally, and in this specific conflict only. There's a difference. Finland isn't crazy enough to trespass into Soviet territory. That would be suicide. That's for your *Wehrmacht* to attempt."

"Yes, I know what the agreement was. But the *Führer* wants to re-negotiate that part of the memorandum of understanding. I'm sure the powers-that-be in Finland will see the wisdom in acquiescing to Germany's revised wishes."

Once again, Kersten was irritated at the arrogance of the Nazis. *Revised wishes!* But he had made his point. He held his tongue.

"But the most important part of the agenda is to talk over the Jewish Question with President Ryti."

There it is again. The Germans and their damnable obsession with the Jewish Question.

"I'm not the president, of course," Kersten said. "But I think you need to be prepared for some resistance when discussing that matter."

Himmler's body straightened noticeably. The blood rushed to his face.

"Your president should not forget that our part of the bargain with Finland is that we will supply adequate foodstuffs and fuel. My intelligence sources report that their stocks of bread and grain have dwindled to the point that they have only three or four weeks' supply remaining. The president will have to choose between hunger for his nation and delivering up their Jews to us."

Kersten was moved by his own anger to respond and let the chips fall where they may. He took a deep breath, and then raised the volume of his voice and took a bold step in Himmler's direction.

"Is this the way your *Führer* treats a brother-in-arms?"

"We will abide no allowances. Finland must do as the *Führer* wishes."

Kersten was ready to risk pushing Himmler's ire even further.

"Let me remind you," he replied, gritting his teeth, "that according to the memorandum of understanding, Finland remains an independent state. You can't treat us like the Poles or Ukrainians. We agreed only to fight the Russians by your side as a sovereign nation. We will do in our own country as we like."

Himmler's back was up. Kersten noticed that Himmler's eyeglasses were beginning to fog up.

"Don't talk horseshit, Kersten! The independence of Germany's neighbors and associates, whatever the agreement, only lasts as long as it suits the *Führer.* Finland is no different."

CHAPTER TWENTY-SIX

Vinnitsya, Ukraine: July 21, 1942

Kersten was dangling between excited anticipation and nervous apprehension about the mission to Finland. He had to wait in any case until Himmler had returned from a quick trip to Poland.

Himmler was gone almost three days. Kersten was anxious for his return because their scheduled departure from Berlin to Finland was less than a week away. The way Kersten discovered that Himmler had arrived back at the field headquarters in the Ukraine was that a breathless SS private had knocked on his cottage door, interrupting his nap.

"I'm sorry to disturb you, Dr. Kersten. But the *Reichsführer* is in great distress. He wants you at his quarters as soon as possible."

Kersten suspected than that whatever the purpose of Himmler's trip to Poland, it had triggered another relentless attack in his abdomen.

Kersten could hear Himmler's moaning in pain even before he took the three small steps up to his cottage. Once he opened the door, the groaning was as loud as Kersten had ever heard coming from Himmler.

"Kersten! I thought you'd never get here. What took you so long? I'm the one who had to travel the kilometers from Poland."

Kersten made no effort to protest that he had come as quickly as he could. "Well, I'm here now."

Kersten rolled up the sleeves of his shirt and launched into another massage session. Within seconds, it seems, Himmler's groans softened into whimpers.

"I should have taken you along with me to Poland," Himmler managed to say. "I don't know why I didn't."

"I'm all ears, *Herr Reichsführer.* But let me say first, welcome back."

"It's the *Führer*, of course, who dispatched me to Poland. He wanted a first-hand report on the conditions in the Jewish ghetto in Warsaw and our progress in cleansing it."

"Cleansing? Whatever do you mean?"

Kersten was well aware that Himmler didn't mean the SS were sweeping the streets and washing the gutters.

"The *Führer* believes the time has come to tear it down and liquidate the population of that cesspool. And I tend to agree."

"Liquidate them? That's over 450,000 people."

"450,000 Jews, Kersten, not people."

Kersten was speechless. He knew better that to object at this time.

"Our German industrial leaders like Többens and Schultz couldn't depend on the ghetto Jews as workers in their plants and factories any longer. It's as though the Jews were working slowly very deliberately. They're truly such a lazy bunch. A stiff-necked race, as their own God himself calls them in the Bible."

Kersten was both incensed and horrified. He decided to maintain a diplomatic silence, however.

"When I arrived in Warsaw, my usually dependable and efficient SS boys were having difficulty getting the Jews to cooperate in gathering at the *Unschlagplatz* to be marched to the trains for resettlement in a camp a little northeast of the city."

"The camp named Treblinka, by any chance?"

"Yes. That's one of our newer resettlement camps. State of the art. You know about it, do you?"

Kersten brought back to mind the revealing, horrific photos by the two Swedish journalists of the work camps just a half-year earlier. He was leaning toward giving credence to the rumors that the Treblinka camp, like Auschwitz and Birkenau, was of an altogether higher order of brutality than even the worst of the others.

"Treblinka is really a camp for extermination, isn't it?" Kersten asked accusingly, "For 'liquidation' as you call it?"

"We have installed gas chambers there, yes. But this new method of liquidation is so much more humane than the crude practice before it of lining the Jews up on the edge of a pit, shooting them in the back and watching them fall on top of one another at the bottom of the pit."

"I should be gratified and comforted by that?"

"Kersten, I don't want to debate the merits or drawbacks of extermination with you right now. I know full well what you think of it. I want to get back to my experience in Warsaw."

Kersten reined in his anger and resumed his neutral professional demeanor. "My apologies. Please, continue."

"So since my men were not succeeding with the obstinate Jews, I decided to order them to set every single block on fire immediately—

every last one. Before too long, one block after another was blazing hotter than hell. I'll tell you, Kersten, that got the Jews to scamper out of their hiding places and dugouts like the rats they are. It was quite a show. Some were jumping out of the third and fourth story windows to escape the smoke and flames."

Kersten gave no visible indication on his face but his insides were sickened to the core.

"You know, Kersten, the will to live even among Jews is astounding to me. Some of those who had jumped from their flat, their bones undoubtedly broken, still tried to crawl across the street to the blocks of buildings that hadn't yet been set aflame, or were just partially burned. It was a pathetic sight."

Kersten could hardly stand to hear any more of this depraved abuse of life. But he knew better than to get up and leave in the middle of Himmler's monologue. As painful as it was to listen, there might be some suggestion of diagnosis and treatment hidden in all the drivel, some constructive reason to justify sitting through it.

"Our SS men shot them before they could get to the other side."

Kersten closed his eyes slowly in sorrow.

"I left the ghetto in short order and went to observe the loading of the Jews onto the railcars at the siding."

Suddenly, Himmler's voice became less strident and confident. He took a deep breath before he continued.

"The Jews who had obeyed the original order to gather at the *Platz* were carrying small suitcases with clothes they would need as they were being resettled. Of course, we knew that they might have stashed whatever valuables they had left in the suitcases. They were ordered to put all the suitcases in one car on the train."

"They were told, no doubt, that they could retrieve their luggage when they arrived at Treblinka?" Kersten commented sadly.

"Well, yes. To be truthful, though, they wouldn't need their suitcases when they got to Treblinka."

Kersten was sure he detected a definite note of wistfulness, a hint of shame even, in Himmler's voice. Strange.

"I watched the whole process impassively in my official capacity. I was making sure that the men were performing their duty properly and efficiently. The Jews being loaded onto the train were just pathetic faceless, nameless specters to me...But Kersten, I must have been exhausted doing my duty. Because what I saw next affected me in a way very few incidents in this war have."

Himmler was no longer giving an objective official report to Kersten. His monologue was edging toward painful personal disclosure.

"Oh? Can you say more about what you saw?" Kersten had to avoid getting too close to Himmler's emotions too quickly lest he panic and shut down completely.

"I saw a young woman, a teacher no doubt, lead a group of little boys to the railcar. I assumed they were her students. She stood by the open door of the car and smilingly supervised as each boy laid his book bag or knapsack carefully, almost lovingly, onto the floor of the railcar."

It was curious to Kersten that Himmler should choose to describe *this* particular scenario in detail.

"Kersten, the scene brought me back to the closing day each year of the Catholic school in München where I was a teacher before I joined the party. Suddenly, I started to feel the same melancholy as I did every summer when my pupils were leaving for holidays. Imagine that. Right there, at the edge of the notorious ghetto, I was reminiscing about my little male students who are undoubtedly grown up by now, maybe serving in the *Wehrmacht* or maybe even the SS."

Himmler's eyes were beginning to dampen. His thin lower lip was quivering.

"There was one particular boy. I could hear him asking his teacher if he'd be able to get his notebook of drawings back after the train ride. 'I'm sure you will get it back when we get to our new home. We'll have a school there just as we did here,' I heard the teacher answer. She was trying her very best to sound reassuring and cheerful, but I could tell from the pained look on her face that she knew she was telling him a white lie. The boy seemed satisfied, so much did he trust his teacher."

"I suspect that the teacher knew that his was not to be any customary relocation out into the country," Kersten added.

"Yes, I suspect so, too. What a sacred thing it is, Kersten, this innocent trust of a pupil for his teacher…I was so very moved…so very moved."

Kersten sensed that silence would encourage Himmler to say more.

"This little boy, he looked almost like one particular boy named Rolf that I had as a pupil one year. Rolf was so bright-eyed, so smart and curious, so respectful that it would have been hard for any teacher not to love him."

"And you did?" Kersten asked.

"Yes," Himmler said sadly. He turned and looked away from Kersten, as though in shame like a little boy himself, confessing some petty act of disobedience to a parent.

"I approached the boy and his teacher near the railcar and lifted him into my arms. He made no effort to resist. 'I will personally see to it that you get your drawing notebook back,' I told him."

"And did you?" Kersten felt like adding, "Did you tell the boy a white lie, too?" but resisted the temptation to rub Himmler's nose in it.

"Unfortunately, I could not," Himmler confessed on the verge of tears. "I couldn't go ahead and meet the train at Treblinka, of course. Besides, I noticed that at that moment all eyes were on me. Globocnik, my appointee to supervise the resettlement, the SS who were loading the Jews onto the train, even the *Kapos;* they all stopped what they were doing and watched me in silence, as if transfixed by disbelief at my actions for a time that felt like an hour."

"And then?"

"And then I gave the *Heil, Hitler* salute and turned and left. I felt thoroughly humiliated by what I had done. They all saw me reveal weakness, their notorious leader having an emotional meltdown."

Kersten delayed saying anything. Then he asked, "Reveal weakness? Or was it love and empathy instead?"

"Love is for the bedroom, Kersten, and empathy is for the priests. I'm the head of the SS. In any case, what I felt in Warsaw was not as harrowing as what I experienced after I arrived back here last night."

"Oh?"

"I didn't sleep a wink. It was one of the few times I regretted that I abstain from alcohol. Perhaps some *Schnapps* might have helped me to sleep…Kersten, I couldn't purge from my brain or my eyes, even when closed tight, the haunting image of the boy being told by his teacher at Treblinka that he was going with the others to the bathhouse to get cleaned up after the train journey with a shower."

Tears erupted from Himmler's eyes and flowed down his waxen cheeks. Kersten nudged his chair closer to Himmler's quietly, careful not to distract Himmler and perhaps short-circuit his confession of regret and shame.

Himmler continued tearfully. "Kersten, the boy went into the shower chamber trusting and believing the teacher. That's sacred. I can't burn from my mind the vision of the boy when he discovers that there is not just water coming from the shower, and his gradually collapsing to the hard concrete floor. Oh, my God! I wept most of the night. Oh, Rolfie! I'm so sorry."

Kersten asked softly, "And do you wonder if he ever asked his teacher where his drawing notebook he had been promised was?"

Himmler was absolutely silent for a moment. Then he almost whispered, "Yes, I do wonder."

Kersten intuited that he and Himmler had arrived at a holy moment, and that it was most fitting and prudent to honor it with a respectful silence.

Himmler raised both hands to cover his face. His body was shaking from his weeping, which was almost uncontrollable now. Kersten had seen Himmler in pain many times, but never so vulnerable as now. Perhaps even some purported to be monsters can feel remorse. Kersten took the risk to rise quietly from his chair, approach the trembling body of Himmler, and gently wrap both arms around him. To Kersten's pleasant surprise, Himmler didn't flinch or resist. He lowered his hands from his face, took out a handkerchief, and wiped his eyes.

"How long has it been since I've been embraced?" Himmler asked as he gradually ceased his weeping. He seemed calmer, as though his confession had been a kind of healing balm. Kersten inconspicuously removed his arms from around Himmler.

Abruptly, Himmler seemed to flip an emotional switch and gather himself and put on his SS face.

"Now today, I woke up with the worst stomach pains I have ever had."

Kersten thought it was a suitable time to shift to a therapeutic approach. "Let me ask you, *Herr Reichsführer,* if you can see any correlation?"

"Correlation between what, Doctor? What are you getting at?" Himmler sounded irritated.

"Between your traumatic experience in Warsaw, last night's bad dream, and today's stomach pain?"

"Oh, I'm too exhausted to try to figure it out myself, Kersten. You're the expert. Illuminate me."

"It seems clear to me, if I might say so, that the emotional distress you felt you couldn't afford to disclose has to go somewhere. Do you know Newton's theorem of the conservation of energy? Energy, especially emotional energy, cannot be destroyed; rather, it transforms from one form to another."

Himmler looked at Kersten as though his therapist had lost his mind.

"For Christ's sake, Kersten, now you're quoting the ethereal, academic theories of an *English* pseudo-scientist. The apple that was said to fall from the tree and hit his head probably caused a concussion, or something, for him to have such a hair-brained idea."

Kersten smiled at the attempt at humor. "Maybe so, but I know of a lot of *German* scientists who no longer consider Newton's ideas as mere theory, but as law, or principle. They couldn't do their work without giving it full credence."

"You're losing me with all this talk about Newton. Get to the point and tell me how you think all this pertains to me and my stomach distress."

"I mean, just think of the times in the last few years, *Herr Reichsführer,* when the distress was so acute you couldn't walk, or sit, or sleep. Think of what preceded each episode...Recall the time, for instance, in February of '40 when your *Führer* was going to put you in charge of forcible transplanting all the Jews in Holland east to Poland. Remember how acute your pain was the next day when I saw you? I wonder about the timing of such intense pain. I wonder what emotional energy in your mind and heart was being transformed into piercing pain in your gut?"

Himmler appeared to be contemplating Kersten's words reluctantly but made no reply.

Kersten gave another example. "Or what about the time after Wannsee back in January when you were made aware of what the *Führer* and Göbbels and Eichmann are calling 'the Final Solution.' You were given the order to transform all the reeducation and work camps into extermination camps like Treblinka. You were deathly sick the next day when Brandt called me to come to the Chancellery immediately to treat you. Again, have you ever thought of the timing of your stomach anguish that day? Once again, I am made to wonder, especially now in light of your account of your experience in Warsaw, what emotional energy in you was being transformed into your stomach *angst.* Some resistance to the notion of this so-called 'Final Solution,' perhaps? Some innate fear of having to send innocent people like that little boy to their deaths?"

Himmler's face began turning red, but Kersten could tell it was not from his weeping. He had seen this transformation of mood and demeanor in Kersten countless times before. His face had become more resolute. His body had resumed the erect, tenacious, unbendable bearing of a Nazi general. He tightened his thin lips as though they were standing at attention. He raised his body emphatically out of his chair.

"You do a lot of wondering. I believe it's time to terminate this session, Kersten. I think if you reflect on your last comments, you will recognize that your wondering has led you far afield. You have said much too much. You have taken too much liberty in your capacity as the personal masseur of the Chief of the *Schutzstaffel*. Don't let it happen again. You're dismissed. You may go. Good day, Doctor."

CHAPTER TWENTY-SEVEN

Helsinki: August 1, 1942

Kersten was riding in the front seat of an Opel limousine. Himmler was in the rear seat with Finnish Prime Minister Johan Rangell and Foreign Minister Rolf Witting. They were returning from a state luncheon given in Himmler's honor. The men sat in a post-luncheon, post-cognac mellowness. Only Himmler, the strict teetotaler ,was fully alert.

He broke the silence with some cheery remarks. "We are very grateful for the cooperation of the Finnish government in the *Führer's* Operation Barbarossa. Allowing our forces to infiltrate Russia through Finnish Lapland is a key element of the strategy. We'll teach the Bolsheviks a lesson or two, won't we?"

Kersten cringed. Himmler was speaking too jauntily for the liking of the more taciturn Finns.

"Likewise, we are appreciative of your support and vital *materiel* for our efforts to maintain our independence from Stalin," Rangell said diplomatically. "Finland has only one desire: to live in peace and independence on our own soil."

"I spoke with the *Führer* yesterday and informed him of the warm hospitality extended to me, and therefore to him, by the Finnish government. I told him also of the relaxing session in the sauna."

"It is our duty, *Herr Reichsführer,* to show our respect," Rangell said, glancing briefly at his foreign minister.

"The *Führer* believes that the time has come to take the relationship between our two countries to a new and more intimate level."

Kersten looked at the Finnish politicians who were clearly apprehensive and unsure how to proceed. His anxiety caused him to inject himself into the conversation and risk transgressing diplomatic protocol.

"I believe I speak for our government when I say we are satisfied with the relationship as it now stands."

"That's very noble of you, Doctor," Himmler said with a

patronizing smile. "But the fact is, you do not speak for your government. These two gentlemen can and do...It is regrettable, sirs, that even before the war you were forced to receive German and Austrian Jews as refugees. The first step your government can do to enhance our relationship is to repatriate these refugees to the *Reich* from which they fled illegally."

Kersten had consulted privately with Witting over dinner the night before. He gave the foreign minister advanced warning that this subject, which Himmler considered paramount, would likely be on the agenda. He and Witting had settled on a strategy of procrastination, which Kersten assured him would be more likely to be accepted by Himmler than outright refusal of the request.

"I can arrange matters back in Germany to expedite the repatriation," Himmler added.

Kersten had informed Witting of what fate would almost surely await the refugees if they were repatriated.

"You are correct, of course, *Herr Reichsführer*, that *Herr* Rangell and I can speak for our government," Witting said. "But within certain constitutional limits, you understand. Such an action would have to be ratified by the supreme authority in our land, the Parliament."

"Democracy is a rather clumsy and inefficient form of government, I must say," Himmler said pointedly. "Like that of the British. But of course, we would want to abide by the customs of our host."

"Unfortunately, Parliament has adjourned for the season," Witting continued. "Not even Members of Parliament are willing to sacrifice their beautiful Finnish summer in the country or beside the lake for which we wait for seven or eight months."

Kersten had to turn his face back to the front in order to hide the giddy conspiratorial smile that was growing on his face.

"I believe it's not until November, isn't it, *Herr* Rangell, when you call Parliament back into session?" Witting asked, looking at the Prime Minister.

"That's correct," Rangell was quick to inject. "November 15 this year, in fact."

"Surely, a special session of the Parliament can be called to discuss this matter?" Himmler enunciated the sentence as a statement rather than a question.

"For a matter of utmost national security, of course," Rangell replied. "But with all due respect, the refugees we accepted—willingly, I must add—have not posed a threat to Finnish national security to this point, and we don't expect them to."

Kersten could sense Himmler through the back of his head, looking to him for some word of support, but Kersten continued to look out the windscreen.

"Then I am sure the *Führer* will be happy to postpone this matter until then," Himmler said, stunning Kersten with his uncharacteristically servile retreat from the power struggle.

Himmler, though, wasn't finished with the subject.

"While you have your Parliament in session in November, the *Führer* would like the members to consider a formal request to round up not just the refugees who have arrived in Finland since 1936, but *all* Jews in your country and to surrender them to the *Reich*. My SS commander in Tallinn has requested such a list from your chief of the State Police."

Kersten was as surprised as Rangell and Witting. Himmler had not divulged this comprehensive request to him earlier.

"If he is doing his job, as we expect he is," Witting said, "*Herr* Anthoni will have responded to the request by informing your commander that no such list exists. To the extent of my knowledge, we do not keep a list of persons by religion. Am I correct, *Herr* Prime Minister?"

"You certainly are, *Herr* Witting."

"I find that strange. Doesn't your government need to know its own people?" Himmler asked, genuinely dumbfounded. "If there is no list currently, as you say, I am sure that one could be generated in little time."

"*Herr Reichsführer,* it would strike the Members of Parliament as totally unreasonable to request such a list, and furthermore, to request that persons named on the list be surrendered to a foreign government," Rangell said firmly, but careful not to offend Himmler if at all possible.

"To us Germans, it is an entirely reasonable request, *Herr* Rangell. Besides, we are allies now working together and marching hand in hand."

Kersten shared the politicians' frustration at Himmler's stubbornly German-centered spin on the unorthodox agreement between the two countries. He was sure Himmler was deliberately misinterpreting the nature of the relationship to gain advantage in his argument.

"As I say, your request is not one that would be received favorably, I'm afraid," Witting said firmly.

"In that case, if the request is considered out-of-hand by your government, there are certain favors to Finland the *Führer* might be moved to reconsider granting," Himmler said, much more menacingly now.

"Such as, *Herr Reichsführer*?" Rangell asked cautiously.

"Such as the food shipments from the *Reich,* which have been keeping you and your countrymen alive during this conflict with your neighbor."

Rangell and Witting were taken aback. Kersten turned back toward the rear seat and shot a disapproving look at Himmler, who pretended not to notice. Rangell and Witting persisted, however.

"*Herr Reichsführer,* such an action by our cobelligerent would be perceived by the Finnish people as punitive, even hostile, and lower the respect of the Finnish people toward Germany quite substantially," Rangell said. "It would be regarded as a breach of our agreement of 1941. Our relationship would deteriorate seriously at such a sensitive moment in our campaign against the common enemy."

Good for you, Rangell.

"Perhaps a breach of the literal words of the agreement, but certainly not the *spirit* of the agreement. Besides, the *Führer* isn't overly concerned about the feelings of the run-of-the-mill people. It's the cooperation of your government and military that interests him."

"You must understand, *Herr Reichsführer,* that without the approval of the Finnish people, the Members of Parliament would be reluctant, to say the least, to continue our relationship as brothers-in-arms."

Himmler seemed to back off for the moment.

Not willing to raise the white flag, Himmler continued, though in a less assertive manner. Kersten could see that the limousine was nearing their hotel.

"We will have to return anon to discussion of the Jewish problem in Finland. I must take up the conversation with Field Marshall Mannerheim when I visit him at his headquarters in Mikkeli tomorrow."

"With all due respect, *Herr Reichsführer,* we do not have such a thing as a 'Jewish problem' in Finland," Rangell said. "Yes, we do have roughly several thousand citizens in this country who are Jewish. But these are decent families and individuals who have contributed to the well-being of the country as a whole."

Himmler responded in a doctrinaire fashion. "My good sirs, I am glad to know that there are relatively so few Jews in your midst. If you have Jews in your country, however, *any* Jews, you do, therefore, have a 'Jewish problem'."

Kersten could tell by his face that the usual stoic Rangell's inner emotions were roiling. When he next spoke, his voice was growing in intensity and passion. He hoped that Rangell would be careful in what he said.

"Many of the sons of those decent families," Rangell continued, "have sacrificed their lives in the Winter War against our common enemy, the Russians. Many continue to serve in the current conflict we share against the same Russians. Even many of the able-bodied Jewish refugees from the *Reich* have volunteered to serve. No Finn, I can assure you, *Herr Reichsführer*, would understand how their own government would be willing to surrender the mothers and wives of such valiant men, or be supportive of it."

Himmler shook his head in disbelief and seemed to admit defeat, for the time being.

"It's hard for me to comprehend, gentlemen. Jews fighting side by side with our *Wehrmacht*."

"So perhaps we can agree that both parties to the agreement have had to make compromises, and leave it at that," Witting said.

After that, Himmler was reduced to silence. Kersten's heart was beaming with pride in the nation that had adopted him, and admiration for that country's Prime Minister and Foreign Minister. The discussion of the "Jewish problem" in Finland ended right there.

Initially, Kersten had regarded accompanying Himmler to Finland as a welcome opportunity to touch down on Finnish soil again after so many years. On the other hand, he had feared it would be an interruption from his *real* work: not just treating Himmler but saving the lives of innocent Jews. It turned out, instead, that the trip was an unexpected and serendipitous occasion to intervene on behalf of more Jews, this time the several thousand who had made Finland their home.

~~~

When Himmler and Kersten returned to the hotel, Kersten was thrilled at the day's events. He was rightly anxious, however, about the bitter fallout from a spurned Himmler that he would have to endure at his next treatment session.

Himmler didn't wait until the next treatment. The telephone in Kersten's room rang almost as soon as he was in the door. It was

Himmler.

"What does that louse of a country of yours think it's doing?" Himmler's furious voice registered on the receiver. "Do they not know that the *Führer* is not somebody to trifle with? The uppity bastards! If he so wishes, the *Führer* could wring the Finns' bloody necks any day he chose and sentence them to the same fate as the Jews they are protecting."

Kersten remained prudently silent. After a while, Himmler's fury was spent. The tone of his voice changed.

"Oh, good night, Kersten," he sighed. "I know this is not your fault. You can't be blamed for the short-sightedness of your government. Our treatment tomorrow morning at the usual time?"

"Yes, *Herr Reichsführer*, the usual time."

Kersten was a little shaken when he put down the telephone receiver. He couldn't help hoping that Himmler would return to Germany with a renewed understanding of the principles guiding Germany's cobelligerent and would transmit that insight to his boss.

CHAPTER TWENTY-EIGHT

Gransee: August 3, 1944

Kersten never felt as fully alive and contented as he did on the few occasions that his schedule, or more correctly Himmler's schedule, permitted him several days in succession to return to the serenity of his country estate, Hartzwalde.

He could tell from Himmler's disposition at any given time how the war was going for Germany. Recently, Himmler had been particularly moody and distracted, confirming in Kersten's mind that the tide of the war had turned in a decidedly unfavorable direction for the Germans. For that reason, Felix and Irmgaard discussed the possibility, the wisdom really, of her and the children's relocation to Sweden. For a variety of reasons, Kersten had chosen Sweden as his next country of residence. There would be no future for them in Germany once the Allies reached Berlin. Holland was too physically devastated by the war. As an officially neutral country, Sweden would be a safe and desirable landing spot for them.

When he had first considered the possibility of having his family relocate to Sweden, he convinced his boss to order the installation of an untapped telephone line at Hartzwalde and his flat so he could call his wife and talk in private. Himmler didn't hesitate a second to oblige.

"You really have Himmler's permission for all of us to leave?" Irmgaard asked.

"Well, no, not all of us. He will make arrangements for you and the boys to leave for Sweden. But I have to return. That's all he asks."

"*All* he asks," Irmgaard sighed sarcastically. "To your family, that's more than all."

Already in June, a massive American, British and Canadian armada had landed on Normandy. Readers of reports of the Normandy landing in the *Deutsche Allgemeine Zeitung* were given the distinct impression that it was a small flotilla of requisitioned British fishing craft. When Kersten checked the *Helsingin Sanomat* at the Finnish legation, however, he was told the landing was the largest naval armada in the history of the world. Even if the truth was somewhere near halfway between the official Nazi organ and the view from Finland, Kersten had a pretty good idea that Hitler's days were numbered.

He and Irmgaard confirmed their decision that she and their six-year-old son Ulf and infant son Andreas would go on ahead to Sweden. He would join them as soon as the war was over. Kersten was able to make arrangements for a new residence for the family through his contacts at the Swedish Red Cross.

Kersten remained alone at Hartzwalde. Thanks to the secret arrangement for use of Himmler's mailbox by Brandt, he kept abreast of the progress of the Dutch government-in-exile at South Mimms in Hertfordshire in England through clandestine Dutch contacts. He had been very concerned and downcast when he heard about a bombing of the old estate at South Mimms that badly damaged the buildings and killed two of Queen Wilhelmina's guards. At the same time, he was relieved to hear in the same report that the bomb narrowly missed the queen. She survived and recovered shortly thereafter. She wasted no time resuming her activity on behalf of her people. Churchill described her as "the only real man among the leaders of the various governments-in-exile in Britain."

To express his gratitude that the stalwart queen of the Dutch people survived, he went out into the Hartzwalde flower garden his wife had laid out and planted, and picked some tulips. He placed a colorful bouquet beside the photo portraits of Queen Wilhelmina and Prince Hendrik on the grand piano in the living room.

He was sitting in his reading chair with his copy of a novel by Mika Waltari in his left hand and a cup of *ersatz* coffee in the other. As he read Waltari's narrative of the rise and fall of various Egyptian dynasties, he thought of the *Deutsches Reich,* which was advertised to endure at least a thousand years.

Not a chance that it will last more than a dozen years.

He heard the crunch of automobile tires on the gravel of the driveway. Kersten looked out the living room window. A silver-gray Mercedes-Benz came to a stop. A driver in a blue uniform came out of the driver's door, circled the vehicle until he came to the rear door on the passenger side, and opened it. An extremely distinguished-looking woman, perhaps in her sixties, and dressed far too formally and warmly, stepped onto the driveway in her stylish black high-heeled shoes.

Kersten rifled through the files in his brain to try to retrieve the woman's name. She looked familiar, but couldn't place her. Eventually, he came upon it: Frau Ingeborg Escher, director of the museum at St. Gallen in Switzerland, a former patient of his.

The two engaged in small talk as Kersten brought out tea.

"It is a surprise to see you, Frau Escher, particularly here at Hartzwalde," Kersten said as he put down the tray with teacups, cubes of sugar and milk. "How in heaven's name did you find me?"

"I have my sources, *Herr* Doctor. I hope you'll forgive me for coming unannounced. One never knows in Germany who is overhearing the conversation if one uses the telephone."

"I fear that has become the norm all over Europe, hasn't it?" Kersten agreed. "If the SS isn't listening in, then some partisan is. You must therefore have something for me to hear that you don't wish to share with the world?"

'Indeed, I do, Doctor. But are you certain this is a secure place to have this discussion?"

"I am. My employer, *Herr* Himmler"—at the mention of Himmler's name, Frau Escher's face twisted as though she had detected the smell of rotting eggs—"has declared Hartzwalde to be quarantined..."

Frau Escher's eyes scanned the room warily. She sat back in her chair as if to be beyond the range of Kersten's exhalation. When Kersten heard his remark through her ears, it occurred to him that his words were open to misinterpretation.

"Oh, let me you assure that there's no health risk, Frau Escher. Himmler has his staff inspect my property very carefully at least every month for wiretaps and other clever gadgets of surveillance. They assure me that the place is clean. *Herr* Himmler has strictly prohibited any other department of the government, or renegade elements in his own outfit, to engage in any spying on Hartzwalde. That's a long-winded way of saying, yes, Frau Escher, that it is safe for us to talk freely."

Frau Escher looked rather dubious. "You actually trust that man's word?" Frau Escher asked.

"I have the luxury of trusting his word because he considers me absolutely indispensable for his health. He does not want to alienate me in any way."

"All right, then, since you have such trust. If details of this conversation were to be fall on SS or any Nazi ears, it would mean certain death for me and you and probably tens of thousands of other people."

"Tens of thousands? Good Lord! Then again, we do live in a time when human life is considered cheap. But it sounds like you have something urgent."

Kersten intuited that another request for a favor was coming. He didn't want to have to leave the tranquility of Hartzwalde. "There's only so much I can do as a therapist, you know," he inserted quickly.

"Don't pretend with me, Doctor. It's because many in the Resistance are aware that you have access to *Herr* Himmler that I have come to you."

"The Resistance?"

She put down her teacup on the coffee table as though slightly offended. "I come on behalf of not just some ragtag peasant partisans, *Herr* Kersten, if that is your idea of the Resistance. Rather, I represent some of the most prominent businessmen and industrialists of Switzerland."

"They are taking a huge risk if they are part of the Resistance. Even in neutral Switzerland."

"Many people in Switzerland, too, are disgusted beyond words by what Hitler and his goons are doing to Europe."

"I sympathize."

"We know you do, *Herr* Kersten. Our sources inform us of your valiant efforts on behalf of Jews."

"Your sources?"

"Yes, we have good sources. Our members have influential connections. But I'm sure you understand, their names are confidential."

"Of course. What exactly do you have in mind?"

"My associates and I have had secret discussions with persons in friendly quarters of our government, and with the International Red Cross."

"I imagine that not every quarter of your government can be trusted or assumed to be friendly toward the Resistance. The Nazis have infiltrated the governments of even neutral countries like yours. And what, may I ask, has been the subject of these secret discussions?"

"Oh, you may most certainly ask, Doctor. In fact, among the subjects we have discussed is *you.*"

"I'm afraid I don't understand."

"I think you're playing coy with me once again, *Herr* Kersten. Once I explain our goal, I think you'll be able to fill in the blank about your role."

Kersten shrugged his shoulders and reached out his open right palm toward Frau Escher as an indication that he was ready, though reluctantly, to hear more. "Please proceed, Frau Escher."

"We have in mind a plan to get as many Jewish prisoners out of those horrendous concentration camps in Germany and Poland as is possible into Switzerland. They would still be in camps, even in Switzerland, but in *refugee* camps, not concentration camps. At least until the end of the war when they will be free to emigrate if they choose, to Britain, or the United States, or the Jewish nation that is being considered for Palestine."

"A commendable goal, of course. How many prisoners does your group plan to liberate in this way?"

Frau Escher didn't pause a fraction of a second before she answered, "Twenty thousand."

Kersten swallowed hard. He raised his bushy eyebrows so that they looked like a pair of hairy question marks.

"*Twenty* thousand? That is an ambitious plan, to say the least. May I also say, respectfully, you understand, that it's a pretty preposterous one."

He leaned back on the sofa, satisfied that he was weaseling his way successfully out of a project that had little chance of success.

Frau Escher gave no hint that she was daunted by Kersten's skepticism. She had the same dignified, almost haughty look on her face. "Why, Doctor, among hundreds of thousands, probably millions, of Jews in those camps, even twenty thousand is just a spit in the ocean."

Kersten nodded his head in a respectful way to concede her point. "And what is the plan to help these twenty thousand escape the clutches of the Nazis? I admit that their grip is not as watertight, you might say, now that the Nazis' hold on the war is loosening. But they still have a considerable security force that must be taken seriously."

"Yet, Herr Doctor, it's a security force that we noticed you have managed to elude successfully."

"So far," Kersten added. "Is your group suggesting that I somehow convince *Reichsführer* Himmler to hand over twenty thousand Jewish prisoners to you?"

"That's what we hear you are good at. But not surrender them to us, *Herr* Kersten; rather to *you*."

~~~

The next afternoon, Kersten left his retreat at Hartzwalde and drove straight to Himmler's office without an appointment. His inertia and reluctance to leave the peace of Hartzwalde was overcome by the prospect of assisting in the mass rescue of concentration camp prisoners. Himmler was glad to see him.

"Kersten, this is a happy surprise. Were you getting bored out in the country?"

"I never get bored when I am at Hartzwalde, even if there all alone, as I have been these last several days."

"When is your family coming back from Sweden?"

"We didn't set a return date." This was technically true. Kersten didn't want to divulge that the move to Sweden was permanent. He'd rather not have to deal at the moment with pressure from Himmler to remain with him in Berlin until...until the inevitable end.

"I came back earlier than I planned, *Herr Reichsführer*, because I suspected your ailment might be acting up again and you might desire a treatment."

"If I didn't know your loyalty to me and your conscientiousness about your profession as well as I do, Kersten, I might suspect you were up to something."

"Shall we proceed with the treatment?" Kersten asked, conveniently ignoring Himmler's last remark.

Himmler had removed his shirt and lain down on the divan almost before Kersten had finished his sentence.

After about thirty minutes of massaging, Kersten tried to broach the subject of the release of the prisoners as casually as he could. "Perhaps you would like to reward me for this treatment, which I'm sure you appreciate, is over and beyond the call of duty."

"Well, you certainly did have a correct intuition that I'd need you. What kind of reward do you have in mind?"

"The usual, *Herr Reichsführer,* the only reward for which I've ever asked—your quietly arranging the release of some more Jewish prisoners."

"Who, and how many this time?" Himmler asked almost formulaically. He was accustomed to the routine, the script, of their post-treatment conversations.

"I'm thinking about...say, twenty thousand."

Himmler burst into boisterous laughter that probably could be heard down the corridor.

"Oh, Kersten, if that is your thinking, then you are fantasizing." Himmler's whole body continued to shake from laughter. He had trouble getting the words out. "Do you wish to hand Göbbels more rope with which to have the *Führer* hang us? How could I possibly release that many prisoners and not be detected? Did you get too much sun at Hartzwalde that would cause you to lose your sense of judgment like this?"

That doesn't sound to me like an outright refusal. Perhaps I can push the matter some more.

"I must admit that twenty thousand is an ambitious number. But say, just twenty *percent* of that number is doable, is it not, Sir?"

"Even that would be impossible."

"*Herr Reichsführer,* allow me to be quite frank. You and I both know that the tide of the war has turned irreversibly. The Russian campaign was a disaster, as I suspect in your heart you agree. The Russians have now advanced to the outskirts of Warsaw. The landing of the allies on Normandy is a back-breaker. I know the *Führer* would not hear of it, but you're a wise and practical man, *Herr* Himmler. You perceive, even if the *Führer* doesn't yet, that the war is, for all intents and purposes, lost."

"I hear the Americans are having trouble with the Russians," Himmler chimed in without much conviction. "They'll probably come to blows over some trivial thing and split up the alliance. Germany will suddenly have a second chance. Don't you think?"

Kersten's face looked very deliberately skeptical, like a teacher's listening to a pupil's lame excuse for not handing in his homework. He didn't need to say, "Oh come on, *Reichsführer.* You know better than that."

Himmler seemed to understand Kersten's facial gesture. He remained silent. He looked straight ahead blankly at the wall behind Kersten. His face looked surprisingly resigned, Kersten thought. He didn't make a sound of disagreement with Kersten's analysis.

Kersten continued, "You need to begin contemplating your own future should the allies succeed. The Russians, especially, will want to get revenge for what they consider German atrocities during the war, especially at Leningrad and Stalingrad. You know how these things work, *Herr Reichsführer.* They will call it executing justice, but we both know it is a form of exacting revenge."

Himmler began to look downright despondent. His head was

bowed, his chin almost resting on his chest.

"*Herr Reichsführer,* you must begin to situate yourself in a more advantageous position in the eyes of the possible victors. They will not look kindly, to say the least, on the senior officer responsible for the construction and operation of the concentration camps."

Kersten read Himmler's face for his reaction. Himmler's body language convinced Kersten that his talk was having the desired effect.

Now for the decisive blow, Felix.

"But *Herr Reichsführer...*" Here Kersten paused for maximum effect. "I rather think that they would look favorably on an enemy officer who took private measures to mitigate his involvement in the running of the camps."

"What kind of 'personal measure?'"

"A personal measure such as arranging for the merciful release of a symbolic cohort of prisoners. Would you not agree, Sir?"

Himmler raised his head. His face, paler and leaner than usual, gave the look of someone hungry, starved, for hope. "You really think they would?" His voice rose as he neared the end of the question and placed a noticeable emphasis on the word "would." It made Kersten think that Himmler actually believed that there was a chance that what Kersten had speculated could possibly be true.

"If I were a betting man, I would wager that they would lean toward mercy on someone who engaged in such acts of mercy," Kersten said reassuringly.

Himmler sat and pondered. "Oh, Kersten, you speak so wisely. It's no wonder the *Führer* sought out the Finns as brothers-in-arms against the Bolsheviks. Since I am so indebted to you...I would consider two thousand. I believe we could pull it off since the *Führer's* generals are distracted by setbacks left and right."

"That would be prudent of you, *Herr* Himmler."

"Kersten, even after all these months and years, it is still beyond my comprehension why you exert yourself so much on the Jews' behalf. Surely you don't think a single Jew will ever thank you. One day, you, too, will learn to know the Jews, what they're really like, how they pose a fatal danger to Europe."

Kersten was too delighted by his success to pay Himmler's remark much heed.

CHAPTER TWENTY-NINE

Gransee: August 12, 1944

Kersten came back to Hartzwalde rejuvenated and brimming over with satisfaction after he and Himmler negotiated the release to the Swiss of the two thousand concentration camp inmates. Brandt informed him that his boss had decided on the Theresienstadt camp in Czechoslovakia as the most likely source of the two thousand prisoners to be released to Switzerland. *Kommandant* Anton Burger had been a particularly soulless and despotic overseer of the camp. But he was also the one who owed favors to Himmler for the times the *Reichsführer* had graciously meted out only minimal punishment for his overzealousness in driving his inmates hard to an early death by physical labor. Himmler was now ready to have Burger return the favors. He dispatched Brandt to Theresienstadt to inform Burger personally of the unorthodox order to prepare two thousand inmates to be loaded onto trains, not to Auschwitz or Birkenau, but to Bern in neutral Switzerland instead. Burger had to swear not to report the action in any way, but to keep it between himself and Himmler.

Kersten had communicated the good news to Frau Escher on the secure telephone line at Hartzwalde. He also called Irmgaard in Stockholm to share his joy and to check on her and the boys' adjustment to life in Sweden.

"Oh, life will be good here, in spite of the cold and long winters the locals have been warning me about," she said, "but not until you get here...and stay here."

She went on to tell him how the Swedish news had reported that Himmler had been ordered by an incensed *Führer* to begin rounding up anyone and everyone whom he had reason to suspect had even the slightest role to play in the nearly successful assassination plot on Hitler's life at the Wolf's Lair in East Prussia the previous month.

"Swedish radio says that thousands have already been apprehended, tried, and sentenced to prison or death," she said almost breathlessly. "That's just in three or so weeks. Do you think your enemies might try to implicate you in that plot somehow, Felix?"

Before waiting for Felix to respond, she continued at a frenzied rate, "Dear, I won't relax until you come here from Germany. Hitler's gone insane. I'm so afraid for you."

Felix remained calm. He didn't want to permit his wife's anxiety to ruin the afterglow of the concession he had wrangled out of Himmler for two thousand Jewish lives.

"Himmler is surely not going to put me on the list of suspects. He can't afford to lose me, remember."

What he left unsaid to Irmgaard, however, was his awareness that there were others at the SS and *Gestapo* headquarters in Berlin who could conceivably use Hitler's close brush with death as an opportunity to be rid for good of the questionable, mysterious Finnish masseur.

~~~

The next morning, Himmler sent word through Brandt for Kersten to report to him immediately at the Chancellery in Berlin. Brandt omitted any explanation or reason.

Kersten's stays at Hartzwalde were becoming less frequent and of a shorter duration each time. It took increasing effort and patience on his part to interrupt his retreats from Berlin. The war had been raging for five years now. The nation was growing exhausted by the allied bombing raids every night. The carpet bombing of Hamburg the year before was a psychological blow to the whole German *Volk*. This was a reversal of the blitz of Britain of 1940 that they had been promised by Hitler would not occur. By the summer of 1944, however, seemingly endless streams of pitiful people left homeless by the bombings paraded through the ruins of former towns and villages—not Poles, or Jews being marched from camp to camp this time, but fellow Germans—following horse-drawn carts containing the meager belongings they had left, humiliated and reduced to the status of paupers. Their aim was to escape as far to the west away from the Russians. Despite routine assurances to the contrary emanating from Göbbels' propaganda office, the refugees knew the Russians were advancing at a furious pace to the German-Poland border in the east.

When Kersten arrived at the Chancellery, Brandt said nothing. Rather, his anxious face served as a mute advance warning to Kersten to be ready to duck his head and take cover—figuratively, Kersten hoped. Kersten nodded that he understood, but had no idea of what might be annoying Brandt's boss. Brandt didn't look as though he wanted to say more.

The source of Himmler's present ill humor could be anything at all. In recent months—in the entirety of the past year, in fact—Himmler's emotional fuse had been unusually short. The occasions of his uncontrolled fits of rage and vicious verbal assaults on anybody who happened to be in his vicinity were increasingly frequent. Brandt told Kersten recently that if there is no one in the office with him, Himmler railed loudly at the air as though it were wholly responsible for whatever blunder had set him off. Predictably, in the aftermath of each emotional explosion came Himmler's familiar inevitable stomach cramps.

Kersten stood a little uneasily behind the door to Himmler's office and knocked. There was no answer. Brandt, however, gave him the signal to open the door and go in anyway. He found Himmler lying on his back on the divan, his eyes covered by a blindfold that was used to help one sleep by blocking out light on summer nights when the sun was late in descending.

"*Herr Reichsführer,* Brandt called me to say you wanted me to see you today."

Himmler remained stonily silent on the divan. Kersten glanced at his chest to make sure he was breathing.

Then, without warning or so much as a "good morning," Himmler tore off the blindfold violently and exploded immediately into an angry tirade. Kersten had witnessed Himmler aim his outsized anger at others, especially underlings whose performance of duties was not up to his standards. Himmler's anger that day was directed at *him.*

Himmler opened with an indignant question. "Have you listened to the radio this morning, Kersten?"

"No, there isn't one in my car." But Kersten knew that Himmler wasn't asking for information.

"You Finns really are a shitty bunch of turncoats. I'd like to know what the Russians paid those bastards, Mannerheim and Ryti, to get them to sell out."

"Sell out? I don't honestly know what you are talking about."

"Don't expect me to believe that you haven't heard from all your contacts back in Finland. Or anywhere else, for that matter."

"No, I haven't. Hear what, exactly?"

"You spineless, traitorous Finns negotiated a separate peace with Stalin behind our backs. Cowards! We had a job to complete jointly. Now you Finns have left the job undone and expect us to finish it. The ingrates!"

Himmler sat up on the divan.

Kersten surmised that any effort at trying to interpret to him the Finnish logic for pulling out of the cobelligerence agreement with Germany would only add fuel to the flames of Himmler's ire. But whenever Finland was being maligned, Kersten felt it as an attack on his own person. He couldn't stop himself from saying something.

"Honestly, I didn't know about yesterday's events. But I do know that since the German disaster at Stalingrad, there's been thought given in Finland to cutting our losses and going it alone against the Russians while they are preoccupied with pursuing Germans and pushing them back west of the Vistula."

"A minor setback, and your leaders switch sides? That's textbook chickenshit. What happened to the vow to be 'brothers-in-arms,' as you Finns euphemistically call our agreement?"

"I've reminded you before, and I'll jog your memory one more time." Kersten was gritting his teeth now. "Once our joint forces succeeded in pushing the enemy back to their territory as defined by the border that existed from 1917 to 1939, the Finns had fulfilled their part of the agreement."

"Not only do you pull out of the agreement, but you, in essence, declare war on us as well?" Himmler was trembling with rage. "My profound regret is that I didn't have Mannerheim and Ryti and the whole gutless bunch of them arrested when we were in Finland in 1942. And hung upside down by their balls, for that matter!"

Now it was Kersten who was growing impassioned. He tried to control the volume and intensity of his voice. "Such schoolyard bullying conduct seems to be the Nazis' default strategy."

"By the terms of this insane separate peace with the Russians, you Finns have been ordered by the Russians to empty your country of all German forces. Aren't you at least minimally humiliated by that? Forced by Ivan to run his errands and muck the shitty barn for him? Kersten, I warn you: You won't be able to turn on us and try to rout us out of your country without our exacting a bloody price."

Kersten resignedly let Himmler rant and rave. He didn't answer this time. Instead, he thought of his own situation should it really be true that Finland had withdrawn from the agreement with Germany. Kersten was relieved in a way that the awkward "brothers-in-arms" arrangement with this conquest-crazed country was off. It was becoming clearer with each passing day that Hitler's goal had been to totally annihilate the populations of Moscow, Leningrad and Stalingrad so they wouldn't have all those hungry Russian mouths to feed. As bitter as the Finnish enmity was toward the Russians, they wanted no part of any such barbaric murder of civilians.

But he was landlocked and isolated in what was now an enemy country. If he didn't act decisively, and soon, his own fate would be inextricably intertwined with that of Himmler. When Germany would have to face the repercussions of this war, Himmler would end up going down with the Nazis. Kersten had been saving others from the Nazis; now in a bitterly ironic twist, he himself was going to need to be rescued.

Once Himmler reached the end of his rant, he put his hands on his stomach and started to rub it ferociously. "You, why are you just sitting there like a bump on a log? Do something, for Christ's sake. Can't you see that I am in pain?" It was not Himmler's usual polite request.

Kersten set to work to relieve his patient's torment. It didn't take long for the magic, which had first helped Himmler in the first therapy session back in 1939, to disseminate throughout his body. Kersten's technique had its usual effect. Himmler felt his nerves relax. His breathing became more easy. His pain gave way and finally seemed to recede completely. He was lost in thought about the man who was treating him.

Kersten belongs to a nation of lily-livered traitors. Kersten's an exception, though. What a telling difference between this doctor, who treats me like no one else, and the flock of cowardly sheep who run his country. For five years, he's been my only friend, my sole confidant. Finland might be proving to be base and cowardly and totally undependable, but Kersten remains my healer, my friend. God help the man who dares to harm a single hair on his head.

"How was your drive to Berlin?" Himmler asked rather contritely, a question Kersten couldn't remember his ever asking before.

Kersten, too, had calmed down after Himmler's angry barrage. "I had a very good drive, thank you. When I left Hartzwalde, at least I was still a free man."

Himmler started up in his bed, as though struck with a whip.

"Do you doubt my goodwill?" he asked. "Kersten, I know I've just given you a tongue-lashing. I apologize. You're in Germany; Mannerheim and Ryti are in Finland. We expected so much more from them. But I cannot blame you for their piss-headed decisions. Please accept my apologies."

"I do, *Herr Reichsführer.*"

Himmler's face lit up with gratitude like that of a little boy who'd been caught cursing by his parents, but then spared the bar of soap in the mouth.

"But I am sure you realize that given the new circumstances between our countries, I am a citizen of a nation now opposed to yours. I no longer have the right to be treating you."

"Nonsense, Kersten. Politics have never come between us before, and they never will. Why should we let the matter of our two countries being in a state of war with each other affect our relationship?"

"I appreciate that. The Finnish legation here in Berlin, however, might have a differing opinion, however. And, I think there are some here, like Kaltenbrunner, of course, who feel differently as well?"

"Kaltenbrunner? Neither that overly-ambitious bootlicker, nor anyone else, will be allowed to lift a finger against you. I will see to it personally."

Himmler seemed to have simmered down completely. For the time being, he had forgotten Germany's humiliation at being rebuffed by a much smaller, less powerful nation. Kersten took the risk once again of seizing what may be an opportunity.

"Since you promise that things between at least you and me will remain the same, I am going to ask you for a favor."

"More Jews again?"

"No, not this time. I'm thinking rather of the two or three hundred Finnish nationals living and working here in Germany. They all have families. Some have even been employed in the offices of Nazi personnel. They are now stranded in what circumstances have rendered officially a hostile country. They have worked hard and honestly here. I ask that you don't arrest or persecute them, or do what you can to prevent others in the party from doing anything to harm them."

"The *Führer* will probably be angrier than a taunted bull that the Finns have made this about-face. But I also know that he's too preoccupied with keeping the Americans and British at bay in the west, and doing his damnedest to stop the criminal advance of the Russian rapists from the east. It shouldn't take much to convince him to leave the Finnish civilians in Germany alone. He can't be bothered with what he'd consider a trivial matter in the scope of things. I'm sure I can persuade him to grant them permission to return to their homeland if they wish. I'll mention it to him when the moment is right. You can imagine he's not himself these days."

Kersten recalled the prescient report on Hitler's health Himmler had shown him and Schellenberg several years ago, and their attempt to warn Himmler.

"I am most indebted to you, *Herr Reichsführer*."

Kersten shook Himmler's hand and turned around to leave the office. Before Kersten was out the door, Himmler was to have the last word.

"At least for once, Kersten, you're not asking for the release of more Jews. I find that utterly refreshing."

CHAPTER THIRTY

Hartzwalde: August 24, 1944

Once again, Kersten received an early morning telephone call from Himmler's lieutenant Brandt. Himmler was back at his headquarters and was sick as a result of difficult meetings of Hitler's inner circle. Brandt said that Himmler had a desperate need for Kersten's services as soon as possible.

"You can imagine, I'm sure, how he is after being in a closed room with a raging *Führer* and the fawning Göbbels, Göring and Bormann," Brandt added.

Kersten called his driver, Markus and ordered the car for three o'clock. Markus was a Jehovah's Witness he had hired in 1939 so that the Nazis could not deport him the way they had so many others of his people. Markus knew the route to Berlin like the back of his hand, for he had driven it umpteen times. He knew every street and turn in Oranienburg, the only town of any size they had to go through. It was there they often caught sight of the Sachsenhausen camp in the distance, not far from the SS training facility.

As they were passing the camp one day several months prior, Markus remarked, "A reeducation camp is what I hear it is, Sir."

Kersten understood that Markus was no fool.

"Yes, so they say," Kersten replied in a tone that Markus recognized as pure Kerstian sarcasm, "I'm sure they employ the most modern pedagogical methods."

On this blistering hot August afternoon, Markus had just opened the door for Kersten when they heard the sound of a motor from around the bend in the private road that led to the highway. As the vehicle came around the bend, they saw a military motorcycle coming toward them at top speed, creating a cloud of dust. The SS soldier, covered with sweat and road dust, stopped at Kersten's feet. He leapt from the motorcycle with deliberate haste and almost comical formality, and handed Kersten a letter.

"From Colonel Schellenberg, Sir," the soldier said. "It's very urgent."

Kersten dug for a key from his pocket and used it as a letter opener. As he opened the sheet of official SS stationary, another letter, just a small tightly folded note, really, fell to the ground. Kersten was intent on reading Schellenberg's letter, so that he didn't notice the second piece of paper on the ground. If the SS soldier saw it, he gave no indication that he had.

The soldier gave a formal salute, got back on his cycle and exited the grounds the way he came, only with less speed. Kersten still felt uneasy whenever he was saluted. He had always maintained that he was a civilian employed by Himmler, but not a member of the German military at all, certainly not the SS. Never did he repeat the "*Heil*, Hitler" mantra. In fact, Kersten had observed a noticeable reduction in the frequency of the ritual except by those most eager to please their superiors or maintain the illusion that things were the same as they had been in 1939.

Kersten began to read Schellenberg's letter. At first, Kersten thought the soldier had delivered it in error to the wrong recipient. The first few paragraphs seemed to be referring to official matters well beyond Kersten's purview, and written in language that was almost gibberish. Embedded in the middle of the letter, however, was a paragraph that most definitely was addressed to him. From the first words of the paragraph, Kersten felt a surge of adrenaline rush through his body.

"Beware, Doctor...Kaltenbrunner has made plans to assassinate you. I'll explain some other time how I came upon this information, but I believe it can be assumed to be true. He suspects you of having drugged Himmler so that he signed the release form for the two thousand Jews from Theresienstadt and their secret transfer to Switzerland. Be on high alert. The danger is imminent. Kaltenbrunner has vowed to eliminate you in spite of Himmler."

Then Schellenberg's letter returned in the next paragraphs to matters with which Kersten was totally unfamiliar. Kersten breathed rapidly and shook his head as if stunned by a blow. Then Markus picked up the folded piece of paper from the ground and handed it to a clearly distracted Kersten. Kersten leaned on the car and read the handwritten note.

"Don't take your usual route back to Berlin through Oranienburg. Take the route through Templin. You risk death if you travel your customary route."

Kersten returned to the house and took from the bottom drawer of his bedroom dresser a revolver that Himmler had given him special permission to carry. It had lain in the drawer ever since. He checked to see that there were bullets in the magazine, and then put the handgun in the pocket of his overcoat.

He paused to consider the letter and note. Should he take Schellenberg's advice? How could he be sure this wasn't a ruse, a trap, set up by Kaltenbrunner himself? Kersten and Schellenberg formed an unspoken alliance, to be sure, and they had partnered to manipulate Himmler into trying to encourage Hitler to resign because of declining health and name a successor. But he had never seen Schellenberg's handwriting to verify if the note enclosed with the official-looking missive was actually in Schellenberg's hand or not. The only true friend he knew of those around Himmler was Brandt. Brandt had undoubtedly seen Schellenberg's handwriting on more than one occasion. But there was no time now to take the note and show it to Brandt.

Kersten wiped the perspiration from his brow with one hand. With the other, he checked to make sure the revolver was in the pocket of his overcoat. Markus stood waiting before him, his left hand on the handle to the passenger door of the Mercedes.

Stay calm, Felix. You must think clearly...No, you must listen to your gut.

His mind reviewed in a flash his various encounters with Kaltenbrunner, his one sworn enemy within the Nazi ranks, the one who perceived him as a deadly cancer within the Chancellery with exclusive access to the *Reichsführer* that he himself coveted. Now political circumstances had rendered Kersten a leprous pariah from a nation that, in Kaltenbrunner's interpretation, had turned against Germany.

Kersten's gut signaled an immediate decision. He went back out to the driveway and stepped into the back of the car.

"Let's go," he told Markus as casually as he could, "but not through Oranienburg today, OK? Let's take the Templin route. I feel like a change today." Markus knew to obey and not object to a slightly longer route.

~~~

Kersten didn't read his book or write notes to himself in the back seat as he usually did on the drive to Berlin. Instead, he scanned the horizon and visually inspected the hedgerows lining the road for any signs of snipers or SS men preparing to launch an ambush. The children of local farmers rode their bicycles on the side of the road and waved as the Mercedes passed. Kersten waved back, just as farmers on their carts had back in Estonia when he and his brothers had waved to them from the side of the stony road. He was relieved that these towheaded children had not been co-opted by Kaltenbrunner to pull out hidden weapons and spray the vehicle with bullets. That wouldn't have been beneath Kaltenbrunner.

They had no mishap on the trip, however. No flat tire that might have made them vulnerable to a deadly assault by the *Gestapo* camouflaged in the bushes. No unannounced roadblock or unplanned detour off onto an isolated side road. No farmer's wife on foot by the side of the road hailing them for a ride to market in town, then once inside the vehicle, pulling out a handgun and killing them both. Forty-five uneventful minutes after departing Hartzwalde, Kersten stepped out of the car in front of the Chancellery on *Prinz Albrecht Strasse.*

Meanwhile, in a small wood along the highway outside Oranienburg, twenty *Gestapo* foot soldiers armed with submachine guns had been dispatched by Kaltenbrunner. The men split into two groups. One group hid in the ditch on either side of the road. They lay in wait for Kersten's familiar gray Mercedes. Their orders were to stop the car and ask to check the identity papers of the occupants. They were then to step away from the vehicle. The car would then be turned into a sieve by bullets from almost two dozen submachine guns from the ditches.

As soon as the men were sure that Kersten and the driver were dead, the squad leader was to report to Berlin that the car would not stop when ordered, and that he had been forced therefore to order his men to fire. All that would remain for Kaltenbrunner to do was to inform Himmler and express his most sincere regrets at the unfortunate incident in which the driver and a passenger had perished.

"The passenger," Kaltenbrunner would report in his gravest voice, "I regret to say, *Herr Reichsführer,* was identified as your Finnish doctor."

Kersten heard on the radio later that evening that a local businessman and his teenage daughter had been gunned down viciously by multiple machine guns as their car was heading toward Oranienburg. As was characteristic of Göbbels' propaganda broadcasts, blame for the killing of two innocent civilians was laid at the feet of Jewish partisans supplied by the Allies.

~~~

Kersten was too unmoored emotionally to go directly to Himmler's office. Instead, he asked Markus to take him back directly to Hartzwalde. He would wait until the next morning to see Himmler.

The next morning, he found Himmler stretched out on the divan, contorted with spasms.

"It's about time, Kersten," was all Himmler said as Kersten rolled up his sleeves and dove into the familiar treatment procedure.

"How lucky I am," Himmler said later during a pause in the treatment, "to be able to see you when I need you…even if it is a little later than I had hoped."

"You might not have been able to see me at all."

"What are you talking about, Kersten?"

"I'm about 99% certain that I escaped being murdered yesterday afternoon on my drive to Berlin."

Himmler looked at Kersten shocked and bewildered. "You're joking, right?"

Kersten raised his voice, trembling with feelings he could not master. "I have good reason to believe that Kaltenbrunner planned to have me killed."

Himmler exclaimed equally loudly, "Come on. Nothing like that happens in Germany without my knowing about it."

"This was at least one time you did not know."

Himmler shot up into a sitting position on the edge of the divan. Without being aware of it, he was pulling feverishly at the buttons of his one-piece undergarment.

"What don't I know about? Tell me," he asked Kersten angrily.

Kersten went over to his suit jacket on the back of a chair and from the breast pocket pulled out Schellenberg's letter and note. "Here, read these."

Himmler fumbled to put on his steel-rimmed glasses and read the letter. He was confused by the initial paragraphs of official-sounding mumbo-jumbo, which someone had composed out of his imagination and which made no sense to him. But his eyes widened as he got to the paragraph inserted into the middle of the letter with the explicit warning to Kersten about Kaltenbrunner's plot.

"My God!" Himmler declared in disbelief. Kersten couldn't tell whether it was disbelief at the notion of a plot against his personal masseur or at the implausibility that someone under his own command could be plotting something like this without his knowledge. More likely the latter.

Himmler reached for the bell on the head of his bed. Brandt was in the office in less than an instant.

Still sitting in his underwear on the side of the divan, Himmler's head was bowed in bitter disappointment. He spoke softly to Brandt, but loud enough that Kersten could overhear. "I want you to read this piece of obscenity, and then proceed to find out if it is true. No one is to know what you're up to, least of all Kaltenbrunner."

~~~

Brandt accompanied Kersten into Himmler's office the next day when he arrived for the daily treatment.

"Well?" Himmler asked Brandt.

Brandt did not explain how he had found out. It wasn't necessary. Like the jungle, Kersten knew, the Nazi secret services had laws of their own. Kaltenbrunner had his undercover agents within Schellenberg's office, and Schellenberg had them planted in Kaltenbrunner's. Wearing the same uniform and reciting the same vows of loyalty to the *Führer* evidently did not guarantee mutual trust between principals. Brandt had procured agents for Himmler in both Kaltenbrunner's and Schellenberg's offices, although undoubtedly both suspected or were even aware of it.

"Schellenberg told the truth," Brandt reported. "Kaltenbrunner had indeed prepared an ambush for Kersten, and would have succeeded without a doubt if the doctor had not been warned."

"Then, damn, it is true," Himmler shouted, slamming his one fist into the other. "My chosen head of the *Gestapo?* I can't believe it's true." He was alternating taking off his glasses and then putting them back on.

Kersten spoke haltingly. "Then if Schellenberg had not..." The remaining words of the sentence stuck in his throat. This was the first time since the murder attempt that he felt shock.

"Exactly, Doctor," Brandt said. "We are fortunate that one of Kaltenbrunner's personal aides is in Schellenberg's employ as well. He warned Schellenberg about the plot."

"It was just in time," Kersten said, shaking his head contemplatively. "Had that motorcycle arrived at Hartzwalde a minute later, we would have been on our way on the Oranienburg route."

Suddenly, briskly, Himmler rose to his feet and started dressing with haste. He looked at his watch. It was almost two o'clock.

He announced abruptly to Brandt and Kersten, "I'm hungry. We're going to eat. Brandt, call the chief of the *Gestapo* and tell him—no, command him— to join us in my private dining room."

~~~

Kersten and Himmler took seats on one side of the table for four. Brandt took the seat beside Kaltenbrunner and directly opposite Himmler. Except for the huge red and black Swastika flag hanging from the ceiling, the room was starkly white. Looming on the wall over the head table at which they were seated was an oversized portrait of Hitler. Judging by the appearance of the subject in the photo, it must have been taken back in '33 or '34 when his face was still virginal and hair purely black. A more recent portrait would have revealed the thinning, graying hair and deep etches and lines on his less confident face.

The meal began with silence except for each person's giving their lunch order to the obsequious waiter who was accustomed to his boss, Himmler, having guests for lunch from among the higher ranks of the SS or *Gestapo*.

Himmler and Kersten were too tense to start the conversation. Kersten was more than curious about where and how this spontaneous confrontational tête-à-tête was going to proceed, or even begin.

Evidently, Kaltenbrunner was anxious as well. The silence was excruciating to him, the delay, unbearable. Why was this sudden, unexpected invitation to lunch? He spoke first to relieve his tension. He addressed Kersten with exaggerated courtesy, which Kersten had learned to recognize as the Nazi way of paving a smooth path for a kill.

"Well, Doctor, how are things going for you in your dear Sweden where you seem to be spending a lot of time lately?"

The question and Kaltenbrunner's tone of voice confirmed to Kersten how much he detested this vile, odious man. It was clear the feeling was mutual. Everything about the *Gestapo* chief exuded a mellifluous hatred for Himmler's masseur that he did little to conceal. When Kersten hesitated in answering the question, Kaltenbrunner provoked him rudely.

"You must be doing very well in Stockholm. I hear that you have found very ample accommodations."

"No, that's not correct," Kersten said straightforwardly. "Not at all well. I have no work there."

Kaltenbrunner was surprised. He put down his glass of water and leaned back in his chair.

"How could that be? A doctor with your expertise and references, and no work?"

The waiter delivered the lunch orders. Conversation halted for the time being.

Once the waiter had returned to the kitchen, Kersten continued. "You ask me as if you didn't know, General. With your expertise in what you do and with all the resources at your fingertips, I cannot believe that you do not know what I really do. Have you not learned that for five years I have been an agent of the British MI6?"

Kersten paused to make sure everyone at the table heard him. Kaltenbrunner's eyes were wide open, his eyebrows arched in the shape of pyramids.

"Yes, the M16 has been paying me to infiltrate the SS and kill the *Reichsführer.* I succeeded in the former, as you know and which irks you to no end. But so far, I have failed in the latter. This is not good enough for them. So I have lost my job."

Himmler had been sitting silently and moving his food about on his plate without having taken a bite. He looked up suddenly at Brandt in absolute astonishment. Brandt looked calm, and Kersten saw out of the corner of his eye that Brandt shook his head calmly at Himmler almost imperceptibly. Himmler looked back down at his plate no better informed, but seemingly satisfied for the moment that perhaps Brandt and Kersten had concocted a surreptitious strategy that he didn't know about.

In point of fact, Kersten himself was astonished at what he had said. This wasn't a premeditated speech or a pre-planned strategy at all. Neither was it a conspiratorial ploy dreamed up with Brandt. He wasn't completely certain of what the aim of this artifice was. He only knew he wanted so profoundly to humiliate the *Gestapo* chief for his own vengeful satisfaction.

Kaltenbrunner looked across the table at Himmler, and seemed as surprised by Himmler's apparent lack of reaction to Kersten's remark as by the confounding remark itself. He was utterly speechless, his mouth agape in disbelief and bewilderment.

Himmler looked up from his plate and began fingering the frame of his spectacles. Each man recognized this idiosyncratic practice of the *Reichsführer* as the prelude to a statement of some importance. Kaltenbrunner braced himself. He was totally flummoxed by the direction of this conversation. For their part, Kersten and Brandt looked at Himmler expectantly.

"Listen to me, you Austrian thug. What's worse, Ernst, is that because of your uninvited intervention, the doctor almost lost his job here with me." He raised the volume of his voice several notches. "In fact, he almost lost his *life* entirely. And it was all done behind my back."

Kaltenbrunner's color turned almost as white as the walls of the dining room. He remained silent, and averted Himmler's angry stare.

"Something like this shall not happen again! You are not to take any actions regarding the *Gestapo* without my signing off on the action! Have I made myself clear, Lieutenant-General?" Himmler was almost shouting.

Whenever Himmler acted in this way, Kersten marveled that such vituperative volume could emerge from such a short, frail man, and that it could elicit such fear as it did in Kaltenbrunner now.

Kaltenbrunner became uncharacteristically sheepish. "Yes, *Herr Reichsführer*, perfectly clear," he said, utterly cut down.

"I surely hope it is, for my sake and yours," Himmler continued in the same authoritative voice. "I thought I had made myself perfectly clear after Heydrich's assassination in '41 when I named you *Gestapo* Chief. This is not a novel condition for your work under my command, is it...*Is* it?"

Nothing had been said about his being relieved of his post. Kaltenbrunner must have been sensing that the punishment he was dreading just minutes earlier was not going to be as harsh or final as he'd feared. He seemed eager to keep it that way.

"No, Sir, it is not. I shall do better from now on, *Herr Reichsführer*, I assure you."

"I can't hear you, *Obergruppenführer*. Speak up so that I can hear you."

"I shall do better from now on. I shall consult you on every decision."

"That's better," Himmler said.

Kersten was surprised, too, and a little disappointed at Kaltenbrunner's relatively light sentence. But he was taking great inner delight in seeing the bastard knocked down a few notches from his haughty throne.

"One more thing," Himmler said, continuing to look sternly at his *Gestapo* director. "There shall not be any more 'accidents.' You are both too important for me to tolerate any more monkey business. Ernst, you are ruthlessly ambitious, too much so for the good of the *Reich*. Honestly, I have never liked or trusted you completely. This is not news to you, I suspect. I am sure, in fact, that you feel exactly the same way."

Himmler had adopted the stern schoolmaster's tone he had used many times undoubtedly in his brief teaching career in München.

"Be that as it may. The *Führer* and I have spoken about this many times. We agree that we have a dilemma. Your selfish ambition makes you a danger to the *Reich* where we must each transcend and deny our private, personal ambitions. Yet, neither he nor I can come up with the name of an officer more suited and with the desired requisite experience and frankly, sheer brutishness, for the post of chief of the *Gestapo*."

Himmler was still exasperated. He calmed down for a moment to say, "So this is what we have. We have to try to make the best of it."

Kaltenbrunner now looked like the contrite, anxious schoolboy summoned to the schoolmaster's office for disciplining and hoping for mercy. The schoolmaster wasn't done, however.

"Get this, Kaltenbrunner, and get it straight: If anything untoward should happen to my personal doctor here, I won't bother to investigate whether the instigator of the plot was you or not. I will simply assume that it *is* you. If Kersten is injured or killed, you won't last twenty-four hours, believe me. I will have you shot…No, let me correct that. In your case, I will make an exception. I will not merely give the order to have you shot. I will take the rifle and press the trigger myself. 'An eye for an eye…' Is that understood?"

The meal ended as it had begun, in an awkward, stone-like silence. No one had eaten much, not even Himmler who had claimed hunger in the first place. Sitting across the table from the man who had almost succeeded in killing him, Kersten didn't even have the stomach for a cup of coffee. He excused himself and promptly exited the Chancellery.

He waited by the front entrance for Markus to pick him up and drive him back to Hartzwalde to take a new inventory of his life.

CHAPTER THIRTY-ONE

Theresienstadt: February 5, 1945

Roll call had been finished for about half an hour on the dark, freezing *Platz* of the Theresienstadt camp. Hannah Hirtschel was not yet twenty-two years of age—the best she could remember at least—since in the camp she had lost track of the months and years. She and the other women in her barrack were too exhausted from the day's work to say more than a few indifferent words to one another that evening, just the familiar mundane goodnight greetings that they had continued to recite almost mechanically. The women had pledged to continue this ritual in order to maintain some semblance of normalcy and sane routine.

Hannah and the women in her barrack considered themselves among the fortunate inmates, at least in comparison to others. They were within what was called "the main fortress," a walled ghetto, really, as opposed to the "old fortress," the former town citadel across the Ohře River in Bohemia. The elderly and more frail inmates were warehoused there until, Hannah had learned, they were virtually shoveled onto trains headed for extermination at the Auschwitz and Birkenau death camps. The main fortress had been reconfigured as an industrial camp utilizing Jewish slave labor. Most of Hannah's fellow inmates in the main fortress were young, like her, although she was among the youngest of those considered to be adults.

Hannah had been apprehended by the SS at the home of her great-aunt in the small village of Bautzen near the Polish border a few weeks before Christmas in 1938. After her train had arrived from Berlin, she had walked nervously from the train station along the unlit street to her great-aunt's home, looking over her shoulder the whole time. She was sure she heard sharp footsteps clicking against the concrete surface perhaps twenty or so meters behind her. She hadn't had a very long reunion at all with her great-aunt before their hearts leapt in unison at the sound of loud banging on the front door and a harsh voice shouting, "SS, *Öffnen Sie die Tür schnell!*"

Later that same night they were put onto a train to Czechoslovakia.

Hannah's great-aunt was assigned to the old fortress, and Hannah never heard from or about her again. When she first arrived at the main fortress, Hannah had been assigned to the dusty mill to slit ore from mica for making tungsten to be used in the manufacture of shell heads. More than one SS officer took note of her feminine physical attributes, and before long she was the favorite sex slave for officers in the camp. Her lusty clients wanted her whole, uninjured by the fire of the ore smelters, and not too overtired, so they arranged with their superiors for her reassignment to the clothing workshop. For five of the almost six years at Theresienstadt, she had sorted apparel confiscated from the arriving Jews, and found skirts, blouses, dresses and underwear in suitable condition to be redistributed to the wives and girlfriends, and Hannah suspected, mistresses as well, of SS guards and officers back home in Germany where supplies were beginning to run short.

Many times, the repetitive routine of her work in the clothing barrack allowed her to think. She dared not think of her great aunt, so sad was it. She had probably grown weary and weak in short order and died of exhaustion, or been shipped to one of the extermination camps. She though often of Algot Niska, the sweet man who had resisted her offer of sexual favors when he had taken her into his flat in Berlin, and then provided the fare for the train to come to Bautzen. He *saw* her. He actually saw her for who she was—a human *soul*. Had any gentile ever looked at her and seen her in that way?

Had he evaded capture and imprisonment? Had he become just another sorry victim of this horrendous war, this brutal and inhuman Nazi system? Was he even still alive?

The *Kapo* shouted to the women in the barrack to settle down for the night and put out the lights. Before long, a few of the women began their chorus of snoring. Otherwise, the barrack was silent. Hannah received sleep as a gracious gift.

All of a sudden, she was awakened by a loud, sharp, thumping sound against the floor at the end of her bunk. She looked down toward her feet to see what had made the harsh, unwelcome sound, but since it was dark, she could barely see. She heard the smacking sound again several times, presumably on the floor by the nearby bunks of one or two women.

The shrill voice of a female SS guard pierced the darkness. "*Wache auf!* You who have been designated, get out of your filthy beds and stand at attention at the foot of your bunks! Come on. Hurry up!

Schnell! You know who you are. The rest of you, back to sleep."

Hannah presumed that the violent slapping of the guard's truncheon against her bunk was the signal that she was one of the "designated." Designated for what? In the middle of the night? How many hours after falling asleep?

"*März auf den Platz!* Form orderly rows. Hop to it!"

Out to the cold *Platz* again? Hannah asked accusingly—silently, of course. She knew such a query uttered openly would be judged as insubordination for which there could be any number of painful, degrading repercussions.

The barrack was still dark. The three women felt under their bunks for shoes or boots for their feet.

"*Nichts!* Take nothing but your shoes," the guard shouted.

Hannah reflexively tossed the thin coat she had picked up back on her bunk.

When they exited the barrack, the women had to shield their eyes from the punishing light of the searchlights from the turrets, which were directed down onto the *Platz.* Some of the women were dressed in nightclothes they had pilfered from the clothing barrack. Since Hannah worked there, she had secured a pair of warm pajamas for herself and traded other pieces of clothing for end pieces of stale bread. Their crime of stealing was now in plain sight in the glaring light. Other women were still dressed in the filthy, ragged clothes in which they performed their daily labor.

Hannah saw that though there were hundreds, maybe a thousand or more, women standing on the snow-covered *Platz,* shivering helplessly, this was not a general roll call. Not all the female prisoners, apparently, had been "designated" the way she had been. This confused her even more. Each woman wore bewilderment, disorientation, fear, in some cases panic, on her face.

Without speaking—though their hearts surely were spilling over with questions—the women organized themselves into orderly rows with an efficiency that comes from habit. Hannah could hear the loud, slow, laboring sound of a locomotive on the tracks just beyond the gate.

What, dear God, is happening? Are they going to march us out into the woods again behind the barracks? Will we be forced to witness once again some obscenity of execution at the pit and ordered to cover the bodies with dirt? Or is it we who will be shot and buried in the pit this time? But why the train? Are we being sent somewhere...Oh God, maybe to Auschwitz? God, no! Not Auschwitz. I knew my time would come.

"The first row, march forward!" ordered the female guard, now joined on the *Platz* by seven or eight others.

Hannah watched as the first row of inmates obeyed the guard's order. They were directed toward the gate that separated the camp from the railway landing, the gate above which the words *Arbeit Macht Frei* mocked them.

The second row marched in the same direction. Then Hannah's row. All was silent but the sharp commands of the guards, the shuffling of the inmates' feet, many in worn and holey socks, and the earsplitting hissing of the locomotive's air brakes. The women dared not look into one another's faces lest they discover there a mirror reflection of the fear and bewilderment on their own face.

"Auschwitz," the woman beside her said quietly. Hannah couldn't tell if she was making a statement or asking a question.

"I don't know," answered Hannah, almost inaudibly.

"It's Auschwitz, I'm sure of it," the despondent women insisted. "Or Solibor. It doesn't matter. It's all the same."

Once they arrived on the train platform, they were ordered to boost themselves into the empty cattle cars. It was a rise of over a meter. Some of the women helped lift others weakened by the previous day's labor so they could climb into the rail car. A guard shouted angrily for the women to hurry up.

Hannah was reliving in her memory the December night she and her great aunt were loaded in the same way onto the train that brought them to Theresienstadt. Neither she, her great aunt, nor anyone of the Jews squeezed onto the train knew what was happening or where they were going. It had been then much like this dark night when not knowing left space for projecting their worst fears.

A *Kapo* poked his head into Hannah's rail car, then with forceful effort, slid the door shut. The whole car shook as the door rolled and slammed shut.

There was an almost knowing silence in the rail car as the door shut. It was a silent, nonverbal, communal statement by every inmate that the night they had feared, in spite all the fervent Hebrew prayers that the bitter cup be passed from them, had now indeed arrived.

There was a collective gasp as the locomotive let out its first churning chug and the rail car was thrust forward. The force of motion after being in a stationary position caused a few of the women who had not found space on the floor to sit to tumble to the floor with a shriek, landing on top of others who were seated.

The intervals between the clicks of the steel wheels against the small gaps in the rails grew shorter as the train picked up speed. No light whatsoever dribbled into the car through the cracks in the walls from the dark night outside, only frozen air.

A woman near Hannah was rocking back and forth and muttering a prayer. A young *Hasid* woman was reciting a psalm quietly. Another woman was moaning mournfully about a pain in her legs. Against all the odds, Hannah's eyes closed and sleep returned miraculously.

At the first hint of dawn the train came to a sudden stop. The inertia of forward movement caused the women to lurch forward into one another. Those, like Hannah, who had been able to sleep were awakened by the abrupt, unannounced halt. One or two women tried to peer outside through the cracks in the walls of the car.

"I don't think we're at a station. All I see is trees, I think."

The car door slid open with a violent thud.

"*Jeder auf und ab!*" a *Kapo* shouted into the car. "Everyone up and out. Time to do your business."

Again, the women were confused. Had they been brought out here to be abandoned in a forest wilderness?

The *Kapo* pointed with his truncheon toward a ditch along the railroad tracks. Once one woman stepped down into the ditch, pulled down her thin, ragged trousers, and squatted, others followed. Then Hannah understood what the *Kapo* meant by "doing your business."

Hannah wondered if the other women had also been asleep, or so overcome by fear and bewilderment, that they hadn't noticed how urgently their bladder was crying out for relief.

"*Zurück in den Zugwagen. Schnell,*" a female guard shouted. "Back into the rail car. Immediately!"

The women again performed the calisthenics of raising themselves or one another from the stony rail bed into the rail car. The locomotive lurched forward once again and resumed the clickety-clack rhythm.

A palpable hunger overtook the passengers. One young woman in the corner near Hannah dug into her pocket and tried to pull out a small dried end of a loaf of bread without being seen by the others. Her eyes met Hannah's as she pulled it out. Without a word she tore the bread into two pieces and handed one to Hannah, who nodded her thanks.

Is this the prisoner's last meal before execution?

One of the woman, trying to look through the cracks in the car's walls, shouted to the others, "I think I see mountains. Yes, they're mountains all right, big, tall ones."

"Are we in Bavaria then?" another woman asked out loud. "Isn't Dachau in Bavaria? Are we going to our death at Dachau? Oh, my God, I'm sure we're going to Dachau. We are going to die."

The mention of Dachau and death caused the women to look at one another for some kind of affirmation or denial of the woman's apprehension. Hannah resented the woman's violating the unspoken code of the rail car that no one articulate out loud the dark, collective thoughts and fears of their hearts, nor pronounce the dreaded, taboo word "death." It was as if to say the word out loud was an act of surrender to it, a capitulation and submission to the dark fear that hung over them all like a black thundercloud about to erupt.

Not long afterward the rhythm of clickety-clack slowed. As the train decelerated the woman peering through the cracks announced, "We're in some kind of city now, I think. Yes, I see houses...I see streets and people walking. Not guards, but real, ordinary people."

Several women scampered up off the floor and rushed to one of the cracks in the wall of the car. They pasted their faces against the crack in order to see if the other woman was telling the truth.

"It looks like we're coming to some kind of station," one announced to the rest of the passengers. "Yes, there are railroad men on the platform...but...that's strange. They're wearing some kind of uniform...but not Nazi uniforms."

"This is no time for a joke," one woman said sardonically from the floor.

"No, I'm sure. Those are the standard-issue conductors' uniforms they're wearing."

The train came to a stop. The women didn't know whether to be in dread based on their fears, or in expectation based on the woman's reconnaissance.

"Listen," one woman said. "Are those violins I'm hearing?"

The women stopped chattering. Hannah could hear a strangely merry tune waft in through the cracks in the walls. She recognized the tune as one she had heard a long time ago, but her mind was too foggy from confusion and interrupted sleep to be able to name it.

Is it Beigalach? How strange for them to be playing such a playful, jazz-like, upbeat song at the entrance to a death camp.

Others recognized the tune as well. *Beigalach?* But they were too drugged with fear and apprehension to smile in recognition, their feet too exhausted from years of standing in the snowy *Platz* at Theresienstadt to tap along the unanticipated happy beat.

The door to the car was pulled open. Daylight streamed into the car like golden honey. The women shielded their eyes from its brilliance and blinked uncontrollably in an effort to see.

The female guards and *Kapos* were strangely absent. There were no *Wehrmacht* or SS soldiers to shout out orders. Though the air was colder even than at Theresienstadt, it was light and sweet and devoid of the amalgam of foul orders at Theresienstadt.

The women slid down from the rail car warily on their backsides as though anticipating that the lightness would end at any moment. They placed their feet on the cold ground gingerly as though to do so any less delicately would break the spell of the wondrous magic of the moment. How long had it been since the women had not been barked at, or ordered to do something?

A very dignified fiftyish woman dressed stylishly and expensively in civilian clothes stood on a podium that had been erected near the violin players.

"Dear women of Germany. Welcome to Lausanne."

Lausanne? Isn't Lausanne in Switzerland? In neutral Switzerland, a nation not occupied by the Germans and contaminated by Nazi lies?

Soldiers in pea-colored uniforms—not the gray of the *Wehrmacht*—formed a line on the street in front of the station and behind the inmates on the other track. They wore bright red berets and held rifles in a stance of readiness. Only, their backs were turned to the inmates, their bodies facing outward to the street and the field behind the station, as though they were guarding against some kind of potential attack from beyond rather than preventing the escape of the inmates. They formed a protective human wall around the station. Hannah looked up to the roof of the station, and there were several soldiers there, too, thoroughly scanning the skies above.

"You will likely not believe me when I say that you have been transported to your freedom," the woman continued. "But I assure you that is precisely the case. You are the fortunate two thousand who have been liberated. You have been brought far away where the Nazi terror cannot reach you."

The women looked around them, but they could not see a single German soldier. They looked at one another in confusion, and eventually, happy disbelief.

"You have been liberated through the intervention of the Swiss government and the International Red Cross, with the valued help of a compassionate private individual, who must remain nameless for his own safety and security. Women, you will be free!"

The word "free" was too profound and sacred, too rarely spoken or heard in the past seven years, a word the women had not dared allow themselves to whisper, even to themselves. Most of the women continued to have a stunned, uncomprehending looks on their faces.

"You will be transported shortly in trucks to a debriefing camp run by the Red Cross, where you will be issued Swiss passports. Do not be afraid. This is a different kind of camp from the one you know. There will be hot food and clean, potable water for you. Please believe me. You will get a pass for the Swiss railroad system and you will be free to stay and make a life in Switzerland unimpeded if you should choose. There will also be a representative of the Jewish Council for Palestine to discuss with any of you who may be interested in applying to start a new life in Palestine. In any case, you will be free from now on. We Swiss take great pride in assisting you."

For Hannah, it was all too much to assimilate. Freedom, Swiss government, International Red Cross. A mysterious nameless compassionate individual. *Another* one? A new life in Palestine.

"I have asked Rabbi Rosenstein of the Beth Yaakov Synagogue in our city to welcome and accompany you in prayer. Rabbi Rosenstein..."

The middle-aged rabbi, with hair graying at the temples and an intelligent face, came forward to the microphone.

"Ladies," he began in Swiss German. The dialect sounded almost foreign to Hannah. But she was able to make out enough words that the rabbi spoke to understand somewhat.

"Meine Damen," he repeated.

How long had it been since Hannah had considered herself a lady?

"You, dear women," he continued in German, "are the *she'arit hapleta,* the surviving remnant, of the Jewish people, the children of the nation that, in these few years, has been suffering more than any nation throughout history. You, who have been blessed to be rescued from your tormentors, are called to strengthen your faith and trust in our God that He will comfort you and help you establish a new life in a new world in which will reign righteousness and justice, in which no nation shall be persecuted because of its race, in which each nation shall live in accordance with its faith, practices and religion."

Hannah's eyes welled up with tears, as did those of the rescued inmates beside her. She still could not believe that there was no SS guard or Jewish *Kapo* nearby to interrupt the rabbi and herd the inmates back onto the train and send them back to Theresienstadt. Is this just a dream from which they will be awakened by the dreaded siren calling them to their breakfast of dried bread and weak tea? The taste of liberation was still too novel and foreign for her palate.

The rabbi switched to speaking in Hebrew. He recited a prayer:

Barukh atah Adonai Eloiheinu Melekh ha'olam shehecheyanu vekiymanu vehigi'anu lazman hazeh.

Blessed are you, Lord our G-d, King of the Universe who has granted us life., sustained us and enabled us to reach this occasion.

Hannah could no longer remember the name of the prayer, but it sounded dear and familiar and washed over her with the sweetness of childhood.

Hannah and the others bowed their heads tearfully and stood transfixed. They had thought they'd never hear prayers in correct Hebrew again. Even the Hebrew of the *hasidim* in Theresienstadt had eroded and evolved until their prayers were recited in a language that bore an auditory resemblance to Hebrew but was almost desecrated by the occasional insertions of words in German, Yiddish and Polish, especially Polish. This prayer, uttered in the sacred language, made Hannah feel an unaccustomed swelling of joy grow within her heart and spread to the farthest limbs of her body.

The rabbi spoke again in German. "Even as we celebrate and rejoice with these *she'arit hapleta*, we remember with profound sadness those whose lives have been snuffed out in concentration camps. We pray also for those who still remain in those camps, their lives hanging by a thin and fragile tether.

"May His Great Name grow exalted and sanctified in the world that He has created as He willed. May He give reign to His kingship in your lifetimes and in your days, and in the lifetimes of the entire Family of Israel, swiftly and soon."

Almost reflexively, Hannah and the Theresienstadt women joined the gathered crowd and responded with "Amen. His great Name be praised forever." This was the Mourners' Kaddish. Many times in Theresienstadt, the women in each barrack had joined hands out of the sight of the guards and *Kapos* and tried to pray these words of sanctification in memory of women who had grown weak and weary and had collapsed from exhaustion or were shipped to Auschwitz.

The rabbi began his chanting slowly in Hebrew again. He waved his left arm toward the inmates, and one by one, they added their weakened, weary voices to the prayer.

Oseh shalom bimromav, Hu yaaseh shalom aleinu, v'al kol Yisrael, Ve'imru Amen.

May the One who creates harmony on high, bring peace to us and all Israel. And let us say, Amen.

The violinists struck up a joyful rendition of *Hava Nagila.* Hannah's sore feet began to move slowly in time with the violins. The woman beside her reached over spontaneously and took hold of Hannah's hand. Hannah, in turn, reached to take the hand of the inmate on the other side of her, smiled at her, and nodded for her to do the same with the hand of her neighbor. A few of the inmates began to sing along, weakly and tentatively at first as though they were unsure that they were permitted to do so. The sound of laughter, so alien and forbidden for these inmates for years, began to rise up like incense to the brilliant sky from the group of two thousand inmates. Hannah and the women whose hands had joined created a space between themselves and another group that had followed suit and formed a larger circle. The human chains began walking around in a circle, slowly at first, and unsurely, but as the violins and singing and laughter infused them with new strength, the circles of dancers picked up speed.

They danced for themselves and the gift of their unexpected sudden freedom. They danced in memory of loved ones and family whose whereabouts they no longer knew. They danced for those she had seen collapse in death from hard labor, and for the women in the barrack who had not awakened in the morning. They danced for those women still confined in the hell of Theresienstadt.

They danced their joy at having survived. Hannah danced for Algot Niska. They danced in thankfulness for the miracle. They danced their gratitude to the Swiss government and the International Red Cross. They danced in thanksgiving for the unnamed individual who acted in some unknown way on their behalf to secure their freedom.

CHAPTER THIRTY-TWO

Gransee: March 16, 1945

Himmler was spending noticeably less time at his office on *Prinz Albrecht Strasse*. He asked Kersten if they could have their next therapy session at Hartzwalde.

"You know how I like to remain here and not venture into Berlin," Kersten said gladly.

"Berlin has become depressing for me as well, Kersten. I need to get out."

Himmler's chauffeur let him out of the car at the front entrance of Hartzwalde, and Kersten led him to a room that he had converted into a clinic to treat patients who were not Nazis.

About halfway through the session, when Kersten noticed that Himmler was no longer in pain but was relaxed, Kersten broached a subject, variations of which they had discussed several times earlier. Perhaps Himmler was more open to it now. And to the new proposal he was going to make.

"*Herr Reichsführer,* we must not fool ourselves any further. Both we Germans and Finns are known for our ability to tell and face up to the truth. We both know that his war is lost, do we not? My sources inform me that you are willing to reach out to the Allies and seek a separate peace for Germany."

"Has Brandt told you this?"

"It doesn't matter who told me, does it? It's true, is it not?'

"Well, yes. I want our forces to be free from the western front in order to concentrate on defeating the Bolsheviks in the east. If the Bolsheviks overrun Germany, it will be a victory not only for them, but for the Jews also."

"Isn't it a little late for that strategy, *Herr Reichsführer?* Surely your intelligence has informed you that the Red Army has already crossed the Oder and is staging at Seekow Heights for a campaign against Berlin. *Berlin, Herr Reichsführer!* On the front lawn of the *Reich!* I advise you once more to begin considering your reputation and possible exoneration after the inevitable."

"You are brutally honest, Kersten. Reluctantly, I have grown aware of our difficult situation."

"Then I ask: Is there any point at all in annihilating the inmates who remain in the camps as Hitler has ordered? That's close to 800,000 lives!"

"If National Socialist Germany is going to be destroyed, then her enemies and the criminals in concentration camps shall not have the satisfaction of emerging from our ruin as triumphant conquerors and likely slaughter us. No, they need to share in the bitter downfall since they were the cause of this war."

"Surely you are smarter than that, *Herr Reichsführer.* You know perfectly well that the great majority of those in the camps are not criminals, but rather innocent Jews and Gypsies and Slavs. Hasn't the time for stopping the carnage arrived?"

"The *Führer's* direct orders are that the camps are to be destroyed by dynamite the moment the Allies are within a few kilometers of them. I must see to it that they are carried out to the last detail."

Kersten raised his right hand and rubbed his forehead. He was beginning to grow frustrated with Himmler's blatant inconsistencies.

"Surely you don't still have the illusion that obeying this ghoulish order will help you supplant Bormann as the *Führer's* favorite one chosen to succeed him as his successor?"

"That is the *Führer's* decision alone. He is the supreme leader now."

"And where, may I ask, has your *Führer* been in the past several weeks, and where is he now? Safe in his bunker, with his head in the sand—with his mistress Eva at his side, I've heard. Not exactly the pose of a brave leader, is it?"

"Neither you nor the Allies know what is about to hit them," Himmler pronounced with a renewed eagerness. "This war is not over by a long stretch, Kersten. The *Führer* still has his secret weapon. The Brits were astounded in '40 by the V-1 and the rest of Europe later by the V-2. But those are only toys compared to what's coming. You'll see; the last bombs of this war will be German ones."

Suddenly, Himmler bent over at the middle and became as pale as a clean bedsheet. His cheeks were hollow, his cheekbones protruded from his skull, and he began sweating profusely. Kersten led him back to the sofa where he had performed his treatment earlier. He sprung into immediate action, partly out of concern for his patient, but at least as much because he needed Himmler to be past the acute pain in order for him to complete his terribly sensitive and fragile mission for the day, decidedly his most important one of the war on which the survival of the values of civilized society depended.

After twenty minutes or so of intensive massage, Himmler seemed comfortable again.

Kersten resumed the conversation where they had left off before Himmler's attack of abdominal pains. He felt the pressure of time and a window of glorious opportunity possibly closing.

"This relapse you just experienced: It is a kind of language, you know?"

"So you keep telling me. What is it saying?"

"It tells me that a part of you, maybe not even all that deep down, knows that the secret weapon is far too late. I strongly suspect that you know in your heart, if not your head, that if the *Führer* has even a milligram of faith that this secret weapon, however powerful and awe-inspiring in his mind, can turn the tide and prevent an Allied victory, then he's hopelessly deluded."

"I could have you shot on the spot for such talk, Kersten."

"Oh, I'm no fool. I'm fully cognizant of that. I appreciate your protection of me and your tolerance of my repulsion of the camps and skepticism of your *Führer*."

"You also know my protection of you has not been totally altruistic."

"Neither, admittedly, has been my service to you."

"Then we're even, Kersten."

"You may not believe me when I say that in a way I have a high degree of respect for your single-minded devotion for your *Führer.* I wonder, though, if in your fits of sweaty sleeplessness, you have entertained secret doubts about his decisions."

Himmler started buttoning up his uniform shirt without saying a word in reply. Finally, he turned back and to face Kersten and met his eyes.

"*Ach*, you know me too well, Kersten. I can't hide anything from you. Lately, I admit, I have been a little unsure."

"Doubts about his vindictive order to execute all the camp prisoners before the Allies and Russians discover and liberate them?"

Himmler didn't say a word in response. Kersten could tell from the look of uncertainty on his face that the tragically isolated Himmler longed to be forthcoming with someone.

"I agree, there would be little point in carrying out the order. Let the damn Allies and Russians inherit the Jews! They'll learn soon enough what a nuisance, what a danger, they are. In fact, I can't think of a better revenge than for the Russian and Brits and Americans and Frogs to have to deal with them."

"There is a way, you know, *Herr Reichsführer*, that you can evade Hitler's order. At the same time, you will be separating yourself in the mind of the victors from Hitler and Göring and Göbbels and Kaltenbrunner and Eichmann and the rest. They will inevitably be captured and hanged in Allied or Russian prisons in short order, I am pretty certain."

Himmler's eyes flinched, and his face grimaced.

"What exactly do you have in mind, Kersten?"

"While visiting my family in Sweden in February, I had secret conversations with the Swedish government, the Finnish legation, and...a representative of the World Jewish Congress."

"I was with you until you mentioned the WJC. They're headquartered in America, are they not?"

Kersten ignored the comment. He didn't want to get sidetracked.

"I have taken the liberty to invite representatives of those bodies to come here to Hartzwalde in several weeks for a conference to which you will be invited."

Kersten noticed that Himmler's face didn't register as convincing a scowl as usual.

"Me? Here? To Hartzwalde. To meet with the WJC?" Himmler asked.

"That's correct, *Herr Reichsführer.* It's time you met a Jew in person."

"A conference with a Jew to discuss what, may I inquire?"

"To discuss, agree to, and together to sign a document entitled 'In the Name of Humanity.'"

"What, in the name of humanity?"

"To preserve the lives of the surviving prisoners in the camps."

"Kersten, you and the Red Cross already succeeded in convincing me to release two thousand inmates to Switzerland last year. You're like a Jew yourself. You're never satisfied."

"In a way, I'm flattered by the comparison, *Herr Reichsführer.*"

"I give up, Kersten. You're a hopeless case."

"I like to think, rather, that I am *full* of hope."

"What do you want from me?"

Kersten went over to the desk in the corner of the room, pulled out a drawer, and produced a two-page document. It was the concrete result of the conversations in Stockholm in March.

"When we meet, we will want you to affix your signature on this document."

There were three points listed in the document.

1. *Reichsführer* Himmler shall not obey, or pass on to others under his command, the Führer's orders to blow up any remaining concentration camps upon the Allies' approach, and no prisoners are to be killed.

2. The present number of Jews, which is not accurate in any case, and is disputable, shall be kept in the camps until liberated by the Allies, and are no longer to be evacuated forcibly by Germany and hidden from Allied access.

3. That all camps in which there will still be Jewish prisoners at the time of liberation shall be catalogued and made known.

Himmler took a long time to read the document. Kersten was mildly surprised at the relative lack of perturbance registering on his face.

"Kersten, you realize that you and the others and this Jew you talk about are asking me to commit treason against my *Führer* and the German *Reich*. Who is ever going to thank me for this? If I follow through as you ask, do you really think that the Jews, even the ones who will be saved by my disobedience to the orders of my superior, will remember with gratitude? If you do, then you're the one who is hopelessly deluded."

"History may remember you as one who released 800,000 concentration camp inmates. Besides, under the current circumstances of the war, what exactly constitutes 'treason?' The word is pretty meaningless and moot now, isn't it?"

Himmler reflected silently. Kersten didn't expect him, really, to respond.

Kersten continued. "If you're concerned about being found out by the *Führer* or any of your former associates, you do not need to. They are either protecting their own skin in Hitler's bunker, or scattering to safe havens like Spain, Portugal or Argentina. Their attention is elsewhere. Believe it or not, they're not paying attention to you."

"Oh," Himmler sighed. "My days are numbered, in any case," he declared rather matter-of-factly without the slightest hint of morbidity. Evidently, he had been envisioning the end, his own end.

He took the fountain pen Kersten was holding out for him and signed his name at the bottom of the document. Kersten then took the pen and signed above Himmler's signature:

Felix Kersten, in the name of Humanity.

Himmler was as speechless as Finns at a wake. His gaunt face looked utterly defeated, yet strangely resigned, even reconciled, at the same time.

Kersten explained that the same document would be presented at the conference at Hartzwalde later in April. This was, he said, just the first step, but an important one, a "dress rehearsal" of the conference, the "down payment" as it were, to guarantee the final agreement.

After Himmler had boarded his car and been driven down the driveway onto the highway to Berlin, Kersten reflected on the session. Never in his life had he felt so sublimely satisfied as the moment he had watched Himmler's trembling, slow and stilted writing appear on the document. When he affixed his own signature on the document above Himmler's, Kersten felt that he was a representative of a great power, not Sweden or Holland or Finland, but of humanity itself. As he contemplated the lives of thousands of Jewish prisoners released eventually from the camps of death, he was convinced that he had been negotiating and conspiring in the name of an unseen power that was immensely pleased.

CHAPTER THIRTY-THREE

Gransee: April 21, 1945

The conference at Hartzwalde went much more smoothly than Kersten had expected, although it didn't begin that way. There was some initial tension among Kersten and his guests, Walter Schellenberg and Norbert Mazur, the representative of the World Jewish Congress, on the evening of the 20th, the time scheduled for the formal negotiation with Himmler. Himmler, however, had not appeared as promised. Schellenberg and Mazur looked to Kersten for some explanation.

"I trust, Doctor, that we have not been wasting our time coming here."

Irrationally, Kersten felt chastised by Mazur's question, even though he understood that Himmler's not being present was not his responsibility, but rather Himmler's own.

Kersten went to bed that might fearing that Himmler wasn't going to keep his word.

In spite of initial impressions, Himmler did keep his word about the release of the two thousand from Theresienstadt to Switzerland. That was a significant risk for him. But to openly defy Hitler's order to dynamite the camps was a risk of a different order. I pray he hasn't developed cold feet.

Kersten was awakened at two in the morning by the sound of a vehicle coming up his stony driveway. He looked out his bedroom window and was as relieved as the father of the prodigal son to see Himmler stepping out of the limousine.

The next morning, Himmler was already up and about when Kersten came down from his bedroom upstairs.

"You probably thought I'd bolted, didn't you, Kersten?" he asked, looking as sheepish and shamefaced as Kersten had ever seen him.

"Well, yes. It was a little awkward for me after having reassured the other parties weeks ago that you had agreed to be present."

"I was at the *Führer's* post-wedding party in his bunker. Eva finally made an honest man of the *Führer.* He had told Göbbels that he didn't want one, that he was in no mood to celebrate. But Eva Braun was fiercely adamant that there be a party. Göbbels resisted, but he knew if word got back to the *Führer* that he or Bormann or anyone else displeased his mistress in any way, there'd be hell to pay."

"I can imagine."

"I knew I was expected here for dinner at seven, but when Göbbels telephoned and explained the situation at the last minute, I knew I had to attend the party. I had no credible excuse not to. I couldn't just tell them, 'I'm going to Kersten's estate to sign a document with a Jew that pledges me to disobey the *Führer's* express orders.'"

"Indeed, you couldn't. I am sure that Schellenberg understands your dilemma and *Herr* Mazur will forgive you."

"I'm not aware that forgiveness is a Jewish virtue. It's Christ who put us Christians in the position where we are obligated to forgive."

As though on cue, Mazur descended the stairs, dressed in a black suit and wearing a black *yarmulke* on the back of his head to match. Kersten cringed inwardly at the patently open display of Jewishness. He wondered if Mazur was wearing the *yarmulke* as a passive-aggressive form of defiance of the Chief of the SS.

The two men met at the foot of the stairs. Kersten made the introduction. Himmler and Mazur bowed to each other very slightly. They were silent long enough to make everyone tense.

Finally, Himmler tried to produce a smile and shook Mazur's hand ever so tentatively. He said something to Mazur so softly that Kersten couldn't overhear. But Mazur responded to the comment with a nervous chuckle, so Kersten relaxed for the time being.

What a miracle this is. Once the predator and the prey, they are now shaking hands in the vestibule of my estate.

For his part, Himmler was dressed in his full black SS officer's uniform with an almost obscene display of military medals on his right chest. Mutual defiance, it appeared, so the two sides had each scored points.

Kersten glanced at Mazur and wondered if he was thinking that each gleaming medal on Himmler's chest represented some act of brutality or depravity against his people in the name of the *Reich*.

Himmler apologized graciously that he had been detained by a birthday party for Hitler the night before. The group sat down at an elegant dining room table, each with a glass of Finnish vodka before them. Then followed the tinkling of cups and glasses and the triviality of small talk, which made the scene almost commonplace and even a facsimile of friendliness. Himmler and Mazur sat opposite each other, separated by dishes of jam, butter, and plates of brown rye bread and cakes.

Both understood that in the space between them hovered thousands, by now perhaps millions, of shadowy ghosts of emaciated skeletons and burned human flesh. How much of the apparition Himmler saw, Kersten couldn't tell. But as he looked at Mazur, he saw a man who was most acutely aware of their presence. In his work, Mazur had followed every occasion of the horrors on the hundreds of killing fields. Everywhere it had been the same, the shattered glass, the yellow stars, the night raids, the forced marches through the snow, the endless convoys where the living were led to the showers and the dead were carried to the crematory ovens.

A wave of sudden despair washed over Kersten. The space between Himmler and Mazur seemed like a chasm too fraught with bitter hate and grisly death to be bridged.

Himmler, however, surprised them all by saying, "I promise to do all I can toward granting *Herr* Mazur's requests. I want to bury the hatchet between Germans and the Jews. As Dr. Kersten knows, if I had had my own way, many things would have been done differently."

The tension around the polite table diminished noticeably. Kersten felt himself slowly releasing the breath he had been holding in suspense. He wondered if Mazur, or he himself, could trust Himmler's sincerity.

It appeared as though Himmler had decided that his opening statement would constitute the entirety of his remarks. He remained uncharacteristically silent during the negotiations. Even when asked his opinion, he demurred by saying, "Dr. Kersten speaks for me." He looked beyond resigned.

"In the Name of Humanity" was signed first by Mazur, then Schellenberg, and then Kersten. Everyone noticed that Himmler was hanging back. Kersten recognized the fear on Himmler's face. At the threshold of signing the document, Kersten knew the abject fear Himmler was experiencing. Even at this last minute, *especially* now, Himmler was terrified that he would be found out by Hitler somehow. He was paralyzed by the possibility not so much that he would be punished by death himself as that he was betraying the man to whom he had dedicated over twenty years of his life and work.

All eyes were on Himmler.

"*Herr Reichsführer?*" Kersten held out the pen to Himmler and gave a reassuring nod.

After yet another pause, slowly, cautiously as though the pen were an explosive device, Himmler took it into his hand. He looked again at Kersten, and then at Mazur. Mazur was looking down at the floor and didn't return the glance. The large standing grandfather clock clicked the seconds that felt like minutes. *Click. Click. Click.* Himmler took a deep, extended breath. Finally, with a trembling hand, he signed the document.

There was an almost sacred silence immediately afterwards. The only sound was the crackling of the flames in the giant fireplace.

~~~

On the morning after the conclusion of the conclave, Kersten met Himmler outside in the driveway as Himmler was trying to elude the others and leave for Berlin before breakfast.

"I give you my word, Kersten, that I have intervened and canceled the *Führer's* order that the concentration camps be blown up before the Allies arrive. I believe that after our luncheon several years ago with Kaltenbrunner, he is sufficiently sobered and humbled to pass on my canceling the *Führer's* order down the line of command."

Kersten and Schellenberg had taken steps in advance to guarantee that he would. They had strategized the evening before the formal signing that even if Himmler were to sign the document, Schellenberg and Rudolf Brandt, Himmler's private adjutant who had been so helpful to Kersten, would take necessary steps to ensure that Hitler's orders would not be passed on, especially by Kaltenbrunner. In fact, Schellenberg had reported to the group after Himmler had departed that Himmler had already intervened after dinner the previous evening to halt the destruction of Buchenwald.

"Himmler ordered the *Kommandant* that if he had information that the Allies were within fifteen kilometers he should raise a white flag over the camp. When they arrive, he was to greet the Allied commander like a proud soldier and surrender his firearm."

The others were visibly gratified by the news.

"I think I speak for the others that we are truly appreciative of your faithfulness to the document shown by your order concerning Buchenwald," Kersten said to Himmler on the driveway beside Himmler's limousine whose motor was already running.

"I know that you never really had faith in a German victory in this war, Kersten."

"How could I have believed in a German victory? You yourself gave me insight into the way in which the *Führer* was imprudently and impulsively unleashing a vast conflict against the whole world. Wasn't it an unequal conflict for Germany right from the start?"

"*Ach*, Kersten, we didn't think so at the start. We have made serious mistakes. I always wanted what was best for Germany, but very often I had to act against my real convictions. But the *Führer* decreed that it be so and so. As a loyal soldier, I had to obey. Can a state really survive without obedience?"

Kersten looked at Himmler with a mixture of woe and compassion and empathy.

"How long I have to live now remains to be seen. What does it matter in any case? My life now has become meaningless. What will history say of me? Petty minds, bent of revenge, will hand down to posterity a perverted and false account of the great and good things we have accomplished. The finest elements of the German people will perish with the National Socialist Party."

It was true again what had happened so many times before in Kersten's complicated relationship with Himmler. No sooner had Kersten felt compassion and even admiration for Himmler one moment than Himmler would pollute the air with the familiar, tiresome Nazi blind arrogance the next.

Both knew the time for parting was at hand. Both were uncomfortable. The spring air was sweet and refreshingly welcome, yet for Himmler and Kersten, heavy with melancholy.

"Don't you think it's rather ironic, Kersten?" Himmler asked. "'You meant it for evil, but God meant it for good.' Do you know that verse, Kersten? It's in the fiftieth chapter of Exodus, as I recall. It's Joseph talking to his brothers, who had sold him as a slave. But ironically, it's precisely because Joseph was a slave in Egypt that the brothers and their father Jacob are saved from starvation."

Kersten was fascinated. Was Himmler actually quoting Hebrew scripture? Down to the point of knowing the chapter and verse? Did Kersten think it was rather ironic, Himmler had asked. *Very* ironic, Kersten thought.

Kersten remembered that before he bowed down on his knees to the Baal of Nazism, the former altar boy Heinrich had been as devoted to Roman Catholicism as he was later to Hitler's sacrilege. Some remnants of it, like the fiftieth chapter of Exodus, still remained buried in the hidden crevices of Himmler's heart.

"I'm not entirely sure I know what you mean, *Herr Reichsführer.*"

"I was incensed beyond recognition when you told me about the attempt on your life, as you surely recall. It wasn't difficult to trace the plot back to your old nemesis—*our* old nemesis—Kaltenbrunner. The despicable bastard meant to do you harm, of course. But the whole vile affair made me realize once again how precious you are to me. I rededicated myself to ensuring your safety and welfare—doing whatever it takes. Rather selfish of me, I know. Now my earnest dedication and selfishness has brought us to this juncture where I am actually conspiring with you against my *Führer* to grant freedom to thousands of Jews, from camps I myself had ordered to be built, of all things. Rather ironic, supremely so, wouldn't you say? I meant it all for evil, for ridding the continent of Jews, but somehow it's ending up for good...for you and the Jews, at least." Himmler gave out a final acquiescent, self-deprecating laugh that was devoid of bitterness, but tinged, Kersten thought, with an ominous note of self-loathing and debility.

"Rather morally brave of you, nonetheless, Sir. And compassionate."

"If the world knew, they'd find it ironic and unbelievable to think that Heinrich Himmler had a compassionate cell in his body."

"But that body has a soul."

At that, Himmler shook Kersten's hand firmly, gratefully, and finally. He got in the car and then rolled down the rear window.

"Kersten, I thank you from the bottom of my heart for the years in which you have given me the benefit of your medical skill. My last thoughts are of your family, which sacrificed so much for me. Farewell, my good friend."

Himmler had tears in his eyes as he spoke. Kersten had never seen tears in Himmler's eyes except when he was in acute physical pain.

The rear window rolled shut, and the car drove off.

Kersten stood in the drive a long time and watched Himmler's vehicle grow smaller and smaller as it drove over the horizon toward Berlin. He contemplated his seven-year relationship with Himmler. No, he thought, Himmler was not the devil personified as he had assumed when he first entered the forbidding Chancellery, nor simply a monster. He was more than that, and less than that, too. Himmler had grown in Kersten's mind into an absolutely fathomless mystery, an inscrutable paradox. Indeed, what a chaotic bundle of contradictions he was. So dogmatic and yet emotionally so insecure. Somewhere on the journey of his youth, the humble village schoolteacher had lost his way. The Roman Catholicism and idealism of his childhood upbringing had eroded as the foul, choking winds of the Great War blew over him and continued to descend on Germany in the decades following. But every now and then, as recently as that very day, in fact, remnants of that childhood idealism and decency would re-emerge from the remote un-tapped corners of his psyche where he had stashed them.

Kersten still wondered if the brutal suffering he had wrecked upon the Jews and others was simply a matter of a deep-seated hatred, or merely a product of his dogged devotion to conscientiousness, unques-tioning loyalty, eagerness to please and methodical efficiency. Most would say "conscienceless efficiency," Kersten supposed, but he was confident Himmler's physical ailments were symptomatic of a fragile, tortured, split, pathetically disjointed conscience.

There will be simplistic minds and readers of history who regard evil as black and white, to be sure, and that the only solution is to elim-inate evil completely somehow, as though that were humanly possible. The Allies and Russians may feel that by defeating Hitler they will have erased forever the kind of evil perpetrated by the Nazis from the face of the earth. "Never again!" people will shout. I truly wish it were so.

Whose hands are completely clean of the Jews' blood, however? Or the blood of the Gypsies, the homosexuals, the mentally ill or re-tarded, the Poles, the Slavs, uncooperative Christian clergy and priests? What about the hands of the ordinary German husbands and fathers who served in the police battalions, conducting routine police duties in the cities and towns, hired to merely maintain the rule of civil law...until they were assigned by the SS to round up Jews and deliver them alive to the train stations? Are their hands clean of blood?

Or the hands of the farmwife who came to market in town and saw a haggard group of exhausted, broken, demoralized Jews being marched forcibly through the center of town to the waiting trucks at the town square? Did it never occur to them to wonder who these Jews were and where the trucks were taking them? Or didn't they have the moral courage or imagination to wonder, and just went about making their quotidian purchases instead?

What about the hands of the engineer of the cattle train that was requisitioned by the SS to transport these Jews from the trucks to the camps? Did he and his fireman ask each other what the Jews in the cattle cars would do once they arrived at the work camp? Did they ever discuss what the working conditions were like at the camp, and how the

Jews were treated by the guards? Or did they consider it none of their business?

Or the hands of the farmer out in his potato field. Did he not notice the unusual odor of smoke drifting downwind from the "work camp" between the neighboring village and his? Did he not know what...or who...was being burned? Did the men with whom he had a glass of beer or two at the local watering hole at the end of a work day ever mention to one another the odor, or the smoke? Did they ever acknowledge, even to themselves, their suspicions about what really went on in the camp?

Or mine? Are my hands clean? Did I not bring comfort and relief to Himmler that, in effect, extended his life? Perhaps Kaltenbrunner and Heydrich were right when they referred to me as "Himmler's whore." Isn't that what I became? Someone who performs an act of providing physical relief, if not even pleasure, to Himmler in exchange for remuneration, unorthodox as that remuneration might have been? Does the worthy end of the rescue of Jews justify the deceptive, manipulative means?

If we don't acknowledge to ourselves our own capacity for evil, won't we, like Himmler, project it and attack it elsewhere?

Yet, no thoughtful person would claim that Himmler was a good man, either, Kersten concluded. *At the start, or at some juncture in his life that remains unreachable now, didn't Himmler have as much potential for good as for evil? Could he not have chosen to continue to shape young lives as a schoolteacher? No, he himself was not the devil incarnate. Rather, someone who somewhere, sometime, must have been lured into the lair of the Prince of Darkness itself, and become its monkish, dutiful acolyte.*

THE FINAL CHAPTER

Stockholm: May 25, 1945

At his new home in Sweden, Kersten had heard on *Sveriges Radio* on May Day the report of the suicide the day before of Hitler and his wife Eva Braun in the depths of the bunker deep underneath the Chancellery in Berlin. Göbbels remained true to character and took his devotion and loyalty to Hitler so far as to administer cyanide pills to his wife and children as well.

Irmgaard asked Felix, "He was close to the Danish border. You don't think he was trying to get to Sweden, do you, to come and seek refuge with us?"

Felix lowered the newspaper so that his face was no longer hidden behind it. He said nothing, but just shrugged his shoulders as if to say, "Your guess is as good as mine."

Back on April 27, a little more than a week before the ultimate Nazi capitulation, Hitler had discovered that with the assistance of the Swedish Red Cross and World Jewish Council, his "loyal Heinrich" had attempted to negotiate a confidential separate peace with the Allies. He had done so with the intention of freeing up all German resources to push back the rapidly approaching Soviets in the east. The Allies refused, telling Himmler that nothing short of a total, unconditional surrender by Germany would be acceptable.

Hitler had been devastated by Himmler's attempted betrayal. He stripped Himmler of the leadership of the SS and dismissed him unceremoniously from the Nazi party. Hitler ordered Himmler's immediate capture and arrest. But the crafty, resourceful ex-*Reichsführer SS* had managed to evade his Nazi pursuers and almost made it out of the country.

Evaded his pursuers, yes, reflected Kersten. But how does a man like Himmler cope with the sudden destruction of his dream and lifelong ambition and the suicide in disgrace of the one man who had given his life meaning and purpose? A fate worse than death, perhaps.

The day after his discovery and arrest by the British, Himmler had swallowed the capsule of potassium cyanide he always carried with him. He was to be buried that very day, May 25, in a secret unmarked place near Lüneberg.

EPILOGUE

Amsterdam: January 8, 1957
TO: The Norwegian Nobel Committee
Henrik Ibsens Gate 51
0255 Oslo, NORWAY

Dear esteemed members of the Norwegian Nobel Committee,

Please accept this missive as an official nomination for the 1957 Nobel Peace Prize of <u>Doctor Felix Kersten</u>, currently a citizen of Sweden, formerly a citizen of Finland, and former resident of Berlin, Germany, and Den Hague, The Netherlands.

I write to you as the Founder and Director of the International Institute of Social History in Amsterdam, and as Professor of Economic History at Leiden University. I have been deputized to write to you by the *Het Nederlandse Rode Kruis*, the Dutch chapter of the International Red Cross, whose board of directors has voted unanimously to recommend Dr. Kersten for the Nobel Peace Prize.

We are joined in this nomination by the World Jewish Congress of New York, NY.

The Red Cross and World Jewish Congress have followed the outstanding career of Dr. Kersten, not only as a medical practitioner, but more importantly and germane to your work as the Nobel Committee, for his extraordinary accomplishments in helping save the lives of untold thousands of Jews during the Second World War. Some of our number, myself included, labored alongside Dr. Kersten in rescuing Jews in the Netherlands. He is held in particularly high regard in this country for intervening with the High Command of the German *Reich* to delay for several years the forceful deportation to Poland of Dutch citizens, Jewish and gentile, after the German occupation of the Netherlands in 1940.

Although not a Dutch citizen during his years in the Netherlands, Dr. Kersten served as personal therapist for the Royal Family, and maintained contact and provided financial and moral support to Her Royal Highness Queen Wilhelmina and the Dutch government-in-exile in Great Britain until the conclusion of the war.

Dr. Kersten was dedicated to the saving of lives, at substantial risk to his life, in a crushing environment in Berlin characterized by gross inhumanity, horrendous violence against whole peoples, and the flagrant conduct of a tragic and unnecessary war that led to the atrocious loss of life of millions of persons throughout Europe and beyond. The World Jewish Congress estimates that through Dr. Kersten's valiant efforts, some 65,000 Jewish lives were spared from the Nazis.

Dr. Kersten's self-sacrificing and courageous acts on behalf of Jews, and citizens of the Netherlands and Finland, are a bright light of hope and virtue shining in the darkness of Europe at war.

Sincerely,
Nicolaas Wilhemus Posthumus,

Amsterdam

The Nobel Peace Prize of 1957 was awarded to Lester B. Pearson of Canada.

Felix Kersten's nomination for inclusion in the list of *The Righteous Among the Gentiles* in the *Yad Vashem* World Holocaust Remembrance Center in Jerusalem was rejected because of allegations made by a prominent Swedish aristocrat, Count Bernadotte, that Kersten had, in fact, been a Nazi and an accomplice in Himmler's crimes against humanity. The charges were to be proven as false in 1949 by a special commission of the Dutch Institute of War Documentation headed by Dr. N.W. Posthumus. Thus, *Yad Vashem* had to decide on the basis of conflicting evidence. It judged that Kersten's own testimony of his rescue operations, *The Kersten Memoirs*, were not sufficiently reliable.

Felix Kersten died in Stockholm of heart disease in 1960 at age 61.

Algot Niska died of a brain tumor in Helsinki in 1954 at age 66.

Hanne Hirsch, on whom the character of Hannah Hirtschel is based, moved to the new nation of Israel in 1950.

A WORD FROM THE AUTHOR

Dear reader,

Thank you for the honor you bestow on me by reading this book. Every writer wants a reader.

The novel you have just read is not a volume of history, but a work of *fiction.* To be sure, it does depict many characters who were actual historical personages: Algot Niska, Felix Kersten, Auguste Diehn, Rudolf Brandt, Ernst Kaltenbrunner, Walter Schellenberg, Toivo Horelli, Rolf Witting, and several others. That list includes Heinrich Himmler, of course.

Other characters are purely fictional.

Likewise, the plot is *based* on actual historical events. Many of the conversations between characters are actual direct quotes from the memoirs of Kersten and Niska, and several other sources. This is true particularly in the case of the dialogue between Felix Kersten and his patient Heinrich Himmler. Information about these memoirs and other sources to which I referred in my research are listed at the end of this volume.

Nonetheless, the majority of events and most of the dialogue depicted in this novel are either pure inventions of my imagination, or are adapted, enhanced, or otherwise modified in the service of the advancement of the plot and the development of the characters.

I say this because I believe there is a substantive difference between historical *facts,* on the one hand, and the kind of *literary truth* that a work of fiction pursues.

Being a historical *novel,* therefore, this work is not an accurate or detailed biography of the "real" people who populate this book, nor an exact record of the history of events between 1938 and 1945, and should not be mistaken for such.

Jack A. Saarela
Wyncote, PA

ACKNOWLEDGMENTS

The popular notion, perhaps, of the process of writing a book, especially a novel, is that the author sequesters himself or herself in a quiet, isolated space somewhere for an extended period of time, sits at his or her computer keyboard, and comes back into the light and the company of other humans with a finished manuscript. There's something heroic about such a notion. It is an inaccurate one, however, according to the testimony of most writers, including this one.

This novel is the product of many minds. The seeds of the story were planted initially in my own mind and imagination by my reading the memoirs of the two principal characters, Felix Kersten and Algot Niska. I also performed the imaginative reworking and telling of their story on paper. However, editor **Karen Hodges Miller** served as a kind of midwife in the birth of the novel with whose expert and patient guidance the telling of the story was rendered more accurate, appealing to the reader, and satisfying to the writer.

Even before chapters were submitted to Karen, *beta*-readers **Kathy Weidner, Marty Weiss, Peter Clark, Jose Cedillos,** and my wife, **Diane Saarela,** were invaluable in detecting inconsistencies in the presentation of the plot, lapses in typing, and weaknesses in the writing as well as strengths. They never failed to be frank and encouraging.

Rabbi Ruth Sandberg of Gratz College was kind enough to give expert advice concerning the Jewish prayers. **Eric Labacz** enhanced the book by telling the story through his stunning and creative design of the cover. **Vivian Fransen** made sure the reader didn't have to plow through spelling and typing errors. **Albert Glenn** flattered me with his photo portrait of me that appears on the back cover.

Librarian and published author **Marietta Levinson** and business writer **Marty Weiss** did a read-through of the final manuscript before publication and kindly wrote positive reviews.

My wife, **Diane,** was wholeheartedly forebearing of my sometime neglect of household duties as I dedicated time and energy to this project. I am grateful for her protection of the integrity of my almost religious "writing time" each afternoon for almost two years.

RESOURCES

Below are listed some of the many resources consulted for this novel.

BOOKS

Bohjakian, Chris. *Skeletons at the Feast.* New York. Three Rivers Press. 2009.

Goldhagen, Daniel Jonah, *Hitler's Willing Executioners: Ordinary Germans and the Holocaust.* New York: Alfred A. Knopf, 2002

Kersten, Felix, *The Kersten Memoirs 1940-1945.* New York: The McMillan Co, 1957

Kessel, Joseph, *The Man with the Miraculous Hands.* New York: Farrar, Straus and Giroux, 2004

Manvell, Roger and Fraenkel, Heinrich, *Heinrich Himmler: The Sinister Life of the Head of the SS and Gestapo.* New York: Skyhorse Publishing, 2007

Niska, Algot, *Over Green Borders: The Memoirs of Algot Niska.* New York: Vantage Press, 1955

Rautakallio, Hannu, *Finland and the Holocaust: The Rescue of Finland's Jews.* New York: Holocaust Library, 1987

Shirer, William, *The Rise and Fall of the Third Reich: A History of Nazi Germany.* New York: Simon and Schuster, 1960

Waller, John H., *The Devil's Doctor: Felix Kersten and the Secret Plot to Turn Himmler Against Hitler.* New York. John Wiley & Sons, 2002

ARTICLES

"Algot Niska." Wikipedia.
https://en.wikipedia.org/wiki/Algoth_Niska
"Felix Kersten." Wikipedia.
https://en.wikipedia.org/wiki/Felix_Kersten
"Heinrich Himmler." Wikipedia.
https://en.wikipedia.org/wiki/Heinrich_Himmler
"Military History of Finland During the Second World War Wikipedia.
https://en.wikipedia.org/wiki/Military_history_of_Finland_during_World_War_II
"Winter War." Wikipedia https://en.wikipedia.org/wiki/Winter_War

"Finland and Germany in World War II: Brothers-in-Arms." *Helsingin Sanomat* *www.hs.fi/english/article/Finland+Germany+in+WWII.*

"The Strange Case of Himmler's Dr. Felix Kersten and Count Bernadotte." *Commentary* *https://www.commentarymagazine.com/articles/the-strange-case-of-himmlers-doctorfelix-kersten-and-count-bernadotte/*

FILM

"Heinrich Himmler: The Decent One." Youtube. https://www.youtube.com/watch?v=EkdvWmMczcg

"Himmler's Doctor." Youtube https://www.youtube.com/watch?v=1b48W-Fz0eo&t=28s

ABOUT THE AUTHOR

Jack Saarala was born in Finland and later emigrated to Toronto, Canada. He studied at Yale Divinity School and in 1981 moved to Florida. He currently lives in Wyncote, PA.

He and his wife, Diane, are the grateful parents of two adult sons: Luke, of Wyncote, PA, and Jesse, of Gainesville, FL.

Jack remains a Canadian citizen, but cheers for the Finnish ice hockey teams in the Olympics and international tournaments, even if Canada is the opponent.

In June 2015, he retired after over 40 years as a Lutheran clergyman. Since retirement, his viewpoint has changed from scanning the environment for sermon material to seeing the world as a novelist. He'd always wanted to write one since reading *The Great Gatsby* in high school and then studying English literature at the University of Toronto. So he did write one. In October 2016, his immigration novel, *Beginning Again at Zero,* was self-published at Lulu Press. His second, *Accidental Saviors*, is published by Can't Put It Down Books.

87484934R00151

Made in the USA
Middletown, DE
04 September 2018